# PASTEL PINK

---

## ZADOK SERIES #1

## NIKKI MINTY

Editing and Proofreading by: Cissell Ink (Amy Cissell and Christopher Barnes)

Cover design by: Indicreates (Indiana Maria Acosta Hernandez)

Digital ISBN: 978-0-6450562-0-4

Paperback ISBN: 978-0-6450562-1-1

Hardcover ISBN: 978-0-6450562-2-8

# ACKNOWLEDGEMENTS

I would like to thank my son RJ for helping form the concept for this novel, and my daughter Lyla and brother Trey, for their creative input.

To my partner Kieran, mother Carrie, grandfather Handel and friend Cheryl, thanks for being my loyal beta readers.

Many thanks to Indiana Maria Acosta Hernandez at Indicreates, for creating such glorious, eye catching covers.

And last but certainly not least, I would like to give a big shout out to my editors Amy Cissell and Christopher Barnes at Cissell Ink, for helping to improve, tighten and smooth out the wrinkles in my story. You have been extremely hands-on and helpful throughout the editing process.

To all my other friends and family members who have given me constant encouragement and support during the writing process, I appreciate the love.

# IN LOVING MEMORY OF RAYMOND MINTY

## 1949 - 2019

*You'll be forever in our hearts*

# ZADOK'S CAPITALS AND RACES

## SUMMER

Extremely hot, barren and two thirds desert. The Royals live in a castle protected by guards, while the rest of the Vallons reside as citizens in the kingdom.

**Leader of Summer:** *Queen Sjaan*

**Race:** *Vallon (Power of heat and fire)*

**Skin colour:** *Black/dark chocolate*

**Hair and eye colours:** *Red, Orange, and Amber (the colour of the irises continually swirl like molten lava)*

**Language:** *Similar to German*

**Facts:** *Vallons are the strongest race and have magical, glowing vertic switz tattoos*

## AUTUMN

Very windy, but self-sufficient land. Rukes live by a waterfall.

**Leader of Autumn:** *Chief Waya*

**Race:** *Rukes (Power of air and wind)*

**Skin colour:** *Grey and white (marble effect)*

**Hair colour:** *Black*

**Eye colour:** *Blue, Aqua, Teal*

**Language:** *Similar to Iroquoian*

**Fact:** *Rukes have wings*

## WINTER

Extremely cold, and the only land on Zadok with an ocean. Zeeks live inside the ice caves.

**Leader of Winter:** *Commander Azazel*

**Race:** *Zeeks (Power of water and ice)*

**Skin colour:** *White/white chocolate (with a shimmer that matches the Zeek's hair and eye colour)*

**Hair and eye colours:** *Purple, Magenta, and Pastel Pink*

**Language:** *Similar to English*

**Facts:** *Zeeks are the smallest race on Zadok. Pastel Zeeks are weak with poor eyesight and a short life expectancy*

## SPRING

A comfortable climate, mostly forest with a crystal-clear lake near the village. Drakes reside in huts and treehouses in the deep of the forest.

**Leader of Spring:** *Chief Dakari*

**Race:** *Drakes (Power of the land)*

**Skin colour:** *Brown/milk chocolate (with a shimmer that matches the Drake's hair and eye colour)*

**Hair and eye colours:** *Green, Yellow, and Hazel*

**Language:** *Similar to Afrikaans*

**Fact:** *Drakes are the tallest race on Zadok.*

# FROM ONE ENDING COMES A NEW BEGINNING

## -RUBY-

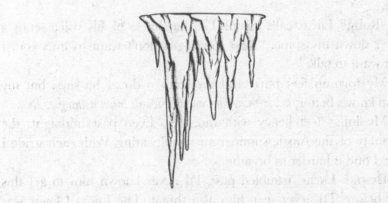

(Earth, eighteen years earlier)

The crunch of dry undergrowth crackles in my ears as his pursuing footsteps grow louder—closer. I gulp. Slowly, shakily, I wipe blonde strands of hair from my sweaty face and take a second to glance behind me. The glimmer of his knife catches my eye, and my stomach lurches. I curse. He's much closer than I'd thought.

"Ruuuby," he stresses the U of my name with a guttural drawl. "Come out, come out wherever you are."

A shudder flickers through my wounded frame. It's only a matter of time before he finds me hidden here. I need to keep moving.

I spring to my feet and my vision swims. I'm met with a crippling surge of pain. I bite down on my lip to hold in a scream, but my hand accidentally brushes past a branch of dried leaves, giving away my location with a rustle.

"There you are." The thuds of his footsteps come rushing towards me.

Panic kicks my heart into overdrive, and I race off deeper into the bush. A sharp branch nicks my shoulder, while another scrapes my thigh. I wince, but I force myself to keep running—*I must.*

Blood oozes from the stab wound at my side, warm and sticky, and I am thankful the night sky is dark enough to conceal my blood trail.

"Ruby," Lucas calls again. The harshness of his voice sends a shiver down my spine. "Stop running. I don't want to hurt you. I only want to talk."

My torn-up feet burn and threaten to do as he says, but my mind knows better; *he's already hurt me. His words mean nothing… Run.*

My lungs feel heavy with moisture. Even past midnight, the humidity of the Aussie-summer-air is suffocating. With each stride I take, I find it harder to breathe.

Despite Lucas' troubled past, I'd never known him to act this way before. I'd never seen him as a threat. The Lucas I knew was shy and introverted. I'd felt sorry for him.

My eye socket and nose throb, and I can taste the metallic tang of blood seeping into my mouth, but these injuries are nothing compared to the gaping stab wound which burns at my side.

"He will never love you the way I love you," Lucas says, and with a rumble, he clears his throat. "He will never make you happy."

My relationship with Josh hasn't always been smooth sailing, but

2

he's never physically hurt me. If this is Lucas' way of showing me love, then I don't want it.

The deeper into the bush I get, the less I can see, and soon, I'm running blind. After only minutes, my foot catches on an obstacle, and I stumble. The left side of my body collides with a tree, causing my knee to twist sideways.

Another curse word erupts from my lips, and I cringe. The pain is unbearable; I want to curl up in a ball and cry, but I can't stop now. I must keep moving.

I lunge forward, willing myself to focus on my destination, not my injury, but after only a measly few metres my wounded leg fails me, and I stagger dangerously on the uneven ground. Frightened of falling, I grab hold of a tree trunk for balance, and then one by one, I use the line of trunks before me to drive myself forward. I'm not moving fast enough, and I'm making far too much noise.

The crunching of dried scrub echoes loud behind me, and before I know it, Lucas is hot on my tail—so close—I can hear the wheeze of his breath.

"Got ya."

Lucas' hand yanks my shoulder back, and I'm too weak to fight it. I lose my balance. My feet slip out from under me, and I plummet into the scrub with a thump. Panic envelopes me. *QUICK! Get back up.* As agonising as it is, I roll onto my back and use my arms to lever my body into a seated position. The shadow of his frame towers above me. He's tall and solid, and above all, he is strong.

"Please," I beg. I hold up my arm to block my face. "Don't hurt me."

"Oh, Ruby." He kneels and puts his hand on my knee, causing me to flinch. "I never wanted to hurt you, it's only that you made me so angry."

He attempts to take me by the arm, but I pull back sharply. "Now, now," he warns. He reaches for my arm again, and this time I let him take it, afraid of what he'll do next if I continue to make him angry. He stands and hoists me to my feet. The movement is swift and causes my entire body to scream in protest. I grit my teeth, holding in a cry. I can't let him see me as weak. A thousand scenarios click over in my head. *I have to trick him—I have to escape, but how?*

His hand cups my cheek, and I long to pull away. I stare at the knife clasped in his other hand. There is limited moonlight, and the tip of the knife is covered in blood, yet somehow it still glimmers. *It taunts me. He terrifies me.*

"Ruby," he says again, only this time there's a hint of warmth to his tone. I never thought I'd come to hate the sound of my own name. "Let's start again." His face leans toward mine, so close, I can faintly make out the risen scar along his cheek. "You should be with me." He strokes my cheek with the edge of his thumb. His skin is rough, callused, and feels like sandpaper against mine. "You should leave Josh and run away with me."

My insides churn. It's clear what he wants from me. He'd said the same thing to me earlier. I'd light-heartedly rejected him, yet I'd paid severely. I'd thought he was mucking around. I don't understand how he could do this to Josh. They are brothers through adoption, they hang out all the time, I thought they were close.

"Okay," I agree, forcing a nod. To give into him sickens me, but I have no other choice. If I fight him, he's sure to kill me.

"That a girl," he says, and his sandpaper fingers slide roughly from my cheek down to my chin. I feel the burn of his gaze upon me and the heat of his whiskey and cigarette scented breath blowing against my face. In the dark, his coffee-coloured irises appear black; it's fitting. He pulls me closer, his intentions clear. He is going to kiss me. His tobacco tasting lips graze mine, and I recoil. I can't help it. The thought of his lips on mine revolts me. I know the cost, yet I can't force myself to cooperate; *I'd rather die.*

Right away he notices my repulsion, and I feel his muscles tighten. *I must act.*

I take hold of his shoulder and launch my good knee straight for the area where I believe his crotch to be. *Bull's-eye.* He groans, bends, and cradles his package. *I run.*

Adrenaline surging, I clear another few metres before he catches up with me and tackles me to the ground. I struggle to break free from his grasp. He is far too strong. Before I know it, he's got me on my back, his legs straddling me, restraining my arms by my sides. I'd hoped he would lose the knife during our struggle. He hadn't; I can see the glimmer of it hovering above me.

Realisation hits me like a slap to the face, *this is it, I didn't make it; I'm a dead girl.* I continue—desperately—to squirm free from beneath his body weight, but his legs are like rock solid vices gripping me in place. I'm completely trapped.

I gasp in horror as the faint glimmer of the knife's blade plunges towards my abdomen.

"NO! PLEASE NO!"

A sharp slicing pain tells me it's too late to plead with him. I let out an ear-piercing shriek as it slices through my skin, not once, not twice, but three times.

"Why?" I cry, "why?"

"If I can't have you," the words hiss from his mouth, "nobody can."

The metallic taste of blood fills my throat, blocking my airway until all I can do is splutter. I feel cold. An image of my twin sister Jade fills my mind. *My rock.* The thought of never seeing her again tears me apart.

"Jade." My last word is merely a gurgle…

## 2

# THE FOREST AWAKENS

## -HARLOW-

(Zadok, present day)

*I* squint. Tall trees shadow the forest floor, making it almost impossible to see where I am going. I pause to listen. There's a rustle of leaves coming up behind me.

"Harlow." A poke to my shoulder causes me to flinch. "Hurry up."

My sister Floss is impatient; she doesn't like it when I dawdle.

"We need to be out of here before sundown, or we're as good as dead."

Goosebumps prickle my arms. Her words hold far more weight than she realises.

Ever since I was a child, I've been burdened by human visions, this one of Ruby and her final moments on Earth being the most disturbing of all.

It's strange, I know, but I feel that I'm connected to Ruby. I see what she sees, hear what she hears, taste what she tastes, and feel what she feels.

As a child, I adopted the controversial theory spread among the minority—we had once lived as humans. But after being shut down time and time again by my own family members for voicing my human stories, I'd given up on the idea, or at least—that's what I'd told them. It was no use arguing the matter, I had no proof. All I had were my visions, and only I could see them.

The topic of humans is a great debate among Zeeks. While Zeeks as a whole, believe in reincarnation, not all Zeeks believe we'd once lived as humans. As far as the non-believers are concerned, Zadok is the only planet we regenerate on, and humans are fictional characters, which have been written about in storybooks for the joy of us SCI-FI lovers. My sister, in particular, is a firm non-believer. She taunted me about my visions when we were children, and although I keep my mouth shut about my visions these days, she still finds other ways to taunt me.

The burn of a sharp object scrapes against my calf and I wince. "I need more light," I say.

Floss huffs, rummages through her sack, and hands me a zoft, which is a small purple glowing crystal. "What you need is a better set of eyes."

Like many other Zeeks in our colony, Floss treats me as inferior. Her magenta-coloured hair and irises make her physically superior. I'd not been so blessed; I was born with pastel-pink hair and irises. *A sign of weakness*, or so they like to remind me. The lighter the pigment of the iris, the worse the eyesight. Sadly, there is no way of arguing it. My eyesight isn't great, and my body strength isn't the best either, but I'm not as ill-fated as others. Some of the paler, less fortunate Zeeks are born blind.

"Well, if you happen to be attacked by a fuegor, and I manage to survive, I'll pinch yours," I say.

Floss snorts. "I'd rather the fuegor eat them."

I think it's safe to say that Floss isn't fond of me. She believes I'm an embarrassment. I am the only non-Magenta Zeek in our family—*shame on me for being born this way.*

"You know, you're right," I reply. "Let the fuegor take them, why aim for magenta eyes when I can aim for purple."

Silence…

Floss hates it when I bring up the word "purple". Being a Magenta, she has it over me, but when it comes to Zeek status, she's only second rate. Purple Zeeks are at the top of the ladder.

The rumble of a fuegor growl echoes through the trees, sounding a little too close for comfort. Daylight is dwindling, which means our nocturnal friends have risen, and are ready to hunt.

Floss reaches for her blade. "I'm refusing to work with you again," she says, eyebrows furrowed. "It's only a matter of time before you get us both killed."

My eyes dart in her direction. "Why blame me? I only stopped once. You stopped a dozen times."

It doesn't matter whose fault it is I get the blame—it's always the same story—not only with Floss, with everyone. *Pick on the Pastel. I hate it.*

"So, I made a few quick stops." She uses her fingers to flick droplets of water at me. It's a neat trick—and one I'll never be capable of—but it's certainly not as impressive as the sharp shards of ice I've seen flying from the fists of an angry Purple. "Your one stop cost us thirty minutes."

I pull out my rattan and jab her sack. "Hey," I say, voice harsh. "I cut down four big bunches of degs in that thirty minutes. If it wasn't for me, our sacks would be near empt—"

"Shhh…" Her finger rises to her mouth, forcing me to stop short. "I hear something."

Doing as I'm told, I remain silent and listen. A twig snaps close by, followed by the sound of a low drawn out snarl. I clasp my rattan tighter, my breath catching in my throat. *A fuegor.*

I glance at Floss and her eyes meet mine, large with alarm. "RUN!"

I don't need to be told twice. Adrenaline kicks in, driving my weak body forward. I hold the zoft out ahead, but the light it gives me is insufficient. Or perhaps it's my eyes that are insufficient, either way, it's difficult to see any further than two feet in front of me at a time. My heart pounds erratically inside the wall of my chest. This scene is sickly familiar. Flashes of Ruby re-enter my mind. *We are the hunted. We are the prey. We are running blind.*

Being pursued by a predator through the forest is something I've feared would happen from the first moment I got this job. I never wanted to be one of the fruit pickers, and I certainly hadn't wanted to work with Floss. Picking fruit with Floss reminds me of picking mangoes with Jade, only this lifetime around my twin sister is not my friend; she is my foe. And this forest—even though the trees are quite different—reminds me of the bush at the back of my parent's old property. It reminds me of being chased down and murdered.

A loud growl erupts close behind me, and within an instant, the fuegor's razor-sharp teeth sink viciously into the meaty section of my calf. A burst of searing pain causes me to see stars, and I trip mid-stride, dropping my zoft.

"HELP!" I thrust my rattan back as I fall, hoping to hit the fuegor. It misses, falls, and is now lost to me in the darkness of the scrub.

Floss is nowhere to be seen, and I don't expect she will come to my aid. Her body is stronger than mine; she is faster. She has probably already made it to the edge of the forest by now.

The fuegor drags me backward. Its head thrashes from side to side, causing its teeth to sink deeper, and rip further into my flesh.

Unable to contain myself, I squeal at the top of my lungs.

It was the night of my eighteenth birthday—as Ruby—Lucas had killed me. There'd been a small group of us drinking and partying at the back of my parent's property. Lucas and I were the only two to make it past midnight. My boyfriend Josh had drunk too much and passed out at eleven. I'd considered going to bed with him, but I was overexcited, and wanted to stay up and dance by the fire pit. A choice I regret dearly.

Tomorrow is my eighteenth birthday. I am only a day younger than I was when I'd died as Ruby. *Could this be a coincidence, or is this all part of some sick cycle life has planned for me?*

I catch hold of a tree trunk, and with all my might, I tug against the fuegor's jaw, hoping to break free. *Bad idea.* All this does is cause the flesh to tear further along my calf. It's useless. Besides, I won't be able to hold on for much longer. We are unevenly matched; the fuegor is far too strong.

Its head thrusts backward with amplified force, and my arms give way, leaving me to plummet into the scrub. The wind leaves my chest with a thud, along with any hope I had of surviving. The jaws of the fuegor are far more powerful than Lucas' hands, and I am far weaker than Ruby. If she stood no chance, I'm certainly done for. If only I'd been given a weapon worth using, like a blade. I could have defended myself, and perhaps I would have stood a chance against the fuegor's might.

Twigs scratch lines along my skin, as I'm dragged helplessly across the forest floor, and I am foolishly thankful my sack remains on my back, because it holds my degs. Not that my degs will do me much good when I'm dead, but at least when the warriors find my body, they will see I've put in a hard day's work.

*I wonder how far I'll be dragged before it kills me.* I quiver. *Will it tear me up slowly, piece by piece, or will it go for my jugular and be quick about it?*

Fortunately, my thoughts are interrupted by a loud yelp, and with an abrupt jerk, my leg falls free to the ground. Caught by surprise, I flip over, my eyes flicking open to discover the fuegor has been hit. Its glowing amber eyes are wide in pain, and I can see the handle of a silver blade sticking out from the top of its slick black neck.

*Floss,* I think in disbelief. *She's come back for me.* My heart skips a beat. I can't believe she's risked herself to save me. I always thought she didn't care—that she didn't love me. But as I lever my torso upright, I see a brown hand dusted with fluoro green, lowering towards me. It's not Floss, I realise, with a pang. Floss' skin is white like mine, like all Zeeks. We Zeeks have the same pasty complexion as human albinos, only we shimmer pink, magenta, or purple, depending on our hair and eye colour.

This is no Zeek. This is the hand of a Drake. I've never met a Drake before, but I've heard of them. They are the forest folk, and they stand over eight feet tall, with brown skin. Like Zeeks they shimmer, only they are dusted in yellow, green, or hazel depending on their hair and eye colour.

Deflated, yet grateful, I take the hand being offered to me, and use it to lever myself to my feet. I grimace with the movement. My leg can barely take my weight. I peer upward to find bright green eyes scrutinising me.

"Dit is nie 'n plek vir jou."

I frown, confused. What she says is foreign to me.

"Thank you," I say with a nod. "You…you saved me."

"This is no place for you." Her words are harsh and laced with a thick accent, making her incredibly hard to understand. "Not after dark."

Her hand wraps around the handle of her blade, and with a strong tug, she wrenches it out from the fuegor's neck. A loud crack fills the air, followed by the squelch of ripping flesh. I shiver.

She throws my rattan towards me. "Go home Bleek Een."

Surprised, I catch it with clumsy fingers. It wobbles a moment, until my grip tightens. I grin. She must have found it.

"Go," she repeats, gesturing for me to shoo. "You are not built for the forest."

My grin quickly vanishes as I gaze back in the direction I need to go. The sun has fallen further, and the shadows from the trees have taken over the forest floor. Without my zoft, all I'm able to see is black.

Tears sting the corners of my eyes. "I can't see."

The Drake woman grunts. "Useless pale one." She brushes past me hastily and beckons me to follow. "Come."

She is much taller and more muscular than I am, with green peppercorn hair shaved close to her skull. We Zeek women are small, averaging from five to five-foot-nine at most. Even our men are short compared to the other races here on planet Zadok. The tallest Zeek in our colony is Jax, the Commander's son. He is six-foot-six, but this is rare. Most other males are lucky to reach six foot.

My eyes focus on the Drake woman. Her tribal clothing doesn't cover much, and her brown skin shimmers fluoro green in the darkness, making it easy to follow her to the forest edge.

My calf burns with every step, and I can feel warm sticky blood seeping into my boot, but I dare not complain, for although the Drake woman was kind enough to rescue me, I don't feel she will show me any sympathy.

As we get to the edge of the trees, I can see a little clearer. The sun lingers above the horizon, casting a deep orange glow over the wide-open, snow-filled landscape.

I turn to meet her gaze and smile. "Thank you," I say again.

She takes one look at my leg and grunts. "You need to fix your leg Bleek Een. You're losing a lot of blood."

Doing as I'm told, I kneel and grab my pocketknife out of my boot. It's coated in blood, which makes it slippery, however, I manage to cut the last few centimetres of material off the bottom of my shirt, before it slips from my fingers, and lands in the soil. Using both hands, I straighten-out the slice of fabric, and then wrap it firmly around my calf. The pressure feels painful, but it'll slow down the bleeding—which is more important than comfort—if I wish to make it all the way back home without passing out.

After I've finished tying the fabric in place, I snatch my grubby knife from the ground and rise to my feet.

The Drake woman takes another look at my calf and nods in approval. "Now go," she says, voice sharp, and then points to the open-white-landscape.

A puff of vapour leaves my lips as I cross over the border, between Spring and Winter—soil and snow. I'm certainly made aware of the variation in temperature. The air is frosty on this side and has a bite to it. Zadok is not like Earth; we don't have seasons that change quarterly. Our planet is broken up into four capitals, Summer, Autumn, Winter and Spring, and depending on our race, we live by our given season all year round. Zeeks are the Winter folk. We hold the powers of water and ice, which is useful, especially for our warriors. Ice can make a mean weapon if you have the strength to use Winter magic to its full potential.

Living in a land of ice comes with its disadvantages, though. We can't grow our own fruit and vegetables, so we need to cross over to Spring on a regular basis. Over the years Zeeks have tried growing fruit and crops on the border of the forest, but it hasn't worked, the fruit and crops die before they hit full maturity. The best soil to harvest in lies deep within the forest.

A sharp pain shoots through my calf, followed by another and another. Here in Winter, it's been snowing heavily, and the slush on the ground is thick, meaning, with each step I take, my feet are swallowed by the white sludge. My wounded leg doesn't like this, nor does it like the scrap of material tightly hugging around it. It's begun to feel a little too restricting, with the harsh jerky movements of my steps.

I gaze above, the air is misty, but I can still faintly make out the pink, purple, and green glowing swirls which light up the evening sky. Glinting below the winter lights is my home. The crystallised caves stand tall and magnificent in the distance, a mix of limestone and ice. *It's not too far,* I assure myself.

It's funny, because as a human I hated winter, I craved the heat, but as a Zeek I've grown accustomed to it. Our skin is thick and rubbery like an orca's, so unlike humans, we can withstand the cold. It's surprising how beautiful a world filled with ice can appear, when you're not too busy freezing your butt off to notice all of its wonders.

When I arrive back at the ice caves, I am greeted by Floss and a pair of Purple warriors. Floss isn't relieved to see me; her forehead is creased, and her eyes are slitted like daggers. They must have forced her to wait at the entrance until I showed up. I will pay for this later. Floss won't care that I've been attacked; she'll say I deserved it for dawdling. All she'll care about is the fact that she's been held here against her will. She will think she's been targeted, once again, because of me, her embarrassing excuse for a sister.

The Purples take our sacks, open them, and examine our goodies. My sack is blood stained and scuffed; yet surprisingly it has kept its contents. Nobody says anything about the bloodstains on the sack, nor do they pay any attention to the ripped slice of blood-stained fabric wrapped around my calf. Instead, everyone seems ticked off about having to work an hour later than usual.

Floss gets a nod from the taller of the two Purples and is handed a generous basket of soms and degs, which are the human equivalent of apples and bananas, only they are larger and much sweeter. I, on the other hand, get a scowl.

"Is this it?" the smaller of the two asks. Her arms are folded, and her brows are puckered. I avoid eye contact and nod. My sack was filled to the brim, exactly the same as Floss', but I'm a Pastel, which means I have a target on my back.

"Just give her some ogs," the taller one says.

She picks up four orange balls from a basket and hurls them towards me one after the other. I catch one, but the rest go flying past. My cheeks flush, not only with embarrassment, but also with anger. I wish I could leave the ogs and walk away except I need to bring them home to my family. Even as it is, I will be punished. Four lousy ogs is not much to offer in the way of food.

Sniggers fill my ears, as I drop to my knees to collect my ogs. Floss doesn't help me. Instead, she turns her face away. It's no surprise, yet it still hurts. Jade, my human twin, would never have turned her face away, she would have helped me.

A towering shadow forms on the ground beside me, followed by another shorter, more solid one.

"What has happened to your leg?" I look up to see Jax, the Commander's son standing straight and tall. His lion sized husken stands by his side—as always, eyes alert and ears pointed.

"I was attacked," I say. My eyes don't meet his, for I'm afraid I am going to get in trouble. I've arrived back an hour later than I

14

should have, and I am wounded. It doesn't look good, especially given I'm the only Pastel ever to be hired as a fruit picker.

When he doesn't respond right away, I dare a peek. I've never seen Jax up close before, to me, he's only ever been that distant figure in the passageways giving orders. His muscles bulge from his leather armour, and his fitted chest plate displays the carved symbol of the official Zeek snowflake.

His eyes analyse me from head to toe, and for a moment, it almost looks like he's going to offer me his hand, however, at the last second, he recoils. *It's probably a smart move*, I think. If he were to be seen helping me, it wouldn't go down well with the rest of the Purples.

"Get up." His voice is deep and matches his stature. You can tell he is the son of our Commander; he looks and sounds strong.

I scoop up the last og and rise to my feet.

"Come with me." He strides forward, motioning for me to follow. "We need to get you some medical attention."

Before I can manage a step, his husken circles me, stopping mid-loop to take a quick sniff of my calf. I wish I could pat him, run my fingers through his thick fur, but I resist. I know better than to touch one of the warriors' huskens.

Huskens look like wolf/husky crosses only they are taller and coloured with shades of purple fading to white. Most of them have purple eyes too, but there are the odd few huskens with one purple eye, and one pastel. Those huskens aren't used by the warriors, they're given to the Magenta hunters to drive their sleds.

After undergoing the sniff test, I limp along behind Jax and his husken around the outer passage to the medical chamber entrance. I gaze across the open chamber; it has a cathedral ceiling spiked with stalactites, and crystallised shawls. Unlike the remarkable ceiling, the floor of the chamber has been altered from its natural state, ground down and smoothed to a slick marble-like surface. Rows of beds and equipment line the chamber, similar to a human hospital, and beeps and vibrations can be heard, echoing off the limestone walls.

Though there are many differences between Earth and Zadok—

and the Zeek way of living is far more rustic than modern day Humans—many things we have, say, or do, are very similar, if not the same as Humans. Zeeks of the past have known about the Human world, they have seen it and lived in it—the same as I have. However, those who were brave enough to write about their past human lives have been forced to label their work as science fiction. The Commander and those commanding before her profess to be firm non-believers and refuse to encourage such nonsense.

My ears prick to the sound of voices coming from the beds behind the reception area. I lean forward and step up on my tippy toes, hoping to see above the desk. I grimace as a sharp pain shoots through my calf, but I'm able to manage a quick peek before dropping back to flat feet. There are two other patients inside, and by the looks of it, they're both Magentas. I roll my eyes… *Great.*

Jax's dreadlocked hair hangs down past his waist, rich in colour. A purple so deep, when the shadows hit it, it almost appears black.

"Wait here," he says, voice firm, his husken straightens at his command, as do I.

He strolls across to the reception area to speak to the young Purple lady behind the desk. She appears to be in her early twenties, around the same age as he is.

Eyes twinkling, her lashes flutter eagerly while she responds. At one stage, she even gives a seductive smile, her fingers fiddling with the heart shape pendant of her necklace, which sits in the valley of her breasts. Embarrassed for her, my cheeks burn. She's blatantly flirting.

Finally, he returns, which causes the husken to wag his tail wildly. "I've spoken to Tansy, she said she will get one of the medics to take care of you." He slips his hand into his pants pocket and pulls out a nauclea latifolia root, which is a natural painkiller. "Here, chew on this while you're waiting, it'll help ease the pain."

I pop it into my mouth and bite down. The root has a potent taste to it, and I have to fight the urge not to gag.

"Come on, Sphinx." He clicks his fingers above the husken's snout. "Let's go."

## 3

# PITIFUL PASTEL

## -HARLOW-

Two hours and multiple stitches later, my calf is all patched up. The medic orders me to keep off my wounded leg as much as possible for the next few weeks while it's healing. I don't see how that's going to be possible. I doubt my father will even allow me to have tomorrow off, never mind the next few weeks. He won't support me; *I know he won't.* I need to support myself.

I breathe a loud sigh of relief as I make it up the staircase to the

Magenta caverns without toppling. Sweat drips from my brow into my eyes, causing them to sting. I'm in dreadful agony. *Please let all of my stitches still be intact under the bandage.*

Up on level two, where the Magentas live, the greetings I receive aren't any kinder than those I received downstairs. If anything, they're worse. Fingers point, and sniggers echo off the icy walls. I feel a small object strike the back of my shoulder and laughter follows. As much as it pains me, I pretend not to notice. Purples are mean, but Magentas can be meaner, especially when you're the only Pastel living on their level. Being born a Pastel from two Magenta parents was unheard of until I came along. *Lucky me.* Purples produce Purples, Magentas produce Magentas, and Pastels produce Pastels. To date a Zeek outside of your colour status is a punishable offence, enforced by Purples. They want their superior bloodlines to remain pure.

I was never meant to stay on level two, I was supposed to be given to one of the Pastel families on the lower level, but my mother fought for me. I wished she hadn't, and there are days when I believe she wishes the same thing.

Two Magentas heading in the opposite direction pass me by. No smiles, no nods, only scowls. It seems strange to me, such beautiful caves are home to such ugly characters. Glowing purple zofts line the sparkling icy limestone passages, and icicle-shaped stalactites hang from above. If I were to look without feeling, this place appears glorious. It reminds me of the Jenolan Caves back in the human world, only prettier, colder, and far more open; like the Werfen Ice Caves in Austria. Ice shimmers in a way bare limestone doesn't. I'd visited the Jenolan Caves with Jade when we were little. Our parents took us there for a weekend away. I sigh at the memory as nostalgia hits. My human life held far more love and joy than my life as a Zeek. I wish I had appreciated it more while I was alive. Here on Zadok, the only Zeek who genuinely cares about me, is Zavier—a Pastel guy my age, from the underground Pastel caverns.

❋

My mother meets me at the entrance of our family's cavern, her face tired and lined with worry.

"What happened to you?" Her gaze leaves my face to look at my calf. It's bandaged now, but the dried blood caked down and around the back of my boot shows just how nasty the wound underneath is.

"A fuegor bit me."

Her jaw drops. Floss mustn't have told her about the fuegor.

I unlace my boots and leave them by the entry, all the while salivating over the delicious aroma of roasted meat and vegetables coming from the kitchen.

I'll need to wash, but for now I would like a rest, even if it's only for a few moments. My leg throbs, and the small cuts and scrapes across my arms, shoulders, and lower back, sting from the antiseptic cream.

My mother shakes her head. "I told them not to make you a fruit picker. Your body isn't strong enough for that kind of work. But your father insisted."

I know she's right, and even though I never wanted this job, I hate to hear her say it. I hate that I'm constantly reminded about how weak I am. Pastels don't usually work outside the cave walls. It's too much for us. We don't have the body strength, sight, stamina, or speed. Most Pastels are servants, cleaners, cooks, dishwashers, factory workers, or help to look after the infants of other Zeeks.

Given that they are hardier, Magentas tend to work outside the caves as harvesters, fruit pickers, gatherers, labourers, fishermen, and hunters; however, the same can't be said for the cream of the crop. Although they are the strongest of us all, most Purples work inside the caves, the same as Pastels do, only their jobs are either high ranking or cushy. They work as teachers, writers, librarians, artists, and medics, or if they're brave and willing, they become warriors like Jax. Warriors are trained in combat, to serve and protect our kind from potential attacks. Jax is the Chief Warrior and is highly regarded, unlike his older brother Nix, who died early last year at the hands of one of his own warriors.

The Summer folk, Vallons—with their dark skin, molten lava

eyes of red, orange, or amber with matching hair and vertic switz tattoos—have attacked us Zeeks over the years, and because of this, the number of our warriors have been increased substantially. Women can now be warriors as well as men, and they too have the privilege of owning a husken.

Pastels like me fear the Vallons, for many of our kind have been stolen during these wars and taken back to Summer as slaves. Vallons know we are the weakest of our race and least likely to fight them off; hence, they use this to their advantage. Our Commander may be cruel, and narrow-minded, but from the stories I've been told, the Vallon Queen Sjaan is pure evil.

I pop my four ogs on the table alongside Floss' abundant basket and sigh. As far as jobs went, my sister wanted to be a hunter like our parents, but she was refused. Father held her back to stay with me. He knew my sight wasn't good enough to hunt, and my mother didn't want me paired with any other Magenta, because she was afraid they would tear me to shreds at the first chance. It's no wonder Floss hates me so much. If I were Floss, I'd probably hate me too.

I go to sit down, and mum stops me. "I don't think so," she says, taking me by the arm. "Look at you, you're a mess. You need to wash-up before dinner and be quick about it. Your father's already furious about you arriving back late from work, never mind the fact he's been waiting over three hours for his dinner to be served."

*This day is getting more miserable by the minute.*

"You should have eaten without me," I groan. "I don't understand why you didn't. You usually would."

"We were too concerned," she says, and sadly, as much as I wish to believe otherwise, I can guarantee it wasn't my wellbeing they'd been concerned about. God only knows what Floss told them. They probably thought I'd lost my job.

After dinner, I stick around long enough to help wash the dirty plates before heading straight for bed. My belly might be full, but my insides feel empty. Floss hardly said a word to me at dinner, and I'd received no sympathy from my father. All I got was a lecture.

His eyes were narrowed. "How many people know you were attacked by a fuegor?"

"Only those at this table," I'd replied with a circular gesture.

"What about Jax?" Floss had asked, a shade of green flashing across her eyes. *How humorous*, I'd thought. She was jealous he'd spoken to me.

"I told Jax I'd been attacked, but I didn't say what by, and he didn't ask."

"And the medic?" my father asked.

"The medic asked, 'What happened?', and I told her 'I was attacked'. She didn't ask any further questions, and I didn't offer any further information," I'd answered.

The sad reality is, she wasn't all that interested. She was more worried about the injured Magenta guy in the bed next to mine. He'd spent the entire time I was there telling his heroic tale about how he'd been impaled through his shoulder by a razor-sharp stalactite. Supposedly, he'd heard the crack before it fell and had selflessly thrown himself on top of his younger sister to save her life. Whether his story had been embellished, or not, I didn't know. Most Magentas have a tendency to over-exaggerate to Purples. I guess they feel the tougher they sound, the more they'll be accepted. Sadly, in some cases, this happens to be true. My father, Saul, is well respected for being a brute. He is the best hunter we've had in years, or so I've been told.

"Well if anyone else asks, I want you to tell them you scraped your leg getting down from a tree." My father had warned. "I don't want you losing your job over this. It's an excellent position and if you throw it away, you'll be sent down to work with the rest of the Pastels." His threatening gaze scrutinised me. "We wouldn't want that now, would we?"

I squash my pillow over my head, attempting to rid tonight's dinner discussion from my mind. It's no good dwelling on my family's lack of love and compassion, it won't change anything; it'll only upset me further.

"Good night, Harlow," I say to myself, pretending to be a family member who *actually* cares about me. "I'm sorry you had such a horrendous day, how terrifying. I hope your leg feels better in the morning."

# 4

# A WORLD APART

## -HARLOW AND HARLOW AS RUBY-

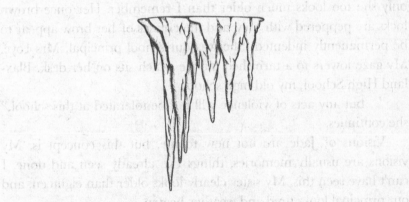

*I* take in a breath and the familiar smell of musty carpet
fills my nostrils.

A blurred figure sits before me. "Why would he do that?" *Jade?*
It sounds like her voice, only her Australian accent is much harsher
than I remember it being.

I blink several times to clear my vision and then gasp. *Jade—it's
really her.*

"You know what he's like," a man replies, his tone hushed. "He's impulsive."

Beside Jade, sits a man in a suit, creamy skin flushed pink, with hair the colour of sand. Jade doesn't look the same as I remember. She looks older and more sophisticated, dressed corporate with her golden hair tied back in a bun. Her fingers twiddle with her bag strap and worry lines mark her face.

"Connor never used to be this way," she says, looking across at someone behind me. "He was always such a good kid."

"He's thirteen," the man beside her says. His pale blue eyes flickering between my sister, and whomever it is that sits behind me. "Teenagers are impulsive; they make bad choices. It's all a part of growing up."

"I understand he is a teenager..."

I glance over my shoulder to put a face to the voice joining the conversation. A woman sits at a wooden desk. I recognise her also; only she too looks much older than I remember. Her once brown locks are peppered with grey, and the creases of her brow appear to be permanently indented. She was our school principal, Mrs Foye. My gaze lowers to a tarnished plaque which sits on her desk. Blaxland High School, my old high school.

"...but any acts of violence will not be tolerated at this school," she continues.

Visions of Jade are not new to me, but this concept is. My visions are usually memories, things I've already seen and done. I can't have seen this. My sister clearly looks older than eighteen, and our principal looks tired and weather-beaten.

I gaze back to where Jade sits. A few lines crease the corners of her green eyes, but not many. It's been eighteen years since I was murdered. If I was still alive as Ruby, I'd be thirty-six. A flutter of excitement blossoms inside me. *Am I back on Earth in the present? Is Jade thirty-six?*

*No*, I shake my head ridding myself of the thought. *I'm dreaming.*

"I understand," Jade says. "And I can assure you we will speak to him."

There is a knock on the door before it opens, and a lady with ginger hair and glasses, pokes her head in. "I'm sorry to interrupt," she says, "but Rueben's uncle is here, and he needs to get away in a hurry."

Principal Foye nods. "Tell him I will be with him in a moment."

The lady nods in return and then disappears, closing the door behind her.

"Since this is his first offence, I'm going to let him off with an afternoon detention, but if this happens again, I'm afraid he will be looking at a suspension."

"Thank you, Janice," Jade says, and rises from her seat. To hear her call Principal Foye by her first name seems odd to me.

"Yes, thank you," the man repeats. He rises next to Jade, bending slightly as he slides his coat off the back of the chair. "Connor will get a firm talking to."

Jade doesn't wait around to chat, and before I know it, she is out the door. I glance around the room. It's strange how clearly, I've remembered this place. My dream seems so detailed—*so vivid*.

The man exits, and I follow behind him; just in time to witness my sister drop her handbag to the floor with a crash. Lipsticks, coins, and a pair of sunnies scatter across the hall. The man quickly kneels to help pick up her things, while Jade stands there staring, stiff as a board.

"Lucas!" Her hands tremble at her sides.

*WHAT?* My gaze snaps to the person standing in front of her. His hair is shaved shorter and dark stubble shades his lower face. He has also thickened out a lot, bulked up, but his coffee coloured eyes are still the same, as is the pink scar along his cheek. *Oh my god it is him.* I shudder. *It's Lucas!*

I wake up with a fright, my sheets soaked in sweat. Thank goodness it was only a dream. I gaze at my watch; almost two in the morning, *good grief.*

Warm and flustered—which is a rare sensation here in the ice caves—I get up to splash my face. I wince as I stand. My leg is much sorer than I'd expected. The stitches are tight and pull savagely with the movement of my leg.

After a few icy splashes of water, I stand there staring at my dripping reflection. Pale pink eyes gaze back at me, tired and red at the corners. As Ruby, I'd loved the colour pink, but as Harlow, I've grown to hate it. If it weren't for my pastel colouring, and shorter, leaner frame, Floss and I would have been identical. We have the same facial structure, almond-shaped eyes, and delicate grooves in our cheeks. We also have the same wild cowlick that swirls on the right side of our hairline, making our fringe appear like a tropical beach wave.

There've been many times over the years where I've wondered what my life would've been like if Floss and I had been born the same. *Would we have been close? Would we have been friends? And if things would have been different had we been born the opposite way around; would I have been as cruel to her as she is to me?* I would like to believe I am kinder than she is, but who knows, perhaps I would have been just as horrible.

The longer I stare at this washed-out face before me, the more resentment fills me. *Why were we born different colours?*

Tearing my eyes away from the mirror, before depression hits, I glance at my watch again. It's much too early to stay up, but after the dream I had, the chances of getting back to sleep again are minimal. The image of Lucas won't leave my mind. His face has been the face of my nightmares for as long as I can remember. I can see the madness in his eyes; smell the cigarettes on his breath. *It's sickening.* I dread the thought of him popping up again in my dreams; so instead of forcing myself to go back to sleep, I throw on some slippers and head down to the water pool to clear my head.

My mind is a million miles away as I hobble down the marble passageway towards the pool, and it isn't until the last minute, I realise someone is walking towards me. It's Jax and his husken

Sphinx, looking all too bright eyed and alert given its well past midnight.

*Crap!* I hadn't expected anyone else to be up at this hour. I don't want him to see me limping, worse yet, in my threadbare pyjamas. The fear of being demoted, and disappointing my father, overwhelms me. I straighten up and attempt to walk properly… *Epic fail.* My calf is too sore to co-operate.

As he draws closer, he asks, "How is your leg?"

"Oh, it's…um…" Nervous, and unsure of how to answer without admitting I'm in terrible pain, I fiddle with my braid. "It's fine."

"It looks like you're struggling a bit."

"I've only just got up," I say, and flick my braid back over my shoulder. "My leg's a little stiff, that's all."

He nods as if he's agreeing with me, but his expression says otherwise. "By the way, I've been meaning to ask," he says, his gaze firm on mine. "What was it that attacked you?"

My father's words hang over me, heavy like a weight around my neck. I don't want to lie, and what he's asked for me to say sounds idiotic, but if I tell Jax the truth, I might lose my job.

My eyes dart away from his. "A tree," I say, and swallow back the bitter taste of the lie. "I accidentally tore my calf on a branch when I was chopping down the degs. It was a minor error in judgement, it won't happen again."

One of his brows shoots up. "Really?"

I nod.

In this lighting, his brows appear black, the same as his hair, but unlike his mother, the Commander, whose irises are as deep in colour as her hair and eyebrows, his eyes are bright, the colour violet. I've never noticed this before.

"Sylvie the medic told me you were lucky." I can feel his gaze burning down on me as he speaks. "She said the creature's teeth hadn't sunk-in deep enough to cause any permanent muscle damage, but she suspects whatever-it-was that attacked you, dragged you, given the gashes were so long."

Embarrassed, my cheeks burn, and I lower my head in shame.

Trees are not creatures, and they don't have teeth. He knows I was lying.

"You know the truth," I swallow. "Does this mean you are going to relieve me from my duties as a fruit picker?"

"Is this what the lie was about?" His voice is curious. "Are you afraid you'll lose your job?"

I nod. "My father was worried. He thought if people knew I was attacked by a fuegor I would be demoted."

What my father actually said, was I'd be sent down to work with all the other Pastels, but I don't repeat the last bit. I didn't want to give Jax any ideas, for although the thought of working with other Pastels doesn't offend me, I know for certain, it will offend my father.

Jax looks baffled. "How did you get away from the fuegor?" he asks.

Afraid of being caught out in another lie, I answer honestly. "A Drake woman helped me. She killed the fuegor with her blade."

Again, this gets me thinking, and perhaps it's something I should bring to his attention. Things may have been different if I'd had a blade of my own. I might've been able to defend myself better. All the Magenta fruit pickers have blades, yet I was given a lousy rattan and a pocketknife. They'd said my eyesight wasn't good enough to carry such a dangerous weapon. Personally, I think they were worried that someday I would snap and turn it on one of them.

"Well it seems you were very lucky," he says. "You're the only Zeek to survive such an attack."

"I am?"

"We've lost over a dozen Magenta's to fuegor attacks this past decade. No one's ever been lucky enough to return and tell the tale." His eyes scan me from head to toe, and I flush. "And you feel okay?" he asks. "You don't feel sick or disorientated?"

I cross my arms over myself in shame. *How embarrassing.* My pyjamas are threadbare, and my slippers have holes in them. They were hand-me-downs from the Zeek woman next door. Unlike my Magenta family members, I don't earn many tradable goods, so I can't afford much. I must make do with the minimum I have.

"No." I shake my head. "I feel fine."

"That's good." He nods. "Hopefully, you'll remain feeling fine, but if anything changes and you begin feeling feverish or start hallucinating, head straight back to the medical chamber, okay?"

"Okay."

Feeling exposed and uncomfortable, I decide against bringing up the blade. *Next time.* Not only am I ashamed of my appearance, I'm ashamed I've been caught lying. I wish to leave this conversation before I embarrass myself any further. *If only the floor would open-up and swallow me whole.*

"I'd best be going," I say, and proceed to step past him.

"Harlow, wait." He spins to face me.

Shocked, I whirl back to meet his gaze. *He knows my name.* I hadn't expected him to know me by name. *I am a Pastel; I'm insignificant.*

"I'm sorry," he says. "I know this isn't what you want to hear, but I'm going to have to take you off your fruit picking duties." He must see the disappointment written on my face, because he quickly adds, "Only for a few weeks until your leg gets better."

I nod, but on the inside, I feel gutted.

"It's for your own benefit," he adds. "You need to rest your leg in order for it to heal. Meet me at the medical chamber at six thirty tomorrow morning, and I will have a temporary job worked out for you."

By the time I get to the water pool, I feel giddy. I guess it's not surprising given the hefty beating I'd taken, both physically and emotionally over the past several hours.

I can't decide what's bothering me most; the fact that my own father and sister don't love me enough to show me compassion, even when they can see I've been badly hurt?

Or that my killer from my previous life—a life which I loved and miss, by the way—can still haunt me in this life.

Or that I'd embarrassed myself by lying to Jax, the Commander's son, in order to keep my job as a fruit picker, only to be told he is going to relieve me from my duties anyway.

Feeling overwhelmed, I sigh. I know Jax isn't relieving me from my position to be cruel, he is doing it for my own health and safety, but it still hurts, especially when I know how terribly my father will take the news. He already treats me as if I'm inferior.

I kick off my slippers and dip my feet into the cold water. It feels good. My forehead throbs with heat, and I can feel beads of sweat forming across my skin. Cupping my hands together, I dip them into the icy water and scoop up a small amount of cool liquid to splash on my face. This seems to help momentarily—until the burn of nausea sets in.

*Oh no, please no.* I sit there for several moments, swishing my feet around in the water, assuring myself this feeling will pass. *You're worked up,* I think. *Take a deep breath and you'll be fine.* Following my own orders, I inhale deeply—this causes the giddy sensation to increase further. *Oh my goodness, I'm not fine. I feel sick, really sick. I need to lie down before I puke.*

※

"Harlow," I hear, followed by a few firm taps to the face, and a nudge to the shoulder. "Harlow, wake up."

Confusion fills me as I open my eyes to find Zavier kneeling above me. His long, pink, wiry locks appear wilder than usual, and he's dressed in his pyjamas. His face is angelic, and his physique is slender, but wiry. Most modelling agencies of the human world would kill to have a face like his on their books. He's the living definition of pretty boy.

"Harlow," he says once again, his pale pink eyes are flared with alarm. "What's going on? What are you doing down here?"

I blink back the blur and gaze beyond his face. I'm not in my cavern, I'm in an open chamber, and the glistening reflection of water glints from the icy stalactites above. I'm still at the water pool, I realise. I'd come here last night to dangle my feet and clear my mind. It obviously hadn't worked; my mind is foggy, and my head feels groggy.

"I must have fallen asleep," I say, thinking aloud.

Zavier puts the back of his hand to my forehead. "You're burning up." His eyes examine me further. "What's happened to you? You're absolutely covered in scratches and bruises. You look like you've been attacked."

I lever myself upright, causing the cavern to sway. A loud yelp leaves my mouth before I can stop it, and I blush. My leg has become too painful to move. I look at the bandage and notice some blood has seeped through to the surface.

"Harlow, what is going on?" Zavier asks, panic filling his voice. "What's happened to you?"

I realise I haven't been answering his questions. Zavier is my best friend, and I trust him, but I don't feel so good, and the last thing I want to do is talk about the attack. I've already made enough of a fool of myself over it.

"It's nothing," I croak. "I'm fine."

I try to get to my feet; it's a struggle. Zavier sees this and hooks his arm through mine to help hoist me upright.

"You don't look fine," he says. "You look terrible."

He's right. I'm not fine. The room sways further, and then blurs, until all I see is black.

# 5

## I LOATHE PURPLES

### -ZAVIER-

*H*er body starts to fall, floppy like a rag doll, and I'm lucky to catch her in time before she hits the ground.

"Frost!" I curse.

My heart thuds wildly in my chest. I wish I knew what was going on. I'd seen her yesterday morning, and she was fine, now here she is, covered in bruises and scratch marks, with a blood-stained bandage wrapped around her lower leg.

Lexan, the man who took me in as a child, had rushed back to our cavern a short while ago, to let me know he'd seen Harlow here on his way to work. He'd said he'd tried to wake her, but she was unresponsive. I know he would have carried her to me, or the medical chamber if he could have, but his strength and eyesight are limited by his lack of pigment. His hair and irises are so pale, they almost blend with his pasty skin.

I drop to one knee and cradle her. A sheen of sweat covers her face, and a few loose strands of hair have stuck to her forehead. I use my fingers to brush them back. Her body may be battered, but her face looks untouched. Clammy and all, she is still the prettiest Pastel I know.

At the count of three, I heave myself to my feet. For someone so small she feels heavy, but then again, I'm not really known for my strength either.

It's around six-forty when I reach the passageway to the medical chamber, ten minutes past my rostered starting time at the Bean-Brew Cavern—or as Harlow likes to call it "the café". I hadn't had the chance to tell anyone I would be late for my shift this morning. This means they wouldn't have covered for me. I hope Minty will be able to cope on her own. She's tiny, but her spirit is strong, and this is more important when dealing with whinging and bitching patrons all day.

My limbs struggle through the entryway, Harlow's body still draped across my arms. I haven't stepped a foot inside this place since I was seven years old—even though there were several occasions when perhaps I should have. My stomach twists as I cross that invisible line. Not only is this place filled with bad memories for me, it's filled with Purples. I loathe Purples, and I hate the thought of them touching me—whether or not it's for my own benefit.

Personal feelings aside, Harlow appears to be in serious trouble, and I'm no medic, so I swallow my own qualms and do what is best for her.

Jax, the Commander's son stands by the reception desk, his

stature large and imposing. He is talking to a young Purple woman sitting behind the desk. When she sees me heading towards them, she rises.

Jax turns and notices me struggling with Harlow in my arms. His eyes widen. "What's happened?"

I stop before them, my muscles screaming in exhaustion. "We need help," I gasp between heavy pants.

Jax is taller than I am and built like a brick. I am five-foot-ten and wiry. Or as others like to say, built like a string bean. Having him standing there directly in front of me, tall, solid, and broad, makes me feel inadequate in more ways than one, especially given he's dressed in his fearsome warrior gear, while I'm in my torn pyjamas.

Harlow's legs hang heavy over my arm, leaving her calf half hidden from his sight. He leans forward and takes her by the ankle, raising her leg upward to get a better look. More blood has seeped through her bandage, and I can see it's smeared along my forearm. It's a good thing my stomach isn't as weak as my muscles.

"I'm not sure." I shrug. "I found her this way this morning. I asked her what happened, but she passed out before answering."

Jax puts his hand to her forehead. "She's burning up," he says, telling me what I've already figured out for myself. His hand shimmers bright purple against her skin, and within an instant, water drips from her forehead, down through her hair and along her temples. A few drops hit my arm. It's ice cold. The cold sensation causes me to shiver, depleting me of what little energy I have left.

"Here." I extend both arms out, my muscles shaking under the pressure of her body weight. "Can you please take her?"

It kills me to hand her over to him, but sadly I have no choice. My scrawny arms burn with the strain of carrying her all the way here.

The Purple lady steps around the desk to join us. Her name is Tansy, I discover. It's written on her nametag. She too lifts Harlow's leg by the ankle to inspect the bloodied bandage.

"Her bi—" she begins to say but stops short when Jax shakes his head at her, eyes warning. Understanding flashes across her face, and they share a look for a moment, before he asks.

"Where should I put her?"

*Her bi?* I repeat inside my head. I can't figure out what she was going to say. I glance between the two of them, somewhat suspicious. They don't seem shocked about Harlow's condition, concerned maybe, but not shocked. *They know something I don't.*

"Take her to bed ten," she says. "It's down the far left." She nods her head in the direction she needs him to go. "I'll get a medic to meet you there."

He turns his attention back to me. "You can go," he says, voice deep. "We'll take care of her."

After the cagey behaviour I'd witnessed, I feel uneasy about leaving her here alone with them. It appears there's a secret going on—a secret I'm not a part of. Perhaps I've made a mistake by bringing her here. I should have known better. *Purples can't be trusted.* This is something I learnt early in life. *Stupid move Zavier, stupid! You should have sought help elsewhere.*

Riddled with concern, my fingers tap frantically against my thigh. If anything were to happen to her, I don't know what I would do with myself, *I'd be lost.*

Jax notices my hesitation and adds, "Don't worry, I can assure you she's in expert hands."

Before I can argue his point, he takes off, leaving me standing there, still wondering if I've made the right decision by bringing her here.

# 6

# HAUNTED BY MY PAST
## -HARLOW AND HARLOW AS RUBY-

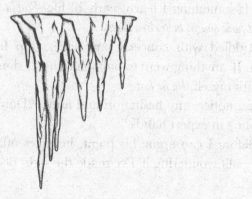

*I*'m slipping in and out of consciousness.

I hear Jax's voice, deep and booming in my ears, along with the beeps of a nearby machine. "Some of her stitches have torn," he says.

It's Medic Sylvie who replies, "Her wounds were extensive…" I recognise her voice. She'd used this same gentle tone with me yesterday. "I told her to rest her leg as much as possible, because I knew there was a chance some of the stitches wouldn't hold." She pokes at the wound on my calf, causing me to whimper. "But it seems she didn't listen."

Beeps continue, followed by vibrations. I feel my leg being lifted, and then lowered, before my body is flipped to its side.

"Did you give her any antibiotics?" Jax asks. I feel another poke.

*Please stop,* I say, only it's in my head. I'm too weak to say the words aloud. Sylvie's voice lowers to a tone far softer than I can grasp. I strain to listen, I want to know the answer, but their voices fade to nothing as I slip back into darkness.

Light finally appears, along with a windscreen, dashboard, and the view of a parked car in front. To my left is a side-mirror, and through the reflection I see a line of houses, scattered with trees, followed by a tall pointed school fence, which stretches over a hundred metres along a curved footpath. The sky above looks angry, spoiled with dark grey storm clouds.

It's warm where I sit, protected by the car, but there's a strong wind blowing outside. The branches of nearby trees whip around wildly.

*Looks like we're in for one hell of a storm,* I think. *Thankfully, it's only a dream.*

A tap at the driver's window triggers me to glance across. My sister Jade sits in the driver's seat, her hair tied up in a bun, and beyond her, is a face which causes me to shudder by looking at it— *it's Lucas.*

*I don't understand why he's not in jail.*

She looks startled by him at first, although to my surprise, after taking a second to recompose herself, she reaches for the window button and presses for it to go down.

*NO!* I think in a panic. I extend my arm across to stop her, but to my disbelief, my hand slips straight through hers, along with a tingling sensation. The hair at the base of my neck prickles. *I'm like a ghost.*

"Jade," Lucas says, the wind howls behind him as he speaks. His tone is tender, unnatural. It makes my skin crawl. "It's been a long time." He smiles, exposing his yellowing teeth. He used to have a chip across his left-front tooth when he was younger, but the whole tooth has been replaced with a gold cap. It's ugly and makes him look meaner. I guess I could say it suits him.

Jade's posture is rigid, and she gives an anxious smile in return. "Yes, it has."

"I didn't mean to startle you yesterday." His lips twitch at the corners. "I didn't even know you still lived around here. Last I heard you were living up North."

"I moved to Queensland, and then to Coffs Harbour for a long while," she says, her finger tracing along her seatbelt. "But as time went on, I missed the mountains."

He nods, face understanding. "I know what you mean," he says. "There's no place like The Blue Mountains."

An awkward silence lingers for a moment before he changes the subject by saying, "Connor seems like a good kid."

"You know Connor?" Jade's voice is neutral, but I know my sister like I know the back of my own hand. I can sense the unease circling within her.

"Yeah, he's become friends with Rueben, Josh's kid, my nephew."

I flinch, as does Jade, but not for the same reasons.

Josh. *My Josh.* An irrational part of me feels betrayed. It's silly and I know it. I died years ago. Of course, Josh would have moved on. People can't mourn forever; they need to get on with their life, move forward, meet someone new, start a family; *it's the norm.*

I hadn't placed Rueben as Josh's kid. When Lucas had said Rueben was his nephew, I'd assumed he belonged to Josh's older sister, Bianca. This new revelation has me feeling oddly wounded until the rational part of me steps in to remind myself that this is only a dream.

Lucas leans forward, resting his forearm across the top of the car. A gust of wind ruffles his shirt, exposing a tattoo of a skull with a rose. "Look." He lets out a long breath, reeking of tobacco. "I want you to know I'm sorry about your sister."

My eyes flash to his face. Dream or not, my wounded feeling is back, along with a plague of bitter emotions.

This isn't something I expected to hear, and I'm not entirely sure I want to hear it. There'd be no apology big enough to make up for taking my life.

"I know you've always blamed me," he says, "and you were right too. For a long time there, I blamed myself." Baffled by his pathetic attempt at an apology, I let out a huff. He continues, "I always thought, if only I was stronger or faster, maybe, just maybe, I could have taken that bastard down before he stabbed her."

*WHAT?* Confusion fills me. *What does he mean by that bastard?* It had only been the two of us in the bush that night. He was the only "bastard" there.

Jade's body remains rigid. "I don't blame you."

I turn to face her, shocked, hurt, but most of all confused.

"Well, maybe I did." Her shoulders slump a little. "But I don't anymore." She glances up at him, face strained. "I know you were hurt on the night of our party too, and perhaps I should have been more sympathetic, but I was hurting, and all I could think was, I want my sister back." Tears form in the corners of her eyes as she speaks. "I resented the fact that you survived, and she didn't." She shakes her head, her cheeks flushing a little. "Gosh, it sounds so wrong, doesn't it?"

The corner of Lucas' mouth curls up in a sympathetic smile—or so it would appear. "You loved her," he says. "We all did."

I cringe. *Please, make him stop.*

He'd used this word the night he'd killed me. He'd told me Josh would never "love" me the way he did. Bile rises in my throat. *I can't listen to any more of this.*

Emotions running wild, I reach across my sister and try desperately to push the UP-window-button. It's no good, my hand goes straight through. Tears sting my eyes, as I continue to pound, pound, pound, through the button to no avail. I can't bear to hear any more of what Lucas has to say, and I don't want him talking to Jade. *I want him gone. Gone, gone, gone, gone…*

"You can try all you like, but it won't work," says a voice, not Jade, not Lucas. "Trust me, I've been there."

I stop dead, my eyes gazing up in the direction from which the voice came.

There, behind Lucas, stands a young guy, tall and broad, with short wavy brown locks. I gasp at the sight of him. He looks similar to younger Lucas, only he appears to be a *much* better-looking version of him. He's cleaner, dressed well—not all in black—and he has a cheeky smile.

This guy doesn't have the scar across his cheek either, and there is no small chip on his left front tooth. Instead he has a scar across his brow, which cuts down to above his eyelid, and there is a thin silver line, which runs down through his lower lip.

*Is this Rueben? And more importantly, was he talking to me?* As far as I was aware, nobody here could see me.

I haven't heard a bell, and no other school kids have come out yet, but there's a chance he could've left class early. I entertain this idea for a moment until something, which should've been obvious before now, occurs to me. Lucas was Josh's adopted brother; therefore, Rueben looking like Lucas makes no sense whatsoever.

I gaze between the pair, searching for answers, until his coffee coloured irises meet mine, sharp and intense. "Hello Ruby," he says, his voice rich with charm. "I've been wondering if I'd ever be lucky enough to see you here."

Panic-stricken, I pound the window button with my finger once again. This time the window shoots upward, startling us all.

Jade turns white and Lucas leaps back from the car, brown eyes as wide as saucers, he slips straight through his lookalike.

And then with a bang it clicks. My heart skips a beat. *Of course.* This is why he can see me. We are the same; *we are ghosts.* Lucas had a twin brother who died a year before I met Josh. Although I knew of him, I'd never met him, so the thought of this person being him hadn't occurred to me right away.

I take a shaky breath. "Alex?"

# 7

# KILLER NIGHTMARES

## -ZAVIER-

$\mathcal{M}$ inty jabs at my chest with the bristles of the broom. "How many times do I have to tell you," she says, her eyes squinting behind her black-rimmed glasses. "Get out of here; come on, get… Shoo." She looks adorable when she's being forceful, although I would never tell her this. If she heard me refer- ring to her as adorable, I'd get the bristles aimed at my eyes. Five foot nothing and almost as pale as Lexan, her sugary appearance is deceptive. She is by far the feistiest Pastel I know.

"Are you sure?"

It's still an hour before I'm supposed to finish, and the limestone bench is littered with food scraps. The kitchen is warm compared to the rest of the caverns; the limestone cavern is bare, no ice. It remains this way because it's closed off from the open icy passageways, sealed by a large solitary door made from wood and then covered in animal skin to provide insulation.

"Yes, I've got it covered, now go."

Gloves off, I slip out of my apron and hang it over the hook. The elastic of my hairnet breaks as I pull it over my head. I screw it into a ball and aim for the bin.

"He shoots, he scores." It's an expression I stole from Harlow. She always uses it when she tosses her rubbish into the bin from a distance. Apparently, it's a human basketball term—*or something.*

I feel a little guilty about leaving Minty to clean up the kitchen on her own, especially after I'd arrived late this morning, but the offer of being able to see Harlow an hour earlier is too good to refuse. She's been on my mind all day, leaving me distracted. Two new painful blisters bubble from my forearm due to the careless handling of a hot frypan. They're not my first burns, nor will they be my last. These things happen when you're the chef. If your head's elsewhere, you get burnt.

I arrive at the medical reception to find Tansy still working the front desk.

She glances up from her paperwork, eyes puffy and circled with shadows, a sign of a long tiring shift creeping towards its end.

"She's still in bed ten," she says, using the tip of her pen to point. "Go on through."

I head along the far aisle, as directed, to find Jax sitting by Harlow's bed. I can't see his face, *exactly*, but I know it's him. His long, dark dreadlocks are a dead giveaway. He and his mother, the Commander, are the only two remaining Zeeks with hair near-black.

I'm surprised to see he's still here after all this time. I'd brought Harlow in hours ago.

Feeling apprehensive, I shove my hands into my pockets. It's a little out of character for a Purple to be so attentive to one of us, especially him, given his supreme status. I would have presumed he'd have far more important things to do than to watch over a wounded Pastel for the day.

When I approach her bed he stands. "You're back," he says.

"Yeah, I left work early." I gaze down at Harlow; no blankets cover her. "How is she?"

"She's still running a temperature." He points to a drip hanging from a pole at the head of her bed. "But they've got her hooked up to IV fluids, and she's been injected with some strong antibiotics."

I place the back of my hand to her forehead, she's still warm, but not like she was this morning. "What happened to her?" I ask. "Has she been awake? Has she said anything?"

"I saw her here yesterday," he says, which causes my forehead to crinkle. I find it more than a little suspicious, that he's waited until now to tell me this. "She was brought into the medical chamber after work. She said she cut her leg falling from a tree."

There is something about the matter-of-fact way he says this, which makes me suspicious. The story sounds fabricated, like it's been rehearsed. Besides, Harlow would have told me if she'd fallen out of a tree. She wouldn't have kept it a secret. When I'd asked what had happened to her, she said it was "nothing", and from what I've learnt, the word "nothing" is generally a cover-up for a much bigger "something".

I ask him several more questions and he answers, but it's clear he's responding out of courtesy, not kindness. He seems tense; his muscles are flexed. He obviously doesn't want to be discussing her condition with me. This furthers my suspicion. *He knows something I don't. He knows what happened to her.*

Seeing him next to Harlow's bed had given me false hope, that unlike his callous, cold-hearted, killer of a brother, he might've seen us as fellow Zeeks, not lower-class citizens. It seems I was wrong. A small part of me is disappointed, yet a large part of me isn't surprised. It was silly, and out of character for me to hope such a thing. Hope against all odds is Harlow's thing, not mine. She's generally the optimist, while I'm the pessimist.

Considering he's still here, watching over her after all this time, has my mind racing with questions.

This morning's scene replays in my head. "Her bi" Tansy had said before Jax cut her off. *Her biological? Her biceps? Her bites?*

"Her bites" gets me thinking. There's a good chance Harlow was attacked by a Purple, and Jax is here trying to cover for them. His concern may not be for her, but for his own kind. I ponder the idea. *For a Purple to get angry and bite Harlow on the leg seems unlikely, but not necessarily unheard of.* On second thought, *I bet it was one of the warriors' huskens who attacked her.*

Jax's eyes meet mine, his brows puckered in thought. "By the way," he says, voice curious. "Do you know anyone by the name of Lucas?"

I shake my head, pretending I don't, but secretly I do. Lucas is the villain from Harlow's reoccurring nightmares, the ones she's been having ever since she was a child. I'm guessing she must have called out Lucas' name in her sleep.

Jax lingers for a moment, but when he realises I'm not about to open up, he reluctantly turns and leaves.

Once he's out of sight, I pinch his seat, my hand reaching straight for Harlow's. "It's okay," I whisper, "I'm here."

From my pocket, I pull out a small bracelet coloured with precious stones and bound by a leather strap. I'd made it myself from the stones hidden in my mother's old treasure box. I gently slide the bracelet over her fingers, and up to her wrist.

"Happy Birthday, Harlow."

I wish I could control her nightmares, change them to blissful dreams. When we were younger, she spoke about her nightmares a lot. She would share the stories of her life before this one, a life where she was a human girl named Ruby. Unfortunately, I wasn't the only one she'd confided in, she'd made the mistake of telling her family, our teacher, and a bunch of other kids at school. Not everyone is open to the idea of us once living as humans, and those who do believe in the idea are usually mocked. Some of them laughed and called her a liar; others made jokes about her and told her she was insane. Even her own family members hadn't supported her. They'd asked her to put a lid on her stories, telling her they were "ludicrous". I was the only one out of everyone, who cared enough to stand by her. Admittedly, I've always been slightly sceptical about the idea, but I believe she believes, and I believe in her.

After half an hour of sitting there, Harlow's hand still clasped in mine, I hear footsteps approaching from behind. A hand grabs my shoulder and gives it a light squeeze.

"How is she?" Lexan stands above me, his hands red-raw from a day's work.

Lexan works in one of the factory caverns, situated deep inside the caves where there's no ice, only limestone. He works with cleaning chemicals now, evident by the blisters on his skin. But over ten years back, when I was only seven, and before his eyesight had deteriorated to a mere 20/200, he'd worked in the sewing factory with my parents.

He'd been working alongside them the day of the accident, when a machine had malfunctioned, and unexpectedly exploded in the adjoining cavern—*or so the Commander would have us believe*. Personally, I think the explosion was the result of sabotage, and I wouldn't be at all surprised if I found out her son Nix and his gang of Purple followers were the ones responsible for the incident. He would have only been fifteen, but he was born wicked, and after his father was killed—seventeen and a half years back—his status rose quickly.

*Anyway*, regardless of how the explosion occurred, the limestone wall between the two caverns had blown to smithereens, causing a large section to cave-in on top of the workers. Forty-nine Zeeks were crushed under the mass of rubble; my parents included.

Lexan suffered three broken ribs, a broken shoulder, and two broken fingers, but amazingly, he'd survived.

After hearing about the accident from a classmate's family

45

member, who'd come back from the incident with only minor scratches, I'd left class and rushed to the medical chamber.

As soon as I got there, I'd hurried through the aisles, scanning the beds, one by one. I'd never seen the medical chamber so full. Pastels upon Pastels filled the beds, some punctured by shrapnel, some missing whole limbs, and others with—*I can't bear to think about it without wanting to puke.*

Blood was everywhere I looked. I could see it, I could smell it, and as I rushed past a Pastel who was bleeding excessively from the spot where his legs were supposed to be, I almost slipped in it.

Overwhelmed by the horrendous sights and the sounds which surrounded me, my heart had pounded so hard, I'd almost believed it would pound right out of my chest.

"Please don't let them be dead," I'd chanted, "please don't let them be dead."

Eventually, after aisles worth of bed searching, I found Lexan laying on a stretcher near the back of the chamber, his face withered in agony. He was fully conscious, but severely wounded.

"Where are my parents?" I'd asked. And that's when he told me the devastating truth.

He'd said, despite the severity of his own wounds, he'd tried his best to help save them, but after pulling back the rubble which covered their bodies, he saw that the injuries they'd suffered were too great—they were unable to be saved. I'd heard the devastation in his voice as he relayed the incident and saw the tears which welled in his eyes as he mentioned my parent's names. He'd been our neighbour, and a good friend to my parents. They'd considered him family.

After the accident, Lexan remained virtually bedbound for nearly six weeks, and I was sent to live with Minty's family, but on the day he was released from the medical chamber, he came searching for me, and told me I was to come and live with him.

There'd been thirteen of us children who'd lost both parents the day of the accident. I was the oldest, and unlike the rest of them, I didn't have any other living/breathing extended family members.

My grandparents on both sides had died, each of them before the age of fifty, and my parents, like myself, had no siblings.

I often question why Pastels breed children; it seems like a selfish, unfair thing to do. Unlike Purples or Magentas, our bodies are not built to last. Our existence is basically a joke, and this is exactly how we are treated.

I shrug. "She's doing okay, I guess. Jax said she cut her leg on a tree." My eyes dart up to assess his reaction, nothing out of the ordinary. He buys it. *Perhaps I'm being paranoid.*

"I take it her wound has become infected." It's more of a statement than a question, but still I nod. "Well, I guess this explains the fever then." He walks to her bed and leans on the rail. Forehead scrunched above his glasses; his eyes observe her from head to toe. The lines of his brow deepen, as he uses his finger to trace over one of the many red lines etched into her arm. "She must have fallen out of the tree. She's all scuffed up."

Unable to help myself, I ask, "Do you really think she fell from a tree, or do you think it's a cover-up?"

Lexan looks at me, a hint of a smirk on his face. "A cover-up for what exactly?"

I knew to expect this kind of response from him. Lexan thinks I tend to overreact, especially when it comes to Purples, but I disagree, I believe he's too trusting.

"I'm not sure yet."

He laughs half-heartedly. "I'd leave this one alone if I were you. I'm sure Harlow will straighten things out when she wakes up."

"Yeah, I guess you're right."

Despite our difference of opinion about those of deeper pigments, Lexan and I are as thick as thieves. He is a good man, and I have a lot of respect for him, not only because he took me in as a child, but also because I deem him trustworthy.

I assume this feeling is mutual, given he has shared with me one of his deepest, darkest secrets. A secret *so great*, it could mean the potential death of him and three others if it were to ever come out. I've never mentioned a word to anyone, especially Harlow, for as much as I hate to keep things from her, letting her in on such a secret would only put her life in danger.

## 8

# REALITY OR A DREAM?

### -HARLOW AS RUBY-

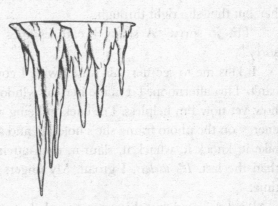

$\mathcal{I}$'m no longer sure whether this is reality or a dream, but nevertheless, here I am once again, a part of the human world—only less alive, and less human.

I lay on a bed, the smell of fabric softener fresh in the air. A chrome fan whirls above me, hung from a plain, white ceiling. My eyes flicker from wall to wall; the surfaces are flat and characterless, painted in a deep shade of beige, which adds no life. I'd never realised how boxlike our human rooms were before now. When I was Ruby, they were all I knew, so I'd accepted them without question, but after living in the caves all these years, this boxlike structure feels odd. Still, I'd leave the beauty of the caves in a heartbeat, if it meant I could come back as Ruby. A beautiful home does not equal a loving home, I have come to learn.

The sounds of sniffles can be heard from the end of the bed, my sister Jade sits on a throw rug, a photo frame clasped in her hand. Curious, I creep over to where she sits and take a peek. It's a photo of us, taken on the night of our year ten formal. Jade's dress was the colour jade, mine ruby red. We'd thought we were so clever buying the same style dresses, long and slimming, sewn in different coloured fabrics, each to match our own names.

A tear falls from my sister's cheek and lands on the photo frame. "I miss you," she says, before melting into heart-felt sobs.

The pain in her voice makes my heart ache. "Jade, I'm here," I try to tell her, but she can't hear me. I try to wrap my arms around her, but they slip right through.

"I'm so sorry." A shaky breath escapes her lips. "I'm so, so sorry."

It kills me to see her this way. I wish I could console her, but I can't. This afternoon, I'd made her car window jolt upwards somehow, yet now I'm helpless. I'm back to being a ghost. I focus all my energy on the photo frame she's holding, and with my hand, I try to take it, knock it, whack it, slam it, each attempt more determined than the last. *It's useless*, I groan. My fingers slip through it every time.

I feel defeated, but this emotion only lasts temporarily, for as I'm about to give up, the door bursts open and I jump, my arm knocking the frame out of Jade's hands with the fright. She jolts as she notices, her eyes bulging at the frame which topples face down onto the beige carpet.

*Yes!* The idea wasn't to frighten her, although it looks as if I might have, I merely wanted her to know I'm here.

"Can I get a little help please?" are the words I hear, but as I turn to the bedroom door—which has been burst wide open—a large box with legs is all I see. A coloured picture of a television is printed on the outside of the box, however it seems an odd shape to fit a television. The box is large, flat, and rectangular, like a table-top.

"I'd hoped to get Connor to help me bring this up, but I couldn't find him." I recognise the voice; it's the man who'd been sitting next to Jade in the principal's office, presumably her husband given the large shiny rock and matching wedding band glistening from her left index finger. He stands and waits a few seconds; however, it appears Jade hasn't registered one word he's said; her focus is still on the frame. With an irritated huff, he struggles through the door unaided and then dumps the box alongside her with a thud.

"Earth to Jade," he says, voice gruff, but his persona instantly softens when he catches sight of her tear-streaked face.

He crouches alongside her, causing his wallet to slip out from his shallow pocket. It falls to the ground, front flap open, to reveal his licence photo. Byron King. I grin at the irony of it. Here I am living at the bottom of the ladder on planet Zadok, and here on Earth, my sister becomes a King.

"Honey what's wrong?" His hand reaches for her face, and with his fingers, he tenderly wipes back the tears from her cheek. "Is this about Connor?"

Jade shakes her head, her eyes flickering. "It was knocked right out of my hand," she says, more to herself than to him. Her voice catches in her throat as she speaks. "I felt it being knocked. I didn't drop it, it was knocked."

Byron glances down at the frame lying skewwhiff at her feet, and his eyebrows knit together. "Jade…" His expression grows serious. "Are you feeling okay?" Before she can answer, he leans forward and picks up the frame, flipping it front ways to look at the picture. "It's your sister," he says, surprise evident in his voice. His eyes linger on the photo. "You two looked so much alike."

Jade's lower lip quivers, her eyes still glassy. "We were identical."

Byron offers the frame to her, and she takes it, wrapping her arms around it tightly to hug it close to her chest.

"Why don't you ever talk about her?" he asks. "You were obviously very close."

She doesn't answer the question, and a moment of silence wavers between them, before she asks, "Do you believe in ghosts?"

The wideness of his eyes tells me he's concerned, although I'm fairly certain it's not "ghosts" he's concerned about. "Why do you ask?"

"I think Ruby is here," she says, sounding mildly delirious.

A glow of satisfaction washes over me, my plan worked, *she knows I'm here.*

"I can feel her," she continues. "I think she's been with me ever since I bumped into Lucas."

"Lucas?" Byron's brows rise, causing his forehead to crease. "You mean the guy from the school, the one you said was nobody, despite spilling the entire contents of your bag at his feet?" He rises to his feet, his face contorted. "What are you keeping from me Jade?" Clearly frustrated, he rakes his hand through his short blonde waves. "Why don't you tell me anything? Everything about your life is always such a secret. Up until last year, Connor and I never even knew you had a sister; the only reason we found out is because your mum let it slip when she and your dad came up to visit us at Coffs Harbour for Christmas. How could you keep that from us? We are your family for crying out loud."

Jade lowers her head. "I've already told you," she says. "It hurts too much to talk about her."

I find it strange to hear she's kept my existence secret, even from her own family. But everyone deals with grief differently, *I suppose.* I've chosen to hang on to mine all these years, whereas she'd chosen to bury it.

"We moved here for you, Jade," Byron's says irritably. "Don't forget that, Connor and I were happy in Coffs, we did this for you, because you wanted to go back to your hometown."

"I know, and I'm sorry. I should have told you everything before we moved here, but it's…" She shakes her head, as if trying to sequence her words into place. "It's too hard to talk about."

"This is what I don't understand." His brows pinch in confusion. "If your past is too hard to talk about, and you've spent this entire time hiding it from us, then why bring us here? Why come back?"

"I didn't want to come back, I was drawn back," she snaps, and then recoils at the harshness of her own reply. "I mean..." Her fingers pinch at the knitted fabric of the throw rug. "I mean it was time to come back."

Byron doesn't respond, however, the mixed emotions which flash across his face, say it all. The tension in the air is thick, suffocating; it makes me feel awkward, especially given that their argument is centred on me. My lack of existence has come between them, causing them pain. If only I could step in, speak up; tell them I'm here; tell them not to argue.

As he slips off his coat, Byron notices the dusty partially open box sitting by the entry of their walk-in robe. Clearly curious, he walks over and peeks inside.

"Is this her stuff?"

Jade nods.

He pulls up one of the flaps. "May I?"

Jade hesitates for a brief second, before giving an uneasy nod.

As if afraid Jade might suddenly re-consider, Byron shows no hesitation, he quickly drops to the carpet, and inquisitively picks through the contents inside the box.

My heart tingles as he pulls out each object one by one. Inside are my most treasured possessions, Billy my blue bear, my soccer jersey, my promise ring from Josh, my favourite clothes, photos, and last but not least, my diary. Jade may not have spoken about me over the years, but she's obviously held on to me, otherwise she wouldn't have kept all of my treasured things.

After inspecting all my other goods first, Byron picks up my diary, and flicks it open to the first page, but he hardly gets a line in before Jade leaps from the end of the bed, snapping the cover shut on his fingers.

"You can't look inside!" Her brows shoot down in a V. "It's Ruby's diary, it's personal."

I wouldn't have minded if he'd looked inside, it's all history now, still, I'm glad to see my sister protecting a piece of me, even after death.

"Well, why don't you tell me something about her," he asks, eyes pleading. "Something, anything."

I love my sister, and I understand how talking about me must be hard, but at the same time, I can't help but feel sorry for Byron. I can see he's hurting and desperate for answers, and a large piece of me hopes she'll open up to him. Thankfully, after a moment of consideration, she nods.

"Okay…fine." She sits down beside him, shuffling close, so she can lean her head on his shoulder. An anxious laugh-cross-cry escapes her lips. "Where do I begin?"

Byron places his hand in hers and gives a compassionate smile. "Wherever you'd like, Honey."

To his relief, and mine, she slowly opens up to him. She even tells him about all the mischief we'd gotten up to when we were young teens. Our grumpy old neighbour gets a mention, as does our year eight English teacher Mr Smellee. Man, did we give that poor helpless teacher a hard time. On reflection, I kind of feel guilty about it, especially given I now know what it's like to be the butt of every joke. Mr Smellee had tried changing his name to Mr Lee, but considering everyone already knew his true name, it didn't stop the name-calling. *But seriously*, what an unfortunate surname to inherit.

As the stories tumble out, more tears spill from Jade's eyes, although, thankfully there are a few chuckles to go with them. Byron interrupts occasionally to ask a question, and she answers without hesitation. It's as if the dam has broken, and her repressed memories are free to pour out. I wasn't expecting her to be so forthcoming, especially given how secretive she's been all these years—but I'm glad. Most of the memories she shares are ones I enjoy reliving, and it's interesting to hear them from her point of view.

Towards the end, a shadow of a frown crosses Jade's face. "It was the night of our eighteenth birthday, when Ruby was murdered."

"Murdered?" Byron's eyes flash in shock. "I didn't know," he says apologetically. "Your mum only said she'd passed away; she didn't say she'd been murdered." His eyes quickly dart to hers, and he squeezes her hand, his expression sympathetic. "It makes sense now. I understand why you've found it so hard to talk about. To lose someone is tragic enough, but to know she was murdered..." His mouth tugs with abhorrence, and he shakes his head. "That's sickening."

Jade gives a strained smile. "Thanks, your support means a lot." They hold each other's gaze a moment, before she launches back into what she was saying. "It was around midnight when the party crasher came—or at least that's what I heard Lucas tell the authorities."

"Lucas, as in the—shady looking dude from the school—Lucas?" Byron asks and Jade nods.

"Apparently Ruby had been dancing to the Chili Peppers, and the guy had gone straight over to join her by the fire pit. They were talking and laughing at first, and Lucas said he hadn't thought much about it, he'd assumed Ruby knew the guy—that they were friends. His opinion changed ten minutes in, when he'd noticed the guy getting handsy with her. Supposably Ruby had yelled at the stranger to back off but was quickly silenced by a forceful punch to the face. After witnessing this, Lucas said he'd leapt up and raced straight over, challenging the guy to back off. Apparently, the guy was irrational and wouldn't listen, and before Lucas had time to register what was happening, he had drawn a knife from his pocket, and stabbed Lucas twice in the abdomen."

Jade cringes, and Byron's grip on her hand tightens. "And once Lucas was down," she says, voice shaky, "the stranger chased Ruby into the bush."

*"WHAT?"* I blurt. Fire swirls inside me, casting a deep red shadow across all I can see.

"I'm so sorry." Byron places a kiss on the top of her head. "You don't have to continue; the rest of the story speaks for itself."

"I don't believe it," I say angrily.

Nothing Lucas told the authorities was true—except for the part about the Chili Peppers *of course*. They'd been my favourite band and I remember playing their latest album on repeat—all night, to the point where Lucas had told me he was going to chuck the CD in the bin if I pressed repeat one more time. *I wonder if he did?* My CD being thrown in the bin seems inconsequential compared to the ending I'd endured.

The confusing conversation I'd witnessed between Lucas and Jade replays in my head. "That bastard," Lucas had said. I scoff, he was the bastard.

Lucas had lied about my death, and he'd made me look like a floosy in the process. The more I think about his version of the story, and how he'd made himself out to be the hero, the more I see red. I clasp my hands together to stop them from trembling.

"LUCAS, YOU BASTARD, YOU HORRIBLE LYING BASTARD!"

"There's one more thing I need to ask." Byron says and then studies Jade's face carefully before continuing. "Did they catch the guy? Has he been locked up?"

Jade shakes her head. "No, they never found him. The son of a bitch murdered my sister and got away with it."

# 9

# SURPRISE BIRTHDAY BOMBSHELL

## -HARLOW-

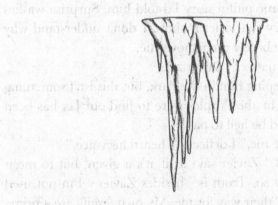

"*H*arlow, shhh, it's okay." The back of someone's hand slides tenderly along my cheek. "It's only a nightmare, wake up." Zavier's gentle voice brings me back to reality, soothing me from my raging hostility towards Lucas. He stands above me, his loose pink hair falling down past his shoulders.

"It's okay, Lucas can't hurt you," he assures me, and dabs a cold damp washer to my forehead. "It's only a nightmare."

Still a little groggy, I blink back sleep from my eyes, causing the bright row of zofts above to burn my irises. Beeps and vibrations ring through my ears, and the smell of disinfectant tickles my nostrils.

"I'm at the medical chamber," I say, and he nods. "How long have I been out?"

"I brought you here yesterday morning after I found you by the water pool, do you remember?"

I rack my memory bank, it's a little hazy, but it's there. "I remember."

As the cogs continue to turn, more memories flicker through my mind. I remember overhearing Jax and Medic Sylvie talking about my leg and discussing whether or not I'd had any antibiotics. I also remember hearing Lexan's voice. He'd been speaking to Zavier about the scratches on my arms—and then with a jolt, I remember something else, something far more important, *Jax had lied for me.* He'd fed Zavier the same pitiful story I'd told him. Surprise washes over me, although I try not to let it show. I don't understand why he'd do this for me. He barely even knows me.

"Is something the matter?" Zavier asks.

I'm not used to keeping him in the dark, but this isn't something I should share. If any of the Purples were to find out Jax has been covering for me, there'd be hell to pay.

"Lexan came to see me," I deflect. "I heard his voice."

"Of course he did," Zavier says as if it's a given, but to me it seems odd—pleasantly so. Truth is—besides Zavier—I'm not used to anyone going out of their way for me. My own family are a prime example. They haven't even bothered to come see me, or at least, I don't remember hearing their voices.

"What about my parents?" I ask, already certain of the answer. "Have they been in to see me?" I don't even bother asking about Floss. She hates me. She would rather poke her own eyes out than waste a second of her time coming to visit me.

"Lexan said he was going to pass by your family's cavern last night when he left." He looks down at his watch, and then frowns. "Perhaps they're coming this afternoon?"

"Or perhaps they're not coming at all."

My childlike desire to be loved—deflates. I keep setting myself up for a fall.

While I know my sister loathes me, and my father thinks I'm a complete and utter disappointment, I had hoped my mother would give me at least five minutes of her time. *Clearly, I'm not that important.*

The same old bitter resentment brews inside me. I doubt they would have even missed me if I'd never returned from the forest. They'd probably consider my death a blessing in disguise. *I should have let the fuegor kill me, save them all the trouble of having to deal with me.* I shudder at this thought.

"What happened to you anyway?" Zavier pops the damp washer on the metal rail and sits down in the chair beside my bed. His eyes meet mine, squinting inquisitively.

Lying to Zavier will be much harder than lying to Jax, he's my best friend, I usually tell him everything, but seeing as Jax had lied for me, it will only make matters worse if I tell the truth now.

I evade his eyes. "I made a stupid error in judgement, when cutting down the degs. My lousy pocket knife wasn't long enough, and my legs weren't strong enough to grip the trunk, so when I reached out a little further to cut down the outer bunch, my thighs gave way and I fell out of the tree." I give a lame shrug. "I guess I got a little cocky."

His head jerks back, and he screws his face up. "That doesn't sound like you."

I give another shrug. "I was showing off to Floss. I'm sick of her always acting as if she's better than I am, because she's Magenta." A dark, weak laugh rumbles from my throat. "Funnily enough, it seems I've proved her point rather than my own."

Zavier's eyes meet mine, warm and sympathetic. "You are a hundred times the Zeek your sister is," he assures me with a semi-smile, "and don't you ever forget that." His hand slips from the bed rail to gently wrap around mine. "You are kind, generous and beautiful, and I am extremely lucky to have someone like you in my life."

His kind-hearted words cause me to blush. I'm not used to compliments, and I'm not certain I agree with all he's said. Too embarrassed to respond, I fidget. My fingers wiggle beneath his, causing him to release his grasp.

A hint of disappointment flashes across his face, and I realise with a pang, I've hurt his feelings.

"Anyway…" His hand retracts. "I'd best be going. Minty had to open and close on her own yesterday, so I'd better pull my weight today before she insists that they fire me." He stands sharply, the chair creaking as he leaves it.

"Zavier, wait." I lever myself up, and reach towards him, but immediately pull back as I notice a band of small precious stones glistening around my wrist.

"A bracelet?" Curious, I bring my hand to eye level and then twist my wrist back and forth, allowing the stones to shimmer brightly under the light of the zofts.

"Where did this come from?" The flash of a memory flitters through my mind, it's a little hazy, but I remember Zavier wishing me Happy Birthday. *I wonder if he bought this for me.* Not to be nasty, but it looks a little out of his price range. Still I ask, "Is this from you?"

A hint of a smile returns to his lips. "Yeah, I made it for you, for your birthday."

*Wow, I really am a jerk.* I feel a pinch in my chest, knowing I've offended him, when he's gone out of his way to make something so nice for me.

"It's beautiful." I give another turn of the wrist making the stones shimmer again. "Where did you get the stones?"

"They were my mum's. I figured she'd prefer to see someone making use out of them, rather than to have them sit in a box for all eternity."

"I absolutely love it." I flash him a grin. "You're amazing Z. I'm so blessed to have a best friend like you."

His smile fades a little, and I don't understand why. He appears disheartened by what I've said. I'm confused.

"Rest up, Harlow." He leans down to kiss my forehead. "I'll come and see you again this afternoon."

As Zavier turns to leave, I spot Jax standing a few feet away, his gaze pointed in our direction. Seeing me notice, he sets down the paperwork he was holding, and then heads over to my bed. Zavier straightens at the sight of him, his body tense. I'm also sure I hear him mutter the word "frost" under his breath, although it was so faint, I can't be certain. If I didn't know any better, it would appear Zavier has a problem with Jax, however, I don't know if it's a colour issue, or if it's personal.

I doubt it could be personal, as far as Purples go, Jax doesn't seem half bad. I might even go as far as to say he seems decent, given he was the only Zeek who'd cared enough to question me about my wounded leg. He's shown me more kindness and consideration than any other Purple has shown in all my eighteen years, and yet he's the Commander's son, *go figure?*

Jax approaches my bedside and gives Zavier an uneasy nod. Zavier returns it with the same unease. The tense feeling is mutual —it seems—yet I don't understand why?

"You're finally awake." Jax leans down to touch my forehead with the back of his hand. "And your temperature is gone, that's good." His eyes inspect me head to toe. "How do you feel?"

"I'm okay, I guess… A little tender, but okay."

Zavier hovers for a moment, and I can tell he feels hesitant about leaving now that Jax is here. But after another quick glance at his watch, he reluctantly says goodbye again and leaves.

Once he's out of sight, Jax un-bandages my calf.

I dare a peek. The wound looks nasty, a mix of dried blood, stitches, and red and purple splotches.

He gives it a poke. "How does it feel?"

I flinch. "Sore when you do that."

"Well it looks much better. A lot of the swelling has gone down." He continues to poke and prod at it, despite my protests. "And it doesn't seem as if the venom has caused any lasting effects."

"What venom?"

"Fuegor venom." He wipes the dried blood away with wet gauze. "Fuegors have venom in their saliva. It's not necessarily deadly—or at least that is what the Drakes say—but it makes you really sick. I've always wondered if it would be the same for us Zeeks, but until you, no Zeek has ever walked away from a fuegor attack."

"Huh, and here I was thinking I'd gotten an infection or something."

"Sylvie gave you a shot of antibiotics the evening she stitched you up. Besides, infections don't set in that fast. It was the venom that made you sick."

"How do you know all this?"

"I was training to be a medic as well as a warrior," he says, and then shuffles in closer to assess the section where my stitches have ripped. "I'd finished my first three years here and I enjoyed it, but after Nix was killed, my mother insisted I was to take his place as Chief Warrior. The role demands a lot of responsibility and left me with no time to continue my studies, so I had to leave my medical training behind." His face constricts. "It was stupid, I should have never let her push me."

It's surreal to hear him say this. He is so powerful looking; I find it hard to imagine him being pushed around by anyone, Commander or not.

For me, being pushed around is an everyday occurrence. I'm small and weak. I have no choice but to nod and agree with those above me. I have no leg to stand on. *No pun intended.*

"I know what it's like, always having to do what's expected of you, rather than living your own dreams," I say with a bitter edge. "It sucks."

He nods. "Yes, it does."

One of the young medics—with big doe eyes—notices Jax and immediately scurries over to my bed, pretending to be interested in my progress, although I'm fairly certain it's not my progress she's interested in. She giggles like a schoolgirl while she speaks, her super-long eyelashes fluttering at the end of every sentence. Jax is friendly with his answers but doesn't flirt in return. I think she notices because she doesn't linger. She quickly checks my vitals and then moves on to the next patient.

"Will I be working today?" I ask.

He examines my wound a little longer, before grabbing a fresh bandage to wrap around it. "Today? Not a chance. You need to rest. As it is, you've already ruptured six stitches."

"I can't afford to rest," I admit with burning cheeks. "My father will be furious. I need to be able to support myself. I'm feeling okay, really. I can keep fruit picking."

"How is it you think you'll be able to go out fruit picking with this injury?"

I shrug. "I have to do something in a similar position, or my father will be disappointed in me."

He considers what I've said for a few moments before saying, "I noticed on your paperwork it was your birthday yesterday." His glittering violet eyes touch my face briefly, and I blush. "Well, being as it was your birthday and you didn't get to celebrate; I'm willing to offer you something in the way of a present."

My brows raise in interest.

"From what I've been told, it sounds like your father is a hard man to please. Therefore, I'm prepared to offer you a temporary position at the library."

"What?" I swallow. "But that's a Purple's job." I wasn't looking to be promoted, I was only hoping not to be demoted.

His generosity towards me comes as a pleasant, yet very unexpected, surprise. I haven't done anything to deserve his kindness. If anything, I've made a nuisance of myself.

"Yes, it is," he agrees. "Which means if you agree to take me up on this offer, I need you to promise me you'll keep your head down and your wounded leg up. It's going to take at least a month for your calf to heal, and I don't want any problems in the meantime."

I press my lips together and nod. The library, *I love the library*. I'm always there in my free time, skimming through old human SCI-FI books. My eyesight's not the best, so I'm forced to squint in order to read the small printed text, but for now, while I'm still young enough, I try to get in as much reading as I can. As I age, my pigments will fade further, the same as Lexan's have, and I will no longer be able to enjoy such things as library books. My life will be nothing but a blur.

"Thanks," I gush. I can hardly believe it. To think, *I now have a job at the library, a job fit for a Purple.*

"I won't let you down," I assure him. "I promise."

# 10

# ELECTRIFYING

## -HARLOW-

*A*fter my cannula is removed, the medic gets my paperwork sorted while I take a few minutes to freshen up.

"Here," Jax hands me a small sack with clothes in it. "Try these on."

There's a long thick fur edged brown jacket inside, along with a cable knit jumper, tights and a pair of brown, fluffy-topped, leather flats.

I take a moment to glance at my reflection. I look and feel like an Inuit which in the land of Winter—is the elite style among the Purples.

Jax claims all the items came from lost property. *I don't believe him.* This jacket, in particular, has golden embroidery on it, and would have cost a fortune in tradable goods. I doubt it could be easily forgotten—even by a rich Purple.

After giving me the nod of approval, he hands me a set of crutches, which feel awkward using. He insists I give them a chance, telling me they'll help take the pressure off my wounded leg.

It's seven-thirty when the medic says I'm free to leave. Sphinx sits in the passageway by the exit, and when he sees his master coming towards him, he jumps up excitedly and thrashes his tail about.

"Has he been waiting out here the whole time?" I ask, and Jax nods.

"He knows he's not allowed in here." He clicks his fingers and Sphinx dashes to his side. "Come on boy, let's go."

The library is a fair distance from the medical chamber. Thankfully, most of the ground between both chambers has been smoothed with only two natural bumpy sections left untouched. Jax asks me several times if I'm okay, and I reply with a simple, "yes", my cheeks burning as I speak. I'm not sure whether to feel flattered that he cares, or embarrassed that he finds me so fragile.

A single set of chiselled stairs lead down to the library entrance. After struggling down the first two on my own, Jax offers me his hand. I hesitate for a second, and look around, unsure whether to take it. It feels wrong, like I'll tarnish him by accepting it.

Sensing my hesitation, he says, "Don't worry, nobody's watching." And then he scoops me up, crutches and all, and carries me to the bottom.

Having his bulging muscular arms wrapped around me, causes my heart to flutter, however, I assure myself it's out of fear—*nothing else*. Jax may be strong, and ridiculously good-looking, but he is a Purple, and the Commander's son, nonetheless. He is not someone I should be interested in. Besides, I don't want to be like all those other girls who "goo" and "ga" over him, I'm just glad he's helping me.

As I enter the library chamber, Jax and his loyal companion by my side, all eyes turn to me, some narrowed, some enlarged, but none indifferent.

I feel vulnerable and exposed, yet somehow, strangely important. *I've been noticed*—not in the way I'd wish to be—*but hey*.

I recognise the librarian sitting at the desk closest to the entry; she is Electra. She'd been Nix's girlfriend—*or so I've overheard*. I've seen her many times when I've come to the library to borrow books, and I've often wondered how she was coping without him.

She is several years older than I am, with deep plum coloured hair and lilac eyes. Her face is beautiful, and her features refined, but there is a hardness in her eyes which leaves me feeling cold.

I also recognise the older, prune-faced librarian, who, until this very moment, has never given me even so much as a glance. I'd asked her where to find a book once, and she'd answered the question without even turning to face me. I'd also handed her a book once—which had slipped from her trolley—and she'd snatched it from my fingers without a word. To her, I'd been a *nobody*, which had hurt, until I came to the conclusion that being a *nobody* beat being a target.

Electra leaves her desk and struts towards us, face tight and eyes narrowed on Jax.

As she approaches, Jax nods, his expression unyielding. "Electra."

"What's going on here?" she asks through gritted teeth. Her eyes flick towards me and then back to him. "Who is this?" The disdain in her voice is mortifying, and I feel myself shrink a little, my insides riddled with regret.

I shouldn't have taken Jax up on his offer. I should've gone down to work with the rest of the Pastels like my father had taunted. He would have been disappointed in me, but perhaps I would be happier. At least I would be with my own kind. *Actually*—come to think of it—I probably wouldn't have been. Most Pastels don't like me either. They resent me because they feel I've been shown privilege over them by being able to live with my Magenta family and work as a fruit picker. I'm always going to be the piece of a puzzle that doesn't fit right.

Despair threatens to consume me as it has time and time again, but this time I don't let it, I push it aside. I love the library, and I want to work here, so screw everyone, Pastels, Magentas and Purples alike. If I'm going to be hated by all, I might as well give them a good reason to hate me.

Jax's expression is an unreadable mask. "Harlow is going to be working here for the next month, or at least until her leg gets better."

A look of horror flashes across Electra's face. "A word," she says, and tilts her head to the right, beckoning him to follow. They step a few metres to the side, and then stop, their frames only inches apart.

"You can't bend the rules for her just because she has a pretty face," she says in a hushed tone, although it's loud enough I'm still able to hear her. "If you bend the rules for her, you set a precedent which opens the floodgate to everybody else."

*Hold on,* rewind, *did she just say I was pretty?*

Jax takes a step back. "Would that be so wrong?"

"Excuse me?" She jolts, horror filling her voice.

"I don't know why we don't integrate all colours together in our working system, I mean, I understand there are some jobs Pastels can't physically do, but there are a lot of jobs they can do, and they should be able to apply for them." His words leave me stunned. "I feel like there is so much segregation between us," he continues, "yet we are all one race—we should stick together, work together, and build towards a brighter future."

Electra's face twists in disgust. "I'm going to pretend you didn't just say that, and I advise you not to repeat this to anybody else. Your mother would convict you for saying such things."

"I'm not my mother, or my brother," Jax says, his tone so harsh, I shiver. "And I refuse to live by their beliefs."

Sphinx senses the tension between the pair. His ears prick up, and his stance becomes rigid, as if ready to pounce if needed.

"You're not thinking like a Commander's son," Electra says,

"you're thinking like a child. Your brother knew better, he understood how damaging it would be to integrate our colour system. With interworking comes inter-friendships, and this can lead to inter-relationships, which means we would be tainted with half-blooded children. Our colour system would be ruined, our bloodlines diluted. The Pastels are weak, they have nothing to offer us."

Her comments hit where it hurts, but as much as I hate to admit it, some of what she says is right. It's true; we Pastels have nothing to offer in the way of breeding. *We would weaken them.*

Jax leans forward, aligning his face with hers. "Nix was already weak," he says bitterly. "He believed what he was told to believe, instead of thinking for himself, and look where it got him."

Electra gasps, and then slaps him across the cheek, so hard, it echoes through the chamber. "How dare you!"

Jax doesn't flinch, even as Electra turns on her heel and storms off out of the library. He remains like a Queens guard stiff and composed.

The hum of whispers can be heard floating across the chamber. I glance around to find three of the four remaining librarians huddled together, watching and whispering; their faces contort.

After a moment of standing there frozen, Jax heads back over to me. "Sorry about that." There is a red hand mark on his cheek with tiny frost shards still clinging to it. She'd given him an ice slap, one of the hardest slaps known to Zeeks, although only Purples are able to give them.

"I don't need to work here," I say. "I can go down and work with the Pastels."

This is not what I want, but I feel the need to offer him an out. He's gone well out of his way to be kind to me, and I don't wish to cause him any trouble.

"Don't worry about Electra." He uses the sleeve of his jacket to wipe the frost residuals from his cheek. "Her problem is with me, not you."

I nod, but I don't entirely believe him. He mustn't realise I'd overheard everything that she'd said.

"Was she Nix's girlfriend?" I ask, wanting to confirm the

rumours I'd heard. I know I should mind my own business, but my curiosity has gotten the better of me.

"She was his nexus," he answers, which is the word we Zeeks use for fiancée.

I would like to ask why Nix was killed, but I resist. It would be inappropriate of me to ask such a thing.

From the stories I've been told about him, I'm not surprised he had enemies. He sounded horrid, ruthless. What does surprise me though, is it was one of his own warriors who killed him, a Purple. I would have imagined it to be a Magenta or a Pastel.

Jax walks me to the furthest part of the reception area toward a young guy my age with short-purple-spikey-hair and black framed glasses. Short hair is uncommon among Zeeks. Most Zeek men grow their hair out, and keep it in either dreadlocks, cornrows, or—in Zavier's case—a tangled mess.

This guy appears almost humanlike to look at. Perhaps it's because in the human world, most males have short hair.

"This is RJ," Jax says, nodding towards the guy with the spikes. He rests a hand on top of the seat next to RJ's, gesturing for me to sit. "RJ, can you give Harlow a quick brief of the tasks she is to perform today?" he asks, his voice rich with authority. "And make sure she stays off her leg as much as possible."

RJ nods, his eyes flicking towards me warily. "Sure, no problem."

My pasty, washed-out eyes shine back at me from the reflection of his glasses, and I quickly lower my gaze. Best if I don't see how truly pathetic I look. My confidence is barely existent as it is.

*Hold on*, come to think of it, my eyes flash to his again momentarily. *Why is a Purple wearing glasses?*

Noticing my double-take, RJ shies away to the furthest part of his desk.

He is different than the other Purples working here; he seems gentle by nature.

Besides my initial entry—which everyone had looked up for—RJ hadn't concerned himself with the rest of the ruckus taking place. Instead, his eyes had remained glued to his desk. Looking to

the far side of his desk, I'm now able to see what has kept his attention. He's been doodling. A detailed, half-finished comic strip sits in
front of him. I lean in closer to get a better look at it, but he notices,
and turns the paper upside down.

"Here," he picks up a pile of paperwork which had been sitting
next to the comic and hands it to me. "You can help me sort out
these." He then hands me a folder with multiple tabs. "The categories are written on the side." He must assume, because I'm a
Pastel, I'm braindead, because he points to the colourful tabs one by
one and gives me a detailed explanation of each of the different
categories.

The hint of a smile tugs at the corners of Jax's lips as he listens
in, and I notice with delight he has a beautiful set of dimples. *Huh,*
it's no wonder he's got Zeek women falling for him left, right, and
centre. He really is the perfect mix of rugged and handsome.

Seeing him so positive, knots my stomach with nerves. *Please don't
let me mess this up.* He's taking a tremendous risk on me, and I don't
want to let him down.

Eyes twinkling in amusement, he says, "Well good luck with it
all." And then he and Sphinx depart, leaving me to feel alone and
vulnerable in a chamber full of Purples.

I get through the day unscathed. Electra never returned, and unlike
the rest of the librarians, RJ had been easy enough to work with. He
seemed nervous, and standoffish around me at times, but he didn't
ignore me, nor was he nasty or impolite. He answered all my questions—*with ridiculous detail*—and showed me how things were done,
which was all I needed to get by.

After finishing my shift at five, I hobble my way down to the
lower level café where Zavier works. He does long twelve-hour shifts
on a rotating roster, four days on, and four days off. Since I know he
was supposed to start at six-thirty this morning, I can only assume
he will still be on duty.

It's only five-thirty when I arrive. I take a seat at one of the empty booths, lifting my wounded leg, to rest on the seat across from me.

The delicious aroma of bean-brew—AKA coffee—mixed with fried foods wafts into my nostrils, making my stomach growl, and I realise with a burst of hunger, I haven't eaten since this morning at the medical chamber.

The café cavern is only small compared to the medical and library chambers, and the ceiling is low, meaning someone like Jax would come close to scraping his head on the longer stalactites hanging from above. Not only do we have stalactites down here, we also have helictites, which stem from the higher parts of the outer walls, appearing like hundreds of glittering swordfish snouts sticking out from the stone.

An image of Jax walking through the café fills my mind. I'm quick to shake it off. Besides, Jax would probably be angry if he knew I'd walked all this way unaided, especially given all the stairs I had to struggle down to get here. And he wouldn't be out of line either—my leg is absolutely killing me. Regardless, I had to come; I needed to let Zavier know I'd been released from the medical chamber, save him heading there straight after work only to find an empty bed.

I can't wait to tell him where I'm working now. I can still hardly believe it myself. *The library*, my favourite place on planet Zadok.

I sit for the next hour, head buried in a book I borrowed. It's another human SCI-FI, *of course*, my favourite. The waiting staff don't bother with me anymore. I come here often, but I never order anything, mainly because I can't afford to, although I'd never tell them this. In the beginning, I'd have to wave them on, assuring them I was only waiting for Zavier. Eventually they got the point and stopped asking if they could help me.

"Hey, you." Zavier slides into the booth next to me, interrupting me mid chapter. "Well this is a pleasant surprise." He gives me a slight nudge. "What are you doing out and about?" Despite being excited to see me, contradictory lines mark his brow. "Shouldn't you be in bed resting?"

I pinch one of the paper napkins off the table and pop it into my book as a bookmark. "I'm feeling much better now," I say with a smile. "Anyway, how was your day?"

"Better than yours, I'd imagine, although, we had an exceptionally large number of complaints made today. You know the drill, the deeper the pigment, the bigger the whingers."

I give a polite smile in response to his comment.

"Actually…" I say. "My day was quite eventful too."

"Oh?" He plants his elbow on the table, resting his chin in his palm. "Why, what happened?" His left brow arches in curiosity as he speaks.

"Let's just say you are now looking at a librarian." I use an open hand gesture for a dramatic effect, but seeing Zavier's eyes pop, I realise with flushed cheeks, I may have overdone it. "Or should I say, temporary librarian," I add sheepishly.

"How?" Is his only response.

I'm about to answer his question when Minty swings into the booth, landing heavily in the seat across from us, barely missing my injured leg.

"I heard you've been tree diving," she says, face smug. "It's not the brightest idea if you ask me, but you never were known for making the best choices in life."

Zavier leaps to my defence. "Knock it off, Minty," he warns.

Clearly unfazed, she pulls a mock face at him. "My bad, I forget how delicate she is." Her eyes flick to mine, a sly grin playing on her lips. "I'm sorry, Precious."

This is her standard nickname for me, "Precious". *I hate it.* But like always, I shrug it off, pretending to care far less than I actually do. I don't want to give her the satisfaction of knowing how much she gets to me.

"Are you done?" Zavier's eyes are slitted.

"I don't believe I even got started. After all, her reckless actions have managed to impact my life. Tell me again, who was it that opened and closed by theirself yesterday?"

"You told me to leave early yesterday, in fact, you threatened me with a broom, so don't start."

"I had to. You were a menace. You were too worked up about her," she says, pointing at me without looking, "to keep your mind on the job." She nods towards his arm—the one that rests on the opposite side of the table to where I sit. "Look at those nasty burns, they say it all, don't you think?"

"What burns?" I glance around to look at them, but Zavier is quick to hide his forearm under the table.

"That's enough Minty, leave it alone."

Minty salutes him, and then leans back against her chair, a smirk plastered across her face.

Feeling on the outer, I shift uncomfortably where I sit.

Minty seems to detest me—for whatever reason—although I presume it's derived from resentment, the same as most other Pastels.

She's always been nasty towards me, even when we were younger. At first, I used to believe it was jealousy over Zavier, I thought she liked him, and that she found our friendship a threat. But then she started dating Tatum, a taller, pink-haired, female Zeek, two years her senior, and my jealousy theory was thrown out the window.

"Tell me..." Ignoring Minty, Zavier steers his attention back to me. "How's this possible?" I presume he's jumping back to our previous conversation; however, I feel uncomfortable sharing now that Minty is here.

Minty doesn't miss a beat. "How's what possible?"

"Harlow's a librarian now."

*Great!*

Her eyes swivel to mine. "A librarian?" She waggles her eyebrows suggestively. "My, my, aren't we working our way up the ladder."

I resent what she's said, and don't want to discuss it any further. I blow the whole thing off. For an incidental promotion I'd been so proud of only moments ago, Minty has succeeded in making it seem cheap and nasty.

I can tell by her expression she's got more to say, but luckily for me, Tatum arrives at the entry, stealing her attention away from me. After greeting each other with a kiss, Minty turns back to face Zavier. "We've gotta go," she says. "Can you lock up?"

He nods. "Yeah, of course."

He picks up my book and hands it to me, face sympathetic. "I should probably lock up now," he says. "Go wait out front for me, and I'll walk you home. We can talk all about your day then."

I wait for Minty and Tatum to go before I get up, *God only knows how much crap Minty will give me, if she sees me hobbling around on crutches.*

It's a good five minutes before Zavier comes out front to join me, and as his eyes catch sight of me, he does a double take. At first, I think it's because of the crutches, but then I realise it's probably because of how I'm dressed. Feeling self-conscious, I cross my arms. After the unpleasant episode with Minty, I no longer feel as enthusiastic about my promotion. I'm starting to question whether I was foolish for believing I was worthy of filling such a position. I must look absurd. A Pastel dressed-up in Purple clothing—pretending to be important—*I'm a fraud.*

## 11

# NAIVE

## -ZAVIER-

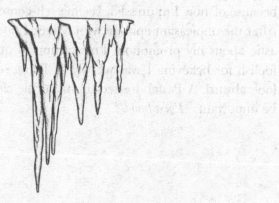

*H*arlow's lips are held in a tight line, and the light I'd seen in her eyes only moments ago has dimmed. She's upset because of Minty, I suspect. Her offensive comments have left her down and deflated.

"Don't worry about Minty," I say, giving her a light, playful elbow. "You know as well as I do, she's rude to everybody."

Minty and I have remained good friends ever since her family took me in for those six devastating weeks after my parents died. She and her parents were very kind to me during my time of mourning, and although I'm sure Minty would die before ever admitting this to anyone, she hugged me to sleep every night for the first week, while I sobbed into my pillow.

I don't have the same relationship with Minty as I do with Harlow, but we're just as close, and I value our friendship. I enjoy working with her—and hanging out when she's not in one of her bitchy moods—and funnily enough, in most situations, it's her outspoken feistiness I love most about her.

That being said, it's a whole other ball game when it comes down to her picking on Harlow. I resent it, and I get really defensive.

Minty knows how I feel about Harlow, and she thinks I'm a fool. She says Harlow's using me, and that someday she'll crush me without a care. Maybe she's right about the fool part, but the rest of what she says is a load of sludge.

Harlow doesn't know how much I care about her, and it's clear from what she said this morning, she doesn't feel the same way. It hurts a little, I won't lie, but I know she'd never hurt me intentionally. She doesn't have a malicious bone in her body.

I'd like to believe one day her feelings for me could change, and she will finally see beyond the *best friend* tag I've obtained and view me in the same light that I see her. *Hopefully.*

I glance her way; she appears to be struggling on her crutches. I slow down to match her pace.

"You're a librarian now, huh?" I flash her a smile, she looks like she could use one. "How exactly did this happen? Last I saw, you were flat on your back in a medical bed, and now, well…I mean… well look at you." I gesture towards her. "In all the years I've known you, I've never seen you so dressed up."

Her cheeks redden. "Actually…" She pushes a stray hair back from her face. "Jax made it all happen."

Hearing his name makes my skin prickle. "Jax?" I repeat.

She nods. "Yeah. He said I could work at the library until my torn calf gets better."

"Your torn calf," I shoot her a sharp look. "You mean the one

77

you hurt falling down from a tree?" Scepticism drips from my voice, and I can tell Harlow notices, because she gives me an anxious sidewards glance.

*Ahuh... I knew it! She's hiding something.*

"Anyway," she says, not taking the bait. "My leg should only take a month to heal, so I plan on making the most of it while it lasts."

She seems happy about this arrangement, and I want to be happy for her, but there's something about Jax that doesn't sit right with me. I don't trust him, and I don't believe his intentions are pure.

"Look, I'm not trying to rain on your parade here," I say, struggling not to sound as cynical as I feel. "But do you not find it the slightest bit odd that Jax has offered you a job in the library? I mean; I know you're a good worker and all, but you're not exactly the right colour for the job."

Lines of hurt mark her face. "I'm not the right colour to be a fruit picker either, yet I've been working as one for the past year now, and you've never said a thing about it."

She pauses, and I follow suit, turning to face her. "But you live with Magentas, so when I heard you'd be working with them, it seemed reasonable."

Her eyes have become glassy, and her lower lip curls down at the corners. "I thought you would be happy for me."

Guilt works its way through me. I hadn't meant to upset her, but I think she's being naïve. Stuck for words, I rake my hand through my hair—or at least I try to—my fingers catch in the knots. "You've taken what I've said the wrong way." I let out a breath. "I am happy for you, I'm merely concerned, that's all."

"Well, you don't need to be," she says sharply. "I'm handling the job just fine."

I can tell by her reply, she still doesn't get where I'm coming from. She thinks I'm taking a swipe at her, when really, I'm taking a swipe at Jax. Afraid of digging myself in any deeper, I drop the conversation, leaving us to walk the rest of the way in silence.

# 12

# ALONE, ANGRY AND AFRAID

## -HARLOW AND HARLOW AS RUBY-

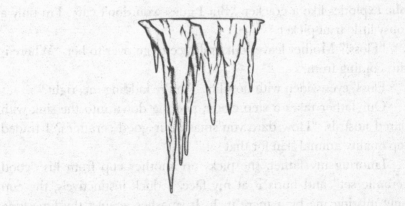

$\mathcal{M}$y afternoon with Zavier hadn't gone as expected. He apologised for upsetting me and gave me a hug goodbye before going his separate way; regardless, it still feels as if there's a wall between us. I'm not used to him being unsupportive. He's usually the one Zeek I can depend on when everything else in my life is falling to ruins.

For the first time in a long time, I feel alone.

My father gives me a nod as I enter my family's cavern; it's a rare event, and not one I'm comfortable with. I would like to believe it's his way of acknowledging he'd missed me while I've been gone, but I know better. He's not that fond of me, it's status he's fond of. Someone must have told him about my new position.

After kicking off my flats, which have left blisters on my pinkie-toes, my mum finally notices me, and flies over to give me a hug.

"My goodness, I've been so worried," she says, and I want to believe her, but I can't shake the bitterness I feel inside. If she really cared, she would've visited me at the medical chamber.

Floss is standing by the sink and welcomes me with an icy glare. *Nice to see you too,* I think sourly.

"I hear we have a librarian in our midst," my father announces, confirming my suspicions. "How was your first day?"

Floss slams her dishes into the sink, causing whatever was beneath, to smash. "I don't remember you asking how my day was." She explodes like a cracker. "But I guess you don't care. I'm only a lousy little fruit picker."

"Floss!" Mother leaves our embrace to go over to her. "Where is this coming from?"

Floss' eyes widen with hostility. "You're kidding me, right?"

Our father takes a step closer, peering down into the sink with flared nostrils. "How dare you smash our good ceramics? I traded top quality animal skin for that set."

Ignoring my father, she picks up another cup from his "good ceramic set" and hurls it at my face. I duck instinctively, the cup only missing me by a mere inch. It smashes against the limestone wall, and a few small fragments land at my feet.

"This is all your fault!" she yells, her finger pointed straight at me. "I'm stuck as a lousy fruit picker, while you're off playing hero with the big shots. How is this even possible? You're a pathetic little Pastel for crying out loud. You're useless."

Our father raises his voice to her again, but Floss doesn't stick around to listen. She storms out, pushing past me with a shove as she leaves the cavern.

Straightening myself, I turn to my father, meeting his eyes for the first time in years. "It's only a temporary position," I say, "so don't go getting too over excited about it."

I see my dinner sitting on the limestone bench waiting for me. I'm starving and desperate to dig straight in, but I can't stand to be near my parents any longer, so along with the growl of my stomach, I leave the living area and head straight to my little sleeping nook.

After an emotionally exhausting day, sleep comes easy to me, however, it's not a restful slumber, for I've slipped back into the human world.

Green grass stretches out before me, along with a path, trees, and beyond that, a river—the Nepean River to be exact, I recognise my surroundings.

My sister sits at a park bench, her hair loose, and clothes casual. She looks different, more relaxed, although it seems ironic, given she's sitting alongside Lucas.

I feel my emotions spike as the memories of last night's dream, or reality—I'm still unsure—comes rushing back.

I gulp. It's not safe for Jade to be alone with Lucas, he's dangerous.

This scene sets off alarm bells, especially given what I now know about him. To kill someone, and then pretend to everybody else you were trying to save them, is sick enough, but Jade said Lucas had been stabbed, and given I hadn't stabbed him, this means he would have had to of stabbed himself—or at least that's the only conclusion I can come up with—which to me—equals next level psychopath.

"I have to admit," Lucas says, along with a puff of cigarette smoke, "I was surprised when I got your call."

"It was Byron's idea," Jade admits, and pushes a loose tendril from her face, tucking it behind her ear. "He thinks I need to come to terms with what happened to Ruby, in order to accept my grief and move forward." Pain flashes across her eyes. "I'm not sure if he's right, but I told him I'd give it a shot."

Lucas shuffles uneasily on the bench seat, flicking ash from his cigarette with his middle finger. "Well, as much as it's nice to have your company, I don't really see how I can help. I'm not exactly councillor material, I'm a fuckin' mess."

Jade flinches at what he's said, and he apologises for cursing in front of her, I however, find myself agreeing with him. He is a mess —a big one at that—and I certainly don't want him hanging around my sister. *Damn you Byron for suggesting such a thing.*

"But you were there the night she was killed," Jade says. "You know how horrific her death was. She didn't die of an accident or natural causes, she was murdered." She sinks back in the seat, leaning heavily against the wooden panels. "It's one thing to accept she's dead, but to know that she was brutally murdered..." She pauses, raising a hand to her forehead. "It's too much for me to let go of, especially when I know her killer is still out there."

Lucas' eyes flicker, and his left leg jiggles on the spot. To me, his behaviour radiates guilt. *How can Jade not see this?*

I suppose she believes he's a helpless victim once again. His actions could easily be mistaken as post traumatic stress.

Because of me, Jade is aware of Lucas' tragic past.

I accidentally walked in on him—nude—in the bathroom one day. I'd gasped when I saw him, not because he was naked, but because of how severely scarred his body was. After closing the door and apologising, I'd dashed out to tell Josh and Jade about the incident, and that's when Josh opened up about Lucas' past. According to him, Lucas and his twin brother Alex, had been subjected to years of child abuse, not only by their natural parents, but by a string of brutal foster parents. A pink risen line, which runs from Lucas' left cheek down to his chin, is the only scar visible for others to see. I'd always noticed it, but until I'd seen the rest of his body, I hadn't thought much of it. People have accidents in life; they get the odd scar.

"Worrying about all of this won't bring her back. You're better off letting it go. Push it aside and move on with your life. It's what I had to do."

His pitiful, selfish advice causes my cheeks to burn in anger, and

I can tell by the way Jade is staring at him, brows knitted and jaw tight, she's not too happy about what he's said either.

"This was clearly a mistake." Jade stands to leave, but Lucas reaches out, taking her by the wrist.

*RUN!* Is the word I scream inside my head. *Flee now before it's too late.*

With his other hand, Lucas flicks his cigarette to the ground, leaving the lit butt to roll away without even stomping on it.

"I'm sorry," he says. "I didn't mean to be so harsh."

Jade looks down to her wrist, and noticing her tense expression, he quickly lets go, putting both his hands up in a surrender position.

"I loved your sister," he admits, causing my stomach to twist. "I really did." His eyes met hers, appearing almost vulnerable. "Probably more than I should have if I'm being honest. I thought she was an incredible person."

The rigidness of Jade's frame begins to uncoil, and Lucas pats the empty seat beside him. "Please, stay."

*No, no, no...* I think nervously, *RUN!*

"You're right," he continues. "I was there the night she was killed, and I wasn't able to save her, do you know how hopeless this makes me feel?"

Pure and utter rage sparks within me. *Don't you dare play the victim card!*

"I've been battling with this for years, and the only way I've truly been able to deal with my pain and move forward, is to flip my switch, turn it off."

Blood hitting boiling point I shout, "HE KILLED ME!" even though I know Jade can't hear me. "AND HE'S A LIAR AND A COWARD!"

Driven by an out-of-control rage, I lash out, and kick him in the head—or at least I try to. I'm well aware my leg has flown straight through his face, but I don't care, I keep kicking anyway, praying eventually one of my kicks will magically make contact.

"YOU BASTARD!" I yell at the top of my lungs. "YOU LYING BASTARD! YOU STOLE MY LIFE." Tears streak my face. "GET THE HELL AWAY FROM MY SISTER."

Strong arms grab me from behind, jerking me back mid-kick, and I panic. I deliver a fast, hard elbow to this person's ribs. There is a small groan, and I continue to struggle, but these arms are vice like, seizing mine to hold me tighter.

"It's okay," he says, though I don't know who *he* is. My breaths are short and erratic. "Take a deep breath and try to settle down before you hurt yourself."

There is a charisma to this guy's voice which sounds vaguely familiar, although I'm so worked up, I can hardly focus.

"It's okay," he says again. "It's just me, Alex."

Hearing who it is, has the opposite effect on me. A small whimper sound gurgles in my throat, and I thrash my head and legs around wildly, landing a few hard heel kicks on Alex's shins.

"Stop it!" he says with a grunt. "You have nothing to be afraid of, I'm not going to hurt you."

His face is close to my ear, and I consider giving him a head-butt, but there's something in his voice which stops me. The compassion in his tone seems sincere.

"Please," he continues. "You need to settle down before you hurt yourself."

Strangely enough, even though he's my killer's brother, and I don't know him all that well—or should I say, *at all*—I believe him. I know I shouldn't, but I do.

Giving up my fight, I do as he says and gulp in a few deep breaths.

"Hey." He gives my arms a light squeeze. "You're going to be okay."

Eventually I settle, and my body relaxes against his, triggering me to notice exactly how skimpy my dress is. I gaze down and blush. Silver sparkles glisten from my *much missed* D-cup chest and reflect on Alex's arm. I feel exposed, yet—sexy. After being Harlow *the scrawny weakling* for so long, I'd forgotten what it was like to be the shape of an hourglass. I'd forgotten what it was like to feel desirable.

*Snap out of it,* I chastise. *This isn't the time to be self-indulgent.* Besides, this is the dress I wore to my eighteenth birthday party, it's the dress I was murdered in.

Tears sting the corners of my eyes. "Your brother killed me, you know." My tone is no longer angry or accusatory, it's raspy.

"I know." His breath is warm against the side of my cheek. "He killed me too."

Taken by surprise, I turn to face him, which—given our proximity—puts our heads in an awkwardly intimate position. "He did?"

He nods, his grip on my arms loosening. "Yeah, I was only nineteen, a year older than you were." He pauses a moment and then adds, "He made it look like a suicide."

# 13

# FILLED WITH QUESTIONS

## -HARLOW-

My eyes fling open. *No!* I have so many questions like: *Why did he do it? Have there been others? And how is it, that he's never been caught?*

And then something far more terrifying occurs to me, Jade is still there with Lucas—*alone*. Besides Alex, of course—assuming he's still there—but he is a ghost, he can't help her if Lucas attacks. Fear fills me, crippling my insides.

*Go back to sleep.* I stuff a pillow over my head. *Jade needs you; you must go back to Earth.* I try desperately to send myself back to sleep, but I'm too wound up; my mind is racing.

I feel like yelling for someone to help, but I'm no longer in the human world, and nobody here could do anything even if they wanted to. Chances are they wouldn't want to help anyway. Nobody here—besides Zavier—likes me enough to stick their neck out.

*I wonder if Jax would help?* Not that he could, but I wonder if he would. We may not be friends, but he did help me with my leg and glorified job. My heart flutters a little, making me instantly push these thoughts aside. Don't be stupid Harlow, this is no time to be thinking of Jax, your sister is in trouble.

The next few hours drag by. I'm motionless, and my eyes are shut tight, yet I'm still wide awake. My thoughts are scattered, and my nerves are on edge.

*Please let Jade be okay, please let Jade be okay.*

I can hear my parents rustling around, which means, I too, should get up soon.

I wait until I hear them leave before I get up. Now that I'm a librarian, my hours have changed. I start later than them. My calf is still tender and screams at me when I stand. I unwrap the bandage to relieve some pressure. It looks multi-coloured today, a mix of purples, reds, browns, and greens.

As I head for the washroom, I pass Floss' sleeping nook. It seems untouched. She mustn't have come home last night. *I hope she's okay.* Floss may hate me, but the feeling isn't mutual. I begrudge the way she treats me, and I resent we weren't born the same, but deep down, I love my sister—not in the same heartfelt way I love Jade, but I still care about her, even if she doesn't care about me.

After a quick rinse over I soon find myself in another predicament. *What am I supposed to wear today?* I don't have any nice clothes. My clothes are all worn and shabby. The only nice thing I have to wear is the outfit Jax had given me, but I wore that yesterday, and I feel embarrassed wearing it again for the second day in a row. As a fruit picker, it never mattered what I wore, I was excused for my ragged appearance, we spent our days trotting the forest, climbing trees, and crawling through dirt. But working alongside Purples, I won't be given any leniency. I'm supposed to look crisp and proper, like they do. I rummage through all my things but come up empty-handed. I don't possess a single piece of nice clothing; everything I own is spoilt with stains or holes. I look down to the end of my bed where the clothes from yesterday lay, and with a disappointed sigh; I scoop them up and slip them on.

*Second day in a row it is.*

Gazing at my refection, I manage a simple side braid in my hair. I would love to do cornrows, or a head full of braids—something much more exciting—but it's too hard to do it myself, and unlike other Zeeks, I don't have any friends to do it for me.

After polishing off last nights' dinner—which had been left on the bench—I slip on my flats, grab my crutches and head out into the icy passageway. Both baby toes sting, as the fronts of my shoes rub against the raw blisters I'd obtained yesterday. I never knew flats could be so painful. *I miss my worn old boots.*

As I pause to re-adjust my left shoe, I hear my name being called. *It's Zavier,* I recognise his voice.

"Hold up," he yells, from down the passageway, and then picks up the pace.

When he nears, I ask, "What are you doing here?" Today was the first of his four days off. He should still be in bed, enjoying a well-deserved sleep-in.

"I couldn't sleep." His mouth pulls crooked at the side. "I felt awful knowing I'd upset you. I hadn't meant to sound cynical; I was just worried Jax might be setting you up for a fall, that's all. You know as well as I do, we Pastels aren't usually handed nice things for free. If a Purple does something nice for us, it usually comes with a hefty price tag." Seeing my frown, he gives a shrug. "Who knows, maybe Jax has honourable intentions, something's got to give even-tually—*right?*"

It's good of him to add in the part about Jax "being honourable", even though I can see by his facial expression he doesn't really believe it. The way he'd responded to my news yesterday wasn't the reaction I'd hoped for, but it seems he has his reasons. And in all honesty, I probably should be more suspicious of Jax. After all, I haven't done anything at all to deserve his help.

"I suppose I overreacted a little," I offer.

He opens his arms to me, and I notice his left forearm is bandaged, probably to cover the burns he doesn't seem to want me to know about. "Friends?"

I step into his embrace, crutches and all. "Friends," I say, giving him an awkward hug. I can't afford to remain upset with him over something so trivial. He is my best friend—*my only friend*. Without him, I have no one.

Zavier offers to walk me to the library, and I am grateful for his company. I need the distraction, not only from the physical pain of my torn calf and two blistered toes, but also from the fear circling my mind. *Jade.* I'm worried about her, *super worried*, especially now that I know *exactly* what Lucas is capable of.

A few times during our walk I consider telling Zavier about my dreams, but I find it difficult to string the right words together. *How do I explain my dreams are actually reality? Only I'm no longer on planet Zadok, I'm on Earth, and I'm no longer Harlow the Zeek, I'm Ruby the human. What's more—I'm not alive on Earth but a ghost of my former self...*

*Geez.* My explanation sounds so crazy—even I struggle to believe it.

When we get to the chiselled stairs before the library, Zavier insists on helping me down. He's not as swift in his movements as Jax had been. His arms strain under my weight, and exertion lines mark his face. I'm too heavy for him to lift comfortably.

As he places me down at the bottom of the steps, I smile and say thank you. A bead of sweat rolls down the crease of his forehead, and he wipes it away. I feel bad for him. I wish there was something I could do to help make him stronger.

"By the way, I brought something for you." He opens his hand to show our small multi-coloured magic rock, and I smile.

The rock isn't really magic, so far as I know. We were only six when we found it. It was wedged inside a deep crevice of the passageway outside of the sewing factory cavern Lexan and Zavier's parents used to work at. We'd been playing around in the passageway, waiting for them to finish up, when I'd spotted it shimmering. I showed Zavier, and he'd carefully dug it out with the pocketknife his dad had given him for his sixth birthday.

"It's magic," he'd said as he handed it to me. "It'll keep you safe."

Less than a year later, the day his parents died, I handed it back to him, telling him the same thing he'd told me.

Over the years we've handed it back and forth to each other, mostly at big turning points in our lives.

Zavier places the colourful rock into my hand and repeats the same line we always say to each other when passing it over. "It's magic, it will keep you safe."

"Thank you," I say, and then I hurriedly slip the rock into my pocket before anyone sees it.

Zavier opens his mouth to say something else, but like the flick of a rubber band, he quickly closes it again, allowing me to hear the patter of footsteps coming up behind me. It seems something—*or should I say someone*—has captured his attention. Given the glare, my guess is it's a *particular* someone—Jax.

The sound of a deep voice confirms my suspicions. "Are you ready?" Jax asks and I turn to face him. "I thought I'd quickly get you settled in before heading to training." His eyes flicker between Zavier and me. "Save any unwanted hiccups."

"Yeah, I'm ready."

I swivel to say goodbye to Zavier, but he has already taken off, his feet now climbing the bottom few steps.

As Zavier continues up the stairs, Jax moves forward, tilting his body to face me more directly. His gaze is so powerful, I can feel it. "I take it your boyfriend doesn't like me much."

I fidget beneath the intensity of his stare. "He's not my boyfriend," I correct, my eyes lifting to meet his. "And he doesn't dislike like you, he just doesn't trust you." I use this opportunity to assess his reaction. There's no shock in his expression. This information doesn't surprise him.

"Do you trust me?" he asks, his right brow pointed with curiosity.

90

"I think so." I tug nervously on the fur of my jacket. "I mean... I don't understand why you're being so kind to me. I haven't done anything to deserve your kindness."

His eyes regard mine. "I have my reasons," he says, and leaves it at that. "Come on." He beckons, before I have the chance to ponder. "Let's get you started for the day."

Before we get to the entry, I pause. My heart is pounding at a ridiculous rate. If everyone looks up, they'll see I'm in the same clothes as yesterday, and they'll laugh, I know they will.

Noticing I've stopped, Jax turns back to face me. "What are you doing?" His forehead is scrunched. "Are you coming?"

Feeling desperate, an embarrassing idea pops to mind.

"I was wondering, were...were there any other nice clothes left in lost property?" It's mortifying having to ask this of him, however, sadly he is the only person I can ask. I'm certain these clothes hadn't really come from lost property; they look fresh and newly sewn. I believe he traded for them. He only told me they came from lost property to save my pride.

At first Jax appears confused by my question, but as his eyes scan over me, understanding flashes across his face. "I will check for you."

I gaze down at the marble like floor, my cheeks burning with embarrassment. "Thank you," I say. "I appreciate it."

Once inside the library, the first Zeek I see is Electra. She appears to have noticed me first, and her face is set in a scowl. I flinch at the sight of her; she's certainly an intimidating woman.

Sensing my unease Jax mutters, "Just keep walking."

When I arrive at my seat, my eyes are immediately drawn to a colourful picture sitting on top of my desk, it's the comic RJ had been drawing yesterday, only it's finished. Pictures from yesterday's uproar fill the boxes, and the words "NO PASTELS ALLOWED" is scrawled across a few of them. Jax's face is sketched tight and rigid, with a ready to pounce Sphinx crouched at his side. Electra has been drawn yelling, with bubbles of capital-letter-words escaping her mouth. The librarians have also been drawn with bubbles; only theirs are faint, and the words are written in lower-case, indicating they are whispering. And then, last but not least, there is a solo drawing of me. I'm standing alone, my face worn and miserable. *Geez, I hope that's not how I really looked.* My miserable expression is so confronting, it almost has me feeling sorry for myself.

I flip the paper over to find a picture of RJ and me, sitting alongside each other.

Our desks are littered with paperwork, but we don't look worried, we look busy. The words **"KEEP YOUR HEAD DOWN—and if you're lucky, they'll ignore you"** are scrawled along the bottom of the page. I squint as I read the words over and over again. I'm not exactly sure what to make of them.

*Where is RJ?* I wonder. I haven't seen him yet. My eyes do a quick scan of the library before returning to the picture. *I'm not sure whether this was done as a kind gesture, or if it was done to torment me?*

Jax peers at the comic from over my shoulder. I crane my neck to look at him. His face is tight, unreadable.

"What should I make of this?" I ask.

"RJ should have been an artist, not a librarian." He snatches the drawing from my fingers and starts to curl it up into a scroll.

In a rush of panic, I throw my hand out to stop him.

"Don't destroy it," I say. It's clear my outburst has taken him by surprise. "I'd like to keep it if I may."

His brows shoot up. "Why?"

"No one's ever drawn me anything before."

His expression relaxes a little, although he still looks doubtful about handing the scrolled piece of paper back to me. "Just promise you won't read too much into it. RJ isn't like the rest of them, he means no harm." He nods in the way of a greeting to someone beyond me. "Speak of the Zeek," he mutters under his breath.

I spin around to see RJ heading towards us, weighed down by a large pile of paperwork in his hands.

"Greetings." He nods, his eyes staring off elsewhere. He is a unique character, both in looks and in personality. His voice is distinct as well. He doesn't sound like most Zeeks, he sounds semi-robotic, like a character out of the human movie Star Wars.

As he shuffles towards his seat, he spots the picture curled beneath my fingers and does a double take. Feeling guilty, I straighten the paper out.

Not knowing what to say, I place the picture back on my desk where I found it and force a semi smile. Not noticing my efforts, RJ dumps the large pile of paperwork on my desk. The stack lands straight on top of the comic.

"Now..." He splits the pile in half, taking the top section for himself. "This should keep you busy for a while."

Once I'm settled in my chair, Jax gives a satisfied nod and turns to leave. Sphinx scurries over to where I sit, giving me one last sniff over as a way of goodbye. His thick, purple coat is so beautiful, I have to fight the urge to reach out and pat him.

Being Head Hunter, my father was supposed to care for one of the heterochromia huskens which are given to the hunters to help to drive the hunting sled. Sadly, he'd refused, leaving Fau, the second in charge, to care for both huskens. I'd begged him to reconsider, but he'd blatantly refused, telling me he hated animals—*heartless grinch*. I suspect this is the reason he's such a skilled hunter. It's easy to kill when you don't have a heart.

During the course of the day I overhear the prune faced librarian say it was because of Jax I'd been able to work with the Magentas. The Commander wanted me to be sent down to work with the Pastels, but Jax had argued the matter, telling her it was unfair—and if I was good enough to live with my Magenta family, I should be good enough to work with them. According to prune face, Jax's decision to help me had caused a huge rift between the Commanding brothers.

"Rumour was," she'd whispered. "Nix planned on having Jax assassinated, but Stavros killed him before he could put the plan into action."

Yesterday, Electra mentioned Nix didn't want any integration in the colour system. He despised the idea of us mixing. He must have felt strongly about this if he was willing to sacrifice his own flesh and blood for the cause.

*Had Jax really helped me? Is this how he knew who I was?* I feel flattered, yet sick. Nix may not have been a nice Zeek, but he was still Jax's brother, and I'd hate to think I'd been a wedge between the brothers.

Hopefully, this story isn't true. Zeeks have spent their entire lives gossiping about me, *the privileged Pastel, or the Defective Magenta, either goes, take your pick.* Prune face probably knew I was listening in and was purposefully feeding a load of lies to upset me.

I lean back in my chair, taking in the magnificence of the crystallised shawls draping down from the high cathedral ceiling. To think how many centuries they've seen pass, continually surrounded by bitching, bickering, and nastiness. If shawls could speak, the tales they would tell.

RJ taps his pencil on my desk. "Keep your head down," he says under his breath. "And if you're lucky, they'll ignore you."

Considering this is the first—and only thing—he's said to me since Jax left, I do as he says and turn my attention back to the leftover papers on the desk in front of me.

I'm not entirely sure what he's been doing this whole time. After Jax left, he'd placed a large hardcover book up in-between us as a blockade. My guess is he's been drawing, not working, but as much as I'd like to peek, I don't.

My theory is confirmed at the end of the day, when RJ hands me another picture he's drawn, only it's not a comic this time; it's a sole portrait of me. Hundreds of tiny words circle my head, most of which are hurtful, yet sadly familiar. They were the nasty words I'd overheard circling through the library today. Clearly RJ had overheard them too. At the top of the page, in big bold letters it says, **"STICKS AND STONES WILL BREAK MY BONES, BUT NAMES WILL NEVER HURT ME"**. It's a common human saying, and one I remember using back at Blaxland Primary School when a girl in my class insisted on calling me nasty names.

I've never heard a Zeek use this saying. *I wonder how RJ is familiar with it.* A shadow forms over the picture, as someone steps up close behind me.

"What's this?" an icy voice says, and with a swift movement, the picture is snatched from my fingers. A snarl escapes Electra's throat. "Really, RJ?" She crumples the picture into a ball and then throws it at him, causing him to cower. My insides burn—*Bitch! I wanted to keep that picture.*

"I don't believe drawing pictures for the newbie is a part of your job description. In fact, if you keep drawing during work hours, I'll personally see to it, you are removed from your position as librarian." Her words are sharp, cutting, and RJ's hands quiver in distress.

"It's not his, it's mine…" the words automatically spill from my mouth. "I drew it."

RJ's eyes dart to mine, wide with surprise.

Electra sniggers. "Is that so?" She knows the truth, but unless RJ admits to drawing it, she can't prove anything, and therefore he can't be held accountable. "Well, well." She circles the back of my chair like a shark. "I didn't realise we had another artist in our midst." She grabs the back of my chair and spins it around, bringing us face to face. She pinches my chin tight between her thumb and pointer, and jars my neck upward, forcing me to look straight up into her chilling gaze. "Know this," she says, her eyes slitted with warning. I feel her nails dig into my skin as her grip tightens. "Jax may be the Commander's son, but I am in charge here, and if I were you, I wouldn't get too comfortable." A zap erupts from her fingers, and within an instant, my whole face stings, like as if a thousand needles have pierced through my skin. From the stinging sensation grows a sharp, icy, burning sensation, which penetrates through my skin and invades my skull. I want to scream but I feel crippled, frozen. Stars fill my eyes, and my body topples from the chair…

# 14

# STILL CONNECTED

## -HARLOW AS RUBY-

*A* high-pitched scream rings through my ears—not mine. *Ouch!* I clasp my head with my hands; afraid my frozen skull will shatter against the sound. And then, like a flash, I realise something, and it's enough to make me momentarily forget about the pain. It's Jade screaming... *SHE'S IN TROUBLE.*

My vision is cloudy, but regardless of my current state, I blink back the blur and rush towards the sound.

She won't hear me, but this doesn't stop me from shouting her name at the top of my lungs, "JADE! JADE!"

A thousand sickening scenarios tick over in my mind, furthering my state of panic. I swear if Lucas has done something to her, *he will pay!* I will make it my mission to make his life a living hell.

As my hazy vision clears, I discover I'm not where I thought I was. I'm exiting the front gates of my old high school—and what's more startling is it doesn't appear to be school hours; the sky is far too dark. *This can't be good.*

Still running, I lift my arm to check the time on my watch—*no luck.* The small round face is nothing but a bouncing blur. My eyes scan the area to find a pack of teenagers hovering around the bus shelter. I frown in confusion. Upon further examination, I notice they are dressed in casual clothes and holding suitcases, some with sleeping bags and pillows. They must be going on a school camping trip. A bus pulls into the empty bay, and the sound of hydraulic brakes, along with the shriek of squealing teens, drown out Jade's screams. Unable to hear her anymore, my panic increases—that is —until I spot a crowd of people gathered in a circle on a lawn, diagonally across from the school. My eyes squint into focus, and between the gaps of bodies, I see her. She is crouched over next to Lucas; her head cradled in her hands.

Adrenaline surging, I dash across the road without looking. A SUV ploughs straight through me, startling me, and my limbs threaten to cease. I refuse to let them, I force myself to keep running to the lawn.

"GET AWAY FROM HER!" I yell, not to the crowd but to Lucas.

"Wait a minute…" Alex's form exits from the crowd, and he dives in front of me, forcing me to a halt. His arms take hold of mine, and I fight against them.

"Before you go in there, guns blazing, I want you to know this wasn't Lucas' fault. He didn't do anything wrong."

"Get off me!" I force his arms away and dash over to Jade.

Lucas' hand rests on her lower back. "I don't understand what's happening?" he says, and if I didn't know any better, I would say he looked worried.

Two teenage boys break their way through the crowd, both appearing frazzled. The smaller of the two, skinny with long blonde locks, races straight over to Jade. "Mum," he cries in a panic, "Mum, what's wrong?"

"Should I call an ambulance?" asks the other teen. He is much bulkier than Connor, and his hair is short, dark, and curly.

Jade's screams may have subsided, but she is still cradling her head in her remaining hand. "I'm okay," she finally croaks, although her body language indicates otherwise.

Lucas' face looks flushed. "What can I do?"

"Back off," I answer sharply, and even though I know he can't hear me, I add, "And keep your filthy hands off her."

"He's only trying to help." Alex now stands beside me, and I shoot him a dirty look.

"I don't care; I don't want him near her." I try to rip Lucas' arm away from Jade's lower back in frustration, but my attempt is futile.

Concerned voices shout from all directions, some asking questions and others giving advice, but my sister doesn't answer, leaving her son Connor to speak for her.

Clearly overwhelmed by the chaos, Lucas' eyes dart from person to person, his brows scrunched in stress. Eventually, he reaches into his pocket and pulls out his case of cigarettes along with a lighter.

"I have no idea what happened to her," Alex says, and my eyes snap to his. "One minute she and Lucas are having a normal conversation, and next thing I know, she's screaming. Lucas didn't touch her—I swear. He hasn't had a drink in years."

Anger causes my cheeks to burn. "Why are you defending him?"

"He's my brother." Appearing genuinely baffled, he adds, "And honestly, he's done nothing wrong this time. I have no idea why she started screaming."

A scoff leaves my lips. "He's done nothing?" I shake my head in disbelief. "Your brother is a murderer, so excuse me if I'm more than a little suspicious. I don't know where you're from, but where

I'm from, people don't tend to scream their lungs out for no reason."

Turning my back on Alex in haste, I step over to where Connor stands, and crouch down to peer up at Jade's face. Her hand still covers one side, but from what I can see, there doesn't appear to be any blood seeping, nor does there appear to be bruising. Her exposed eye is shut, and her lashes are wet with tears.

Connor holds a small screen of light in his hands, which shows a photo of a girl on it, along with several rows of small squares, each with different symbols and colours.

"Mum, what should I do? Should I call Dad?"

She gives a slight shake of the head, and he slips the screen back into his pocket. *Hold on… That device was a phone?*

Jade remains in a crouched position until a short, chubby, bald man comes racing through the crowd with a chair.

"Here," he says, placing it down behind her. His eyes dart to Lucas. "Get her to sit down."

An elderly woman with salt and pepper hair emerges from behind the man, a glass of orange liquid held tight in her hands. "Here." She hands the glass to Connor. "Get her to drink this."

After being aided to sit, Jade slowly lifts her head, allowing her hand to drop from her face. She looks okay, unmarked—*as far as I can see*—only a flush of pink has spread across her cheeks.

Her eyes lift to meet Connor's. "I'm so sorry, Son." She appears flushed and confused. "I don't know what happened. It felt like a major brain-freeze came over me; only I wasn't eating or drinking anything cold. It occurred out of nowhere." Her forehead scrunches. "I don't understand."

"It's okay, mum." Connor hands her the drink. "Here, drink this."

Realisation hits me, like a slap to my—already sore face. "Holy cow, it was me…" I raise my hand to my gaping mouth in disbelief. *The awful pain she'd felt was because of me.*

Admittedly, this isn't the first time something like this has happened to us. Jade and I shared a lot of strange experiences when we were younger, although, it'd never been to this magnitude.

Strange occurrences weren't unheard of with twins, so we'd accepted it. But I'm not her twin anymore; *I'm dead. This makes no sense. Our connection should be severed.*

"What was you?"

Pushing my earlier resentment aside, I spin around to face Alex.

"The brain freeze," I say. "I was given a brain freeze by someone back on Zadok only seconds before I got here. It must have transmitted to her somehow, she must have felt it. We must still be connected."

His brows knit at first, but after giving what I've said some thought, he simply says, "There you go. I told you Lucas didn't do anything."

Annoyed by his remark, my resentment reignites. I glare into his eyes, teeth gritted. "This isn't really the time for I told you sos."

"You're right." He leans forward and cups my shoulder with his hand. "I'm sorry." His eyes gaze into mine, earnest with sympathy—and even though I'm angry—I can't help but stare back into them with wonder. Coffee brown, with a hint of golden warmth, they are so similar, yet so different to Lucas'. It's hard to know if he genuinely cares, or if it's some kind of act to lure me in. Lucas is deceitful; he may be too. They are twins after all. Besides, I don't understand how he can be so quick to defend his brother, knowing what he knows. Lucas is a cunning, cold-hearted killer. *He is scum.*

The longer I stare at Alex—trying my best to figure him out—the more I take in the rest of his features. His skin is olive, and smooth, and he has a lovely shaped nose and cleft chin. His lips are full, and unlike Lucas, his teeth are all white and straight, with only a minuscule gap between the top two front teeth to add character. He looks nearly identical to the young Lucas I knew, only he's a *much* better-looking version. I would even go as far to say he is quite good looking.

*Oh my goodness, what are you doing?* The rational part of my brain kicks in, and I give an abrupt shrug of the shoulder, causing his hand to slide right off.

"Don't worry about it, it's fine." I step aside, putting distance between us.

"Hey Connor." The teen with the curly hair walks straight through me. "We'd better go; the bus is about to leave."

"That's Rueben in case you're interested," Alex says, appearing to overlook the fact I'd given him the shrug off. "Josh's Son."

My eyes examine the teen standing before me. He's quite different to what I'd pictured Josh's son to look like. His skin is the colour of cinnamon, and his hair is black. Considering he was sticking close to Connor, and I'd heard Lucas say they'd become good friends, I had wondered if it was him. *He must get his looks from his mother.*

"Here, let me help you," I hear Lucas say, and through my peripheral, I watch him help Jade up from her chair, so she can kiss Connor goodbye.

Connor's forehead is creased. "Are you going to be okay?"

"Don't worry," Lucas says, along with a puff of smoke. "I'll drive her home. Your Dad can bring her back to pick up her car later this evening."

I open my mouth, ready to protest, and then quickly remember —*they can't hear me.*

I don't like the idea of her being driven home by Lucas, *he's dangerous.*

My expression must be readable, because Alex puts his arm around me and says, "Don't worry; we'll go with them."

# 15

# IRRITATING YET INTRIGUING

## -HARLOW AS RUBY-

*J*ade's house is only a few blocks away from the school. We could have easily walked back to her place. It seems humans have become even lazier than I remembered.

Zeeks don't have cars, and only the warriors and hunters are able to drive the sleds. The rest of us have to use our feet to get wherever we need to go, and for some of us, that involves a whole lot of walking. Drakes are the same, they go everywhere by foot, but Rukes and Vallons have the luxury of getting around by other means. Rukes, the Autumn "wind" folk, have wings. They can fly to wherever they need to go. And as for Vallons, the Summer "fire" folk, they have horsens. Horsens are horse equivalents only they are much larger and faster. Their fur is brightly coloured, a mix of reds, oranges or yellows, depending on the horsen. I'd seen one once when I was younger, back when the Vallons had attacked our caves. I was very small, but I remember being mesmerised by its magnificence, until...

*Don't think about it!* I warn.

The car finally pulls into the driveway of a modern two-story home. From the front, Jade's place looks *absolutely* massive; it's got to be at least double, if not triple, the size of the family home we grew up in.

Thinking of our old place gets me thinking about our parents. *I miss them.*

Alex gives me a gentle nudge. "You look lost in thought." He cranes his neck to face me, his golden eyes gleaming. "What are you thinking about?"

Not wanting to share, I say, "Your brother's car stinks," and then exit through the door, onto the driveway. It's the truth. Lucas' car is old, dirty, and absolutely reeks of cigarettes.

Jade rustles through her handbag, searching for her keys. After a few seconds I hear a jingle, and out they come, clasped in her hand.

"Thanks again," she says, giving Lucas a small wave. "I really appreciate your help."

Lucas leans his head out of the driver's-side-window, watching her intently. *Creep.* "Are you going to be alright?"

Jade gives a nod and proceeds to the entryway, but to my dismay, she spins back around to the sound of Lucas' car reversing out.

"Lucas wait," she calls, and he stops to look over at her. She appears anxious and hesitates. "Would you like to come in for a coffee? I found something I'd like to show you."

The world comes crashing down around me. *No Jade.* She's making a terrible mistake.

Lucas pulls back up the driveway, eager to accept. "Sure, I could use a coffee."

Once inside, Lucas follows Jade to the kitchen, helping himself to one of her sleek silver designer bench stools. His eyes wander as she fills the jug, inspecting the floor-to-ceiling windows which line the back wall, offering an amazing view of the valley of trees beyond her professionally manicured backyard. The inside of her house is jaw dropping too, furnished in a modern style far beyond what I could have ever imagined. There are a few mint feature walls which work perfectly with the rest of her mint and jade home-wear. She always loved the colour of her name.

"You've done very well for yourself," Lucas says.

"With my and Byron's combined income, we haven't had to struggle," Jade says, her face flushing slightly. "We both studied hard and have good paying jobs." She pauses, then backtracks. "Well, I mean we both *had* good paying jobs. Byron is the only one working at the moment. I've had a few interviews since moving back here, but I haven't had any luck as yet."

Lucas' stool creaks as he rocks back and forth on it, and I can tell by the creased lines along Jade's forehead, she is not happy about it. "What is it you do exactly?" he asks.

"I'm a forensic scientist."

His stool comes to a halt. "A forensic scientist," he repeats.

She nods. "After Ruby died, I spent every afternoon of the following year searching every square inch of the bushland behind my parents' place, but sadly, like the police, I came up empty hand-ed." She shrugs. "The problem was, I was out of my league, I didn't know what I was looking for, or how to go about retracing some-body else's footsteps." She dumps her handbag at the end of the bench, causing the buckles to clink against the stone. "After wasting a year wandering helplessly through the bush, I entertained the idea of becoming a detective."

Lucas swallows hard as she speaks, his left leg jiggling wildly, as it'd done when he was sitting by the river.

Seemingly oblivious to this, Jade continues to speak. "After talking to a few people in the field and doing a bit of research on the ins-and-outs of it all, I changed my mind and decided I wanted to study forensic science instead."

"Huh…" he murmurs. His gaze drops to the benchtop in front of him. "Well, you always were the brains of the group. I'm sure Ruby would be proud."

He's right, I am proud, in more ways than one. Regardless, I don't appreciate being spoken for, especially by him.

I hadn't known Jade was a forensic scientist, never mind the fact that she'd become one because of what had happened to me. My heart swells in my chest. *Oh*, how nice it is to have a sister who honestly cares about me.

"Talking about Ruby," Jade says, breaking me away from my unpleasant thoughts. She places two mugs on the stone bench. "That's kind of what I invited you in for." After pulling out a teaspoon, along with the sugar and coffee containers, she adds, "I'm going to quickly duck upstairs for a second while the jug's still boiling. I'll be back in a tic."

A few moments later she re-enters the kitchen with a box —*my box.*

"No!" I scream ineffectually.

She takes it to the bench, and I follow, hoping against all odds I can get through to her somehow.

"Please don't show him," I beg. "They're my treasured things." I try to snatch the box from her hands, but I can't; my fingers slip straight through. "He'll taint them with his murderous hands."

Unable to hear my pleas, she reaches into the box and pulls out an old photo. "I was going through some of Ruby's stuff the other day and came across this."

She passes him a photo of the five of us, me, her, Josh, Dale— her boyfriend at the time—and Lucas. The photo was taken at the Hawkesbury Show in front of the Ferris wheel. Josh had been majorly hungover that morning and hadn't wanted to go on many of the rides. This meant I'd spent most of the day pairing up with Lucas—who at that point in time—was too shy to speak more than two words to me.

As I stare down at the photo now clasped in Lucas' hand, my memories from that day flood in. Besides bickering with Josh all morning—which wasn't unusual—I was happy. I'd loved everything about the Hawkesbury Show, the rides, the showbags, and best of all, the games. I'd been an absolute master at the target game; I'd nailed every single shot right on the centre of the bullseye. Come to think of it—*that was the day I won Billy.* My gaze falls to the soft blue teddy bear squished in the corner of my box of treasures, and I realise with a heavy heart, I'm not able to pick him up. *I am dead. I'm dead because of Lucas.*

My eyes hurl daggers in his direction. "You bastard," I say under my breath. I attempt to snatch the photo from his hand. It's useless. "You stole my life."

Unaware of my efforts, a rumble of a laugh leaves Lucas' throat, and I cringe at the sound of it. "Gee whiz, look how young we were." He uses a finger on his free hand to point. "Dale Purdy, tell me, what did you ever see in that guy?"

Jade smiles. "I know, right? He's certainly no Byron."

My body trembles as hurt and resentment rip through me. I find it disturbing how he can sit there, casually looking at a photo of me, and yet, show no sign of remorse. I was only eighteen years old when he killed me. I had my entire life ahead of me. I had a family who loved me.

A lone tear escapes my eye and runs down my cheek.

"Hey," Alex taps my shoulder, and I jump. "You don't wanna watch this. It's only going to upset you."

I whirl around to face him, gaze sharp. "What do you care?"

He blinks in surprise, making me feel guilty.

I hadn't meant to be so rude, but I still haven't forgiven him from earlier. I don't like how protective he is of his brother. Lucas is a murderer. He killed both of us. Yet for reasons I can't fathom, Alex is intent on defending him.

"Oh Rubes," Alex says sympathetically.

*Rubes?* I'm taken aback. Only Jade has ever called me Rubes.

He uses the back of his pointer finger to wipe the moisture away from my cheek, and I flinch, my eyes quickly darting upward to meet his. His coffee-coloured irises appear warm and full of compassion, yet somehow, I still don't know whether I can trust him.

Although he may seem decent and caring enough in this moment, he's still Lucas' twin, and this alone leaves me feeling guarded.

"Why don't you come and check out the pool with me," he offers. "It's pretty amazing."

"Is that where you've been this whole time?"

I'd wondered where he'd disappeared too. I was beginning to question whether he'd even followed us inside.

He takes me by the hand, causing a swirl of mixed emotions to run through me. "Come on, come with me."

He's clearly not afraid to get up close and personal with someone he's just met. I don't exactly know what to make of him, and this bothers me. He irks me yet intrigues me all at once.

I jerk my hand back and shake my head. "No." My gaze turns to Jade. "I don't want to leave her here alone with him. I have to stay and protect her."

"We won't be far, it's just out back. Come on, you've got to see this pool." A thin smile plays on his lips. It's cute, he's cute. *No, you can't think that!*

My gaze flicks between him and Jade. I know he's trying to distract me with that charming smile of his, but it won't work. I don't want to leave Jade alone with Lucas.

Sensing my hesitation, he says, "You're not always going to be here to protect her, you know this—*right?*"

"I know, but she's not always going to be alone with Lucas *either*," I point out.

He holds out his palm, fingers spread to show all five, "Come on; give me five minutes, it's all I'm asking for. I haven't got much time left here, anyway. I won't hold you up, I promise." He ends his sentence with a flirty wink, which again leaves me emotionally confused.

I blush. *How embarrassing.* I'm not sure what's come over me. I'm never usually like this. It's been a while since I've received this kind of attention from someone. I'm letting it get the best of me.

Giving Jade one last glance, I take in a deep breath. "Fine," I say, finally giving in to him. "But I'm only giving you five minutes."

I follow him to the back of the house, and out through two floor-to-ceiling glass doors which lead to a patio.

The magnificent resort style pool catches my eye, and I gape. "Wow." It hadn't been visible from the kitchen due to the hedges.

It's shaped like a jellybean with an adjoining circle spa sitting in the belly of the bean. On the opposite side to where we stand is a rock wall, built with several waterfalls which trickle from the top rocks, all the way down to the water. Jutting out from the middle of the rock wall is a curved slippery slide, and it too has water flowing down from it.

"You're right," I say. "This pool is amazing."

Alex steps off the patio and goes and sits by the pool steps, allowing his long legs to dangle down into the water.

"Can you feel it?" I ask curiously.

"No, not really, but I imagine I can." He pats the spot next to him. "Why don't you come see for yourself?"

I hesitate, a part of me wants to rush back inside to check on Jade, yet there's another part of me that's curious—not only about the feeling of the water—but about him. So much about Alex is a mystery to me.

Going against my better judgment, I make my way over and sit beside him.

"Connor's one lucky kid being brought up in a place like this," Alex says, a hint of envy lacing in his voice. "Lucas and I were lucky if we had shirts on our backs."

I dip my legs into the water and discover once again, he's right. I don't feel anything.

"Josh told me you guys had a rough upbringing," I say. "I'm sorry, it must have been hard."

His eyes meet mine. "You've seen his scars, haven't you?"

The memory of accidentally walking in on Lucas *naked* in the bathroom turns my cheeks hot.

"Yeah." I nod. "I have. How did you know that?"

"Lucas mentioned the incident to Josh a few years back. I guess it's always bothered him."

*Huh...*

"Our childhood was horrendous," Alex says, and I sense deep, dark resentment boiling inside him. "Our parents were junkies of the worst kind. Drugs were their life. They'd do anything for that high." He turns to face me, and even though I know it's wrong, I find myself staring at the scar along his brow. "As toddlers, when Lucas and I were too loud, they would inject us with heroin to keep us quiet, or worse yet, if they had none, they would beat us into submission." Noticing my curiosity, he points to his brow. "This here, was from being head-slammed into the corner of our kitchen benchtop." He then points to the scar on his lip. "And this here, was from my father's ring."

The thought causes me to cringe. "I'm sorry," I say once more.

"Don't be." He shakes his head. "It's not your fault they were low-lifes." Breaking eye contact, he stands up and wanders down the pool-steps until finally he gets to the bottom.

Guilt courses through me—*poor guy.* His parents abused him, and then his own brother killed him; and to think, I thought I'd been given a bad hand. I may not have a family who loves me back on Zadok, but at least they don't beat me into submission.

I suppose I can see why Lucas has turned out violent. I've heard that children who have been brought up in abusive families often grow up to be abusive adults. I don't understand it though—but then again, I'm no shrink.

Knowing this does not mean I can forgive him. A rough upbringing doesn't give you the right to murder people, especially your friend—or worse still—your own flesh and blood.

My gaze trails Alex as he wanders along the bottom of the pool. I take it he's forgiven Lucas.

I'm not sure whether I'd forgive Jade for killing me; it's hard to say, when I know deep down, she'd never do it.

"Ummm." My voice catches in my throat. I need to change the subject. "You said you don't have much time left here. What does that mean?"

His gaze snaps to where I sit. "I've got to wake up soon."

"Wake up where?" I kick my legs around, trying desperately to cause a splash. *No such luck.*

Alex chuckles at my failed attempts, and I'm glad to see there's a smile back on his face. "The same place you're from."

"Zadok?"

He nods.

"Huh…" I place my hand in the water, hoping I'll feel something. *Nope. Nothing.* "What does this make us?" I ask. "Are we ghosts?"

"I guess so." He shrugs. "Ghosts, Spirits. I'm not really sure what else you'd call us."

I ponder for a moment. "Are there others like us?"

"I've only seen a few others, but I'm sure there are more of us out there—there'd have to be." He strolls over to the deep end, until all that is visible above the water is his head. "I haven't spoken to any other ghosts though, the only ghost I've spoken to is you."

"Why do you think we're here?" I ask. "Do you think it's because we're still connected to our twins?"

"I assume so." He gives another shrug. "But I don't really know. I know as much as you do."

I heave myself up and make my way down the steps. It feels strange. I'm surrounded by water, yet it's not touching me. I'm as dry as a chip. It's like I'm caught in some optical illusion.

"I don't understand," I continue as I reach him. "This whole *being here* scenario—whatever it is—has only just started happening to me. I've always remembered my life as Ruby, but until a few days ago I'd never revisited Earth." My fingers fiddle with the hem of my dress. "I didn't even know it was possible. The first few times it happened, I thought I was dreaming."

"And you're sure now that you're not?"

"Am I?"

He chuckles. "You're not dreaming. Trust me, I've been coming here for years."

"Years…? How many years are we talking?"

I suddenly feel ripped-off. Until recent days, I'd spent every waking hour wishing I could see Jade again, and now I find out Alex has been coming here for years.

I get no response, so I rephrase. "When was your first time here?"

Alex's playful expression darkens. "It was a long time ago," is all he says.

"How long is long?" I push. "How old were you?" When he doesn't respond—yet again—I continue to push harder. "Where did you appear? Was Lucas there? Jade was there for my first—"

"Wow, hold up," he says, gesturing for me to pause. His gaze locks on mine. "Talk about the Spanish inquisition." He swallows, his eyes dimming a shade. "Look, I think it's best if we don't talk about this."

"Why?"

"Trust me, you don't want to know."

"Why?"

His expression grows stern. "Stop pushing."

"Why won't you just tell me?"

I know I'm frustrating him, but I can't help it. I want to hear his answer.

He forces a puff of air from his nostrils. "Do you honestly want to know?" he asks irritably. "Because I will tell you if you really want me to, but I promise you, you're not going to like it."

I nod. "Yes, I want to know. Please… Tell me already."

His eyes evade mine. "I was only four years old on Zadok, the first time I woke up here—looking exactly the same as the day I died. I was even wearing the same clothes." He gestures to himself in emphasis. "I could tell life on earth hadn't stood still though, because Lucas looked four years older than when I'd last seen him.

"Despite my initial confusion, the body swap between my two lives hadn't been an issue. My mind was advanced compared to your average four-year-old's, because I still had all my memories from this life. It was quite the advantage." His eyes flick to mine momentarily. "You know what I mean, right? I'm sure you were the same. Always much older and wiser than your peers."

I nod, and he gazes off again.

It's true. From the time I was two—as Harlow—I remembered

everything about my life as Ruby. It was like I was an eighteen-year-old, stuck in a toddler's body.

"I had no idea that everything I was seeing was real," Alex continues. "Like you said earlier, I'd thought I was dreaming." He pauses, a look of angst washing over his face. "No, this isn't right." He shakes his head. "I can't do this. I can't talk about this with you."

His strained reactions tell me that his first experience here was a bad one. And given the way he's holding back, I'm guessing it has something to do with me.

He said he was four at the time, so I do the figures. I dated Josh for three years before I was killed, and from what I'd been told, Alex had died around a year before Josh and I met. Even with adding a four-month Zeek pregnancy to the mix, it's plausible he was around the four zone on Zadok when I died.

"You saw me die, didn't you?" I say thickly, and his eyes dart to mine. "You saw Lucas kill me."

He nods, a shadow of guilt shading his face. "When I first arrived, you were having fun. You were singing and dancing by the firepit to the Chili Peppers. You looked so happy and radiant. I couldn't help but smile watching you." A pained breath escapes him. "But within the hour, Lucas had had one too many drinks and snapped, and everything turned to shit. Like I said, I didn't know it was real; I thought I was dreaming." He scratches the back of his head. "I tried desperately to save you, only I couldn't. I couldn't touch you. I couldn't touch anything." Sorrow glints from his eyes. "I'm sorry, there was nothing I could do."

As my memories of that horrid night flood back in to haunt me, a sick feeling grows inside me. He'd witnessed his brother kill me —*how awful.*

Before I get the chance to respond, Alex's face flickers. "Alex?" Concerned, I automatically reach out to touch his cheek. "What's happening to you? You're flickering."

"I'm sorry." His flickering hand cups mine, making all my nerves light up. "I have to go, it's time to get up," he says before disappearing altogether.

# 16

# FOUL PLAY

### -ZAVIER-

*I* sit by the steps of the library impatiently waiting. It's almost five forty-five, three-quarters-of-an-hour past Harlow's finish time, yet she still hasn't come out. I can't really blame her for taking her time. She didn't know I was coming to meet her, but the longer I sit out here, the more frustrated I get.

Chances are she's dawdling through the SCI-FI aisle searching for another book to read. Since the age of four she's been addicted to them. She'd learnt to read much earlier than most Zeeks, and as a result, she would often quote bits and pieces of her favourite novels to me. Her face would light up as she compared herself to the human characters, telling me about all the same places she'd been to, and some of the similar things she'd seen.

Strangely enough, her father had been somewhat proud of her back then. *Okay*, maybe *proud* is an overstatement. Let's just say, he'd been more accepting of her. Our teacher had told Saul, Harlow was very advanced compared to her peers and had a bright and promising future ahead of her. She'd also gone on to say that Harlow's academic level far surpassed Floss', her Magenta twin, which I believe helped to drive a wedge between the two girls from a young age.

Sadly though, as Harlow grew older, our teacher's opinion of her changed dramatically. She got fed up with Harlow's ongoing "fanciful human stories"—her words, not mine—and went from labelling Harlow incredibly intelligent, to delusional. She was a firm non-believer.

I glance down at my watch for the hundredth time. If the situation were different, I'd probably go inside to see what she's up to, but with this new work arrangement she's got going on, I don't feel comfortable. Harlow has a better opinion of Purples than I do. I don't crave their acceptance; I despise them, and I think she's made a big mistake by accepting Jax's offer. Purples are selfish and untrustworthy, and they don't give a damn about us Pastels.

The fact that Jax has given Harlow a job which is supposed to be reserved for Purples tells me there's something major he wants from her. However, I still haven't worked out what this *something* is.

Footsteps echo from behind me, along with the pitter-patter of canine paws.

"What's going on? Why are you sitting here?" asks a deep voice, and I don't even have to turn my head to know whom it belongs to.

*Rude!* "Isn't it obvious?" I grunt with irritation. "I'm waiting for Harlow."

His shadow passes over me as he continues down the steps with a large hessian sack slung over his shoulder.

"Harlow should have finished ages ago," he says, and as he

reaches the bottom step, he spins around to ask me, "Has she not already left?"

His husken lurks on the stair above me, and I feel a drip of saliva hit my forehead as it sniffs through my hair. Annoyed by this, I swat it away. "Get out of it."

"Has Harlow left?" Jax asks impatiently. "Have you seen her?"

I begrudge the urgency of his tone. I've been waiting here for over forty-five minutes without any answers, yet here he is, getting impatient over the matter of a delayed reply.

Giving the husken another swat, I shake my head. "No," I say irritably. I pull my hoodie up over my already drooled in hair, to protect it from being further slimed. "Not since I've been sitting here."

A shadow of a frown crosses his face. "When did you get here?"

I shrug. "I don't know, a quarter to five maybe. Why? What's the urgency?"

"Electra!" he hisses through gritted teeth, and then without answering my question, he tosses his sack to the ground and storms towards the library.

Unsure whether I should be worried or not, I quickly follow his lead. To presume Harlow had stayed back to rummage through the SCI-FI section had seemed like the most likely scenario, but I'm now starting to second guess my assumption. If Jax is worried, then chances are I should be too.

He's much faster than I am, and before I know it, he's already halfway across the library. His frame now towers above one of the librarian's desks. As I get closer, I recognise the librarian seated in front of him—Electra, the one whose name he'd hissed. She'd been in the same level as Nix at school, which would make her at least nine years older than me. You'd never know it by looking at her. If I were to guess without knowing, I'd say she was early twenties.

She's been working here for quite some time. I know this, because Harlow would often drag me to the library against my will, assuring me it would only take a few minutes of our time. Her few minutes often turned out to be hours' worth of aisle searching, hence the reason I hadn't been too worried about her taking so long —*until now.*

I scan the dust-covered aisles before me; the SCI-FI aisle appears empty, as do most of the others. There are three bays up the far end of the library, but I can't see into the aisles from where I'm standing.

"To what do I owe the pleasure?" Electra asks. Her question comes across as taunting rather than welcoming, but by the looks of her menacing expression, I'm guessing that's the whole idea.

Plum coloured locks cascade down her hard face, deep and rich, much like her pockets, *I'm sure.*

Jax leans closer, his face mere inches away from hers. "Where is she?" His voice booms.

Amusement flashes in her eyes. "I'm sorry, but there's been an accident. I've had to send your little pet for a lay down at the back."

*Accident!* My insides twist. Meanwhile Electra's lips are curved up at the corners. She's treating this as a joke. I almost feel like slapping her, although I wouldn't. I'm not that kind of guy.

"A couple books fell from one of the top shelves Harlow was stacking," she continues. "The poor little Pastel was knocked out cold." Turning her attention toward a young Purple guy, sitting a few desks away, she asks, "Isn't that right, RJ?"

RJ's eyes dart from side to side, and the pencil in his hand quivers. He looks as if he doesn't want to agree, but in the end, he concedes.

Jax's eyes briefly flash to RJ, and then back to Electra, every muscle in his body tensed. "Harlow shouldn't be filling bookshelves; she's supposed to be here on light duties. You know this!"

Not wanting to waste any more time watching these two idiots fight it out, I race to the back of the library hoping to find Harlow. I scan the first aisle, nothing, and then the second, nothing, but as I get to the third aisle, I see her. She's stretched out across the floor in an awkward position, her arms above her head, as if she's been dragged there.

"Harlow!" I crouch down to tap her face but stop short when I notice two angry burn marks on both sides of her chin. "What the frost have they done to you?"

Guilt courses through me, I should've come inside to check on her. I'd been so certain she was aisle gazing, I hadn't thought beyond that, even though I'm the one who's always telling her not to trust Purples. I mentally slap myself for being so stupid.

I lower my head to her chest. It's rising and falling, which tells me she's still alive, but her skin colour's off, she looks paler than pale —no pink shimmer. I straighten her body into a better position and use all the strength I can muster to scoop her up in my arms.

"It's okay," I say. "I'm going to get you out of here."

As I turn to leave Jax comes racing over to me at lightning speed. "What's happened to her? Is she okay?"

I shoot him a glare. "Does she look okay to you?"

His gaze snaps to the red marks on her chin, and his nostrils flare in anger. "Here." He holds his arms out. "Let me take her."

I jerk away, almost stumbling backwards as I do. "You're not touching her. It's your fault she's like this. It was your kind who did this to her." I go to storm past him but realise I'm trapped. Tall aisles filled with books block both of my sides.

"Please." His eyes grow serious. "At least let me look at her."

He holds his arms out once more, and again I jerk away. "No! Now get out of my way."

He doesn't move, causing my fuse to burn shorter by the second. I'm not strong enough to move him by force. I'm hardly strong enough to hold myself upright. My muscles have barely recovered from the last rescue mission, and yet here I am, rescuing her again.

"Where are you going to take her?" he asks.

I groan in frustration. *Enough with the hold up.* Not only is he wasting my time, he's wasting my strength. To carry her home, I needed to preserve as much strength as I possibly can.

Sweat drips from my hairline, down to my brows. "I'm taking her home. Now move already."

I go to shoot through the gap he's left, but he side-steps me, aggravating me further.

"You need to take her to the medical chamber." He puts out his hands again. "You're struggling. Please, let me help you. I'm stronger than you are; I'll be able to get her there faster."

His words are true, and cut deep, which triggers my defences. "Why?" I ask, my voice dipping with anger. "So, you can fabricate another big cover story for this injury too? I know her leg wasn't an accident. I know you're all hiding something. Harlow's too afraid to tell me the truth because you're blackmailing her somehow."

His eyes plead with me. "Trust me, it's not what you think."

"Isn't it?"

Electra comes strutting over to us, putting a pause on our argument. "Who's this scrawny unkempt thing?" she asks, her lilac eyes analysing me from head to toe with disapproval. "Another one of your pet projects?"

*Pet projects?* I scowl and she laughs.

"You really are taking this to the next level, aren't you, Jax?"

Ignoring her comment, Jax's eyes meet mine, his expression tight and serious. "Don't take her home," he says, voice hushed. He steps aside for me to pass. "Take her to your place where you can watch over her."

Not prepared to waste another minute speaking to him, I jump at the opportunity to split, and despite my inner protests, I do exactly as he says. I head towards my place.

The trip home takes much longer than I'd anticipated. My inner frustration has become my enemy, causing my energy levels to burn at twice their usual rate. In the end, I become fatigued, and have to stop every five minutes to take a break.

Jax was right, he is much stronger than I am, and although I know it wasn't his intent to offend me, I still resent his comment. I've spent years trying to build up my body strength, forcing myself through a nightly routine of sits-ups, push-ups, squats, lunges and planks, yet it seems to have done nothing for my physique. I am still weak, *damn it!* Pitifully so. Jax could have carried her all the way to the Spring border and back by now, yet here I am, only now reaching the entryway to my cavern. And to add insult to injury, I'm so drenched in sweat; I look like I've taken a dip in the pool. Thank goodness Harlow isn't awake to see this, or she'd discover how pathetic I truly am.

Noticing me stumbling through the entry, Harlow hanging low across my arms, Lexan leaps from the lounge to come and help me. "What's happened to her now?" he asks, lines of worry marking his face. "Is she okay?"

"I don't know."

Between the two of us, we get her to my sleeping nook and into my bed. Although, given the tight proximity; it proves to be a bit of a contortion act.

Our cavern is not very big, but then again, no Pastel cavern is. All of us lower class insignificants are forced to live in tight spaces and survive with the bare minimum. Anything we can get our hands on after that is deemed a luxury.

After pulling up the blankets, Lexan runs his index finger along her jawline and squints. "What's this on her face?"

"They look like ice burns to me," I reply.

"They?"

"She has one on the other side too," I say, and then slump down onto the floor, next to the bed.

"How did she get them?"

"I'm not sure, *exactly*. But I intend on finding out."

Lexan's brows crease further as he inspects the other side of her face.

"I'll ask her when she wakes up," I say. "Although chances are, she won't tell me anything." Feeling frustrated, I let out a long breath. "I think they've got her blackmailed."

"Who?"

"The Purples." My eyes lift to meet his. "You know she's working with them now—*right?* She's landed herself a job in the library."

"No." He shakes his head. "I'm not told much. Krista tends to leave me in the dark. It's a bit of a one-sided relationship that way, always has been." His eyes flash between Harlow and me. "Is this where you carried her from? The library?" He assesses my current state with knitted brows. "Frost. It's no wonder you're beat."

"Tell me about it." I slump down even further, until I'm lying on the floor. My muscles burn like fury; I feel as if someone has set my entire body on fire. There's an old stale shirt on the floor next to where I now lie, and I bunch it up in a ball to use it as a pillow. It doesn't smell the best, but at this very moment the shirt on my back smells far worse. "I need to rest for a bit," I say bitterly, knowing it's the truth. "Can you please watch her?"

"Of course." He pulls up a chair and takes a seat. "By the looks of it, I need to keep an eye on both of you."

I feel like I've barely nodded off when I'm disturbed by the hum of voices. However, after checking my watch, I see over an hour has passed since I got home. My muscles still burn and my head throbs. After sweating profusely this afternoon, I've become dehydrated to the point where my tongue feels like sandpaper.

*Get up and get a glass of water before your brain fries*, is what I tell myself, but my limbs don't want to co-operate. They despise me as much as my head does.

With a great deal of effort, I drag myself up off the floor, using the edge of my bed as leverage. Boy does it hurt. I've severely over-done myself this time. I should never have carried Harlow all the way here by myself, but my pride got the better of me. *You're paying for it now aren't ya*, I groan. My body struggles with every movement I make. *Thank goddess I've got the next three days off work.*

When I rise, the first thing I see is Harlow's face, which brings a smile to mine. She is still unusually pale, and her burn marks have darkened to a brownish-red, yet somehow, like always, she remains the most beautiful Zeek I've ever seen.

My blankets hug tightly around her, her body lying exactly as I'd positioned her over an hour ago. *I wonder if she's even stirred.*

Now that I'm up, the voices become more distinct. Lexan's voice is soft, speaking in hushed tones, but the other voice is deep and rumbling. Hearing the rumble causes my blood pressure to increase. *For crying out loud. Everywhere I turn lately, there he is.*

"How very kind of you," I hear Lexan say, and it makes me want to gag. I hate how everyone falls at Jax's feet. *Okay, yeah, he's strong, rich and powerful, but come on…he's deceitful, they all are. It's part of the Purple DNA.*

I refuse to show respect to anyone who forces us to live in squalor, while they live in the lap of luxury. We have next to nothing, and they have everything, yet there's not a goddamn thing any of us can do about it. If we were to put up a fight, we'd lose. We don't have the strength or capability.

As I leave my sleeping nook to step out into the living-kitchen-dining room, I catch Jax slip something off his shoulder.

"This is hers too," he says, dumping a hessian sack by the entryway.

It's the same sack I'd seen him carrying earlier. Knowing it couldn't possibly be Harlow's, I eye it with suspicion.

Jax's husken is the first to notice me, and lets out a loud bark. *Annoying mutt,* so much for my tiptoeing out here in order to spy a little first.

Both Lexan and Jax glance up and see me.

"Look who's here!" Lexan says, and despite what I've told him about the Purples blackmailing Harlow, he seems sickeningly delighted to have Jax visit our cavern. It irks me so much, I don't dignify what he's said with a response. Instead, my eyes zoom in on Jax.

"What do you want?"

Lexan looks shocked by the bluntness of my question. Jax however, grins. He'd obviously expected this kind of greeting from me.

"Harlow will need her crutches tomorrow." He points to a set of crutches leaning against the limestone wall of our living area. "She will also need her clothes."

"Clothes?" My eyes dart between the hessian sack and him. "Why do you have her clothes?"

Ignoring my question, he turns his attention back to Lexan. "How is she?" he asks. "Has she woken up yet?"

"No," I answer before Lexan gets the chance. "Now please leave. You're not needed here."

Lexan's head whips around to face me, his eyes surveying mine with shock and disappointment. "Zavier." His voice is firm. "That's no way to treat our guest."

"Guest?"

Undeterred by my rudeness, Jax continues to speak—only it's to me this time, not Lexan. "I don't plan on staying for long," he says. "I'd like to take a quick look at Harlow, and then I'm happy to go. I want to make sure she's okay."

"She's fine," I say, folding my burning arms over themselves. "Like I said, we don't need your help. We're taking perfectly good care of her."

"I don't doubt that, but I'd still like to see her regardless."

"Of course, you can see her," Lexan quickly chimes in. "Here, come with me." He motions for Jax to follow him, meanwhile, shooting me a look of warning. "Never mind, Zavier," he adds. "He's always grumpy when he first wakes up."

Between Lexan, Jax, and his mutt, the area to my sleeping nook is well beyond capacity. I'd like to get in and keep an eye on the situation, but there's absolutely no room left for me to squeeze in.

"What's that?" Lexan asks, and I'm straight up on my tippy-toes, trying desperately to peek in.

"It's a cream for her burns," Jax says. "She should have it applied every few hours. It will cool the skin and help to prevent any scarring."

Despite my efforts, I can't see a thing. I give up on spying, grab a glass of water, and head over to our lounge. My muscles ache like crazy, and there's no point in standing around aimlessly.

Over the next few minutes Jax and Lexan continue to discuss Harlow's condition. Jax is worried that she hasn't woken yet, saying he's afraid she might have slipped into a coma. He also says he believes she needs to be taken to the medical chamber where she can get proper medical attention, and to my dismay, Lexan agrees.

After discussing the matter further, Lexan leaves my nook to come over and speak with me.

"I already know what you are going to say," I warn. "And my answer is no. She's staying here."

"I wasn't planning on asking you, Zavier, I'm telling you. She needs proper medical attention, and you know as well as I do, we can't give it to her."

My face turns to fire. "You're only mimicking what he said," I argue.

"Well the fact of the matter is, he's right."

*You've got to be kidding me.* I shake my head. "Don't you remember our discussion from earlier? You can't trust Purples. They are liars and cheats."

"That's enough." Lexan's voice is stern.

"They're the ones that did this to her."

"Zavier, I've said that's enough." His expression hardens. "I don't want to hear one more word from you, you got it? Jax is taking Harlow to the medical chamber, and that's final."

# 17

# I'M STUCK AS A GHOST

## -HARLOW AS RUBY-

I've never been Ruby for quite this long before, it's been over thirty-five hours, yet here I am, still wandering planet Earth as a ghost of my past life. *I wonder what's happened to Harlow*—or should I say, *what's happened to me?* I know I'm not dead, because last night I heard familiar voices filtering in from back home, they'd hummed in my ears, continually waking me from my sleep.

Most of what I'd heard came through muffled. I do, however, distinctly remember hearing Lexan mention Krista's name. He'd said, "Krista tends to leave him in the dark"—*whatever that means.* I hadn't realised he and my mother knew each other that well. She's never mentioned him, but then again, my mother doesn't share things with me. I'm sure there are a lot of things I don't know about her.

I gaze at Jade, snuggled on her lounge under a fluffy mint-green throw rug, her fat grey cat nestled by her feet. She stares intently at the large theatre sized TV screen mounted on the wall in front of her, attempting to distract herself. Connor is still on school camp and will be for the next three nights.

I overheard her telling Byron over breakfast that she was already struggling with his absence. "He's never been away from us for this long," she'd said.

"You need to relax," Byron had told her. "It's only been one night, and if you continue to worry like this, you are going to give yourself another stomach ulcer." He had taken her in his arms and placed a kiss on her forehead. "Connor is out having fun with all his school mates. Now take a deep breath and try to be happy for him."

An image of an alien fills the screen and Jade jumps. I don't really understand what was going through her mind when she chose this particular series to watch. Stranger Things, I believe it's called. It's about a young boy who's been abducted by aliens. It's very captivating, and I've enjoyed watching the past few episodes with her, but I don't believe it was the smartest choice she could have made, especially when her nerves are already on edge about having Connor away from home for the next few nights.

"Ah… Not this rubbish again," says a cheeky voice from behind, and Fat Cat—or so I've decided to call him—leaps from Jade's feet to hiss.

Taken by surprise, my head whips around, as does Jade's.

"Alex?" Feeling self-conscious, my face instantly flushes. I must look like a proper mess.

"Lucas has been watching this crap too," he continues unaware of my embarrassment. "Only he's up to the next season." He gives a mischievous grin. "Want some spoilers?"

I stand up from where I'm seated, my whole frame shifting to face him. "What are you doing here?" I brush my hand through the ends of my hair. "Have you been here long?"

Unaware of our presence, Jade tells off Fat Cat—or should I say Mittens—for scaring her and goes back to focusing on the show.

*Huh…* I think to myself. *Unlike Jade, the cat must be able to sense us somehow.*

"Why? Am I not welcome here?" he asks, brows arched.

"No, of course you are. It's nice to have someone around who I can actually talk to." Truth be told, I'd been hoping I'd see him again. Our last interaction was cut short, and there are still so many questions I'd like answered.

He gives a warm smile. "Well I'm glad to be of service."

I gaze down at my watch. "It's almost two-thirty," I say. An image of the first time I saw Alex flitters through my mind. It'd been at around this same time. School pick up time. "Do you often come to Earth at around this time?"

He shrugs. "Besides yesterday, I usually end up back here, anywhere between two and five—give or take. It varies depending on what time I get back from hunting." A satisfied grin plays on his lips. "We had a successful night last night, so I'm here on the earlier end of the gauge. Between me and my brother Kenneth, we managed to fill our cart to the brim within the first few hours of being out in the forest."

I frown, not only at the thought of him being a hunter, but also at the thought of him hunting at night.

"You hunt during the night?" I blink in confusion. "Why would you do that? It's dangerous. Besides you'd struggle to see anything."

"We filled a whole cart in four hours. Trust me, we don't struggle."

I take what he's said and try to connect the dots. "How does this work?" I ask. "How often do you visit Earth? Are you here daily?"

"I've been coming here every single day since…" His gaze lowers. "Well, you know."

"It's a never-ending process then, day in, and day out? How do you do it? Do you ever sleep?" I feel exhausted thinking about it.

"You sure know how to roll out the questions, don't you," Alex says with a chuckle. "Don't worry, when I'm here Slater is sleeping."

"Slater?" My brows pucker. "Is that your name from back home?"

He nods. "Yeah, but my friends just call me Slate."

"Friends," he said—*plural*—as in more than one. Clearly, he's far more popular than I am.

"My name back home is Harlow," I offer. "And unlike you, I only have one friend. He just calls me Harlow."

"Harlow," he repeats with a smile. "It's pretty, I like it." His Nescafé Gold coloured eyes gaze into mine, warm and bright, unlike Lucas' plain Nescafé 43 coloured eyes.

Lucas hadn't stayed long yesterday. By the time I came back inside, he was gone. I'd been worried he might linger, but it seems Jade's little talk about detectives and forensics must have scared him off. I had hoped it would be for good, but since Alex is here, chances are Lucas may be here too.

"Where's Lucas?" I ask. "Is he here too?" I crane my neck to gaze past Alex's figure, but all I come across is an empty corridor.

"No need to stress. I'm here alone." He rocks on his heels. "Our last encounter didn't really end the way I would've liked it to. I wanted to come and see if you were okay."

"Oh." I blush. "Well, thank you, that's very kind of you, but how'd you know I'd still be here?"

"I didn't. I took a stab in the dark." He stiffens when he realises what he's said, his cheeks flushing. "Shit..." He scratches his head. "I'm sorry, that was an unfortunate choice of words, I...um..."

Sensing his embarrassment, I wave it off. "Forget about it."

Dramatic music vibrates from the surround sound speakers in the ceiling, and I gaze back at the TV just in time to see Barbara being taken by the Demogorgon.

"No." I put my hand to my mouth. "Not Barb."

Alex sniggers at my reaction. "Okay, enough of this rubbish. You need to walk away now before it rots your brain." His tone is light and playful. "Besides, I've come up with a plan—which I assure you—is MUCH more exciting than lounging around watching phoney aliens all day." He holds out his hand, in a gesture for me to take it. "What do you say?"

Feeling unsure, I hesitate. "What's your plan?"

Golden eyes sparkling, the side of his mouth hitches up in amusement. "Here she goes again folks, the girl of many questions." A faint laugh escapes his lips. "Come on," he says holding his hand out again. "I'd like it to be a surprise."

I still don't know for sure that I can trust him, but I want to. I don't suppose it really matters at the end of the day. I'm fairly certain I can't be killed twice.

"This had better be good," I warn. "Because I can't rewind this show, and by the looks of it, it's getting exciting."

Giving in, I place my hand in his, and to my astonishment, my desire to stick around and find out what happens to Barb, suddenly diminishes. Electricity zaps between our palms, causing my tummy to do a backflip.

Stunned, I almost snatch my hand back, but something compels me to hold on.

*Please don't blush. Please don't blush.* I don't understand why he's having such a powerful effect on me. Sure, he's appealing, and sure he's showing me some sort of kindness, but he is still my killer's twin brother for crying out loud. Something must be terribly wrong with me.

*You can't feel anything for Alex,* I scold. *It would be WRONG on so many levels.*

Unable to control myself, I dare to meet his gaze. His expression is full of eagerness and excitement. *I wonder if he can feel the electricity too, or he's just excited about revealing his big surprise.*

"Don't worry," he says, his voice laden with confidence. "It'll be *well* worth it."

## 18

# SO CLOSE, YET SO FAR

## -HARLOW AS RUBY-

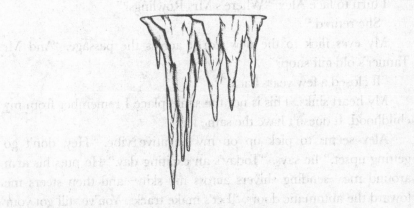

*A*fter strolling past a few blocks, lost in conversation, I gaze up at familiar surroundings.

I pause mid-sentence, my eyes light up. "I know where we are. We're at the back of Blaxland shops."

Cars made in all shapes and sizes litter the car park. Most of them far more modern and bubble shaped than the cars I remember from over eighteen years ago, but there are a few recognisable oldies parked here and there, and I take comfort in seeing their familiar shapes.

"I'm guessing a lot has changed since you were last here."

I eye one of the bubble shaped vehicles parked across the way and sigh. "You're not wrong."

Plagued by a hollowness I hadn't expected to feel, I cross the road and head towards the shops, hoping to evoke that same familiar, homely feeling I used to get when coming here as a kid. Once inside, my disappointment deepens. Most of the small shops along the passage, have either changed hands, or been replaced by new businesses altogether.

Following the aroma of freshly baked goods, I make my way to the other end of the passage and pause by the bakery, looking for the same familiar smiling face I'd seen every Sunday morning when buying a hot loaf of bread. It isn't there. Instead, a fresh young face comes to greet the customer standing by the cakes display.

I turn to face Alex. "Where's Mrs Rowlings?"

"She retired."

My eyes flick to the new florist across the passage. "And Mr Tanner's old gift shop?"

"It closed a few years back."

My heart sinks. This is not the same place I remember from my childhood. It doesn't have the same feel.

Alex seems to pick up on my negative vibe. "Hey, don't go getting upset," he says. "Today's an exciting day." He puts his arm around me—sending shivers across my skin—and then steers me toward the automatic doors. "Let's make tracks. You've still got your surprise to see yet. It's further up the road."

We head out the front doors and veer left. The path runs along the main highway, and we follow it upward until we get to a street by the bend in the road.

Alex beckons me with his hand. "Come on, your surprise is this way."

I can tell he is eager because he's picked up the pace and is now charging ahead of me at full speed.

"Wait up," I call.

He slows a little, but doesn't exactly wait, and it isn't until we pass another dozen houses that he finally stops.

"Here we are," he says, pointing to a small brick house with a quaint rose garden out the front. The scent of the roses fills the air, and as I sniff in deeper, the scent tickles the inside of my nostrils.

Unsure why he's brought me here, I stare at the house, trying desperately to figure out its significance. I rack my brain for answers but come up blank.

Feeling puzzled, I frown. "This house doesn't ring any bells. Why are we here? Do I know the person who lives here?"

A smile flitters across his lips. "You'll understand once we get inside. Here, come on, we'll head in together." His hand wraps around mine once more, and my heart swells.

Feeling embarrassed, I try using humour as a distraction. "Well at least I know you're not luring me in to kill me," I say, forcing a smile. "I'm already dead."

Alex frowns, not appreciating the joke. "Hilarious," he says dryly.

As we enter through the front door, a small tan-and-white fur ball appears, greeting us with three consecutive ear-piercing yaps.

I cringe at the high-pitched sound. "Can the dog see us?" I ask.

Alex shrugs. "It appears that way."

"And what about Jade's cat?" I add. "He could see us too —right?"

"No matter where I go, dogs always bark, and cats always hiss." His lips twist. "I get the feeling they don't like having me around."

"Yeah, I noticed Fat Cat wasn't your biggest fan."

Fur Ball scurries back and forth through our feet as we make our way down the corridor, and with every step Alex takes, another round of ear-piercing yaps escape the dog's throat. For such a tiny dog, he makes one hell of a racket.

"Jersey," a voice shouts, and the dog pauses mid yap, his ears perking up at the sound of his name. "Shut up would you, nobody's here."

*Hold on…* My heart skips a beat. *I recognise that voice…*

"Mum?"

Letting go of Alex's hand, I quickly race off in the direction the voice came from. This leads me through a side archway and back towards a pale blue lounge room with a zig-zag, navy-white rug.

A woman with short red hair and an hourglass figure stands by the window of the room; her back is towards me, as she carefully peeks through the gaps in the blinds. The last time I saw mum, she was a stick-figure with long blonde hair.

"Mum?"

Unable to hear me, she mutters, "Stupid dog," and then steps away from the window, her frame automatically turning in my direction.

"It's her," I gasp—*it's really her.* Her face is as I remember, only rounder, and slightly more lined.

Overcome with joy, I charge towards her, attempting to give her a hug. She may not be able to see, hear, or feel me, but it doesn't matter, I still act as if she can. "Oh mum," I say. "I've missed you so much."

There's no doubt about it, for a woman in her late-fifties she looks absolutely amazing. It's no wonder Jade looks younger than her years.

Noticing Fur Ball scurrying towards her, tail wagging, she unknowingly dumps me mid-air-hug, and leans down to speak to the dog.

"Get over here Jersey, you noisy little rat." Her voice is playful. "No more barking or I'll have to take you to the pound." He scurries to her feet and rolls on his back, asking for her to scratch his tummy. "I tell you what dog," she says, allowing him the scratch. "You're lucky you're so cute."

"Well…" says Alex, and I turn around to find him leaning by the open archway, his warm golden eyes seeking mine. "What do you think? Better than watching phoney aliens?"

A tear of joy escapes down my cheek. "Yes," I say, using the back of my hand to wipe the moisture away. "It's a wonderful surprise. Thank you."

He smiles. "I thought you'd be eager to see how your parents were doing."

"How'd you track them down?"

"They've been living at this address for a long time now," he says. "They sold their old house and bought this one, around about a year after you died. You were gone and Jade had been accepted into a course at The University of Queensland, so I guess they felt it was finally time to move on to somewhere new. Josh was still in contact with them back then and offered to help move their furniture across in his work truck." His gaze lowers before adding, "Lucas gave him a hand, which meant my spirit tagged along for the day."

My eyes snap to his, and he shifts awkwardly where he stands.

"I learnt a lot about you that day," he says. "Josh had a lot to say during the moving process and then, your parents threw a barbeque as a thank you afterwards, and everyone sat around sharing their favourite stories."

A lump forms in my throat. Imagine how my parents would feel if they knew that my killer was one of the guys who helped them move to their new house.

*And as for Lucas, the psychopath, how could he possibly bear to face my parents, knowing he'd murdered their daughter?*

The thought of Lucas sharing his fond memories of me makes me sick to my core. I'm glad I hadn't been around to witness it. I'd rather listen to the sound of someone scratching their nails against a blackboard.

Letting out a long breath, I take in my surroundings. To my delight, the lounge room has been made up like a gallery, spanning a lifetime's worth of memories. Photo frames upon photo frames decorate the blue walls, all of them in various shapes and sizes.

Seeing these pictures displayed before me, sends me on a trip down memory lane.

On the top row, there's a picture of Jade and me dressed up like princesses. And in the next row down from that is a very 1990's shot of us posing as Michael and Janet Jackson. I smile to myself. *How cute were we?* We were always dressing up.

While scanning along the bottom row, I spot a picture of me with Ouzo—our Maltese/shih-tzu cross. It was taken in our old back yard by the pink-and-white frangipani tree. Without thinking, my gaze wanders beyond our faces to the bush backdrop, and I cringe. No wonder my parents moved to a new house. Not only would they have felt lonely with us girls gone, the day-to-day view of that bushland would have been a constant reminder of my death.

Feeling a little queasy again, I try to squash these thoughts and move to the other side of the room.

On the top row of this side, there's a photo of Jade's wedding day. *She looked stunning.* Tears prickle my eyes. I wish I could have been there for her.

Two frames across from this is a picture of Connor and her, standing alongside each other, shoulder to shoulder. *Far out.* It seems odd to think she's thirty-six now with a teenage son who is as tall as she is.

Stranger still, this could have been my life too, had I of not been murdered. I could have been married with a child, or maybe even children.

This idea causes my thoughts to take flight.

*Jade and I could have hosted family barbeques together every other weekend.* I close my eyes to imagine it.

*Our husbands could have cooked snags and chicken skewers, while drinking beer, and squabbling over who was going to win the next game of rugby league.*

*Our children would be there too, of course, either mucking around in Jade's celebrity style pool or playing cricket together in Josh's and my overgrown backyard.*

*Josh and I would have bickered, because that's what we were good at, and Jade would have lent me her ear as I complained about his inability to pick up after himself, or keep our lawn freshly mowed.*

*Despite the ups and downs of our own personal family drama, Jade and I would always have each other to turn to, and for the most part, we could've been happy.*

To prevent myself from becoming lost in this fairy-tale idea, I force my eyes open. *If only I hadn't been murdered.*

I continue to scan along the next row of pictures, one by one, until I come across a photo of me in Josh's arms.

The picture was taken on the evening of my and Jade's year ten formal. Lucas had driven the three of us to the Nepean River, so we could meet up with some friends and take photos. Seeing Josh's face causes my insides to knot.

*Look at him with his thick, honey-brown hair and those piercing blue eyes. Gosh that boy drove me crazy.* The top few buttons of his shirt were unbuttoned—*God forbid*—and the corsage he'd bought me was yellow, which hadn't at all matched the red of my dress—or his blue shirt for that matter!

I'd been annoyed about this, but I'd managed to hold my tongue. I was surprised he'd even accepted to be my date given he was a senior, and I hadn't wanted to wreck our whole evening over silly little details.

Alex makes his way over to where I stand, and I stiffen. I'd been so caught up in my memories, I'd almost forgot he was here with me.

"Do you miss him?" he asks curiously.

Josh had always been a selfish jerk—there's no denying this—but despite his flaws and our constant bickering, I'd somehow fallen head-over-heels for the guy. He would excite me yet infuriate me in ways I couldn't describe. Not to mention he kind of resembled the actor Jared Leto from the TV show My So Called Life. It was all so long ago I barely even remember the show anymore. *I wonder what Josh looks like now.*

I stare at the picture a little longer before answering.

While it had been fun to fantasise about Josh being my husband, the cold hard reality is, we were toxic for each other. I hardly think we would've made it through another year together before busting up.

"I don't really know how I feel about him anymore," I say, and it's true. "Besides, what does it matter? It was literally another life-time ago."

"I know he spent a long time mourning you," Alex says, leaning forward to inspect the picture. "It took him several years to move on, and even then, I've heard he still carries this same picture of you two in his wallet."

"Really?" I gaze back at the rebel-with-no-cause in his unbuttoned shirt and find it extremely difficult to imagine him becoming sentimental.

"You know it's funny," I say, feeling sceptical. "Because I'd always felt like I was way more into Josh, than he was me."

"Well, I wouldn't name my kid after someone I 'wasn't all that into', would you?"

I frown. "What do you mean?"

"Rueben, it's the boy version of Ruby, wouldn't you say?"

Unable to believe Josh would go that far, I shrug it off. "It could be a coincidence. The names aren't that similar."

Alex shakes his head. "You're wrong. Nearly everyone, bar Sarah, picked up on the similarity, however, it wasn't until Rueben's first birthday, Josh finally admitted it."

"Who's Sarah?" I ask.

"Josh's wife."

"Oh…" I flush at the obviousness of the answer. *Duh.* Curious, I ask, "What's his wife like?"

One of Alex's brow's rise. "Ahuh!" He uses his index finger to poke my shoulder. "You do still miss him. I knew it."

Embarrassed, my cheeks flush yet again. "No," I say, swatting him off. "I'm merely curious."

"Honestly, I don't really know her well, but she seems alright." He shrugs casually, and then adds, "I guess…" His eyes meet mine, bright and intense. "She's no you, I know that much."

I feel my pulse quicken while heat flushes my skin. It's ridiculous. I'm seriously getting all worked up over a compliment from a guy I hardly know—and if I'm being honest with myself—shouldn't get to know.

*Come on, Ruby—Harlow—or whoever you are,* I warn. *Pull yourself together, he's your killer's brother.* But even with all my warnings, I can't help but feel a spark between us. Thankfully, the sound of the front door opening, mixed with Fur Ball's yaps, is enough to distract Alex from my beetroot-coloured face.

He cocks his head to the sound. "That must be your dad."

"Shoosh you," says a firm voice in the distance, and Jersey abruptly stops yapping. "Mandy, I'm home."

"You're right," I say. "It's him. It's his voice."

Alex's brows pinch. "Well, what are you waiting for?"

I shake my head, ridding myself from chastising thoughts. "Right."

I exit the lounge room, and head towards the corridor, but I don't quite get there before his figure rounds the corner. At first glance I'm taken aback. *Eek!* He's put on a lot more weight than I'd expected, and he's grown a beard.

"Dad?"

I hesitate. I hardly recognise him. He looks *so* different. He used to be lean and clean-shaven, with dark brown hair, but now he's fat, hairy and grey all over. Mum may not have aged *much*, but he's aged significantly.

As he advances, I get a whiff of his cologne. Good old Brut. He may not look the same, but at least he smells the same.

Alex taps me on the shoulder, and we step to the side, allowing my dad to pass by without walking through us.

"Hey Rubes, I'm gonna head back to Lucas' caravan," he says.

Disappointment washes over me. "You're going? Why?" *I don't want him to go. I want him to stay.*

"You should have some alone-time with your parents."

My gaze lowers, as does my mood, for even though I'm happy to have been brought to my parents' place, it's not like I can spend any real quality time with them. They can't see or hear me, it's all one sided, *I'm a ghost.*

Feeling overtired, my emotions plummet into a semi depressed state. It's the closest I've been to my family in years, and yet they're still out of arms reach. I'm unable to hug them or tell them how much I've missed them. All I can do is watch on silently as they go about their everyday routine.

Alex is the only *real* company I've got here. Without having him around to talk to, I have no one. I'm even worse off than Harlow.

I can't bring myself to look desperate by pleading with him to stay. Instead, I pretend to agree with him. "Yeah, I suppose you're right."

Seeming to recognise my disappointment, he asks. "Will you be back at Jade's around this time tomorrow? If so, I can pop back in again if you'd like? We can hang for a bit."

Unsure, I twiddle with a loose sequence on the hem of my dress. "I might be," I reply. "But I can't say for certain."

"What do you mean?" He gives me a sidelong glance. "What time do you usually appear here?"

"Well, I don't really have a routine like you do. The first few times I appeared here were random and short lived, but this time it's different. I'm still here from early yesterday morning, I never left."

"What?" He glances at his watch and his brows crease. "It's four-thirty," he says. "Are you telling me your body back on Zadok has been asleep for over thirty-seven hours?"

"I don't think I've been sleeping," I say and then swallow. "I think I'm in trouble. I'm starting to worry that the Harlow side of me isn't going to wake up."

He rubs his forehead with his hand. "Shit!" He paces a little. "Shit! Shit! The brain freeze. I should have realised."

"Alex?" His reaction is more extreme than I'd expected. I don't understand why he's so upset. I can't mean that much to him. We've only just met. Unless, of course, he feels the same spark between us as I do.

His eyes swivel towards me. "I can't help you," he says in frustration.

My forehead crinkles. "It's okay. I haven't asked you too."

"No." He shakes his head, his feet coming to an abrupt halt in front of mine. "What I mean is, I want to help you, but I can't. It's too risky."

While I'm flattered to see how much he cares, I'm confused, and I'm certain it shows.

Sparks or not, he doesn't know me as Harlow, he only knows me as Ruby—and even then—most of what he knows is from other peoples' shared memories of me. Besides how can he…

His warm hands gently cup my upper arms, and I try my best to disregard the electrical current which charges through my body. "Look, never mind," he says, breaking me away from my thoughts. "I'll find a way to help you." He leans in closer, his face pausing only inches away from mine. "You're going to be okay. I'll make sure of it."

He is close, *very* close. I feel the warmth of his breath on my face, and my heart races. For a guy I don't know all that well, he feels so familiar, and going by his intimate behaviour, I assume he must feel the same way about me. The thought of him leaning in those last few inches—to kiss me—flitters through my mind, and I stiffen. However, to my disappointment, or maybe it's relief—*I'm not quite sure*—he pulls back.

"I still need to go, there's something I've got to do, but I'll come back to your sister's place around this time tomorrow afternoon, okay?" His golden-brown eyes stare into mine. "Let's hope you've been home and back by then."

# 19

# THREATS

### -ZAVIER-

*A*s I enter the medical chamber, Harlow's SCI-FI book in my hand, I'm surprised to find a guy with purple-spikey-hair sitting by her bedside. At first glance I pause, I recognise him—well his unusual style hair and thick-rimmed glasses, anyway. I'm certain he's the guy from the library.

I eye his semi profile with suspicion. The movement of his jawline indicates he's speaking—but *what about* is the question I'd like answered.

During yesterday's row between Jax and the plum haired Mega-Beast, he appeared nervous. I could see it in the way his eyes darted side to side. My guess is he knows the truth about what really happened but was too afraid to speak out.

I creep a few steps closer and cup my ear to listen, however given the distance between us, and the constant beeps of a nearby machine, I can only faintly make out the muffle of his voice.

Afraid that he'll see my shadow if I step any closer, I force myself to crouch down, and shuffle forward on squatted legs. I groan internally as my sore, stiff thighs threaten to buckle beneath me.

Lexan had pleaded with me to stay home and rest for the day. He'd said I'd overdone myself these past few days, which was true, and insisted my body needed a chance to recoup before starting back at work tomorrow for another four days on. Regardless of his pleas, I'd ignored him, finished getting ready in silence, and then left without saying goodbye. I wasn't prepared to take his advice, even if it was for my own good. He hadn't had the decency to consider my advice. I'd told him that Purples were trouble, and he shouldn't trust them, yet he'd let Jax drag Harlow to the medical chamber anyway, even with my warnings.

"...can be a monster." I hear Spikes mutter as I near him, and I crane my neck to improve the clarity. "I tried warning you, but it backfired. I'm sorry. I should have owned up to the drawing, it's..."

*No, no, no. Frost!* Harlow's book slips from my fingers, causing me to overbalance on my unforgiving thighs. I fall abruptly, accidentally knocking over a medic's trolley stationed diagonally in front of me.

To add to the commotion, a metal bedpan flies from the trolley's top, along with a bag of liquid, which splits on impact and sprays across the marble floor.

Startled by the loud crash, Spikes jumps up from his chair, his head whipping around sharply. Initially distracted by the chaos, it takes him a second to notice me, but once he does, his eyes widen, and he shuffles back and forth on his feet with unease.

*Shoot.* He's going to make a run for it.

"Wait!" I jump to my feet, causing every single muscle in my body to scream profanities. "Please, hold on a second. I'm not looking for trouble; I only want to talk."

He continues to shuffle, but to my amazement—as much as it looks like he wants to—he doesn't run.

"It was my fault," he rattles off like a race commentator. His eyes dart side to side. "It was my fault. I tried to warn her, only it backfired."

I grit my teeth, trying to keep my composure. I'm furious about what's happened to Harlow, but I'm afraid if I appear aggressive, he'll take off.

"Hold on," I say, attempting to sound calm. I take a step closer to him, and gesture with steady palms. "Now slow down, take a breath, and start again."

He doesn't take my advice, which shouldn't surprise me. *If my own father-figure hadn't taken my advice, why should I expect a Purple to?*

"It was my picture, mine, mine," he continues to ramble. "I should have spoken up. It should have been me."

"What are you talking about? What picture?"

He slips his hand into his pocket and pulls out a crumpled piece of paper.

"Here, take it." He hands it to me. "You can give it back to her for me."

Curious, I unravel the crumpled paper to find a well-drawn portrait of Harlow, with the words **"STICKS AND STONES WILL BREAK MY BONES, BUT NAMES WILL NEVER HURT ME"** printed above her. There's smaller writing in-between the saying and her portrait. Unable to see it clearly, I lift the page up closer and squint. To my disgust, it's an array of malicious words.

"I don't get it?" I say with scrunched brows. I feel offended on Harlow's behalf. "Why would you draw this for her? It's cruel."

Spikes cowers. "She could hear all of their nasty whispers," he rambles anxiously, "and she was getting upset. I was trying to help her. I wanted her to ignore what they were saying. She needs to be resilient. They can't hurt her if she's..."

He stops as a delicate hand shoots in-between us, holding

Harlow's book. Caught off guard, I pivot to find a scowling face gawking at me.

"I take it this is yours?" The young lavender haired medic says, her voice filled with annoyance.

I snatch the book from her fingers with my free hand and mutter, "Thanks".

Much to my disappointment, this doesn't get rid of her. Instead she turns her attention to Spikes, her face still fixed in a scowl.

"RJ," she says with a rigid nod, and Spikes—or should I say RJ—nods anxiously in return and then takes off.

"Wait!" I go to sidestep him but I'm too slow. "RJ."

He races down the aisle without looking back, and before I know it, he's exited the medical chamber altogether.

*For frost sake.* I turn to the medic and give her a filthy look.

This could have been my one chance to get some answers, and she'd blown it for me.

"Don't you have work to do?" I spit, for which she returns my glare, and then struts off.

Frustrated, I hastily fold the crumpled picture in four and pop it inside the back of Harlow's book. I don't see why she'd want to keep it. Still, it was drawn for her, so I figure I'll let her decide what to do with it.

I hear a scuffling sound and look to see one of the Pastel cleaners mopping up the mess I'd made as a result of my fall. I had no idea such a tiny bag held so much liquid.

I notice the trolley is still on its side, and I help to set it right again, before plonking heavily on the chair by Harlow's bedside.

"I brought your book," I say, giving her hand a warm squeeze. "I thought I could read a few chapters to you, what do you think?" She remains unresponsive, but I know what her answer would be. "You might have to bear with me though," I add. "My reading's not exactly up to scratch."

*

The next few hours seemed to disappear, with only a few minor interruptions from a wrinkle-faced medic. I'd tried to pry some information out of her while she'd taken Harlow's vitals, but it'd been like trying to draw blood from a stone.

Luckily for her, I have Vinnie's story about becoming a big time, notorious drug dealer in America to keep my mind occupied; otherwise, I'd be more persistent about getting some answers.

*Who knew a human SCI-FI book could be so interesting?* Perhaps I should stop giving Harlow flack about her addiction and join her.

As I pop the book down on her bedside to take a breather, I notice the elderly medic—who'd been working close by at the time —look up. She must have been enjoying the story too. I snigger inside. *Oh well, it looks like she's going to have to wait.*

My stomach rumbles for the third time since reading that last chapter, and I realise with a sigh, I'm going to have to walk all the way back home again to make myself some lunch. I should have packed something. *How stupid of me!* I was so caught up in the thrill of bringing Harlow's book in to read to her, I hadn't thought beyond that.

I rise from the chair, legs creaking, and turn around just in time to see Jax stroll through the entryway. *For crying out loud, I've had enough of this guy.*

He greets Tansy with a friendly nod as he passes and then continues down the aisle in my direction.

As he approaches, I catch his eyes examining Harlow from head to toe, and I bristle.

"How is she?" he asks firmly.

"How would I know?" I retort, "I'm a useless, brain-dead Pastel. You said it yourself, I'm incapable of caring for her." I gesture to the elderly medic standing a few beds down from us. "Why don't you ask your friend over there for an update, she's the one who's qualified in this department."

His jaw clenches. "All I want is what's best for Harlow. Perhaps it's time you swallow your pride and start thinking along the same lines." His eyes flick to the SCI-FI book at her side. "Sitting here reading books to her all day isn't going to keep her alive." He points to the drip, followed by the machine feeding her oxygen. "These machines are, so get over yourself and deal with it."

Too stunned for words, I ponder. *Maybe he is right. Maybe I am letting my pride get the better of me.*

Doing as I've suggested, Jax leaves Harlow's bedside to speak to the wrinkled old medic, and as I watch them converse, I can't help but feel resentful. It's unfair that she's willing to give him a progress report, and not me. I'm Harlow's best friend; I should be the one she gives updates to, *not him.* He barely even knows Harlow, *or at least I hope he doesn't.*

An image of the hessian sack leaning by our cavern entryway flashes into mind, along with a bunch of unanswered questions, like:

*Why did he have her clothes?*

*Why did he give her a job at the library?*

*Why is he so interested in her all of a sudden?*

*And, is it possible that something's going on between them?*

Not willing to go there, I shake away these thoughts. Harlow is a smart girl; she wouldn't go there knowing the consequences.

Loud footsteps sound behind me and I turn to discover two warriors entering the chamber. *This can't be good.* The warriors flank a blood-stained Magenta. As they near I discover I recognise him. It's Saul, Harlow's father.

Jax, quick to notice them, rushes to meet them mid aisle, which works well for me, because it stations them in a position that's close enough for me to listen in without having to strain my ears.

"What's happened?" Jax asks.

Saul straightens. "I was attacked by a Vallon in the forest. He grabbed me from behind."

Jax's forehead crinkles as he regards Saul with concern. "Where are the rest of the hunters from your group? Are they still out there?"

Before Saul has time to answer, the taller of the two warriors cuts in. "They're safe," he says. "Fau received a few bruises and a scratch to the head, but otherwise, he appears fine. And as for the women, they came out unscathed. Zannah is downstairs questioning all of them as we speak."

Jax's eyes flick from the warrior to Saul. "Tell me what happened starting from the beginning."

Saul clears his throat. "Fau and I saw a deetra between the thick scrub on the outskirts of the forest," he says. "It was a big one, and we wanted to catch it, so we parked the sled as close as we possibly could and walked the rest of the way on foot." He pauses for a breath. "Rae and Krista distracted the deetra, while Fau and I crept up on it, which allowed us to take the animal down before it had the chance to make a run for it."

Saul appears sickeningly pleased about sharing this information, and I'm glad—for Harlow's sake—she's not awake to hear it. She hates listening to all of his hunting stories. She says they only prove how heartless he truly is.

"Once we'd killed it," he continues, "the four of us carried the deetra back to the sled together without any issues, and it wasn't until the huskens started barking on our arrival, that we realised something was off." His eyes flick between Jax and the two warriors. "The huskens never usually bark unless there is a threat," he points out.

"After we'd placed the carcass down in the back tray, Fau and I left the women to tie it down, while we went to investigate." Saul's eyes flick between Jax and the warriors again. "My first thought was, we may have disturbed a fuegor while killing the deetra, but as we returned to the area where we'd made the kill, a Vallon jumped us from behind."

Saul doesn't add anything further, so Jax asks. "And then what? How did you manage to get away?"

He gives a sheepish grin. "I have to admit," he adds reluctantly. "The Vallon was much stronger than I was prepared for. Before I had a chance to retaliate, he'd knocked me to the ground and pinned me with his foot, which made it impossible for me to put up a decent fight." He pauses for a moment. "Fau got a few good hits in though." There's pride in his voice. "But eventually the Vallon managed to overpower him too. He caught Fau off guard with a hefty punch to the stomach, and while Fau was buckled over, he snagged his blade. 'Get! Go on, get!' he yelled, pointing Fau's own blade back at him."

"Hold on a second," Jax's cuts in with knitted brows. "Are you telling me the Vallon just let Fau go?"

Saul nods. "He didn't just let Fau go, he let me go too. I wrestled with him for a minute or two longer, before he told me to 'get' as well."

Jax's brows pucker further. "That doesn't seem right."

"I know it doesn't, but it's the truth, you can ask Fau."

"I'm not saying I don't believe you, I'm..." Jax pauses, deep lines marking his forehead. "There has to be more to this story than we're aware of." After saying this, his eyes flick between the two warriors. "Oscar, Kieran," he says. "Get a dozen warriors ready. We'll get Fau to lead us to spot where they were attacked."

They jump at his command and turn on their heels, leaving Saul standing there with Jax.

He shifts uncomfortably where he stands. "Do you need me to go too?"

"No, you're wounded," Jax answers, and then turns his attention to the elderly medic, who appears to be listening in—the same as I am. "Iris," he says. "Can you get Saul cleaned up?"

She nods at Jax before gazing towards Saul. "Come with me," she calls, beckoning him with her hand.

Saul holds up his pointer. "One second," he says, and then to my astonishment, he turns in my direction and begins limping over. Initially, I go to step aside, for I assume he must be coming over to see his daughter, but he stops me mid step. "Can you mind this for me," he says, handing me his pack.

I give an uneasy nod. "Sure."

And then...furthering my astonishment to the next level —*SHOCK HORROR*—he leans in to give me a hug.

*What the heck?* I stiffen. *What is he doing?* I quickly realise he's whispering something to me.

"There are two voltz in my pack. When you get a chance, place one at each of Harlow's temples for half an hour, but don't let anyone see you do it." He taps my back firmly with his hand, attempting to make the hug look genuine. "And don't forget to take them back home with you when you leave." He pulls back from our embrace.

"Thanks for always looking out for her," he says loud enough for the others to hear. "You're a good kid." After this he steps around me to place a kiss on Harlow's cheek. "You get better now, you hear me!"

He straightens, and we share another glance before he leaves her bedside and limps across the aisle to meet Iris.

"Iris, Saul," Jax calls, and they both look. "I'd like you to keep a lid on this until we know more." They nod and his gaze flicks from them to me. "This goes for you too," he adds, his voice sharp.

I offer him a salute in return, for which he huffs, rolls his eyes, and then strides off.

To play it safe, I wait at least ten minutes after his departure to do a thorough scan of the chamber. As far as I can see, everything has settled down, and everyone is going about their business. I open Saul's pack and peek inside. Two bunched up rags glow brightly from an open inner pocket. I've never seen a voltz in real life before —only textbooks. The thought of actually being able to hold one excites me. I reach for one of the rags and unravel it, making sure to do so without taking my hand out of the pack. Once the rag is removed, a blinding glow of red, beams out from Saul's pack, and I find myself doing another quick scan of the chamber, making certain nobody has noticed. Mesmerised, I twirl the red voltz around in my fingers. It's both warmer and brighter than I'd expected it to be. It's almost as warm as a mug of bean-brew.

These precious crystals would have come with a hefty price tag. Saul must have done something major to pull this off. I hope he hasn't bitten off more than he can chew. Vallons aren't known for making deals with our kind, they are known for killing us, or stealing us for slaves.

It's sad to say, but I never would have thought Saul loved Harlow enough to stick his neck out for her like this. He's always struck me as a heartless, self-centred jerk. It seems I may have misjudged him.

I unwrap the remaining rag and clutch the second voltz with my free hand. The second voltz is smaller, and much rougher to touch, but its unique shape makes it prettier to look at.

Placing a voltz on each of side of Harlow's temples seems like an odd thing to do. I assume they're meant to help to bring her back from her coma, but how it's supposed to work is a mystery to me.

As far as I've been taught, voltz hold the power of heat and light, just like our zofts hold the power of cold and light, that's it—nothing more.

My gaze flickers between Harlow's face and the voltz. I want to follow Saul's instructions, but I'm nervous. I'm afraid the voltz will make Harlow's condition worse. *Worse yet*—what happens if I don't use the voltz and she... I shake my head. I don't even want to think about it. I can't afford to lose her.

My stomach churns with hunger and stress. *Just do it. Do it now while no one is around, and you have the chance.*

After another quick glance around the chamber, I lift my hands out from Saul's pack, and hurriedly shove both voltz through the opening of Harlow's pillowcase, making sure to place one crystal at each side of her head. As I take a step back, I panic. The voltz shine so brightly, I can still see them though the material. I grab two fist-fuls of Harlow's hair and strategically place them over the visible glow. It's still not a perfect solution, but I'm hoping it will do. Please don't let anyone come near us for the next half an hour.

# 20

# HOT HEADED

## -HARLOW AS RUBY-

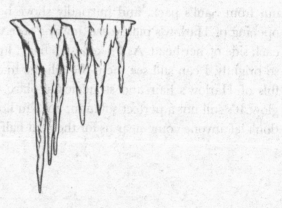

(Several hours earlier)

It's been almost three days since I've stepped foot on Zadok, and I'm feeling more like the Ruby part of myself than Harlow, only, I'm isolated from those I love. To be this close to my family members, without being able to communicate with them, is torture. It's like being handed a scrumptious slice of chocolate cake, only to be told not to eat it.

Jade and Byron went out for drinks with their friends last night, and haven't yet returned, leaving me home alone in a dimly lit room with Fat Cat. I had contemplated going with them, but I didn't see the point. Firstly, I couldn't physically join in on the fun, and secondly, I was too tired and grumpy to deal with waffling drunks.

*Admit it, those aren't the only reasons.*

I gaze down at my watch, which is vaguely visible in the dim light of the full moon. *It's almost midnight,* I sigh. *I don't think he's coming.*

When Alex left my parents place yesterday afternoon, he said he would come back to see me today, but he hasn't shown. Consequently, I've spent the past five—Jade-free-hours—wallowing in disappointment. *It's probably for the best,* I try to assure myself. *He's your killer's twin brother. You shouldn't get too friendly with him,* but despite my inner reservations, I'm secretly hoping he'll still show up.

I toss and turn where I lay. My eyes burn from sleep deprivation, and my head feels like it's been zapped by a taser. I need to give up on the idea of Alex coming, and go to sleep, but between the hum of RJ's voice mixed with the beeps of a nearby machine—filtering in from my unconscious Zeek body—the possibility of getting any sort of rest seems near impossible.

The majority of what RJ says comes through rushed and muffled, except for his warning. "Promise me you will stay away from the library," he says, putting added emphasis on each and every word. "Electra is dangerous, and you've made an enemy in her."

He goes on to say a few more indistinguishable things after this, but is soon interrupted by a crashing sound, followed by Zavier's voice.

*Uh-oh! This isn't good.*

I fiddle nervously with my watchband, while trying desperately to listen in. I hope RJ isn't planning on telling Zavier the truth about what happened to me in the library. Zavier tends to be a hot head. He acts out on his emotions without weighing up the consequences, and I don't want him confronting Electra or he'll end up getting hurt—*or worse.* I shudder. *I don't want him getting killed over me.*

Thankfully, RJ's voice doesn't stick around for long, and I hope, with crossed fingers, Electra's name wasn't mentioned.

"I brought your book," is the first recognisable sentence I hear Zavier say, and a tingling sensation envelopes my hand, like he's giving it a light squeeze. "I thought I could read a few chapters to you, what do you think?"

He sneaks in a joke about his poor reading abilities before getting started, and despite my aching head, I smile. The last time he'd read to me, he'd sounded like a scratched CD. I manage to catch a few lines here-and-there, and it seems he's improved, but I eventually give in to exhaustion and doze off.

Voices blast through from the other side, rattling me awake.

I'm so tired at first, I try to ignore them and go back to sleep, but I soon come to realise—by the urgency of their tones—something's wrong. Curious as to what all the fuss is about, I strain to listen.

"And then what?" I hear Jax ask, which is followed by the sound of another Zeek's voice. I try hard to concentrate on the voice that's now speaking, but it's coming through muffled.

*How frustrating!* I think. *I can't make out a single word.*

After a few more minutes of catching nothing but wishy-washy-mumble, I give up on listening. If I can't make out what they're saying, I'd rather be sleeping. I've almost drifted off again, when suddenly a voice rings through loud and clear. "You get better now, you hear me!" and then a tingling sensation brushes against my cheek.

My eyes fling open, and I lurch forward, my body nearly toppling from Jade's lounge. I swear that was my father's voice. *Surely not.* He's not that fond of me.

Still dazed, I go to right myself, but a hand takes me by the shoulder, and I panic. Instinctively, I snatch the person's wrist and yank it backwards with a twist.

"Owww... Owww..." The hand lets go of my shoulder. "Ruby, stop!"

The room is dim, and my eyes are still glazed from sleep, but I recognise the voice, and quickly release my grip.

I blink back the blur to find Alex hunched above me, his face scrunched in pain.

"Geez, Alex, what were you thinking?" I grumble, before breathing a sigh of relief. "You scared the life out of me."

He huffs and gives his wrist a good shake. "Yeah, well you almost broke my wrist."

"I'm sorry," I say. "I was half asleep, I didn't realise it was you."

Truth is, I was confused. I hadn't known which body had been touched, Harlow's or Ruby's.

Alex kneels to my level, the white of his eyes shining brightly in the pale moonlight. "Why were you so freaked out?" he asks. "Were you having a bad dream or something?"

"Or something," I say bitterly. Now that the haze has cleared and I'm fully awake, the resentment I feel rears its ugly head. I can't understand why it has taken him up until now to come and see me.

He frowns. "What's that supposed to mean?"

"Where were you?" I ask without answering. "You said you were going to come over and hang out with me yesterday, but you didn't, and I sat around all evening waiting for you." I cringe as soon as I've said this. Not only have I come across as desperate; I've also verged on possessive and controlling. *This is not you. Don't be this person.* I really need some proper sleep.

Alex doesn't seem put-off by my stormy reaction, instead, his eyes gaze into mine, large with sympathy. "I'm sorry." He places his hand on my knee, giving it an affectionate squeeze. "I meant to be here before this, but I ran into a few obstacles back home."

Despite my inner resentment—which happens to be decreasing by the second—the touch of his hand still gives me butterflies.

"Exactly what kind of obstacles did you run into?" I ask, trying to shift the focus from my fluttering insides. "Fuegors, Vallons…"

"None that I couldn't handle."

Mentioning the word fuegor causes my calf to ache, and I wonder if the pain is imaginary, or real. I know the pain sifting in from Harlow's head is real. The more I tune-in through-her, the more I can feel it. Her sinus passages are frozen shut, and the pressure surrounding her teeth and gums is unbearable.

I glance at my watch and ask. "Have you only just arrived back on Earth now?"

His lips pull up at the corners. "No, I arrived a while ago but you were sound asleep, and I didn't want to wake you. I've been sitting around waiting." His eyes drift towards the window, and I follow his gaze. "Jade's cat, on-the-other-hand has been desperate to disturb you. He's been hissing like crazy since the moment I got here."

As if on cue, Fat Cat gives another hiss. He doesn't look like the same chilled-out cat who'd been sitting at my feet only a few hours ago. His back is arched, and his tail is bristled.

"I wonder why he doesn't like you?" I ask with furrowed brows. "He doesn't seem to have a problem with me. If anything, he seems to like me. He spent most of last night sitting at my feet, purring like a steam engine."

"Well, I can't really blame the cat." Alex grins, his eyes doing a quick trace of me. "You are much more appealing than I am."

"Stop it," I say with burning cheeks, and I pray the room is dim enough to hide the rouge. "You're embarrassing me."

Snippets of the young nurse who'd been flirting with Jax, flitter through my mind, and I scoff. I hope to never come across the way she did. She'd gushed at his every word like a love-struck schoolgirl.

*Besides,* I think. *Alex is wrong. Look at those grooves when he smiles.* He's gorgeous.

Unaware of where my thoughts have taken me, he asks, "Have you been back home at all?"

"No, not yet." Feeling self-conscious, I adjust the straps of my dress to make sure that my lace bra isn't showing. "But I can still hear all of their voices, so I must still be alive."

Lines mark his forehead. "What do you mean you can still hear all of their voices?"

"Can't you?"

His frown deepens. "No." He shakes his head. "I can't."

"Oh." My shoulders slump. "I assumed it was normal—not that any of this is normal." My gaze snaps to his. "You know what I mean."

From his frown, grows the look of curiosity. "Can you hear anyone now?" he asks.

The incessant hum of Zavier's voice vibrates through my skull. "Yeah, I can hear Zavier."

"What's he saying?"

A strange sensation of warmth filters through my temples as I close my eyes to listen. "He's reading to me again."

"Is that it?" Alex tilts his head. "Can you hear anything else?"

"No, but a commotion broke out earlier," I say, re-opening my eyes. "I don't know what it was about though. I can't always make out everything that's being said."

Alex gazes off, his forehead crinkling once again.

"What's wrong?"

"Nothing," he answers, although his frustrated expression says otherwise. His hand leaves my knee, and he stands. "I hope you get to go home soon, that's all. Your other family must be terribly worried about you." With a concerned look, he strolls over to the window, causing Fat Cat to hiss, pounce off the sill, and then scurry away.

Little does he know how wrong he is. My Zeek family are probably willing me to flatline.

Alex peers out the window, the tip of his nose and chin jutting through the glass, as he gazes at the moon. "It's a full moon tonight," he says. "There's enough light for us to go for a stroll to Glenbrook lagoon if you're interested?"

I am interested. The last time I'd been to the lagoon was during one of our scorching hot Aussie summers, when bushfires had raged up the Blue Mountains. We'd gone to watch the helicopters fill their buckets with water to douse the fire in Warrimoo—the next suburb up from us. It'd been horrific and burnt on for days, taking out a dozen houses, and damaging a handful of others. Our two good friends Natalie and Amelia were left with significant damage to their family home. I hope their parents coped with paying for the repairs. I'd never found out, because it was only a few weeks after this I was killed.

The thought of fire leaves me feeling overheated—*literally*. My head has gone from, being painfully cold, to burning up.

"I am interested," I say, "but I'm not sure if I'll be able to." I clutch my burning head. "I don't feel so good. I think there might be something wrong with my body on Zadok."

Alex whips around to face me. "What do you mean?"

"I'm not sure, I think…" I attempt to stand but my legs buckle beneath me, leaving me to crash to the floor with a thud.

"Shit!" Alex races over and scoops me up in his arms. "Ruby." Using the support of his knees, he quickly manoeuvres me into a cradled position. "Rubes, what's going on?"

His warm coffee coloured eyes stare down into mine with alarm. "Please, talk to me. What's wrong?"

A tingling sensation brushes along my arm, and the heat at my temples intensifies. I moan.

"Rubes, you're flickering." Alex's irises turn pink.

"Harlow? Harlow? Can you hear me?"

*Hold on*, it's Zavier speaking, not Alex.

I feel someone shaking me.

"Rubes, please, why won't you answer me."

No, it's Alex.

"Alex," I murmur.

I try to say more, but Zavier cuts me off.

"Frost!" he says. "Someone's coming." He reaches towards my head, and then proceeds to toss my skull about like a hacky sack.

"Ouch," I groan. "Knock it off." My head is far too tender to be tossed around this carelessly.

Zavier's Pastel eyes flash to mine, filled with a sense of warning. "Shhh…" he whispers fiercely, and as his hands pull back, I'm momentarily blinded by a flash of red light.

# 21

# TRUTH BE TOLD—OR NOT

## -ZAVIER-

"Hey…" Iris comes charging over, her face crumpled up like a used tissue. "What do you think you're doing?"

My heart pounds erratically. Afraid of being caught, I hastily stuff both voltz back into the side pocket of Saul's pack, and snatch out his torch, flicking the switch to ON as I rise my hands up into a surrender position.

"I wanted to see if she'd react to the light." I gaze down at Harlow and watch as her eyes flicker groggily from one side of the chamber to the other. "I think it worked," I say. "Her eyes are open."

Hearing my voice, Harlow's groggy eyes snap to mine. "Zavier?" she croaks. "Is it really you? Am I back?"

*Ah, that's much better.* Only a moment ago, she'd called me Alex.

*Alex,* I repeat to myself, trying to place the name. I don't remember her ever mentioning an Alex before now. The only male names she's ever mentioned from her past life have been Lucas, her killer and Josh, her boyfriend.

*Phft...Josh.* I might not know the guy personally but going from the stories Harlow's told me about him, I don't understand why she ever dated the selfish jerk-off.

*I wonder who Alex is, another EX?*

*Don't go there...* I warn.

I smile down at her. "Hey, it's really me. Welcome back to the land of the living."

She doesn't smile in return, instead, she raises her hands to her temples and groans. "My head." She lets out a dry cough. "It burns."

Her reaction alarms me... I hope I've done the right thing.

Iris approaches the opposite side of Harlow's bed and leans across to snatch the torch from my hand. "Give me that," she says, and then turns her attention to Harlow. "Harlow, honey, it's Iris."

Harlow blinks several times, confusion written all over her face.

I'd accidentally knocked out her oxygen tube when resurrecting the voltz, and I watch as Iris carefully positions it back into place.

"Do you know where you are?"

She lets out another dry cough, and then croaks, "I'm at the medical chamber."

"That's right, good girl."

*Good girl.* I scoff. "Condescending much?"

Iris pays no attention to me, which is probably a good thing, considering from the corner of my eye I notice that Saul's pack is emitting a faint reddish glow. I didn't have enough time to re-wrap the voltz in the rags before shoving them into the side pocket. I wasn't aware it would make such a difference.

I shift back a step closer to where the pack sits, hoping to hide the glow behind my wiry legs.

Oblivious to my efforts, Iris continues to ask Harlow a few more questions. Harlow tries her best to answer, but her throat is dry, and her words come out hoarse.

"I need some water," she rasps.

I know I should be paying more attention to Harlow's answers, but despite my concern, my gaze keeps gravitating to Saul's glowing pack. I've got to get it out of here. I can't afford to be caught with these voltz. If the Commander thinks I've been fraternising with the enemy in order to get these crystals, I'm a dead man.

"I'm starving," I blurt, which is true. "I haven't eaten anything since breakfast."

Iris grunts, her gaze focused on the monitor situated at the side of Harlow's bed. "Well do us both a favour and go eat something."

While her attention remains on the monitor, I squat down and slip the packs straps over my shoulders, making sure to keep the glowing contents hidden directly behind my back.

"I won't be long," I say to Harlow.

It's Iris who replies. "Enough with the threats," she says, and I detect the hint of a smirk hidden beneath her wrinkles.

Harlow's eyes flick to mine, wide and filled with worry. "Are you coming back?"

I feel terrible leaving her now that she's awake, but it's way too risky for me to stay. I barely know how I'm going to get out of here undetected.

I take her hand in mine and give it a light squeeze. "I'll be back in an hour or so. Is there anything you'd like me to bring?"

She gives a sad smile. "Can you bring back a family who loves me?"

My lips tug at one corner. Harlow's father may have helped to bring her back, but I don't believe his motives were love-driven —more like status-driven. Harlow works among Purples now, which makes her valuable to him.

"I can bring you back a friend who does."

I scoot towards the medical chamber exit at record speed, keeping my back faced away from Iris at all times. If she finds my awkward fast-paced-side-steps strange, she doesn't let it show, chances are she's too busy seeing to Harlow to concern herself with my idiocy.

Tansy isn't working at the front desk today, which is a blessing, it's a new girl who doesn't know—or care—who I am. She gives a quick flash of the eyes as I pass, and then goes on doing her work without so much as a second glance.

I anxiously scan the glistening passage left to right. It's empty.

*Score,* I think. *Now be quick.* I hurriedly duck to the side wall and slip the pack off my shoulders, placing it directly in front of me to block it from the view of others. I make sure to keep my back towards the medical chamber, as I re-wrap the soil stained rags around the voltz with shaky hands, and then shove them back into the side pocket.

*Pull yourself together,* I chastise, *it's only possible DEATH if you are caught.* I roll my eyes. *Why worry at all?*

A Purple warrior rounds the corners just as I toss the pack back over my shoulder, and my pulse picks up. Sweat beads on my brow. That was a little *too* close for my liking.

What's worse, I realise, I have to pass him to get home. I discreetly wipe the sweat from my forehead, take in a deep breath, and then try to play it cool as I stroll his way. Clearly my acting skills suck. He eyes me with suspicion as we near each other, and before I can pass him, he puts out one of his large mitts, gesturing for me to stop where I stand.

"You look distressed," he says with a voice of steel. "Is there a problem?"

I keep my eyes low and shake my head. "No problem," I answer. "I'm stiff and sore. I'm finding it hard to walk properly." It's a partial truth.

He lowers his arm. "Go back to your cavern and rest. Jax wants these passageways to be kept clear until further notice."

I nod and take off as quickly as possible without looking back.

By the time I get back to my cavern, my thighs burn from overuse, and my back and shoulders ache from carrying such a heavy pack. So much for taking it easy on my last day off. My body hates me with a passion.

I search high and low for the perfect hiding place to stash the voltz. Thankfully, Lexan is at still at work. I trust him emphatically, but I'm afraid if Saul or I get caught, it will end up making him an accessory to our crime, and I don't want him involved. He has enough of his own incriminating secrets to worry about.

After a quarter of an hour searching, the perfect spot clicks into mind. Located between my sleeping nook and the wall of the living-kitchen-dining area, there's a deep circular pit in the cavern ground. I helped Lexan make a hard cover for it, years ago, during my first night here. We'd nailed a few pieces of old firewood together and then sawed the joint pieces to shape and size. We'd then wrapped the surface in animal skin to protect our feet from splinters, before wedging it firmly into the pit opening.

I snatch my old pocketknife from my limestone bedside, and with burning arms, I use the blade to lever the old wooden cover out from the opening. It takes a few goes of using all of my weight to get it to lift, but eventually I feel it release. *No doubt*, we did a good job of wedging it in firmly all those years ago.

I unwrap the voltz and take one last look at them before rewrapping them and hiding them away.

Before heading back to the medical chamber, I swing by Harlow's family cavern. I'm hoping Saul will be there—alone. Not only would I like to return his pack, I'd really like some answers regarding the voltz.

At the cavern entrance I sing out, "Anyone home?" before entering, and then head straight to the kitchen. There's a half-eaten plate of roasted deetra sitting by the sink, and it smells delicious. I have to fight the urge to lean across and take a bite.

Within minutes, Saul rounds the corner of his sleeping nook, shirt off and looking dishevelled. He's in worse condition than I'd realised. One of his eyes is swollen shut, and he still seems to be favouring his left leg over his right.

"Are you okay?" I step forward to help him, but he puts his hand up to ward me off.

"I'm fine," he grunts.

In other words, *I'm too proud to accept a hand from a scrawny little Pastel like you.*

I stare in envy. Even past double my age, his taut muscular torso is far more impressive than mine. He's not as intimidating as Jax, but he's still a unit. One of his arms is the size of both of mine put together. Nevertheless, his powerful physique had obviously been no match for the Vallon. Purple splotches and nasty scrapes cover a large section of his upper right side.

"It looks like you took quite the beating," I say, thinking aloud. As soon as the words leave my mouth, I realise I've said the wrong thing.

A scowl crosses his face. "It's nothing," he spits harshly. "Now why are you here?"

There's the Saul I know and despise. The show is over. The friendly act is gone.

I slip his pack from my shoulder and dump it on the limestone benchtop with a thud. "I thought you might need this for tomorrow."

Saul eyes the pack warily. "Where are the voltz? Did you use them like I told you to?"

I nod. "Yes, and they worked," I say. "But I haven't brought them with me. I've hidden them somewhere safe. I didn't think it would be wise to cart them around at the moment. Jax has his warriors patrolling all of the main passages."

His gaze snaps to mine. "How safely is 'safe'?"

I'd gone to a lot of effort to hammer the wooden cover securely back into place.

"They'll never be found," I say.

"Good." He nods, and I'm glad he doesn't push for specifics. "Keep them there, and don't tell anyone about them, not even Harlow—if she ever wakes up." He snatches his pack from the bench and turns to leave.

"If she ever wakes up?" I repeat with puckered brows. He obviously hadn't known what the voltz would do. I'm confused. This conversation is far from over. "They worked," I say again. When he pays no attention to me, I shout his name. "SAUL, did you hear me? They worked."

He reluctantly turns back to face me.

"They brought her back from her coma," I say. "She's awake."

His brows shoot upward, and his eyes grow round.

"You did know they'd bring her back—*right?*" I ask. However, going by his expression, I fear the worst. "That's the reason you sought them from the Vallon, isn't it? You knew they would help bring her back from her coma."

The sound of a scoff leaves Saul's lips. "I didn't sought anything," he says. "The only thing that got sorted was me. I'll be lucky if I can go out hunting tomorrow."

A spark of anger ignites inside me. I had a strong feeling Saul wasn't helping his daughter out of the love of his heart, but regardless of his motives, I'd still assumed he was trying to help her. If he hadn't known what the voltz would do, then he should never have asked me to use them on her.

"Please don't tell me I just risked Harlow's life in unmerited blind faith." My voice comes out like a roar. "I trusted you. I thought you KNEW the voltz would help bring her back."

"Keep your voice down," he growls. "She's awake, isn't she? So quit interrogating me and get back to her." He gives the flick of his hand, gesturing for me to shoo, but I'm nowhere near done.

"How did you even get the voltz?" I ask, my voice still raised. "Did you steal them? Did the Vallon drop them during the struggle?"

"Shhh!" His brows scrunch. "Keep it down or the neighbours will hear." Saul might be an intimidating man, and sure, he's much stronger than I am, but at this point in time I've got the upper hand.

If I were to be sent to death over this, I'd lose Harlow, Lexan and Minty, but if he were to be sent to death over this, he'd lose everything. He is well known and respected—for reasons I can't fathom—and he lives far more comfortably than most Magentas do. His family cavern is more than double the size of mine and Lexan's little hole, and as far as tradable goods go, he's got more items of value, than all of his neighbours combined.

"You'd better start talking," I say, "or my voice will continue to raise."

His eyes flare, and his fists clench at his sides. "You're not as tough as you think you are Pasty."

"I may not be tough, but I have an extremely loud voice, so unless you want the neighbours to start asking questions, I'd get on with the details."

Saul's face fills with rage. He lunges forward, arms raised with the obvious intention of punching me. I know I'm not fast enough to dodge his fists, and I brace myself for the blow. To my astonishment, at the last second his tensed biceps recoil. He must be too sore to put up a fight. Or perhaps he's afraid I'll squeal too loud.

His eyes glare into mine. "The Vallon gave me the voltz," he says, his voice dripping with resentment. "There, are you happy?"

"Right—he just handed you the voltz and then let you go." I snort. "How gullible do you think I am?"

Saul stiffens on his good leg. "It's the truth."

"Well I don't believe a word you're telling me, and by the looks of what I saw earlier, neither did Jax."

He snarls and then leans backwards, resting his weight against the side of the bench. "Believe what you want, it's the truth. Now get out!"

I throw my hands up, "Okay fine," I say, toning my aggression down a notch, "let's pretend for a second I do believe what you're saying. If the voltz were 'given to you' out of the kindness of the Vallon's heart, then why wouldn't you keep them for yourself to trade? Why give them to me to use on Harlow? You obviously didn't know what the outcome would be, so what was the point in having me use them on her? It doesn't make any sense."

"It was the Vallon who wanted the voltz used on her," he says with a huff. "After he'd sent Fau away, he asked me if I knew a female Zeek called Harlow—who he'd suspected was in a coma. I told him I did, and he gave me the voltz demanding I place one at each of her temples for half an hour, immediately, or he would come back tomorrow and kill me and the rest of my team."

"Are you for real?" I frown. "That is the worst story I've ever heard. How on Zadok would a Vallon know who Harlow is—or that she's in a coma? Vallons don't know us Zeeks by name, and they certainly aren't looking to save any of us. They want to kill us all. They want our land."

"It's the truth."

"So you keep saying."

"Listen here, boy." He stabs a finger at me. "I have no interest in investigating why Harlow has a Vallon looking out for her. The only reason I had you use those voltz on her, was to protect myself and my team."

I force out a ragged breath, which sounds like a roar. "Forget it fabulist, this was obviously a waste of my time." I pivot to leave, but not before adding, "You'd better hope that Harlow survives, because if not, I'm the one who's going to kill you, not the Vallon."

My mind wages a war the whole way back to the medical chamber, and as I pass by a small section of uneven ground, I trip, nearly crashing headfirst into a young Magenta.

"Watch it!" he yells, giving me a shove. His eyes meet mine, and he snarls, "Stupid Pastel."

I'd love to retaliate with something equally-as-offensive, but if things were to escalate—which they would—I'm way too sore to put up a decent fight. Besides, I have no idea why I'm getting all-riled-up over a one-off senseless comment. I should be used to receiving this kind of abuse by now, I cop it daily when working at the Beanbrew Cavern.

I'm furious after my conversation with Saul. What father, in his right mind, would put his own life before his daughter's? Not that I believe his ridiculous story about the Vallon. If anything, I'm offended by it. You'd think someone as well regarded as he is could come up with a better lie to tell.

I arrive at the medical chamber, feeling physically and mentally drained. Jax is back and talking to Iris. *Yippee.* I'd hoped he'd be on Vallon watch for the rest of the evening. *I should be so lucky.*

"Zavier," He breaks away from his conversation with Iris and heads straight over in my direction. "Good. I've been wanting to speak with you."

I don't know about "good".

I gaze over to Harlow's bed and rock impatiently on the balls of my feet. The last thing I want to do is waste time chatting with Jax, I'm desperate to know how Harlow is.

He pauses in front of me, his light tan jacket spoilt by dirt. "Harlow's awake," he says. "But according to Iris, you already know this."

I clear my throat. "Yeah, she woke up before I left."

His gaze rests firm on mine, he's waiting for me to elaborate. I don't. Instead I ask, "What happened with the Vallon? Did you catch him?"

"No." He shakes his head. "We searched the area where Saul and Fau were attacked, and the majority of the forests edge, but we didn't come across any threats." He lets out a long breath. "Honestly... I don't know what to make of the whole scenario. I'm not saying I don't believe Saul's story, but I'm afraid there's more to it than he's letting on." He pauses and then adds. "Something's off."

Curious, I ask, "What did Fau and the girls say?"

"They confirmed Saul's story."

I shrug. "Maybe he's telling the truth."

"Maybe." His mouth twitches. "But I don't think so. What did he say to you when he handed you his pack?"

I swallow. "He said, 'thanks for always looking out for Harlow'."

"Yeah, I heard that part, but what did he whisper?"

*Jax caught that? Damn he's perceptive.* I shuffle uncomfortably. "He asked me to look after his pack."

"Why?" he asks firmly. "What was in it?"

A trickle of sweat slides down the curve of my back. "I don't know; I didn't look inside."

"Iris said you woke up Harlow by waving Saul's torch in her face, which means you had to have looked inside." His eyes interrogate me. "Come on, Zavier, we both know Saul and your relationship isn't as chummy as he was leading us to believe. The only reason he went over to you was so he could offload his pack."

Jax is switched on; he knows he's been played, and he wants answers. What he doesn't know, though, is whether I've been played too, or if I'm in on the conspiracy. Problem is, I'm not so sure myself!

Saul may have confided in me about the voltz and how to use them, but given our last conversation, I have no idea where his motives lie.

"Saul and I might not be friends," I say bitterly, "but neither are you and I. If you believe Saul's hiding something in his pack, then go ask him about it. Don't stand here pressing me for answers."

Air puffs from his nostrils. "You're impossible...you know that?"

## 22

# SECRETS AND TRUST

## -HARLOW-

Zavier's back, I can hear him speaking to Jax in the distance. I wince as I lift my head from my pillow to listen. My skull feels tender, like it's been taken to with a mallet. Zavier told me he'd only be gone an hour, but it feels like he's been gone at least two. I don't understand why he'd been so quick to leave once I'd woken. I would've thought he'd be busting to speak to me. It's been days since we've spoken properly.

Jax arrived at the medical chamber about twenty minutes ago

and was relieved to see I'd finally regained consciousness. He stopped by my bed for a bit and asked a few questions, yet all the while he'd seemed somewhat distracted. I'd wanted to ask him what was the matter, but Iris was quick to call him away before I got the chance.

*It's tragic.* While a part of me is glad to be back, another part of me is sad. I wanted more time with Alex. He's the only one who knows the truth about my past and my dreams. He's the only one who sees me as Ruby.

"Hey." Zavier steps up to my bedside. "You look a lot better. Your shimmer is back." There's relief in his voice.

"I missed you," I say.

A smile flitters across his lips. "I missed you too." He picks up my book from the side table and hands it to me. "I've been reading you this."

"Yeah, I know, I heard you."

His eyes brighten. "You did?"

I nod.

"RJ brought in a drawing for you this morning, it's a portrait. I folded it up and popped it in the back." He collapses heavily into the seat alongside my bed. "It's not exactly a keeper though." He screws his nose up. "It's not very nice."

I chuckle and then pop the book down beside me without opening it. I have a good idea which drawing he's referring to, but I'm not about to check if I'm right. If I pull out RJ's drawing now, Zavier will ask questions.

As if reading my mind, he says, "We can discuss the meaning behind the drawing later." His gaze flicks to Jax and Iris momentarily. "Actually." He shifts uncomfortably where he sits. "There are quite a number of things I'd like to discuss with you later."

Brushing the prickly subject of the drawing aside, Zavier goes on to tell me how he's enjoyed reading Breakdown so far, and adds that he may have to borrow it off me some time to find out how it ends. I smile and then proceed to tell him about another two SCI-FI books that I think he might enjoy.

He pretends to be interested in what I'm saying, but I notice his gaze keeps drifting to where Jax and Iris stand. I try to ignore his preoccupied behaviour at first and continue to babble on about the overall gist of the books, but in the end, I pause and ask, "What's wrong?"

"It's nothing," he replies.

"You seem distracted."

His gaze snaps to mine and his eyes refocus. "No, I'm fine."

"Are you sure?" My eyes survey his. "Because you seem distant, and when Jax came in earlier, he seemed distant too. Plus, I could have sworn I heard a commotion break out earlier. I even thought I heard my dad speaking to me..." I pause a moment and then add, "Did I?"

His posture straightens, and I catch a flash of worry flicker across his face. "You heard that?"

My heart gives a small flutter.

"Yeah," I answer. "But I wasn't sure if I was dreaming or not. I was so startled by the sound of his voice, I almost fell off the lounge." I cringe and then say, "I mean the bed."

Zavier doesn't notice my slip-up.

"Did my mum come with him?" I ask. I hadn't heard her voice, but then again, I was slipping in and out.

Zavier's expression grows strained. "Something did go down while you were out of it, but I'm not supposed to discuss it with anyone. Jax's orders."

"What?" I frown. "What does that—"

"Later" he says, and then he does a quick tilt of the head towards Jax.

I take the hint and drop the subject.

We fill the silence with small talk a little longer, but the conversation feels stilted. Eventually he stands, and places a kiss on my cheek, but before leaving, he asks, "By the way, who's Alex?"

I freeze momentarily. I must have called out Alex's name while I was asleep.

With so many secrets already between us I decide to answer honestly. "Alex is Lucas' brother."

Zavier appears puzzled. "Your killer's brother?"

I nod. *Yes, that's right—rub it in,* I think dryly.

"Oh..." He scratches his head. "You've never mentioned him before now."

"He died a year before I met Josh," I say. "I never really knew him; I only knew of him."

✳

Despite the constant beeps, voices, and occasional whimpers of the patients in the medical chamber, I'd slept well last night—a little too well. I'd hoped I would appear back on Earth. I wanted to reassure Alex that my Zeek body is alive and well.

Thinking of Alex sparks a curious thought. When Alex isn't on Earth, he's here on Zadok, the same as I am, we've discussed this superficially, but I've never thought to delve any deeper than this.

*Heck*, Alex could be living right down the passage from me for all I know. We could be walking straight past each other every day, on our way to and from work. He'd said he was a hunter, which would make him a Magenta. This means our caverns would be on the same level. We could literally be neighbours. The idea overwhelms me with excitement, until an earlier conversation pops in my head shattering the thought. Alex had also said he hunted at night, and as far as I'm aware, no Zeeks hunt at night, it's far too dangerous for our kind to be out in the forest after dark.

He might not be a Zeek. He could belong to one of the other races here on Zadok.

This new revelation causes my stomach to churn. *If he's not a Zeek, then please tell me he's not a Vallon, or even a Ruke for that matter. If he's not a Zeek then I pray he's a Drake.* At least Drakes tolerate our kind. We have a good trading system setup with them, where we provide them with top quality seafood in order to use their land to grow crops and hunt. Winter has the only ocean on our planet. The other capitals have rivers, lakes and dams, but no oceans. And this is a large part of the reason why the Vallons are always waging wars on us. They want to wipe out our race so they can claim our land and ocean.

I shiver as an awful childhood memory floats to mind. Back

when I was only six, the Vallons invaded our colony. I was on the Pastel level at the time of the invasion, and I'd seen a Vallon on horsenback riding through one of the passages. *Don't think about it* I warn myself, but my mind doesn't listen.

I swallow hard. I'd watched helplessly as the red eyed Vallon snatched an innocent Pastel girl by her hair and dragged her up onto his horsen. I'd screamed as she did, causing his wicked gaze to snap in my direction. His irises had been horrifying to look at. They were like two bright red pools of swirling molten lava.

I give a shake of the head, forcing this horrific memory aside. I don't know whatever happened to that Pastel girl, and I'm not sure I want to know. She was only young, ten at most.

I gaze up at the glorious cathedral ceiling, which glistens brightly above me, with clusters upon clusters of purple zofts. I can understand why Vallons are envious of our land, it is breathtaking. From what I've been told, their land is awful in comparison. It's hot, barren, and two thirds desert. I imagine this is why they've grown to be so tough. You'd need to be tough to survive in the desert.

A breakfast tray is placed in front of me with two mouth-watering deg fluffy cakes, which are similar to banana pancakes, only fluffier and way sweeter. The food you get served in the medical chamber is certainly above and beyond what you'd get served in a human hospital, but in saying this, besides me, there are only ten other Zeeks in the medical chamber today, and this is high.

While Pastels are weak, and will die much younger than most humans will, Zeeks as a whole, rarely get sick. We don't get viruses, and diseases aren't widespread.

I gaze around the chamber. Besides two Pastel men in their mid-fifties, most of the Zeeks lying here are Magentas. It's not surprising, they work highly physical jobs, which makes them more prone to injuries.

"You should try and eat," comes a deep voice from behind me. "You need to build some strength."

I laugh inside at the use of the word "strength". It's not the usual term that's tossed about when referring to a Pastel.

The aroma rising from the deg fluffy cakes fills my nostrils. It smells absolutely scrumptious, but after some of the dark places my thoughts have taken me this morning, I'm afraid my churning stomach might reject the food.

I push the tray aside. "I'm not all that hungry."

Jax scoots across to my bedside and pushes the tray back in front of me. "Well I'd like you to eat anyway, if you can. The quicker you build your strength, the quicker you can get out of here." He scans the chamber with suspicious eyes. "Now that you no longer require the machines, I'd prefer you to be somewhere less exposed."

My gaze flicks to his. *He doesn't think I'm safe here.*

"Okay." I pick up a fluffy cake and take a bite. Queasy tummy or not, I'm keen to get out of here.

He sits. "How are you feeling?"

I cover my food-filled mouth to answer, "Good enough to be sent back to work."

"About that." He leans forward on the chair, lowering his voice to a light rumble. "RJ told me what happened with Electra." His gaze touches mine, his expression sympathetic. "And I've dealt with her as best as I can; but given she's under my mothers' protection there's only so much I can say or do." His eyes darken. "I'm sorry. I would never have sent you to work in the library if I'd known this would be the result. I hadn't realised Electra would go to this length to prove her point."

"What does this mean for me? Will I be sent down to work with the Pastels?"

"No, it just means it isn't safe for you and RJ to work in the library anymore."

"Oh…" My heart sinks. I'd enjoyed working in the library, but I'm afraid he has a point. If I were to stay, Electra might end up killing me. "What about hiring books?" I ask. "Can I still go to the library to borrow?"

His lips tug in deliberation. "Perhaps you should steer clear from the library altogether, at least for a little while." My disappointment must show, because he adds, "If you're desperate, I can go hire something for you."

"You'd do that?" I ask, and he nods. I shuffle up in my bed. "Why?"

His brows pucker in confusion. "Because it's better I go, than you."

I shake my head. "That's not what I mean." I prop myself up further. "I still don't understand, why are you going out of your way to be so kind to me, when all I seem to do is cause you problems?"

"You're not the problem," he says. "Our colour system is the problem, but I'm hoping you'll be the one to help me change this. I've been trying to fight the colour system for years. My closest friend Stavros had tried fighting the system with me, and together we'd gained a number of supporters. But due to unfortunate circumstances arising, we lost those supporters, and he's no longer around to help."

I'd heard Stavros' name being thrown around for months after Nix's death. He was the warrior who'd stabbed Nix through the heart during an outdoor training session. His betrayal had been a shock to everyone in our colony, including me. I would never have imagined Nix dying by the hands of another Purple.

I'm not familiar with any of the warriors or their names, but I'd always noticed Stavros, because his hair made him stand out. He had long thick dreadlocks which hung from his crown, while the rest of his hair was shaved short with the symbol of the official Zeek snowflake etched at each side of his head.

"I'm sorry, about what happened to your brother," I say. I may not be sorry Nix is dead, but I am sorry for Jax's loss.

"Don't be, I'm not. Nix was pure evil."

Not knowing how to respond without agreeing, I ask, "What happened to Stavros?"

Jax's eyes scan the chamber before answering. "Rumour is I killed him."

Brows raised, I ask, "Did you?"

"For the sake of not causing an uprising, it's best that everyone in the colony believes I did."

By nine A.M. I'm released from the medical chamber.

"Where's Sphinx?" I ask, as we step into the empty passageway. Even with the use of crutches, the stitches around my calf feel tight while I limp.

"I've left him with RJ as protection."

"Oh…" I pause. He must be far more worried than I'd thought. "So where are we going?" I ask.

"You'll see."

"You're not going to tell me?"

The hint of a smile flitters across his lips. "Now where's the fun in that?" His playful tone catches me off guard—in a good way. I've never seen this side of him, he's usually the serious type.

He wants to keep my new workplace a surprise, I realise. *Huh.* I've had two surprises from two guys, in less than a few days. I'm not feeling so insignificant anymore.

The conversation we'd had about Stavros keeps replaying in my mind. "For the sake of not causing an uprising, it's best that everyone in the colony believes I did". This seems like Jax's way of saying, "I didn't do it". I don't understand why he would admit this incriminating information to me, we're not that close—*are we?*

As we continue along the passageway, I fatigue easily, however I try not to let it show. I don't want Jax to see me as a weakling. He's finally admitted the reason he's been so kind to me is because he wants me to help him fight our colour system, and if I'm going to be of any use to him, I must appear strong.

I understand by setting the example of the privileged Pastel, I am treading on dangerous ground, but I'm okay with this. I'm honoured he's chosen me in particular to help him. *Although,* come to think of it, I suppose I was the obvious choice. I'm the only Pastel to have ever been born from a pair of Magentas, and what's more, I live and work with Magentas. I've already brought about change, Jax just upped-the-ante by throwing me in the deep end with a pack of Purples.

I swallow back the disappointment I feel, now realising that I'd been picked for obvious reasons and not because Jax had seen me as someone special.

*Snap out of it,* I chastise. *Regardless of the reason you were picked, he wants YOU to serve as a key player in fighting the colour system. You will go down in history as someone who made a difference to the lives of Pastels, possibly even Magentas—if you don't die first. What more could you want?*

*Him...*

*NO.* I'm quick to rid myself of this thought. *You fancy Alex—which is not too smart either. I must be a sucker for forbidden love—or I have a death wish.*

Thinking of Alex, leads me to think of Jade, and thinking of Jade makes me think of our bond, which in turn, leads me to thinking about Electra and how she'd given us twins a shared brain freeze. Electra could have easily killed me if she'd wanted to. I'm surprised she didn't. She is cold and hard and seems capable of committing murder.

The memory of her telling Jax, if he allowed me to work in the library, he'd be setting the precedent for all of the other less fortunates, pops into mind. She clearly doesn't want our colours mixing any more than Nix did, and I believe this is why I was threatened and tortured. She wanted to make an example of me. She needed to prove that a Pastel like me doesn't belong in her workplace. She needed to let Jax know that his dream of integrating our colour system is never going to happen.

I straighten my shoulders above my crutches and hold my head up high. If Electra has eyes watching me, I want her to receive my message—*YOU CAN'T BREAK ME, BITCH! I'm here to help Jax, and I'm willing to die trying.*

I would like to believe Jax and I can make a real difference, but I'm doubtful. He is only one Purple, and to make a proper stand we would need many more Purples on board. We'd need to regain followers.

From what I've heard, Nix had an army of followers, which I find terrifying, given his beliefs were to eradicate all of us paler Zeeks from the face of Zadok. If Jax isn't careful, and continues to push all of the wrong Zeeks, he may end up with the same fate as his brother, only it would be for the complete opposite reason. He would die trying to help us.

Eventually Jax pauses by the opening of a small cavern, and Sphinx comes running out to greet him, his tail whipping my legs as he wags it excitedly.

I wince. "Are we here?"

I squint to see inside. At the far end of the cavern there are twin desks, and there sits RJ looking very much at home.

"I was hoping it was only you two," RJ says, his eyes not meeting ours. "I got worried when Sphinx flew out the door."

I give a weak smile, but on the inside I feel sad. I hate that RJ's wellbeing is under threat because of me. "It's only us," I say.

I hop further inside to find two easels stacked in the corner with a box of paints sitting on the floor next to them. On the desk where RJ sits is a tin of pencils along with a stack of paper, and directly in front of him lies another of his half-drawn comics.

"What exactly are we supposed to be doing here?" I ask.

"I thought you might enjoy a few art lessons," Jax says.

I arch a brow. While I am thrilled by this, and I imagine it will be a lot of fun, I doubt this could be classified as work.

"What about earning tradable goods?" I ask. "I can't go home empty handed, or my father will kick me out. I need to be able to support myself."

"If your artworks are good enough, you might be able to find someone who will trade goods for them," Jax says, a look of amusement flashing across his eyes.

"Okay…" I stammer, biting down on my bottom lip. "Well… I hope you have a backup plan, because I can assure you, nobody in their right mind will trade for my artworks."

Another smile flitters across his lips and I lap it up. "Don't worry," he says, his dimples showing. "I've got you both covered for the next few weeks, so sit back and enjoy the lessons."

He steps over to the twin desk and squats. "That there is yours," he says pointing. My eyes catch sight of a large old wooden box squashed at the back. "There's enough food and tradable goods in it to last you for the rest of the week."

My cheeks flush with embarrassment. "Thanks, I owe you."

"No." He shakes his head and pushes against his thighs to stand. "I owe you, I'm the one who got you into this mess."

"My wounded leg is what got me into this mess."

"That's on me too," he says, his gaze dropping to my bandaged calf. "I was the one who pushed for you to be able to work with the Magentas. I thought I was doing the right thing. I hadn't considered that I might be putting you in danger."

*It's true*, I think. *The prune faced librarian hadn't made the story up.*

"Sphinx and I were leaving to search for you when you arrived back wounded," Jax continues. "We would have left earlier, only I wasn't informed right away. I'm thankful the Drake woman found you when she did."

Stunned at yet another of his admissions, I blink.

"She was calling me Bleek een, do you know what it means?"

"It means pale one."

I puff out a laugh. "Well I guess it's fitting."

The sound of RJs pencil dropping to the floor causes my tummy to do a backflip. *Oops*, I've spoken more freely in front of him than I should've.

Jax senses my unease. "Don't worry," he says, "RJ's knows the truth about everything. We can trust him." His eyes flick to RJ's. "Isn't that right?"

RJ nods in agreement.

# 23

# BEWARE OF THE OGRE

## -ZAVIER-

"*Y*ou're never going to guess who just walked into the dining area together, hand in hand."

I drag my attention away from the pan of frying deetra to find Minty grinning from ear to ear. *Please don't let it be Jax and Harlow*, I think apprehensively.

"Ummm…" I ponder a moment. "I don't know. Who?"

"Floss and Elgar, Rae's son."

"Floss is here with Ogre?" I let out a long breath. "Why?"

179

Minty shrugs. "Beats me. Stupid girl. You'd think she'd know better."

Elgar is bad news, and everybody in our colony knows it, including his own mother Rae, who happens to be a member of Saul's hunting team. As a young child, Harlow was forced to see a lot of Elgar. Rae and Krista often hung out together during their weekends off, which meant Harlow and Floss had to endure his wrath. Harlow believed he was evil, and she'd nicknamed him Ogre, which—according to her—is a legendary monster of the human world, who eats ordinary humans. Ogre constantly tormented Harlow during these visits. He'd call her names, thrown stuff at her, pulled her hair, hit her, and there'd been one occasion where he'd broken her collarbone.

Going by his reputation, not much has changed. He'd been locked away in a prison cell for over a year for beating his last girl-friend black and blue, and since his release, he's become well known for distributing mind altering substances to those who are silly enough to use them. *Not bad for a Zeek who only just turned nineteen*, I think sarcastically.

I turn down the stove heat and place the stirring spoon on the bench. "Can you keep an eye on this for me for a few minutes," I ask.

Minty tilts her head forward and frowns at me from above her glasses. "What? Why?"

"I need to talk some sense into her, before she finds herself in trouble."

"Ahhh...I'm sorry, am I missing something? Don't you hate Floss?"

"I don't hate her. I just don't like her." I pause and then add, "There's a difference. Besides, she's Harlow's sister. I've got to do something."

I slip off my apron and hairnet before leaving the kitchen and its warmth. The dining cavern is abuzz with rowdy Magentas, which is standard for this time of the afternoon. Magentas tend to come here straight after work to socialise and get a decent feed. Purples, on the other hand, are few and far between. They prefer to dine at the more elite seafood caverns where you pay more for less—*if you know what I mean*. It's absurd if you ask me, but then again, the food might be much nicer—*I wouldn't know*. I'm a poor, deprived Pastel who can barely afford food in general, never mind eating out all of the time.

I'm quick to spot Ogre, he's not hard to miss. Not only does he have a shaved head and a chin full of stubble—which is completely un-Zeek like—his arms are marked with ghastly pictures caused from deliberately cutting into his own flesh with a pocketknife. Harlow calls it scarification. She'd said there were humans on Earth who'd pay lots of money to get it done for aesthetic purposes. *Whatever*—I think it's strange. She'd also mentioned they get tattoos for atheistic purposes, which she'd explained look similar to the vertic switz Vallons have drawn on them, only human tattoos are not limited to a certain theme or style. Vallons vertic switz are only done in amber, orange or red depending on their status, and then the pattern they get will depend on their family bloodlines.

Floss sees me heading towards her booth and turns her face away.

"Floss," I say, as I approach their table. "Just the Zeek I needed to see."

Her face flushes with humiliation and as she dares to gaze up at me, I notice her eyes are glassy and red at the corners.

"Are you here to take my order?" she asks sneeringly. "Because if so, I'll get an og juice and a stack of deg fluffy cakes."

"No, one of our waiting staff will take your order in a moment. I'm here because I'd like to show you something in the kitchen," I lie. "I'm making a surprise for Harlow and I need your opinion."

"My opinion would be for you to get lost. I have no interest in helping you or my sist—" She pauses mid word and shakes her head. "No, I'm not even going to call her that."

"Please," I say. "I'm in desperate need of someone with your creative flare." Okay, so perhaps that was an overkill. I don't even know if she is creative.

She scoffs. "Get lost, Zavier." Her glassy eyes flick to Ogre's. "Can't you see I'm busy."

Not able to contain myself, I say, "No, but I can see you're high."

Ogre's wicked eyes snap to mine, and he cracks his knuckles in warning. "You heard the lady, now back off and make her fluffy cakes before I turn you into the batter."

I don't respond well to threats. Just because I'm on the weaker side of our race doesn't mean I'm a walkover. *I'm nobody's doormat.* Feeling ticked off, I abandon my discretion.

"You shouldn't be here with him," I say, focussing my attention firmly on Floss. "He's bad news and you know it. You saw what happened to his girlfriend Nikita; he beat her senseless."

"What did you just say?" Ogre pounds one of his meaty fists hard on the table, causing the cutlery to jump.

I puff out my chest in an attempt to look more threatening. "She deserves better than you."

Ogre rises from the booth, and the chatter of the dining area quietens to whispers. "You're dead," he says.

He stalks towards me, biceps bulging, and I automatically raise my fists. I know don't stand a chance-in-hell of beating him in a fight, but regardless I'm prepared to give it my all. He's quick to get in the first hit, landing his fist hard against my cheekbone. I stumble, afraid the power of his punch may have left a permanent fist print.

I groan and then lunge forward, throwing out a few punches of my own. My fists make contact but carry very little weight. He gives a guttural laugh.

"You're pathetic," he says, before delivering another powerful punch, this time, to my chin. The sheer force of it sends me flying onto the table directly behind me, and the two Magenta girls who'd been sitting there—happily eating—lurch back in their seats and scream. The closer of the two, accidentally spills her cup of steaming bean-brew on me, and it burns, but it's only a minor complaint in comparison to the sharp pain coming from my head.

I blink serval times over. Green and purple splotches distort my vision. I must have bitten my tongue, because it stings, and I can taste the metallic tang of blood seeping into my mouth.

*Too bad, you need to get up, this fight isn't over yet.*

182

As I lever myself upright, half eaten scraps of food fall from my back onto the table, which has since become a mess of shattered-dirty-dinner-plates.

Ogre comes charging at me, eyes flared, the serrated knife from his table clasped firmly in his hand. A wave of panic washes over me as he draws near, but to my surprise, a Magenta guy jumps between us, saving me from being stabbed—*or worse.*

"ENOUGH, ENOUGH..." he shouts.

"Get out of the way, Trey," Ogre warns, giving him a shove with his free hand. "You're lucky I let Nikita live."

Trey's eyes blaze, and it looks as if he wants to take a swing at Ogre, but eventually he regains control of himself and holds both hands up. "Think about it, if you kill him, you'll end up back in the cell, is that what you want?"

Ogre hesitates for a moment, his whole body shaking with uncontrolled rage. Finally, he drops his knife to the floor and grunts.

His eyes glare into mine. "This isn't over," he warns with a pointed finger, and then he grabs Floss by the wrist and drags her out behind him.

Once they've left, Trey scolds me, "Are you out of your frosty mind?" He shakes his head at me, his brows scrunched. "Elgar is not the type of Zeek to mess with. Trust me, you could've been killed."

I swallow my pride and say, "Thanks for your help."

He scoffs. "I might have stopped him this time, but I can assure you he'll be back, and next time you might not be so lucky." He puts his hand out to help pull me up, and despite my inner protests, I take it.

*Not all Magentas are bad, and he did just save your life.*

"I'd start watching my back if I were you," he warns. "Elgar is vindictive and will have it in for you now. And as you can see, he's not the type to hold back."

"I'll try to be more careful next time," I say, without promising anything. "Thanks again."

He nods, picks up the knife Ogre dropped, and then slides back into the booth with his lady friend.

"You idiot," Minty spits from behind me. This is followed by a firm whack to the side of the head. "How could you be so stupid?"

"Awww…" I wince and turn around to find her scowling face gazing up at me. "He got to me," I say.

Her eyes scan me from head to toe with anger. "Yes, I can see that," she replies sarcastically.

From the corner of my eye, I notice the two Magenta girls, whose table I'd landed on, are both staring my way. The shorter of the two looks shaken. Her hands are trembling, and there are gravy splatters all over her shirt and the side of her face.

"I'm sorry about the mess," I say to them. "I'll make you some new meals on the house."

I bend forward to pick up a chair which had been knocked over during the scuffle, but Minty grabs hold of my arm and jerks me upright.

"Leave it," she says angrily. "I'll clean up here. You get your arse back in the kitchen where it belongs."

The last hour of my shift drags, each minute feels like an hour and my face aches terribly. Minty is super peeved, and she isn't afraid to show it. The only time she's spoken to me is when it's been work related.

By six-thirty, the Bean-Brew Cavern is empty. *Finally,* I think with relief, *no more customers.* I bin the scraps, wipe the benches, sweep the floors, and then prepare to lock up.

"Not so fast," Minty says. "We need to talk."

"Now you wanna talk?" I say, and she rolls her eyes at me in frustration.

"Why in Zadok, would you start a fight with Elgar? Do you have a death wish or something? That Zeek is seriously dangerous."

"And that's exactly the reason why I needed to speak to Floss, I wanted to talk some sense into her, but things got kinda out of hand."

Her eyes flash to my swollen cheek. "You think?" She crosses her arms over her chest. "What you did was beyond stupid, you could've been killed."

"But I wasn't."

Her gaze sharpens. "Don't start with me, Zavier. If it wasn't for that Magenta guy who jumped in, you would've been mincemeat."

"Okay, okay." I sigh. "It was a stupid move on my part, I hadn't intended on getting into a fight with Ogre, I was only trying to get a message across to Floss before she made a tragic mistake."

She gives an exasperated groan. "I would have never told you about seeing the two of them together if I'd known you were going to get all macho about it. I thought you'd have a chuckle and say they were well matched. You're always telling me what a bitch Floss is to Harlow, and how you can't stand being anywhere near her, so tell me please, am I missing something?"

*Actually, you are,* I think but I don't say it. I want to share what I know with Minty, but I can't, it's not my secret to tell.

I shrug. "I didn't want to see anything bad happen to her. She is Harlow's twin sister after all."

Her eyes survey mine with suspicion. "I know when you're hiding secrets from me. You do this weird thing where you tap your pointer against your thumb." As soon as she's said it, I realise I'm doing it and stop. "What is it?" she continues to push. "Are you into Floss too or something?"

I jerk my head backwards in disgust. "Pfft. Are you kidding me?" I can hardly believe my ears. I'm offended Minty would think such a thing. She should know me better. I'm in love with Harlow.

"How can you even ask that?" I blurt.

"So, you're not into her?"

"Frost no."

"Good." She looks relieved. "Because not only is Floss a mega bitch, she's also a Magenta, which means you wouldn't solely be on Elgar's hit list, you'd be on the Commander's hit list too."

I swallow hard. *If only she knew the truth about what's really going on here.*

I jiggle the keys in my hand. "Now we've cleared the air, can we go?"

"Not yet, I'm waiting for Tatum." She pokes my chest with her pointer. "And so are you. You've provoked the Ogre—as you and Harlow like to call him—which means you've got a target on your back. Tatum and I are going to walk you home to make sure you get there safely." Her eyes narrow. "Besides, I'm not quite done with you yet." She steps up closer and brushes the top of my shoulder with her hand.

I jerk back. "What are you doing?"

"I'm brushing the chip away," she says, and I shoot her a dirty look. "Let's face facts," she continues. "YES, we are the weakest of our race, YES people walk all over us, and YES it sucks, but we can't change the way we were born, so quit trying to be something you're not. You've become a perpetual hot head lately, you lose control too easily, and this afternoon it almost got you killed." Her expression softens. "I'm only telling you this because you're my friend, and I love you. I enjoy having you around, so smarten up your act, okay."

I feel slightly offended by what she's said, but I know she's right. I have resentment issues and no self-control. "I'll try," I say, which is the best I can offer.

Tatum arrives a few minutes later and Minty fills her in on what happened between Ogre and me.

"You're crazy," Tatum says, scratching her head. Her hair is thick, and a much deeper shade of pink than mine, but it's not quite dark enough to be classified as Magenta, so unfortunately for her, she's been labelled a Pastel. "I've heard terrible stories about Elgar, he sounds really dangerous."

Hearing Tatum's apprehension for my safety, Minty scurries back to the kitchen and grabs a handful of utensils, which she says we can use as weapons, if needed.

I take a look at the utensils in her hand and frown. "Why those things? Why not bring some of the knives?"

"Because we don't want it to look like we are about to go on a killing spree. We just need some sort of protection."

As she hands Tatum a tenderiser, she apologises about having to change their plans. Apparently, they were supposed to be meeting up with some friends by the water pool after Minty finished work. I try telling them I'll be fine and that they should still go, but Minty won't have a bar of it.

"Forget it," she says. "We're walking you home whether you like it or not."

# 24

# WHAT THE FLOSS?

## -ZAVIER-

The stroll back to my place ends up being far less dramatic than Minty had anticipated. The biggest showdown was when Tatum accidentally dropped the heavy tenderiser—spikes down—on my big toe.

"Frost," I'd cursed. "I thought you were here to guard me, not add to my injuries."

"You have shoes on, don't you?" Minty said, jumping to Tatum's defence. "So, what are you whinging about?"

Now, standing at the opening of my puny cavern, I thank both girls for walking me home.

"Remember to sleep with one eye open," Minty says.

"And keep your pocketknife under your pillow," Tatum adds.

I nod anxiously. "Will do."

Once inside, I place the pin dough docker Minty had given me as a weapon on the table, and then head to my sleeping nook to grab some clean clothes. As I'm about to round the corner, I hear a creaking noise and stop dead in my tracks. *Frost, he's here waiting for me*, I think in alarm. *Or could it could be Lexan?* I consider this idea, but I'm doubtful. Lexan isn't the snooping type.

Not willing to take my chances unarmed, I pullback quietly and sneak to the kitchen to grab a sharp knife. *A real weapon.* When it comes to the crunch, killing Ogre beats Ogre killing me. Now armed and ready, I head back to my nook and dive around the corner with the blade of the knife held out in front of me.

A high-pitched girl's scream fills my nook, and I'm *that* startled to see who it's come from, I almost drop the knife.

"Floss?"

Floss had been sitting—curled up in a foetal position—on the end of my bed, but upon my warrior entry, she'd leapt up in fright, her hands flung upwards to ward me off.

*What is she doing here?* It's not like her to visit us "lower level, bottom-feeders"—as she'd once called us. Come to think of it, I'm surprised she even knows where I live.

She collapses back onto the bed, trembling. "What the frost, Zavier?"

"Me? Hey! You're in my nook!"

I toss down the knife and step over to where she sits. As I get closer, I can see she's been hurt, her face is marked with bruises and her lower lip is smeared with dry blood.

"Did Elgar do this to you?" I say, feeling my inner-rage reignite.

She nods, tears streaking her cheeks. "You were right," she says between sobs. "I should've listened."

I drop down beside her to get a better look at her face, and she catches me off-guard by throwing her arms around me. *Awkward.* I stiffen. Floss is not someone I feel comfortable being near, let alone having to console her on an intimate level. We're far from being friends. Our brief encounters are usually made up of snide comments and dirty looks. Regardless, I do feel sorry for her.

I give her back a few gentle taps with my hand. "You're okay," I say, attempting to comfort her. "We'll find a way to fix this." I'm not exactly sure how but I'll find a way. I want to see Ogre pay for what he's done.

Lexan isn't here which concerns me. He's not usually out and about this late. I know he'll be upset to find the two of us here, battered and bruised. I'm also well aware I'll cop a scolding for my part in this. Nevertheless, I still find myself wishing he would hurry up and get home. I'm not entirely comfortable handling this situation with Floss, and I could really, really use his help.

"Have you seen Lexan?" I ask. "Was he here when you arrived?"

A delirious laugh escapes her lips.

*Great,* she's still high.

I pullback from her embrace. "Floss," I say more determinedly.

Her eyes gaze up into mine revealing pupils as big as saucers. Silly girl. I don't understand why she would go anywhere near Ogre and his toxic concoctions.

Keeping my gaze firmly on hers, I retry. "Have you se—" but before I even finish re-asking the question Floss dives in for a kiss.

*What the...!*

Her cold lips graze mine and I panic. *This is not okay. This is not Floss.* I push her back with a shove. "What are you doing?"

"Isn't this what you want?" she says. "Isn't this why you fought for me?"

I lean back further and scowl. "No... Frost no."

Another delirious laugh escapes her lips. "Oh, come on, Zavier, you're no fun. Don't you want to be like Lexan? Wouldn't you like to have one Magenta baby and one Pastel?" She jiggles her brows suggestively. "Don't worry, you can always palm them off to some other sucker to raise." She sniggers and then adds, "We can pretend that they are Elgar's kids, what do you say? If my mother can slum it with Lexan, then I don't see why I can't slum it with you."

My next breath catches in my throat. *How does she know the truth?* This was supposed to be kept top secret. If Floss lets this kind of info slip, all four of them could be killed.

"Why the surprised face?" she taunts. "It's not like you didn't know. Heck, Harlow probably knows, you and Lexan would have told her. She is the golden child after all. Everybody loves her, even our own Commander's son."

I cringe at that last part, but I try to shake it off. There are more pressing issues to deal with at present.

Being careful not to confirm anything, I ask, "Where is this coming from? What makes you say all of this?"

"Please," she snorts. Her eyes fluttering as she speaks. "Is it really that hard to work out? Magentas don't breed Pastels from other Magentas, it's not genetically possible. How no one else has picked up on this before now, I'll never know."

What she's saying is right—and from what I've been told by Lexan—she's not the first Zeek to question their parentage. Apparently, there had been several cheating allegations thrown around after the girls were first born, but Saul was so adamant that Krista had been faithful, he'd convinced everybody of her innocence. In the end, everyone was left believing Harlow's pale colouring was the result of some sort of rare birth defect.

Lexan also confessed it was lucky for them that Saul was so egotistical, because regardless of whether he truly was suspicious or not, he was always going to deny the allegations—point blank—to save face. He was way too proud of a Zeek to admit he was unable to keep his beautiful, sought-after, trophy-wife, happy.

I'm surprised someone as sought after as Krista went for the likes of Lexan. He's not bad looking, but he's a Pastel, and Pastels have nothing to offer.

"What's the matter, Zavier? Has a fuegor got your tongue?"

I don't quite know how to handle this topic without admitting to anything, so in the end I say, "Despite what you *think* you might know about your mum and Lexan, you can't go throwing these kinds of accusations around. If anyone hears what you're saying, you could all be killed."

Without warning, she bursts into full-fledged tears. *Far out*, I think anxiously, *I need Lexan to get home pronto*. I'm not equipped to handle her in this state, her emotions are all over the place.

"I HATE THIS," she lashes out. "I HATE EVERYTHING." She picks up my pillow and hurls it across the room, knocking a few of my better shirts off the exposed hanging rail.

"Hey!"

"My whole life has been ruined because of their selfishness. I've been stuck living in the shadow of my Pastel twin." Her gaze darts to mine. "What is it about Harlow that makes her so damn special? Huh? I'm the one who's Magenta. I'm supposed to be superior."

"Maybe it's your attitude that lets you down," I say, and her eyes flare.

"Screw you."

I hold up both palms. "Cleary I'm mistaken."

My sarcasm seems to aggravate her further. If looks could kill, I'd be dead. But after taking a moment to settle down, she wipes her eyes dry with the sleeve of her jacket and says, "I'm sorry."

Shocked, my gaze snaps to hers.

She's shaking. "I don't mean to be so awful. I'm just bitter."

I grab my throw rug from the end of the bed and wrap it around her shoulders. "I think we're all bitter," I say. "Some of us just hide it better than others."

"To answer your question from earlier," she says, her voice much calmer. "Lexan is with my mother in their secret hiding spot."

I almost fall over. *This is news to me*. I didn't even know they had a secret hiding spot. I didn't even know they still met up. I thought things were over between them years ago. Only the other day, he'd said, "Krista tends to leave me in the dark". Perhaps what he meant to say was Krista leads him into the dark.

"I don't want to go home," she adds with a sniffle. "I don't belong there. I don't belong anywhere. I want to disappear."

*That sounds like the chemicals talking.*

"Well, no one wants you to disappear, so why don't you stay here tonight?"

Her eyes brighten a little. "Really?"

It's not ideal, *but what other viable choices do I have?* She's too high to be sent out alone, and if I were to walk her home, Ogre might spot me and finish me off.

"Really," I reply. "You can have my bed, and I'll take the lounge."

I grab some fresh clothes, have a wash, and then grab a spare blanket before curling up on our *not so inviting* lounge. It's only a two-seater—definitely not designed for a five-foot-ten guy like myself. *Looks like I'm in for a very comfortable night's sleep—not.*

I can't believe Floss figured out Lexan and Krista's secret. You'd think they'd be a little more careful. If Floss has caught on to their rendezvous spot, *what's to stop others from catching on?*

I'm tired and aching all over, but my mind's racing a hundred miles an hour. It won't shut down. I'm still awake when Lexan arrives back around nine. He sneaks in quietly, taking light steps as he heads towards his nook. As he passes by the lounge, he must catch a glimpse of me, because he nearly trips over his own feet.

"Zavier? Is that you?" he asks, in alarm.

I stifle a yawn. "Yeah, it's me."

"What's wrong?" he asks. "Why are you sleeping out here? Are you sick?"

"No, not exactly." I stretch out my arms and then, push the blanket back to sit up. *Here we go…* I think. *Let's get this over with.*

As soon as Lexan catches sight of my face, he gasps. "Zavier, your face… What happened?"

I gulp in a breath before filling him in on the evening's events—starting with my fight with Ogre, and if I thought Minty's scolding was harsh, Lexan's was next level. In all the years I've known him, I've never seen him so worked up.

"The whole reason I even confronted Elgar was because of you," I argue. "I was trying to protect Floss."

Back when I was a young boy, Lexan had told me to always look out for the twins. He'd said Harlow and Floss were very special to him, and he wanted me to make sure nobody ever hurt them.

"While I appreciate you trying to protect her," he says with a sigh, "I still think you did the wrong thing. Elgar is a bad egg, and by the sounds of it, you've put yourself in a very dangerous position." Looking tired, he parks himself on the lounge beside me, his knees cracking as he sits. "I'm sure there were a number of much safer ways you could've handled this."

"Yeah, yeah, I know, I know, hindsight is a wonderful thing."

"You should've spoken to Jax," he continues. "He might have been able to help. He's been helping out Harlow quite a bit since she hurt her leg."

I scoff. "Please," I say. "Jax isn't as noble as you and everybody else thinks he is. I'm sure he's only buttering Harlow up for some big scheme he's got planned."

Lexan shakes his head in disagreement. "No," he says. "His brother Nix may have been on the crooked side, but Jax is good, I can feel it. His father Arlo was a good man, and I think he takes after him. I gave Harlow her name in honour of Arlo, did you know that? Krista named Floss and I named Harlow."

"Enough about Jax and Arlo," I growl. I like Harlow's name, and I don't want to associate it with our Commanding family. "The point is, I knew Elgar would hurt Floss, and guess what—I was right —he did." I run my fingers across my swollen cheek and wince. It feels double the size it should be. "If you think my face looks bad, you should go and take a look at hers." I nod towards my nook. "She's a mess."

His eyes bulge. "Floss is here?"

"Yes," I say. "Which leads me to the next part of the story." My eyes flick to his. "Floss knows the secret you and Krista have been keeping safe for all these years."

His face stops shimmering, making him look paler than pale. "What?"

"She knows you're her father."

I watch as a multitude of expressions flicker across his face and after giving him a moment to process what I've said. I share a detailed account, making sure to skip the part where Floss tried to kiss me. I don't want anyone else knowing about that—*especially Harlow.*

"You've got to talk to her," I finish up, and he nods, his eyes gazing off into the distance. "Make sure she doesn't slip away tomorrow morning before you speak to her, okay? You don't want her spilling your secret to anyone, or we'll all be in trouble."

A grand marble table spectacularly arranged with colourful foods of all shapes and sizes stands before me, begging me to pluck from it. Forcing my hands deeper into my pockets, I gaze beyond the array of tempting treats, to find Purples of all ages, gathered in groups. All of them dressed to impress. They flash their sparkling jewels brazenly at one another as they chatter, each trying to outshine the other.

I look down at my threadbare shirt and my shoulders shrink. I feel underdressed and out of place, and there are too many Purples about for my liking. I don't want to be here. I have no interest in being a part of their celebrations.

My eyes scan the zoft filled chamber—which is larger than both the medical and library chambers combined—hoping to find an exit close by. Instead, I spot Harlow. She stands by an ice sculpture, admiring it, her pastel hair pinned back in a bun set with glistening crystals. I swallow down hard while taking in the rest of her. She wears a beautiful white dress, dusted with pink, and her neckline sparkles brighter than any other Purples in this chamber.

"Zavier," somebody says, taking me by my shoulder. "It's already past six."

I try to ignore them. I don't care what time it is.

The shaking grows more insistent. "Stop it," I groan. "It hurts."

I try to brush the hand off. I need to get to Harlow and find out what's going on. I'm about to take another step, when Jax appears from behind the sculpture, embracing Harlow tenderly, before bending down to place a passionate kiss on her lips.

"NO!" I yell.

The shaking of my shoulder ceases replaced by a full body slam, which leaves me winded.

"Zavier."

The grand chamber around me flickers.

"Zavier, it's me, Minty, wake up, would you? We're going to be late."

My eyes flutter open to find Minty sitting on top of me. I puff out a breath of relief; I'd been dreaming.

"Awww…" I moan. My body feels like it's been hit with a sledge-hammer. "Why'd you have to jump on top of me like that? It really hurt." My arms and core muscles struggle to lift me upright. "My everything hurts."

"Good," she says unsympathetically, and hops up. "Hopefully, this means you're too sore to start any fights today." She rips my blanket back. "Now hurry up and get ready, or we're going to be late."

I flop back down and snuggle deeper into my pillow. "I don't think I can get up. I think I need to have a sick day."

"Oh no you don't," Minty warns. "This was self-inflicted. You're coming to work with me today whether you like it or not." When she realises I'm not budging, she lets out a huff. "I'll grab your clothes for you, where are they?" As she turns to the direction of my nook I'm suddenly struck by a wave of panic, and I leap off the lounge with a start.

"No, its fine…" I say hastily, "…I'll get them."

Minty jerks back to face me, sniggering. "Is it really that bad in there?"

"You have no idea."

She shakes her head, letting out an exasperated breath. "This, my friend, is exactly the reason why I don't date boys." She throws two nauclea latifolia roots at me, and I catch them with swollen hands.

"How'd you manage to score these?"

"The medics gave some to Tatum's father to help him slip away painlessly, but he died before getting to use them. Now hurry up would you, and don't forget the pin docker. I'll meet you out front."

## 25

# ENLIGHTENMENT

## -HARLOW-

"No, no, no, no..." RJ says, clearly stressed, "slowly... Lift the paintbrush slowly while your hand is still moving."

I've spent the last twenty minutes attempting to master the skill of tapering off at the end of a brush stroke, yet somehow, I've gotten nowhere. I gaze across at RJ's page of perfect strokes. How he makes it look so easy, I'll never know. All I can manage are thick unsightly blobs.

Trying to mimic him, I attempt another stroke, but once again it's an epic fail.

I groan and pop my paintbrush down on the easel. "Maybe I'm not made to be a painter," I say.

"You might not be a natural born artist, but this doesn't mean you can't teach yourself to be good. It just takes practice, lots and lots of practice."

The still-life drawing I had attempted yesterday sits on the desk staring up at me accusingly. I frown. *Yuck! What a mess.*

"I don't know about that."

He picks up his brush and demonstrates yet another perfect stroke. "It's only your second day here, give it time, you'll see. You can do this. You just need to persevere and believe in yourself."

Sphinx sits at my feet panting heavily with a smile. I think it's his way of laughing at me. I'm sure he could do a better job at painting a smooth stroke with his tail.

Jax had chaperoned me home yesterday, and then here again this morning, while Sphinx had escorted RJ.

"It's merely a precaution," he'd told us, but I know he's more worried about our safety than he's letting on.

I'd planned on stopping by the café after my lesson finished yesterday, but it's probably a good thing Jax had insisted on walking me home instead. Last time I'd spoken to Zavier, he'd said he had a few things he'd like to talk about—and while I am curious about what went down when I was in a coma—I'm not too keen on letting him in on how I ended up in a coma. I know exactly how he'll react. He'll retaliate, and that's precisely what I don't want.

As if feeling my gaze lingering on him, Sphinx looks up at me with his big lavender eyes and lifts his head to my knees. He is so beautiful, and so, so close. I can no longer resist the urge. I give into temptation and run my fingers through his fur. The texture of his coat is far wirier than I'd imagined, but it feels warm and wonderful, all the same. I imagine leaning down further and burying my face in it.

RJ's glances over wide-eyed, and I draw back in haste.

"Don't worry." His eyes evade mine. "I won't tell anyone, I would never." He shakes his head. "Never, ever."

I smile. "You're different than other Purples." I pause a moment and then add, "Which is a good thing."

"Most Purples aren't as bad as they appear," he says, robotically. "They're just sheep, mindless sheep. They follow orders from the barking dog in fear of being nipped at."

"Sheep?" I repeat in surprise. Here on Zadok, we don't have sheep, we have woollies, and we don't have dogs either, we have canines.

"You remember the human world," he says without so much as blinking. "You know what I mean."

My heart skips a beat. "You remember the human world?"

He nods. "I remember the human world and the world before that. I remember a lot of things I shouldn't."

"How do you know I remember the human world?"

"I've got a sixth sense, but I don't speak openly about it. Not since Nix got a few of his corrupt warriors to hold me down while he tipped an entire bottle of vinegar over my eyes."

"He did what?" I ask in shock.

"It was my own fault in a way," he says, his eyes darting side to side as he speaks. "I knew Nix was dangerous. I should've kept my mouth shut about my premonition of him blowing up the sewing factory, but I didn't, I told my friend—who told his brother—not knowing that his brother was one of Nix's followers."

"So, it's true," I say, my throat constricting. "Nix blew up the sewing factory caverns."

To discover this truth makes me sick to my core. Forty-nine Zeeks had been killed during that explosion, and countless others were injured. From day one, Zavier was adamant that Nix was responsible for his parents' death.

"This is just the beginning," Zavier had said with clenched fists. "Nix won't stop until he's killed every last one of us. He and his gang of followers want to put an end to all of us. Pastels are only an embarrassment to them, a stone around their neck. The Zeek race would be much stronger without us."

These were big allegations for a seven-year-old to make, but I knew where they'd derived from. Zavier's father Xander hated Purples with a passion, and he'd conditioned Zavier from a very young age not to trust them. Although I'd never argued the point, I hadn't believed he was right. It appears he was. *Shame on me.*

It scares me to think Nix had been this ruthless at the mere age of fifteen. To intentionally plot and kill a bunch of innocent Pastels purely because of their colouring is barbaric. We might be pale, weak and have poor vision, but we are all the same race, *damn it.* We're all Zeeks. We should stand united.

RJ's eyes flick to mine momentarily. "Please don't repeat this to anyone. Jax promised me I could trust you."

It startles me to hear this. I don't feel I've done anything to deserve Jax's unconditional trust.

"He's right," I say. "You can trust me."

I redirect my focus to his thick, black rimmed glasses, which had sparked my curiosity the day I first met him. "Is this why you need the glasses?" I ask. "Did the vinegar cause permanent damage to your eyes?"

Again, he nods. "I wasn't able to wash the vinegar out straight away, and the acidity burnt the corneas of my eyes. I can still see, but the outer protective layer of my eyes have been damaged, which means I find it hard to focus on closeup objects without my glasses." His gaze lowers, and then he adds, "As Nix poured the vinegar into my eyes he laughed and said, 'Tell me... What do you see now Freak?'."

"That's terrible." I knew Nix was corrupt; I'd heard stories about him, but I don't think I realised the true extent of his evilness up until now. I shake my head in disgust. "I can't believe he did that to you, or that he intentionally blew up the factory caverns. What a monster! My best friend lost both of his parents that day. They were crushed to death under the rubble."

"Nix was corrupt and ruthless, but don't fool yourself by thinking you're safe now that he's dead. His mother, Azazel is far crueller than he ever was." RJ takes off his glasses to wipe the lenses clean with the edge of his shirt. "She was the one loading the bullets

Nix fired—so to speak. Some even say she was the one who had Arlo killed. He wanted to bring about change, the same as Jax, and she didn't want a bar of it." His eyes flick briefly to mine again, before popping his glasses back on. "Arlo is the reason you were able to stay with your parents after you were born. The warriors thought you should be placed with a Pastel family, and Azazel wanted you killed. She'd said you were 'an abomination', and you would 'bring about conflict to our colony', but Arlo wouldn't have it, he thought you were special and that you would bring about a much-needed change to our colour system. "

I swallow hard, my tummy twisting inside. I hadn't known any of this. My mother said she was the one who fought for me. *Liar*.

It seems I've caused a lot of problems—even deaths—with our Commanding family over the years, and yet here I was, believing I was an insignificant Pastel. Nix and Arlo's blood is partially on my hands.

It's amazing Jax is willing to be so kind to me, when I've inadvertently played a big part in his father's death. He may not have been fond of his brother Nix, but I'm certain he would've loved his father. If I hadn't been born this way, and if Arlo hadn't tried to help me, he might still be alive.

"He was right you know," RJ says, cutting into my thoughts. "You are special. I've seen it. You will bring about change."

"What... Me?" I'm shocked—not only by what he's said, but also by his conviction. "What do you mean I'm special? And what do you mean by 'I've seen it'? Have you had a premonition about me too?"

"I'm always seeing flashes of what the future holds, but these flashes are forever changing depending on the choices we all make."

"What could I possibly do to help bring about change?"

He turns to his easel in an awkward, stiff motion and picks up his brush. "You'll see, I don't want to jinx anything."

I'd like more insight, some clarification, but I bite my tongue. Deep down I understand that his answer is fair.

The rest of the lesson flashes by in a blur. It's been one enlightening week. I'm struggling to wrap my head around everything.

As if worrying about all of the drama, past and present, in this world isn't enough, my thoughts slip to Alex. I wonder how he is, where he is, what he's doing... I wonder if he is wondering about me? I'd hoped I'd see him in my dreams last night, but I hadn't. I hope I'll see him again soon.

By five o'clock, Jax is back and Sphinx leaves my side to bolt over to him. I'm quick to notice he's brought someone with him—a very attractive someone—with lilac eyes and long lavender locks. She looks younger than he does, but not by much. She'd be twenty, twenty-one at most.

"Zannah, this is Harlow," Jax says, gesturing to me. "Harlow, Zannah."

I rise from my seat and nod in the way of greeting. "Nice to meet you," I say.

She adjusts the collar of her special edition warrior jacket, while giving a nonchalant nod in return.

"Zannah is Stavros' younger sister," Jax offers.

"Oh... Right," I manage to squeak. I'm not sure what's got me feeling so self-conscious. *Is it because I'm meeting the sister of the notorious Stavros? Or is it because she is so damn attractive?*

"I'm taking Sphinx this afternoon," Jax says to RJ. "But Zannah said she'll walk you to your cavern, okay?"

RJ nods but doesn't give eye contact. "Okay."

Zannah treads impatiently where she stands, her pants clinging tightly to her muscular legs. "Are you ready to go?" she asks.

As I continue to gawk, despite myself, I can't help but feel envious. She has the tall powerful physique of a female basketball player from the human world—only curvier, sexier. What I wouldn't give to trade bodies with her.

RJ picks up a handful of loose pencils and pops them back into the tin before standing. "I'm ready."

While they head for the passage, Jax heads to the easels. I cringe as he glances from RJ's masterpiece to my disaster. His brows raise, and he gives me an enquiring look.

"It turns out using a paintbrush is harder than it looks," I say.

His lips curve up at the corners, causing his dimples to show.

"It's lucky I brought in those extra supplies for you then. It looks like you're going to need them."

I smile despite myself. *Smart aleck.*

On the way back to my family cavern, Jax chats casually about his day's training session. His demeanour towards me has changed a lot over the past week. He's less formal than he used to be, it feels like we've become something along the line of friends. He tells me how he'd taught some of the new recruits how to zone-in on their magic and produce sharp, lethal, shards on command. The shards created by the warriors are used as weapons against our enemies and can be made in a flash by stealing the moisture from the air surrounding them.

"It takes a lot of power and concentration," he says. "But the new recruits are all pretty switched on. I'm sure they'll have it down pat in no time."

These shards have helped to take down many Vallons over the years. While Vallons are much stronger than Zeeks and have the power of fire; fire doesn't perform well in a land filled with ice. They have trouble summoning a spark due to the dampness in the air, and even if they're lucky enough to ignite a spark, the fire balls they create burn out within seconds of leaving their hands.

As soon as we enter my family cavern, my father leaps off the lounge and hobbles over to greet Jax with an over-the-top welcome. Cringing, I continue towards the kitchen, hoping to avoid round two of humiliation. I knew to expect this ridiculous, fawning behaviour from him, he'd reacted the same yesterday, and I'd almost died from embarrassment.

Funnily enough, even with all of my father's larger-than-life efforts to impress, I get the feeling Jax isn't all that fond of him. His aura radiates "GET LOST". Father doesn't appear to notice. He's too busy bragging to even realise he's splashed bean-brew all over the front pocket of his favourite jacket.

"Thank you for walking her home again," my mother says, leaving the kitchen to join my father. "We really do appreciate it."

Enough... Please... I want to gag.

"It's my pleasure," Jax replies courteously, however, his jaw clenches as he gazes between the pair. He knows my parents don't really care about me. Besides, he isn't walking me home to please them, he's doing it because he's concerned for my safety.

"Would you like a drink?" my father offers. He's virtually frothing at the mouth to get Jax to stay and socialise.

*Read the body language; Jax doesn't like you.*

"Maybe some other time," Jax answers. "I still have a few things I need to take care of before I can sit down and relax." His gaze shifts from my parents to me. "I'll see you tomorrow," he says with a nod.

I nod in return, my cheeks flushed with embarrassment. "You will," I say. *Now please go,* I add in thought, and thankfully he obeys.

As I pass by the dining table to get to my nook, I notice there are only three dinner plates set out.

"Is Floss eating out again?" I ask curiously.

"I assume so." My mother walks over to the pot on the stove and gives it a stir. "We haven't seen or heard from her since yesterday. Your father told me not to bother serving her a plate."

*That's rude.* I haven't seen or heard from Floss since she threw our fathers good ceramic cup at my head and then stormed out.

"Are you not worried about her?" I ask, but before my mother can answer, my father butts in with his two cents worth.

"Floss is a big girl," he says, void of any concern. "I'm sure she can take care of herself."

# 26

# THE WRONG SISTER IN MY BED

## -ZAVIER-

Standing for over twelve hours on sore legs with a splitting headache, while cooking for a pack of Magenta whingers, is what I call torture. I've never suffered so much pain or endured so much worry in my life. I hope Lexan got to speak to Floss before she left, or we'll be facing far worse problems than just Ogre.

After locking up, Minty insists she and Tatum will walk me home.

"You do realise I'm going to have to walk home on my own

eventually—*right?*" I say in protest. "I can't rely on you and Tatum to be my personal bodyguards forever."

"We'll re-evaluate the situation once you're feeling better," Minty says, handing me my pin docker. "But at this very moment, you're in no shape to take on anyone, let alone Elgar."

"I'll never be in good enough shape to take on Ogre, so what's the difference?"

She hands Tatum her mallet, before fixing me with an irritated glare. "Quit arguing and start walking," she demands. "Tatum and I have places we need to be."

I eye the mallet in Tatum's hand with unease. "Sure thing, as long as your girlfriend promises not to tenderise my toes."

Tatum smiles. "Better your toes than your—"

"—Okay I get it," I say. "I'm walking."

When we arrive back at my cavern, I'm stunned to find Floss sitting on the lounge alongside Lexan, but needless to say, I'm not nearly as flabbergasted as Minty and Tatum.

Lexan stops what he's saying mid-sentence to look up and greet us, while Floss puts her head down and says nothing.

"What's going on?" Lexan asks.

"Not…much…" Tatum answers uncomfortably, but Minty doesn't respond, instead she grabs me by the collar of my shirt and drags me back out to the passageway, causing me to drop my pin docker.

"What the frost is she doing here?" she growls, as she slams my poor, aching body into the passageway wall. "Is Floss the reason why you didn't want me going into your nook this morning? Was she in your bed?" Her eyes flare, and her grip tightens, making it hard for me to breathe. "Tell me she wasn't."

"I can explain," I rush to say in a gasp, but as soon as I've said it, I realise it's not true. I can't explain the real reason why Floss came here—*not really*—I'll have to lie.

Tatum comes out after us to see what's going on. "Minty what are you doing?" she says with concern. "Let him go before you choke him to death."

"Tatum, I love you, but stay out of this. Zavier and I need to talk. He has some serious explaining to do."

Lexan appears behind Tatum, his eyes ringed purple due to a lack of sleep. "Actually, I think we all need to talk."

Alarm bells start ringing in my head. I struggle against Minty's grip. "Lexan, no! I've got this. Let me sort this out."

Minty fixes her angry eyes on me with suspicion. "What exactly is going on here?"

Lexan pushes past Tatum to get closer to us. "Let's bring this back inside shall we. We don't want to arouse the curiosity of the neighbours."

Minty gives me another small shove before letting go. "This had better be good," she says. "Because Tatum and I aren't willing to risk our lives for you, if you're not willing to tell us the truth."

As we pile back inside, I notice Floss is no longer sitting on the lounge. I can't see her anywhere. I'm not sure how well the conversation with Lexan went down, and this frightens me. If she is still anywhere near as messed up as she was last night, things could turn dangerous fast.

"Where's Floss?" I ask anxiously.

"She's gone back to bed," Lexan says, motioning his head towards my nook. I sigh internally realising how bad this looks. "She said her head was hurting and she needed to lie back down."

"Back into your bed, huh?" Minty fixes me with another one of her angry glares. "You're unbelievable."

I wave my hands over one another and shake my head. "No-no-no-no, don't go there, it's not what you think. Elgar hit her, and she didn't want her parents knowing. She was upset. she wanted me to console her."

"Please!" Minty crosses her arms over her chest. "Am I really supposed to believe she was merely here for consoling? Come on, Zavier, I saw how you reacted to her being with Elgar. You were jealous."

"For frost sake, haven't we already been through this? I wasn't jealous. I'm not into Floss, I was concerned about her, and for good reason. Did you not just see her face? It's black and blue."

Tatum fidgets uncomfortably with the bottom button of her jacket. "I don't really have to be here for this," she says.

"Oh yes you do," Minty insists.

"Tatum," Lexan says, gazing at her sympathetically. He gestures to the lounge. "Why don't you take a seat." His eyes then swivel towards Minty. "I think it's about time I set a few things straight."

"Lexan, wait!" I say in a panic. "Maybe we should talk about this first. You and I alone."

From the corner of my eye, I detect a look of hurt pass over Minty's face. She's thinking, *if we're such close friends, then why am I keeping secrets from her.* I get it, but a secret is not a secret once too many people start knowing about it, and let's face it, this secret is to die for—*literally.*

"It's okay," Lexan says, leaning his hip against the edge of the lounge. "You trust these girls, don't you?"

My eyes flick to Minty's, and I cringe with guilt. I would love for her to know the truth, but the more people we involve, the riskier it is for all of us.

"Of course I do, but that's not the point, and you know it," I say. "Besides, we can't tell them, I haven't even told Harlow."

Minty gazes between Lexan and me, her eyes filled with a mixture of hurt, anger and interest.

Lexan takes one look at Minty's rigid stance and sighs. "I can't have you and Minty fighting over my secret," he says, straightening himself from the lounge's edge. "Now that you've gone and put yourself on the wrong side of Elgar, you'll need her support more than ever. Tatum's and hers."

"I'll be okay," I say, only half believing it. "Elgar hasn't come back yet, and there's a chance he won't. I'm sure I'm not the only Zeek dumb enough to piss him off. He's probably got a long list of others to get through first."

Lexan fixes me with a long-measured look and then shakes his head. "Enough with this absurdity, I'm being serious."

"I know you are, and so am I."

Taking a big a gulp, I look Minty straight in the eyes, and say, "I'm sorry, but I think you should go. As much as I would love to let you in on what's really happening here, I don't think it's safe for you to be involved."

"Excuse me?" The hurt in her voice causes my insides to twist.

"Being a part of this secret will only put you and Tatum in danger."

"Nonsense," Lexan blurts. "Minty, don't listen to Zavier, you're staying. I need you lot to stick together." He glances between Minty and Tatum, drawing in an anxious breath. "Despite what this looks like, Floss isn't here because of Zavier, she is here because of me."

Minty's eyes enlarge with horror. "What! Are you suggesting you and Floss are..." She pauses, her expression saying the rest. She looks as if she's about to gag. "Ewww...Floss is young enough to be your daughter."

"Floss is my daughter," Lexan says, and Minty and Tatum both jolt in surprise. "Zavier was only trying to protect her, because of a promise he made to me."

"Oh..." Minty struggles to pull her words together. "Oh, I see. Does this mean Harlow is—"

Lexan nods.

"Well I guess that explains her colouring."

"You can't say anything," I jump in quickly, before anything more can be said between them. I look Minty straight in the eyes once more. "Please Minty, promise me you'll keep this secret. You said it yourself, our Commander has a death policy when it comes to interrelationships within our colour system. Lexan, Krista, and the girls would be killed—they might even go after us. This secret is too dangerous to spill, there are lives at stake."

Minty stares up at me, the hurt in her eyes replaced by resolve. "I promise," she says. Her eyes flick to Tatum's and then back to mine. "We both promise."

# 27

# BACK TO EARTH

## -HARLOW AND HARLOW AS RUBY-

*W*hile mum's stew was delicious, having to sit at the table with my parents and play happy family leaves a bitter taste in my mouth. Little do they know I resent them both with a passion—my mother especially. My father may be a heartless brute by nature, but I don't believe my mother is. I think she's fully capable of showing us girls love and compassion, only she chooses not to because she is too weak to stand up against our controlling father.

To him, life is not about love; it's all about status, which is exactly the reason why, now that I've been spending a lot of time with Jax, he suddenly finds me worthy enough to speak to. He tries to involve me in all of his courageous hunting stories—which I have absolutely no interest in—by rewarding me with loads of eye contact.

I laugh inside. To think, after all these years of craving his acceptance, I've finally got it, and now I find myself wishing he'd go back to ignoring me. *The irony of it!*

I don't stick around for dessert. I don't think I can deal with anymore of his heroic tales, and I'm certainly done with answering questions.

How is Jax? What work has he got you doing now? Why has he been walking you home from work? How much are you making in tradeable goods? Who are you working with? Has he said anything about me? And, have you spoken to Zavier since you left the medical chamber?

These questions would seem pretty standard for most caring fathers, but not mine. I'm not used to speaking to him about what's going on in my life, and I don't feel at all comfortable. Besides I know for sure, had I been sent down to work with the Pastels—like he'd initially feared—his interest in my work life, or social life for that matter, would be non-existent.

*Come to think of it,* I'm surprised he even bothered to ask about Zavier. Whenever Zavier comes to visit, he usually treats him like an annoying fly he'd like to swat. *He's not asking out of kindness* I realise. *He's fishing for information.* He and Zavier were both in the medical chamber around the same time—I'd overheard a commotion break out. I'm now beginning to wonder if he was the cause of it. After all, he hasn't offered any explanation as to why it is he's all battered and bruised.

On the way to bed, I stop by Floss' nook. It's strange, maybe even foolish, but I kind of miss her. As fruit pickers, we were made to work beside each other five days a week, but now I barely see her at all. Admittedly, she's never been very nice to me, and when the fuegor came after us, she had left me for dead, but she's my twin nevertheless, and there's a childish part of me that craves her love and friendship.

"I have to quickly duck to Rae's," I overhear my mother tell my father. "I promised I would help her with something."

"You're always over there helping her with something," my father grunts. "Can that woman do nothing herself?"

"Don't worry," she says, her voice quivering slightly. "I won't be gone for long, only a couple of hours max."

Alex's loud excited voice startles me from the blackness.

"Holy shit, you're back! You're alive!"

I feel his embrace before my vision has time to clear, but without hesitation I reciprocate. I throw my arms around him tightly, blinking back the blur.

"Alex," I say, smiling. "Thank goodness."

"Thank goodness indeed. You're finally back." His warm brown eyes gaze into mine with relief. "I was starting to get worried. I thought I was going to have to go and pay someone another visit."

I frown in confusion. "Pay whom another visit?"

"It doesn't matter anymore." He cups my cheek with his hand, his lips curling up at the corners with affection. "You're here again, that's all that matters."

Overwhelmed with emotion, I dive in for another hug. Blissful warmth spreads through me, but this feeling only lasts a moment before I'm distracted by a hissing sound. My sister's voice follows.

"What is up with you lately, you grumpy cat?" She rolls her eyes. "Do we have mice or something?"

Alex lets out an irritated sigh. "Your sister's cat really hates me. It hisses incessantly the whole time I'm here."

His sentence replays in my mind. *He's been here a while. He's been worried about me. He cares about me.* My heart thumps.

"There doesn't appear to be any mice," Jade tells Fat Cat, who's too busy hissing at Alex to notice. "But there is an empty chip packet, and two pairs of dirty socks," she groans in frustration. "When is that boy ever going to learn to pick up after himself?"

I reluctantly leave Alex's embrace and turn to look at my sister. She's crouched by the lounge, peering underneath it.

"Your sister is always talking to herself too," Alex says.

"She's not talking to herself," I say defensively. "She's talking to Fat Cat."

"Sure." He grins. "And here I was thinking she was crazy."

I pivot back around, fixing him with a pointed gaze. "Your brother is the one who's crazy, get it right." My tone is playful, but I mean what I've said.

"I believe the correct term they use for him is schizophrenic, but let's not go there shall we, it's a depressing topic. We should do something enjoyable, like walk by the lagoon."

"Good idea," I nod. "Let's do it." I scan my surrounding and scratch my head.

He glances over at me curiously. "What's up?"

"I feel like I should tell you to wait a minute while I go and grab some sunscreen and a hat, but somehow I don't think I'll be needing them."

"What do you know... There are some perks to being a ghost after all."

"I will miss feeding the ducks though."

"Don't worry," he says with a smirk. "You'd only be wasting your time bringing the bread. They'll be too busy quacking at me to eat anything."

It's sunny outside with a light breeze, and there's not a single cloud in the sky.

"I used to love days like today," I say, gazing above the tall gumtrees across the way. "The clear sky looks so incredibly blue."

The silver sparkles of my dress reflect in the sunlight, casting small shiny dots over the arm of Alex's leather Jacket. "I prefer over-cast days," he replies. "I like feeling brighter than the weather."

The rest of our walk to the lagoon is filled with small talk, mainly about our human lives. Alex reveals he was a bit of a lost, angry, teenager who was forever getting into fights. He admits if he had the chance to do it all over again he would, and he would show a lot more respect and appreciation to Josh and Bianca's parents for taking him in and giving him a good home. He doesn't mention Lucas' name once—since our little dig at him earlier—and I'm glad he doesn't. The thought of Lucas being his twin is still something I'm struggling to get past.

When we get to the lagoon, we take a seat on top of a large smooth rock facing the water, and I think to myself uncomfortably, *I've sat here before with Josh.* My gaze drifts to Alex who is smiling, none the wiser. *Your adopted brother,* I continue to think, but don't say.

There are so many reasons why I shouldn't be into Alex, yet I can't help the way I feel. There's something alluring about him. He draws me in like a magnet.

It's funny, because back when I was Ruby, I'd never thought of Lucas as a good looking guy—I'd never thought of him as bad looking by any means—but he'd never captured my attention like Alex. Then again, he was always unkept, smelt of cigarettes, and was perpetually sullen. He barely ever cracked a smile, and on the odd occasion he did, I was always distracted by his chipped yellowing teeth.

Despite his few serious moments, Alex often gives a cheeky grin, and he also appears to have taken much better care of his teeth. I mean look at those perfect pearly whites, and those cute grooves softening his cheeks. *He's gorgeous.*

"Are you okay?" he asks. "You look deep in thought."

I gaze to where the sun hits the water and watch as the ducks glide along the surface, rippling the reflected light.

"Yeah, I'm okay. I'm just capturing mental pictures to take home with me. Who knows if I'll get the chance to come back or not?"

"You have to come back, or else it's unfair to me." He nudges me playfully with his shoulder. "I feel like we're only just getting to know one another."

I smile, unsure what to say. I like Alex, and from what I can tell, he seems to like me, but the dynamics between us are so messed up, it's not funny. He is my killer's brother, and my ex-boyfriend's adopted brother, and not only that, we're ghosts. We won't get to move forward or build our lives together here; we are stuck as we are. We'll forever be the teens we died as.

"So, are you seeing anyone back in Zadok?" Alex asks, and I blush at the boldness of his question.

"No," I say, fidgeting with the hem of my dress. "I haven't really been with anyone since Josh."

His eyes trace my outline, and he gives a suggestive grin. "I find that hard to believe."

A strained laugh escapes my throat. "Yeah, well my new form leaves a lot to be desired."

"Why? Are you a Pastel?"

Startled, my eyes jerk upward to meet his. "I never told you I was a Zeek."

He smiles smugly and shrugs. "It wasn't hard to guess. You gave your sister a brain freeze."

"I didn't give her a brain freeze," I argue. "Electra gave me a brain freeze which transmitted." I shake my head. "Anyway, that's not the point. Why didn't you say anything earlier? Why have you waited until now to bring it up?"

"Does it matter?" He looks surprised by my outburst. "I don't understand why you're getting so upset?"

He's right. Just because he knows what I am, and I don't know what he is, doesn't mean I have the right to be upset, all I've got to do is ask the question.

After taking in a deep breath to calm myself, I hesitate. The truth is, I'm secretly afraid of his answer.

"Tell me," I say, attempting to hide how anxious I really feel. "What are you? If you hunt at night, you can't be a Zeek."

"Ah, you picked up on that," he says, lifting his brows. "You're right, I'm not."

"Okay… So what are you?"

"I don't know if I should tell you. You might hold it against me."

A shiver runs up my spine. "You're a Vallon, aren't you?"

I stare anxiously, hoping he'll deny it, but he doesn't, instead he gives an uneasy nod.

My heart sinks. Not only is he my killer's brother, my ex-boyfriend's adopted brother, and a ghost—he's also a Vallon. *Holy mother of God, what have I gotten myself into?*

The terrifying image of the Vallon I had seen as a young girl flashes into my mind, and I cringe involuntarily. He was by far the scariest creature I had ever set eyes on.

Noticing my reaction Alex slowly reaches for my hand. "There's no need for you to be alarmed," he says. "Here, I'm just Alex."

Unable to shake the terrifying image of the Vallon from my mind, I pull my hand back.

"Your kind hate my kind," I say. "They steal us Pastels; they kill us."

"We're not all bad." He lets out a pained sigh. "At least I'm not. Besides, your kind are no angels. Your Commanding family has fought our kind for years, telling us that we are not to fish in their oceans or we'll be killed, when all the while, they hand over seafood by the bucket full to the Drakes."

"The Zeeks have an agreement with the Drakes," I say. "We trade seafood for the use of their land."

"Yes, and we trade gemstones and minerals with the Drakes for the use of their land, which is exactly what we'd offered your Commander, but she refused. She wanted to be paid in voltz."

"Why?" I ask. "What good would voltz do us Zeeks?"

"It's not as much about what it could do for you Zeeks, but about what it would do to us Vallons. Without the added power of our voltz, our fire summoning would be weakened. We would be easier to kill."

"Forgive me for saying this, I don't agree with what our Commander has asked for, but it does make sense. Vallons are the strongest race on Zadok, and they're always waging war on us. I'm not surprised that she was looking to even the playing field."

"Our kind wouldn't wage wars on your kind if your Commander was reasonable, but let's face it, we all know what she —and those commanding before her—are really after, they want to weaken our kind so they can invade our land, raid our tombs, take our ancient treasures and steal our magically strength-infused vertic switz ink."

I frown. "Your veritc switz ink?"

"As long as we have the power of fire on our side," he continues, "they'll never be strong enough to take us down on our own turf."

Information overload. I edge away from him with a shiver, trying to hash everything out in my mind. "Look, I don't know much about any of this, I'm way too far down the colour system to be involved in any of the politics. All I know is that your kind have done some cruel, unspeakable things to my kind over the years. Especially to us Pastels."

"Funny you should say that, did you know that after the last war was done and dusted, your Commander handed over a hundred Pastels to be used as slaves. She called it a peace offering."

"What? No?" I shake my head, not wanting to believe him. "Our Commander didn't hand them over; they were taken by the Vallons during the war. I saw a Pastel girl being snatched away with my very own eyes. She was young. She was taken by a Red."

A pained look flashes across his face. "Some Pastels were taken by the Vallons who attacked, I know, but most of them were sent to us by your Commander."

I swallow hard. If what Alex is saying is true, then I wonder if Jax knows about it.

"Even if this is true, your kind still took the offering. They were still happy to use us as their slaves."

"I'm not saying my kind are good, we're not. Like you said, we've done cruel, unspeakable things. I'm just saying your race isn't perfect either."

Tears sting my eyes. I don't think I can take any more unsettling revelations this week. I feel like my whole life has been turned upside-down, and now my two worlds are threatening to destroy me like a volcano erupting from the inside.

Here on Earth my killer walks free—a predator prowling around my sister—pretending to be the hero who tried to save me. And to make matters worse, not only did he kill me, he also killed his own twin brother, who I—for some ridiculously insane reason—have taken a fancy to, only to learn that he's a Vallon—the Zeeks greatest enemy on planet Zadok.

My life on Zadok is already complicated enough without throwing a Vallon into the mix.

I need to walk away now, and I know it. Nothing good can come from starting any kind of relationship with Alex. Besides this isn't realistic. I'm not even alive here, I'm a ghost.

"Hey," Alex says, shuffling over to close the gap I've made. "Don't think too much into what I said, I shouldn't have carried on like that. It was stupid. None of the Zeek and Vallon bullshit politics matter here. This is our escape."

"But none of this is real," I say. "We aren't real. We're ghosts."

He leans forward and cups my cheek with his hand, causing me to flinch.

"Does this feel real?" he asks, and then leans in, touching the top of his forehead against mine. His breath is sweet and warm on my skin. "Does this feel real?"

*Oh, it feels real alright, it feels very real, a little too real.* My heart pounds hard against the wall of my chest.

"If something looks and feels real, then what's to stop it from being real?"

I draw my face back from his hand. "Reality."

"And what exactly is reality?" he asks with scrunched brows. "To me, this world is half of my reality, I'm here nearly as much as I am—"

My attention is abruptly stolen by a few loud crashes nearby. I fling my finger to his lips. "Hold on shhh..."

"What's going on?" he asks, his lips vibrating against my finger.

I let my finger drop. "I can hear something." I pause to listen again. Next, there's a loud bang, and I jump. Startled, I scan the area to see if I can pinpoint where the noise came from. I don't spot anything out of the ordinary. All that surrounds us is trees, dirt, water, and overgrown grass.

My eyes dart to Alex's in apprehension. "Where are the sounds coming from?"

Brows puckered, he cocks his head to the side to listen, but after a couple of seconds he says. "I don't know what you mean, I don't hear anything."

## 28

# OUCH—DOUBLE OUCH!

### -HARLOW-

*A*n explosive bang echoes in my ears, and my eyes fling open to reveal the creviced ceiling of my nook.

"Damn it," I curse, I hadn't been ready to leave. *I still don't know what I want, or how I feel.* Actually, that's a lie. I know exactly what I want and how I feel, the only problem is my heart and my head are saying two conflicting things.

Another huge bang erupts, along with the sound of glass shattering. I jolt. The sounds must have been filtering through from here all along. *That's why Alex couldn't hear them.*

Alarmed, I jump from my bed and rush to the sound of the noise. I see light emitting from the opening of Floss' nook and notice her favourite ornament is on the passageway floor in pieces.

I sigh. She must be super angry about something.

I know deep inside, the best thing for me to do right now would be to stay away. My presence will only provoke her further. Regardless, I can't help myself. I leave my nook anyway and wander across to hers.

As I get to her nook opening, a shoe goes flying past, missing my thigh by a mere fraction, before crashing to the floor with a thud. How my parents can possibly sleep through this racket is a miracle.

"Floss," I say gently, as I continue to creep forward.

I'm hoping—against all odds—I'll be able to settle her down. She needs to stop throwing her things around before she wakes up our father. I know from personal experience how livid he can get when he's woken up during the night. I went to our parents' room for comforting one evening after one of my Lucas nightmares, and it was like I'd poked a grizzly bear. I never made that mistake again.

"Floss," I continue, "what's wron—" I come to a sharp halt as a tall frightening figure stalks out to greet me. It's not Floss making all the racket. I shudder; it's Ogre.

His eyes are flared, and he lets out a guttural growl. "Where is she?"

I gulp and stagger backwards. "Who?" I ask shakily. "Floss?"

*What is Ogre doing here in the middle of the night?* I ask myself. *And what exactly does he want with Floss?*

My eyes do a quick scan of her nook, it looks like a cyclone hit it. Not a single thing has been left unturned, and shards of glass glisten from the floor. *She must have something he wants.*

Ogre stomps forward and grabs hold of my upper-arms with his big, calloused mitts. He looks unkept with dark magenta stubble shading his face. He also smells bad, really bad, like he's been dragged out of a trash can. I screw my nose up. I'm guessing it's been a while since he last washed.

"Where is she?" he roars again, all-the-while lifting me off the ground, to give me a bone rattling shake. A few droplets of his spittle spray onto my face. I wince.

"I..I..don't know," I stutter. "Floss doesn't speak to me."

His grip tightens, crushing the flesh of my upper-arms. "You're lying."

"Owww," I cry in pain.

My breath catches in my throat. I'd fallen victim to Ogre's rage back when we were kids, and I have a long scar across my collarbone to prove it. I gaze towards his self-mutilated, bulging, biceps and cower. They're double the size of what they were when we were kids. *Double the size, means double the power,* I think in fear.

"What's going on here?" My father shouts. He rounds Floss' nook, still dressed in his pyjamas, and thrusts his blade towards Ogre's neck, bringing it to a standstill a fraction short of his actual skin.

Ogre drops me with a thud, and I feel the thump-thump, of my blood making its way back to where he'd cut off the circulation of my arms.

"I'm looking for Floss," he grunts.

"She's not here," my father says harshly, "Now get out!"

Ogre snorts. "But she said she w—"

My father presses the edge of his blade to Ogres skin. "I said get out! And don't you dare come back, or next time there will be blood, you got that?"

Ogre grunts a mocking, "Whatever you say, almighty Saul."

He's using sarcasm to deflect his fear. Ogre may be an infamous badass, but my father is the best hunter our colony has, and Ogre knows it. When we were younger, he wanted desperately to grow up to be exactly like him. Saul was his idol.

With his point made my father lowers his blade, and Ogre storms out, his shoes crunching heavily on the shards of glass scattered on the floor beneath him.

My father turns his enraged eyes to me. "Where is Floss?" he growls.

I stop rubbing my thumping arms to shrug. "I don't know, I haven't seen her in days."

His eyes scan her nook, and he hmpfs in anger. "Well she'd better hurry up and get this mess cleaned up, or there will be serious consequences."

I swallow hard, nod, and then head straight back to my nook, praying for Floss' sake, that she doesn't arrive home anytime soon.

*Wherever she is, please let her be safe,* I add, not knowing exactly who it is I'm praying to.

Zeeks don't follow a Godly force, they pray to the stars. They say the stars above have been set here to help guide us through the many different lives we will face. They believe they hold the power of strength, courage, and healing. I don't know what I believe, but I pray regardless, fully aware that my prayers may never be heard or answered. It makes me feel better. It makes me feel like I have some sort of control over what happens, even though, deep down, I know I don't.

I wait until my parents leave the next morning before getting up. I'd overhead them bickering about what happened last night. My father blames my mother.

"If it wasn't for you inviting Rae and that meat-head son of hers over all the time, we wouldn't have this problem."

"Elgar hasn't been here in years," my mother argued, and I could hear the tinkling of shattered glass being swept across the floor. "Not since he sent Harlow to the medical chamber with a broken collarbone."

"Well, you'd better have a word to your other daughter before things get out of hand," he'd said coldly. "Because I don't want a degenerate like him for a son-in-law. It sends the wrong message."

I shake off their conversation and slip into some of my old threadbare fruit picker clothes. Jax told me he'd gone and retrieved a few extra outfits from lost property for me like I'd asked, but he'd left them at Zavier's the night Electra had put me in a coma.

After I've finished getting ready, I wander over to Floss' nook and peek inside. All the shards of glass and broken bits of ornament have been neatly swept into a pile, while the rest of her belongings have been dumped on top of her bed.

Her jewellery box is mangled and empty, and the bow and arrow that Fau had given her for her sixteenth birthday has been snapped in two.

When Fau had asked me what I wanted for my sixteenth, I'd told him I wanted Lollie, the heterochromia husken which was originally supposed to be given to my parents.

He'd laughed and replied, "As much as I'd love to give you Lollie, you and I both know your father would kill me".

Subsequently, he commissioned a small carving of Lollie for me, which sits on my nightstand. I treasure it.

I manage to get a fair chunk of Floss' belongings sorted out and put away before being disturbed by a set of footsteps entering our cavern.

I set down the shoe in my hand and exit Floss' nook, expecting to see Jax standing by the entry, but instead I find Zannah.

Surprised, I do a double take. She looks fierce in her protective warrior gear, and her hair sits immaculately in a thick off-side fish braid.

I exhale an anxious breath. "Hi."

"Not the face you were expecting, huh?" She laughs cynically. "Sorry for the disappointment but Oscar's been hurt, so Jax asked me to escort you instead."

"What happened to Oscar? Is he okay?"

I don't know Oscar personally, only to look at, but according to what I've been told, he's Jax's right hand man, and one of his more trusted warriors. Jax mentioned his name several times yesterday when walking me home. Oscar and Kieran had been the ones helping him to train the new recruits.

"Oscar needs to learn to keep his mouth shut," Zannah says. "He had a few harsh things to say about Nix to one of his old followers, and it came back to bite him." She grins, which gives me the impression she finds his misfortune somewhat humorous. "Don't worry," she adds, mocking, "he'll live."

I shift uncomfortably. "You don't like Oscar?"

"I like him fine," she says, "But I don't think it would hurt for him to be taken down a peg or two."

I stare her way, waiting for her to elaborate. She doesn't offer any further details, and I don't know her well enough—nor do I feel comfortable enough—to start prodding. In the end I drop my gaze, grab my crutches and say, "I'm ready to go when you are."

Our walk to the art cavern is a little awkward, and I get the overwhelming impression Zannah isn't all that fond of Jax spending so much time with me.

"It's not that I don't see your Pastel life as valuable," she'd said at one point, sounding less than sincere. "I do. But I don't see why he feels the need to tend to you himself. He should get one of his new low rank warriors to babysit you."

*Ouch!*

"If he keeps spending all of his time protecting you instead of helping to rule our colony, he'll end up losing the respect of his warriors."

*Double ouch!* But sadly, I know she's right.

By the time we arrive at the art cavern, I'm exhausted. Sphinx rushes out to greet us, his tail thrashing around wildly as he pants. I realise with flushed cheeks—I'm panting too.

I think Zannah was too busy giving me a piece of her mind to notice I was struggling to keep up with her long brisk strides. I'd thought to remind her that I have a wounded leg, and my crutches are heavy and awkward to use, but I was already feeling humiliated enough after the whole "babysit" comment.

She doesn't linger, which I'm happy about. Please don't let her be the one to pick me up. She can take RJ, and Sphinx can take me.

RJ is all revved up and ready to go. I haven't even made it to my seat before he jumps into a very detailed spiel about the day's lesson. He rambles so fast and excitedly, I only catch half of what he's saying.

"Do you remember him?" he asks.

After Zannah left, he'd started speaking about a human artist named Vincent Van Gogh.

"Sure," I say, "He was the artist who cut his own ear off in a fit of lunacy, and then gave it to a prostitute—am I right?"

"So, some say." RJ blushes. "But it has also been speculated his good friend Paul Gauguin lopped it off with a sword during their row, and that Vincent had lied about doing it himself in order to protect his friend." He waves a hand. "Enough about his personal life, do you remember his artworks?"

An image of blue swirls lit with stars enters my mind. "The Starry Night was one of his works, right?"

RJ's face lights up. "Right." He nods. "'For my part I know nothing with any certainty,'" he rants, "'but the sight of the stars makes me dream.'"

"One of Vincent Van Gogh's quotes, I take it?" I stare at RJ in fascination. "How do you remember stuff like this? You're always quoting things and throwing out random, detailed facts."

"I have a photographic memory," he says robotically, "and I get fixated on subjects that interest me, it's a trait I've always had." His cheeks redden. "In the human world, they diagnosed me with a developmental disorder called Asperger's syndrome, which is the category most humans with unique abilities like mine, fall into."

"Asperger's," I repeat. "Yeah, I've heard of that. Luke, at my school, had it. I didn't really know him all that well—actually none of us did—he was completely introverted, but I remember he could play Beethoven's Moonlight Sonata on the piano and make it look as easy as playing Three blind mice." I smile. "He was a brilliant pianist. Our music teacher Mr Anderson had said, in all his years of working, he'd never come across someone with so much talent. He said Luke was the only person he knew who could learn an entire piece by ear."

RJ taps the wooden end of his brush against his chin, face knowing. "Those of us born of magic, hear and see patterns in things that 'normal' humans/Zeeks can't. It's distracting and over-whelming at times, but it can also act as a gift if you have the concentration to tune in to certain patterns and follow them."

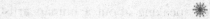

Come five-thirty, I'm relieved to hear the sound of Jax's voice. I'd spent all lesson worrying I'd have to endure another torturous ego bashing, power walk with Zannah.

"I'm impressed," he says making his way over to me. "You've managed to capture Electra's face just so."

I gaze at the sorry self-portrait I've painted and chuckle. "It's supposed to be me," I say with flushed cheeks. "But it's not finished."

His eyes flick between my face and the portrait. "How long has it been since you've looked in a mirror?"

My cheeks grow hotter. "I didn't want to paint myself, but RJ insisted. He said that there's no better way to practice achieving a likeness, than with the face with which you are most familiar."

Jax's lips curve up at the corners. "Right," he says in amusement. His eyes flick to RJ's self-portrait. It's only partially done, but it looks a hell of a lot better than mine.

"Wow," he says leaning in closer to get a better look. "How do you manage to make the eyes look so realistic?"

"You need to understand light and how it reacts on certain surfaces so that you can adjust the element of shadow accordingly," RJ rambles, and I imagine Jax now regrets asking the question. "As long as your light and dark values are in harmony with one another the painting will appear more realistic—given your dimensions are all done accurately of course."

"Of course," Jax replies, however, I don't think RJ picks up on his sarcasm.

"Hey," I say, diverting Jax's attention back to me. "Do you think it would be okay if you walked me to the Bean-Brew Cavern this afternoon instead of taking me home? I'd like to catch up with Zavier, it's been a few days since I've seen him."

Jax stalls a moment before answering. "No problem."

# DAY OF RECKONING

## -ZAVIER-

here's a loud crash followed by a scream from inside the dining cavern. Minty and I share a glance and then roll our eyes in unison.

"Please tell me that wasn't table two's order toppling from the waitress's hands," I say with a groan. "That chicklet omelette took me forever to make."

Minty sighs. "Can you watch this?" she says, nodding to her batter filled frypan. "I'll go see what's happened."

"Sure."

I glance at my watch, it's a quarter to six, and there's still a dozen orders waiting to be cooked. I feel like quitting. I'm way too sore for this, and I still have two more twelve-hour days to get through. *Kill me now!*

A few more bangs filter in from the dining cavern. *What in Zadok is going on out there?* It sounds like chairs being knocked over.

A few seconds later Minty comes flying back through the kitchen door. She accidentally trips over a deg peel I'd dropped earlier, knocking into my legs from behind. The jolt causes me to drop the end of the stirring spoon into the pot, and hot sauce splatters onto the healing burns on my arm.

"Owww!" I jerk backwards, almost tumbling on top of her. "Owww, owww, owww. Geez, Minty!"

I go to race to the sink to rinse my burning arm under cold water but Minty leaps to her feet to stop me.

"There's no time," she says in a panic. "You've got to hide. Now!"

"But it burns," I retort.

"Elgar's in the dining cavern causing a scene. I told him you weren't working today, but I doubt it'll stop him from charging in here." She shoves me towards the pantry nook. "A Magenta has him stalled. Hurry! You have to hide."

She sees one of the large empty flour sacks lying on the ground, and races over to pick it up. "Here," she says giving it a shake to open. "Get in here."

I frown. "Are you serious? I won't fit in there."

Flour residuals rise from the disturbed bag. They fill my nostrils and make me sneeze.

"You will if you contort yourself right." She holds the sack open for me to climb into. "Quick! Hurry!"

Another smashing sound echoes from the dining cavern, along with several screams.

"Okay fine." I do as she says and quickly climb into the sack, making sure to shield my sauce-covered-burnt-arm from the scratchy texture of the hessian material.

"Frost," I curse, as I try to contort my long skinny frame into the sack.

My whole-body aches to move, never mind adding the extra strain of having to bend and flex. This week has been the most physically challenging week I've ever faced. I feel like I'm a seventy-year-old, not a seventeen-year-old.

After I'm in, and the top's tied closed, Minty pushes with all of her might to wedge me into the back corner with the rest of the flour bags. My body feels tender to touch, and with each and every shove she gives, I bite down on my lip to stop myself from crying out in pain.

"Now stay still and be quiet," she commands, which is easier said than done.

I hear the tap tap of her footsteps leaving, and then Ogre's voice. *Here we go.* I cringe.

"I know he's in here," Ogre bellows.

"Who?" Minty says, playing it cool.

A metal clank rings in my ears. "Don't mess with me, little Pastel," he says with a dangerous edge. "I'm not here to hurt you, I'm only here for Zavier."

"I'm sorry, but as I've already told you Zavier isn't here. He hasn't been back to work since the scuffle. He was badly hurt."

"He ain't seen nothin' yet."

The heavy thuds of his footsteps enter the pantry nook, followed by a few bangs and crashes. Nervous, I take shallow breaths, trying hard to keep as still as I possibly can.

"Excuse me, but the pantry is restricted to staff only," Minty says. "If you'd like something to eat, then you must take a seat in the dining area and order through the waiting staff, the same as everyone else."

A few more items crash to the ground, and something sharp collides with my side. My eyes fill with tears, but I bite down on my lip to refrain from crying out.

"If you continue to smash everything in the pantry, then I'm afraid I'm going to have to give you a bill." Minty's voice is firm. "We need these supplies to cook with."

Ogre's thudding footsteps recede, and Minty yelps.

*Frost!* Maybe tying me in this sack was a bad idea. There's no easy way out.

"Do you really think it's wise to threaten me, Pip Squeak?" Ogre roars.

Minty lets out another yelp, and I tense.

There's no way I can hide here quietly while he hurts Minty, *I have to do something.* I try to force the sack open. It's near impossible. Not only am I restricted by the tied top, I'm pretty sure the sharp object which collided with my side is actually wedged in my flesh, because it hurts terribly when I move.

"You've proved your point, you're stronger than I am," Minty says, attempting to sound brave. "Now can you please let me go. I'm understaffed, and I've got over a dozen dinners to make."

A loud crunch fills my ears, along with the sound of Minty's blood curdling scream. *Frost!*

"Elgar," I yell in panic. "Elgar, if you want me come and get me."

"Zavier, no!" Minty shouts. There's an undertone of agony in her voice.

"I knew you were in here," Ogre roars.

The thuds of his footsteps come trotting back towards me and I brace myself for the worst. I'm trapped in this bag, unable to defend myself. I don't know what he's planning to do to me—but I'm preparing for the worst.

Ogre's powerful hands seize the top of the hessian sack, and my folded body is reefed from the floor with a forceful heave. A few strands of my hair must have gotten caught in the tie, because I feel them being yanked from my skull, and I yelp.

"Elgar, please," Minty cries. "I'll make you whatever you want on the house, just please don't hurt him."

"One more word out of you—you lying little Pip Squeak—and you're dead too, you hear me."

The creak of the kitchen door opening fills my ears.

"Elgar, that's enough," a familiar voice calls out. It's Trey, the Magenta guy who stood up for me last time I was in trouble.

Ogre snorts. "You again."

I feel the bag swing as Ogre steps forward.

"I said that's enough, now put the kid down."

*Kid?*

Ogre gives a guttural roar, and then hurls the bag around wildly, using me as a weapon. I feel agonising pain as my body collides with Minty and Trey, as well as several hard objects. I hear grunts, screams and words being shouted, however, after a large knock to the head, I'm no longer able to focus on what's being said. The pain is so horrendous, I feel like I'm going to pass out—*or die.*

My earlier thought comes to mind, *kill me now,* I hadn't meant it literally. I'm not ready to die, not yet. Eventually the side of my body collides heavily with the hard floor. The impact knocks every last wisp of air from my lungs, leaving me feeling winded. Stars dance before my eyes and then I lapse into darkness.

# 30

## BAD FRIEND

### -HARLOW-

*A*s we reach the rugged staircase, which leads down to the underground passages, Jax automatically goes to assist me.

"You're struggling," he says. "Here let me help you."

"No." I thrust my palm out. "I've got this. I've managed to get down these stairs a couple of times on my bad leg, it's just a bit of a long-winded process."

"I could easily carry you down. It would save a lot of time and effort."

I cast him a pointed glance. "And what if somebody rounds the corner and sees you carrying me?"

He shrugs. "Would it be so wrong for others of our kind to see that I have compassion?" he asks. "I mean, ultimately it's what I want for our colony. I want us to learn to care for one another, to support one another."

I carefully place my crutches down another step and then hop to it, my gaze leaving his. "Don't get me wrong," I say, thinking back to the harsh statements Zannah had made this morning. "I believe in what you're trying to do, but I think you need to take a slower approach. Our colony isn't ready for such a dramatic colour revolution, and if you move too fast you might end up losing the respect of everyone, including your warriors." I bite my lip nervously before adding, "Perhaps protecting me personally, isn't such a good idea either. Maybe you should get somebody low ranking to look out for me for a while."

Keeping my gaze locked on the stairs in front of me, I notice Jax's shadow has grown still. I hope I haven't offended him, although I'm afraid I might've.

*It needed to be said,* I assure myself. *I can't have him losing everything, possibly even his life, over me. I'm not worth it.*

Unable to look back at him, I challenge another stair, putting me two steps in front. "Don't get me wrong," I say, attempting to smooth things over. "I really appreciate everything you've done for me, but I'm feeling much better now, and I'm sure you have far more important things to take care of than me."

A deafening silence hovers a moment before he asks, "What exactly did Zannah say to you this morning?"

Zannah and my one-sided conversation rehashes in my mind and causes my insides to clench. "Nothing that wasn't true."

His shadow moves sharply as he clears two steps at once, bringing him down to my level. "I should have known better than to send her to fetch you," he says with irritation. "She needs to learn to keep her opinions to herself."

"Funny," I say, endeavouring to lighten our conversation. "She basically said the same thing about Oscar. How is he anyway? Is he going to be okay?"

"His forearm needed a few stitches, but he'll be okay. I doubt it'll keep him down for long. He, Zannah and Kieran are my best warriors now that Stavros is gone." He pauses a moment and then adds, "By the way, that reminds me, what's going on with your sister? Is she okay?"

I tense anxiously, my crutches positioned a step below where I stand. "I'm not sure what you mean?"

"She hasn't gone out fruit picking for the past two days. I figured she must be sick or hurt."

I hop to the step below, putting me level with my crutches again. "I'm not really sure what's going on with her," I answer carefully, yet all the while I'm plagued with worry.

I hadn't known she wasn't going to work. *I wonder if it has something to do with Ogre. I wonder if she's in trouble. Furthermore, I wonder if I should tell Jax about Ogre's early hour rampage?*

"Floss and I don't really speak to one another," I continue, sparing any details for now. "She detests me."

"But you two are twins?" he says with furrowed brows. "I thought you were supposed to share a connection."

"When one's born Pastel and the other is born Magenta, I suppose it's inevitable the bond will be broken."

Jax responds with a sympathetic glance.

If Floss and I had been Purple and Magenta as opposed to Pastel and Magenta there's a chance we might've grown up to be closer than what we are. Most Purples and Magentas get along okay. When it comes down to it, the difference in their physiques is quite minimal in comparison to frail Pastels. The biggest divider between them—besides colouring of course—is the fact that Magentas can't summon winter magic fully. They can beckon water, but they are unable to transform the moisture into shards of ice.

While I continue to struggle down the stairs one by one, Jax remains by my side, his hand extended, ready to catch me if I fall. I can tell he's frustrated about not being able to help me to the bottom, but he allows me this brief moment of independence.

Stairs done, and a few passageways later the Bean-Brew Cavern finally comes into sight. My breath of relief falls short, when a group of Magentas spill out from the cavern entry, some bloodied and yelling for help. The youngest of the group notices Jax and comes bounding over, his eyes filled with panic.

I step forward, mouth agape, my chest tightening in fear.

Jax's posture goes rigid and he raises an arm out to stop me in my tracks. "Wait," he says firmly.

"Jax," the Magenta calls as he nears. "You need to get in there fast! Elgar is high and reaping havoc. I'm afraid he's going to kill someone."

My heart skips a beat. "Ogre?" I say loudly, and Jax's gaze snaps to mine, his brows puckered like—*what?*

I don't bother to correct myself, instead I leap forward on my crutches. "Zavier's in there," I rattle in fear. "We need to get in there now." I go to take another leap forward but Jax grabs hold of my upper arm and jerks me back.

"You're not going in there." His eyes are fierce. "It's too dangerous."

My heart pounds with fear. "But Zavier's in there. He might be hurt. I have to get in there."

"No, you don't, I'm going in there. If Zavier is in trouble, I will help him." He steps in front of me and cups my shoulders with his hands, causing my heart to go from pounding to a standstill. "You need to stay here where it's safe, okay?" His gaze locks firm on mine. "I mean it."

Releasing me from his grip, his attention snaps back to the Magenta who's been waiting apprehensively for Jax's response. "Stay here with her," he says, nodding in my direction. "And make sure she doesn't follow me inside."

The Magenta guy nods at his command, but he doesn't look happy about the arrangement, and quite frankly, neither am I. I don't want to be sidelined. I want to get inside. I need to see what's going on.

I watch as a few more Magentas stumble over each other at the exit, yelling and cursing. Undeterred, Jax races straight towards the chaos, his dreadlocks whipping around his lower back as he moves at warrior speed.

Feeling frustrated, I turn towards the Magenta guy and sigh loudly.

I notice he has dreadlocks too, only his hair is shaved at both sides, with only a small section of long dreads hanging down from his crown. The style is like that of Stavros', minus the indent of snowflakes at each side. *I wonder if he wears it the same way on purpose—or if it's a coincidence.*

He doesn't notice me studying him, instead he watches with knitted brows as his friends disappear around the bend in the passageway.

"You should go with them," I say. "I'll be fine out here on my own."

"Are you sure?" he asks, sounding hesitant.

I know he'd much rather be assisting his wounded friends to the medical chamber, and I don't blame him. I'd much rather be inside the café where Zavier is.

*Please let Zavier be okay,* I pray.

He shifts uneasily where he stands, wanting desperately to take me up on the offer, but he's probably afraid he'll get in trouble with Jax for not following orders.

"Go," I assure him with selfish intent. "Help your friends."

He doesn't need to be told a third time; he takes off, zooming straight towards the passage where his friends have disappeared.

I don't waste a moment. As soon as he rounds the corner, I hastily hobble straight towards to café.

Once inside, I'm confronted by a terrible mess. It looks like Cyclone Ogre has struck again. Most of the chairs have been turned on their sides, and shattered dinner plates—along with half eaten dinner scraps—litter the floor.

There is nobody left in the dining area. My gaze darts to the kitchen door, bile rising in my throat. Ogre must be in the kitchen.

I quickly zig-zag forward, avoiding debris, and then force the heavy swing door open. A staunch Magenta charges over, his intimidating expression screaming, "YOU DON'T WANT TO MESS

WITH ME RIGHT NOW!", but upon seeing me cower, his body language relaxes a little.

"It's only a Pastel," he says waving me off as a non-threat.

There is blood on his hands—*whose blood?*

"A Pastel?" Jax repeats, and within an instant he's at the doorway, fixing me with an irritated glance. "What are you doing in here? I told you to stay outside."

There is blood on his hands too. *A lot of blood.*

Ignoring his lecture, I say, "Where's Zavier, is he okay?"

I can tell he's attempting to keep his face neutral, but a slither of concern crosses his eyes, betraying him. "You can't be here right now, it's not safe." He motions to the Magenta. "Trey, take Harlow somewhere safe and then fetch me some warriors. I need some extra hands."

"No, I'm not leaving." My grip on my crutches tightens. "I want to see Zavier, where is he?"

"I think you should let her in," Minty says, taking me by surprise. Her voice sounds strained, like she's holding back tears. "Elgar's down, and Zavier would want her here."

My heart hammers in my chest. If she's speaking for Zavier, it means Zavier is unable to speak for himself.

Appearing undecided, Jax's gaze flickers from mine, to something on the floor inside. *Oh God no! Tell me Zavier is not dead on the floor.*

"Please," I beg. "Please let me in."

Exhaling a deep breath, he opens the door the rest of the way. "He's in a very bad way," he warns. "I haven't had the chance to determine the extent of his injuries yet, all I know is he's bleeding heavily from his side and the bleeding needs to be stemmed before I can carry him to the medics." Casting a sympathetic glance, he reluctantly steps aside to let me in.

The kitchen floor is even more chaotic than the dining room floor, but I don't bother with the zig-zagging, I dump my crutches by the doorway and hobble straight over to where Zavier lies facing upwards on top of a torn hessian sack. I fall to my knees by his head, my eyes instantly filling with tears. His face is black and blue, and his body is covered in blood. I wince. Jax wasn't exaggerating, he's in critical shape. My lower lip quivers. *Please don't let him die.*

Minty sits by his feet. Feeling the burn of her eyes on me, I look up to meet her gaze. Her face is battered too, her glasses cracked, and I notice her left arm is sitting at an unnatural angle.

"Minty," my voice comes out strangled. "Are you okay?"

"I'll live," she says, emitting strength. "It's Zavier I'm worried about."

A Magenta woman—I don't know nor recognise—kneels by Zavier's side, her hands applying pressure to his blood-soaked wound.

I gaze beyond her to see Ogre's body lying on the floor, the handle of a carving knife sticking out from his chest. His wicked eyes are open, yet they show no emotion. They are lifeless. He is dead.

Jax rummages through the first aid box and grabs gauze, blister tape, and a bandage before coming over to kneel by the Magenta woman. "I need you to lift your fingers for a split second while I put some gauze down."

She nods and does as he says. They work quickly and efficiently.

"Trey," Jax calls, "I need a quick hand before you leave. After I apply the tape, I need you to lift his body up so I can wrap the bandage around him tightly."

I move aside to make room for Trey. "What should I do?" I ask.

"Pray for his survival," Jax says, without a trace of humour.

After Zavier is bandaged, Jax gently scoops up his limp body with his strong, powerful arms.

"Do you still want me to fetch some warriors?" Trey asks.

"Change of plans," Jax says. "I think it might be best if you stay here with Elgar's body instead. Make sure nobody enters the kitchen until the warriors come. I don't want the body being tampered with. If anyone needs me urgently, tell them I'll be up at the medical chamber." He nods towards the Magenta woman. "Ambre, can you escort the girls to the medical chamber and then fetch the warriors?"

She nods.

"Good, thank you. I'm going to race ahead. This boy has lost a lot of blood, and his pulse is growing weaker by the minute."

I wish I could race off with him, but I know I physically can't, I would only slow him down.

Feeling helpless, I turn to Minty. "Is there anything I can do for you?" I ask.

"Yeah," she says her expression tight. "Stop setting your sights so high and open your eyes up to what's right in front of you."

I frown, unable to make sense of what she's saying. The knock to her head must have been a hard one.

The first half of our trip to the medical chamber is devoid of proper conversation. I try asking Minty about the incident, but she isn't forthcoming.

"Maybe if you gave Zavier a bit more of your time instead of chasing after Jax, you'd know that he's been in rough shape for days."

I suck in a breath. "Why, what happened?"

"Elgar happened," is all she says.

I give up on speaking to her. She's not offering any proper information, and I resent what she's said. I haven't been chasing after Jax, he's been protecting me. I've got Zeeks trying to kill *me* too.

My shoulders slump in disappointment. When Minty told Jax to let me in, I thought it might have been her way of extending an olive branch, *apparently not*. I don't understand what her problem is.

Ambre must feel sorry for me, because going against general Magenta behaviour, she strikes up a conversation.

"I wonder how Trey feels," she says. "If he's relieved or worried."

"I think a lot of Zeeks will be relieved to see Ogre dead...I mean Elgar," I correct. "He was a danger to everybody, including himself." I run my finger over the scar on my collarbone. He might be dead, but he's left his mark on me. My eyes flash to Minty cradling her arm. He's left his mark on her too, and Zavier, and Nikita, and countless others.

Thinking of the young Ogre who broke my collarbone gets me thinking about my sister, and another wave of panic washes over me. She's been M.I.A for the last couple of days. *I hope Ogre hasn't killed her.* My heart starts hammering again. *Please don't let Floss be dead. She may not be kind to me, but I still love her.*

Ambre continues speaking. "Did you know that Trey is Nikita's brother?"

"Nikita," I swallow. "The girl Elgar bashed to within an inch of her life?"

Ambre nods and I wince.

"Who stabbed Elgar?" I ask curiously. "Was it Trey?"

Again, Ambre nods.

"Elgar got what was coming to him," I say with conviction. "I'm surprised Trey didn't kill him before now."

"Oh, he wanted to," Ambre insists. "But his mother and sister made him promise that he would stay out of Elgar's way. Elgar is too dangerous to mess with, they were afraid Trey would get killed." Her glistening magenta eyes flick to mine. "They were also worried if Trey succeeded in killing Elgar, there would be backlash from Rae and your father. Zeek's like Elgar become untouchable because no one is ever brave enough to stand up to them."

"My father?" My brows dip. "I understand Rae, but why my father?"

"Rae is on your father's hunting team, and they're good friends. Trey's family were worried, together they would seek revenge."

I highly doubt my father would stick his neck out for Rae and Ogre, but I don't mention it. My father is too selfish, he doesn't even stick his neck out for his own children, never mind someone else's.

"Elgar broke my collarbone a few years back," I say. "He's dangerous. My father knows that, and he isn't his biggest fan."

"I just hope that the Commander doesn't put Trey in the cell. He doesn't deserve it."

"I don't think Jax will let that happen," I assure her. "He's a good guy. He'll stand up for Trey."

Minty sniggers behind us.

*Shut up Minty,* I think. *I'm allowed to say Jax is a good guy. He is.*

# FOR FLOSS SAKE!

## -HARLOW-

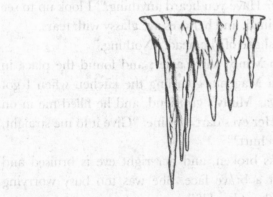

When we arrive at the medical chamber, there's a medic waiting for Minty.

"Come with me," she says, waving Minty over, and then they disappear down the aisle, to one of the beds.

"I'll have to leave. I need to fetch some warriors to send down to Trey." Ambre's gaze is compassionate. "I hope your friends will be okay."

"Thank you." I manage a weak smile. "I hope Trey will be okay, too."

Ambre leaves, and I take a seat. *What you should do is inform Lexan about Zavier's condition, and then go searching for Floss.* It makes the most sense, but I can't bring myself to leave the medical chamber. I fiddle with the bracelet Zavier made for me watching as it shimmers radiantly beneath the bright zofts above.

As soon as Jax finishes helping Zavier, I'll tell him about Ogre ransacking Floss' nook during the early hours of the morning. Hopefully, he'll get his warriors to help search for her. *Hopefully, it's not too late.*

I spend the next half an hour sitting by myself, worrying, praying—waiting for answers.

"Hey, how are they? Have you heard anything?" I look up to see Tatum. Her face is strained, and her eyes are glassy with tears.

"No," I say, with a shake of the head. "Nothing."

"I went to pick up Minty and Zavier; and found the place in shambles. There was a Magenta guarding the kitchen when I got there. I mentioned I was Minty's girlfriend, and he filled me in on what had happened." Her eyes dart to mine. "Give it to me straight, how badly has she been hurt?"

"Her left arm looks broken, and her right eye is bruised and swollen, but she's kept a brave face. She was too busy worrying about Zavier to worry about herself."

"And what about Zavier?" She ties her hair back to keep it from falling in her face. "How bad is he?"

Tears prickle my eyes. "He's…" The image of him lying on the kitchen floor limp, bloodied, and bruised enters my mind, and my lower lip starts to quiver. Unable to elaborate without bursting into tears, I manage, "He's in really bad shape."

She places her hand on my thigh and gives it a light squeeze. "I'm sorry; I really am."

Her compassionate gesture is unexpected. Embarrassed, I turn my face away, wiping the moisture from my eyes. I don't want to be seen crying. *Breathe, Harlow, breathe.*

*Until I receive news, I have to remain strong.*

Silence lingers a moment, while I pull myself together. After taking a few deep breaths I ask, "Tatum, why does Minty hate me so much?"

"I'm sure she doesn't hate you. She's just protective of Zavier."

I frown. "But I'm not a threat. He's my best friend."

She shrugs, her lips curling sympathetically at the corners. "I think this is something you should address with Minty."

*Yeah right,* I think. I tried talking to her on the way here and got stung. Minty is pricklier than a cactus.

A few warriors come and go, but none of them look our way. I want to ask what's become of Trey, but I'm sure they'll only tell me to mind my own business.

A quarter of an hour later Lexan arrives at the medical chamber, his face drawn and far paler than usual.

"Lexan," I call, and he turns my way. His mouth pressed in a grim line. Forgetting my crutches, I leap from my seat and hobble over to him. "Thank goodness you're here."

Seeing the dread in Lexan's face makes the reality of the situation all too real. *We could lose Zavier.* Unable to control myself any longer, I burst into tears.

"Now, now." He wraps his arms around me. His one arm holds me tight, while his other hand strokes my hair. It feels warm, comforting. "Zavier is strong at heart. He'll pull through. You wait and see." The quiver in his voice tells me he's not quite as sure as he'd like me to believe.

"I hope you're right," I say between sobs.

I admire Lexan. He's a bit of a recluse, and he doesn't usually say much, but he's got an extremely big heart. After Zavier's parents died, Lexan took him in and raised him as his own son. Zavier's reckless and impulsive nature has caused him some grief over the years, yet he's loved and supported him regardless.

I wish he'd taken me in too. *What I wouldn't give to have a father figure like him. A Zeek who would love and support me, no matter what.*

"Tatum," a medic calls, snapping me away from my thoughts.

I draw back from Lexan's embrace and spin around to see what's happening.

"Minty is asking for you," she says.

"What about Zavier?" I blurt.

The medics lips twist. "I'm sorry, but he's still in surgery."

It feels like hours until Jax finally appears, and Lexan and I both leap from our seats in anticipation.

His gaze flicks between the two of us. "He's stable," he says, and my insides flood with relief. "His injuries are extensive, but it looks like he's going to pull through."

Gratitude fills me, and I have the overwhelming urge to throw my arms around him and kiss him on the cheek. I control the impulse and settle on a plain-and-simple, "Thank you."

"Yes, thank you," Lexan repeats. "I am forever in your debt."

"I can take you both in to see him," Jax offers, "but I warn you, he's still very out of it."

I'm dying to see Zavier, but there's something important I need to address first. "Hold on a second," I say, voice uneven. "There's something I need to tell you first."

His gaze anchors to mine, his eyes wide with concern. "What is it?"

Lexan's eyes zone in on me too.

I swallow nervously. "Elgar came to my family cavern early this morning looking for Floss, and when she wasn't there, he began trashing her nook like a madman." I pause and give an anxious breath before continuing. "Initially I didn't know it was him. I thought it was Floss throwing a tantrum." I pull up the sleeve of my threadbare jumper up to reveal a big purple and blue handprint. "I went to console her only I found him instead, and because I interrupted him during his fit of rage, he picked me up and shook me. He probably would have done worse, only my father charged in and threatened him to leave or else there'd be trouble."

Jax straightens, the muscles at his jawline clenching. "Why didn't you tell me any of this earlier?"

I lower my head in shame. He is well within his rights to be angry. I should have told him.

"Where is Floss now?" he presses. "Has she been hurt?"

I shrug uncomfortably. "I'm not sure, Floss hasn't been home the past two nights, and I personally, haven't seen her since before my coma."

He forces out an angry puff of air from his nostrils. "I'll go and get a search party ready," he says, his tone firm, harsh. "Wait here, I'll get Tansy to take you to Zavier."

He turns to leave, but Lexan stops him. "Ah...Jax...wait," he says, stammering on his own words. "I...I know where Floss is."

Shocked, I snap to face him.

"Zavier found her in a bad state a few nights ago. She'd been on a date with Elgar, and he'd bashed her up pretty badly." He swallows hard before continuing, "We've been looking after her ever since, keeping her safe."

My jaw drops. I can't believe what I'm hearing.

Jax's eyes are filled with a mix of anger and relief—more anger than relief. "Why didn't you inform anyone about this?" His whole frame stiffens, his muscles tightening, making him look every bit the fierce warrior he is. "By the sounds of what you're both telling me, Elgar's been on a rampage for days. If I'd been made aware of this earlier, there's a chance I could have stopped him before things got to this stage." His angry eyes swivel between the two of us. "Zavier could have been killed today. He almost was." He shakes his head in frustration. "And Minty, her ulna and radius were snapped clean in half."

"Zavier and I should have told you about Floss," Lexan admits, "but I've had a lot of personal issues going on, and Zavier's been working long twelve hour shifts ever since the incident."

Without giving any kind of response to Lexan's lame excuses, Jax calls out Tansy's name, and she leaves her desk to come over to us. "Can you take these two in to see Zavier? I've got the warriors waiting for me, and a big mess to clean up." His eyes brush mine driving home his frustration. "I'll send someone up to walk you home later." At this very moment, he sounds more like the Commander's son than my friend. Turning his stern gaze to Lexan, he says, "Make sure she doesn't leave before they get here. I don't need any more drama tonight." He gives me one last sharp flick of the eyes and adds, "I mean it."

Despite being told Zavier will survive, I sit by his bedside sobbing uncontrollably.

Lexan comforts me by rubbing my back. "You heard Jax," he says, trying to assure me. "Zavier is going to be okay."

I nod but continue to sob anyway.

Minty's words from earlier weigh heavily on my conscience. "Maybe if you gave Zavier a bit more of your time instead of chasing after Jax, you'd know that he's been in rough shape for days."

I still take offence to the Jax comment, but she's right about one thing. I should have come to see Zavier before this. Guilt stabs at me, not only because I've been an absent friend, but also because I've upset Jax. I should have told him about Ogre. I did consider telling him. It was silly of me not to.

"Rough shape for days"—this particular sentence repeats over and over in my mind. *Why has Zavier been in rough shape for days? Did he catch Ogre hitting Floss? Did he fight him? I wonder why he brought Floss back to his place—not ours?* Something inside me claws at this thought. It's silly, and I know it. Zavier is my best friend and according to Lexan, Floss needed his protection. Him helping her is a good thing. I have no right to feel put out by this.

Lexan's arm rests around me, attempting to bring me comfort. *I wonder why has he never married—linked?* As far as Pastels go, he's not bad looking. His face is similar to the human actor Brad Pitt, only it's thinner, paler—slightly more angelic. His height would be similar too, around the five-eleven mark, only he's not as brawny, he's wirier like Zavier.

Zannah and Oscar appear an hour later. *Please let Oscar be my escort.* I'm too emotionally unstable to deal with Zannah's belittling remarks.

As if on cue Zannah walks straight up to Lexan, "I've got you old man, Jax's orders."

*Lexan isn't an old man,* I think defensively. *He's only a year off forty.* Although, forty is on the downward slide for a Pastel. We weaker Zeeks only usually last to age sixty—maximum.

Zannah's sharp gaze swivels to mine. "He doesn't want me filling Harlow's head with my biased opinions."

I shrink back into my seat. I hadn't purposely meant to dob on her. *If only Jax wasn't so switched on and perceptive.* He figured out right away that I didn't come up with those ideas on my own.

Oscar lets out an exasperated breath, which is aimed at Zannah, before turning his attention to me. "Are you ready to go, Harlow?"

"Make sure to be a good boy now won't you," Zannah taunts. "You don't want to cause an upset with his little girlfriend."

Lexan fixes her with an irritated glance, while Oscar humfs and spits, "Worry about yourself, Zannah."

Oscar doesn't say much during our walk back to my family cavern, and I don't blame him. He probably thinks I'm a trouble-making big mouth who has her sights set on Jax. There's no point in trying to defend myself. It'll only make matters worse. The more you try to defend yourself, the more it looks like you've got something to hide.

I can see his forearm has been bandaged and I consider offering him my sympathy, but in the end, I press my lips together and keep them sealed. It's probably better if we don't speak. If neither of us say anything, there'll be no issues to be brought forward later on.

As soon as I get to our family cavern my mother pounces on me. She smells like garlic. The whole cavern does. My tummy rumbles with jealousy. My dinner plans were de-railed by Ogre, leaving me starving.

"Did you hear what happened at the Bean-Brew Cavern this afternoon?" she asks. "Were you there? Did you see who killed Elgar?"

I shake my head, unwilling to share. "No, I didn't see anything."

"Oh, I thought you might have gone to visit your friend Zavier."

"I heard it was Trey who did it," my father puts in his two cents worth. "It makes sense, Elgar did beat up his sister."

Not wanting to talk about this any further, I resort to being blunt. "I'm tired," I say. "I'm going to bed."

"Hold on a minute." My father slings his arm out like a barrier. "What's happening with your sister? I haven't seen her in days."

I shrug. "How would I know?" *And why the sudden interest?* I add in thought. *It's not like you actually care.*

"Well, she'd better not be caught up in this mess, or she's out on her own. We don't need her actions dragging the rest of us through the mud."

"Saul!" Horror fills my mother's expression. "She's our daughter, you can't say that."

*Hold on a second, is she defending Floss? This is a first.*

"Anyway, I'm sure she had nothing to do with it."

"Yeah, well where is she now, Krista?" Acid sprays as he speaks. "Why haven't we seen her in days? And why was Elgar here in the early hours of the morning, huh? Tell me, why was he ripping apart her nook. He was clearly upset about something."

"Let's not jump to any conclusions, shall we?" My mother tries to keep her voice calm, level. "Hopefully, Floss will come back home tomorrow, and we can all sit down and discuss the matter as a family."

*Yes, one big happy family,* I think sarcastically.

My father grunts at the idea.

"I don't believe she had anything to do with Elgar's death," mother insists. "You said it yourself, you heard Trey killed him. Trey has motive."

While my mother might be concerned about who killed Elgar, she doesn't appear at all concerned about Floss' whereabouts. This strikes me as odd. Her daughter is missing, she could be dead for all she knows, *why isn't she concerned?*

A memory of something I'd overheard springs to mind. "I'm not told much. Krista tends to leave me in the dark. It's a bit of a one-sided relationship that way, always has been."

*She knows where Floss is. Lexan's told her.*

# 32

# BARRIERS DOWN

## -HARLOW AS RUBY-

The squeak of sneakers skidding against a hard-shiny floor, echoes in my ears, matched with the continual reverbera-tions of a bouncing rubber ball. Hearing these familiar sounds gives me a feeling of warmth. It takes me back to the days when I'd sit around in the school stadium watching Josh play basketball.

As my vision clears, a whistle blows, and the black-and-white-striped ref calls foul on a young teen in a blue singlet.

"Oh, come on!" A voice beside me bellows, and I gag on the

scent of stale cigarettes coming from his breath. "He barely even touched him."

*Lucas.* A wave of hatred mixed with resentment surges inside me.

I whirl on him, teeth clenched, only to discover that my sister Jade is seated beside him. Her posture is casual, and her expression is relaxed. *This is not okay.* I don't like how familiar they've become. I wish she knew to stay away from him. I wish she knew the truth about him being my killer.

"Hey." A tap to my shoulder causes me to spin around. Alex's warm golden eyes are alight. "Have you seen the score? Our boys are destroying the other team."

My eyes flick to the scoreboard. Twenty-four/nil. *Impressive.*

I scan the court. Connor is easy to spot, his hair is light, shoulder length, and looks like a shaggy mop. You can tell he didn't originate from the mountains; he looks like he belongs at the beach. Rueben is not so easy to spot. The majority of their players have short dark hair, and four of those have dark skin. After a doing a quick head search of the four, I soon work out which one is him. Number six. The player who'd been given a charging foul.

Alex lowers himself down a step to join me where I sit. "There's only five minutes left, do you mind if we stay and watch the rest?"

"No, of course not."

Over the next five minutes our boys manage to sink another four hoops, leaving the game to finish with a score of thirty-two/nil.

The final horn sounds, and all of the team's supporters clap noisily. "I wish I could give the boys a pat on the back," Alex says, clapping along with the crowd. "I'm so proud of them. They played such a good game."

I sigh. "Yeah, if only. It would be nice."

He turns to face me, and I notice an instant shift in his mood.

"Come on, let's get out of here." He takes me by the hand, causing sparks to sizzle between us. "It's too noisy in here to talk."

I glance over at my sister, Lucas still seated close beside her— and I hesitate. "Maybe we should stay."

"Don't worry." Alex gives my hand a tug. "Lucas is heavily

medicated these days, and like I've told you before, he hasn't touched a drink in years."

"So? What's that supposed to mean?"

"It means he's not going to try anything, and even if he does—which he won't—this place is packed, he won't be able to hurt your sister and get away with it."

I let out a long breath. "If he hurts her, I'll hurt you for luring me away, you got that?"

"Got it."

Outside the stadium, Alex leads me to a seat hidden under the shade of a rustling gumtree. "This looks as good a place as any."

We sit in unison, my eyes automatically drifting to the endless bush just outside the back school fence. It's not the exact same location I was killed in, but it's the same bush. Realising this causes unwanted memories to flash to mind. I see the madness in Lucas' eyes and the glimmer of his knife. I feel the burn at my side and taste the blood on my tongue. *Don't go there,* I warn.

I gaze down at Alex and my entwined fingers and begin to fidget. I can't keep holding on, not until I know for certain where I want things to lead with him.

*You already know where you want things to lead with him,* says the voice inside my heart, *but there's so many reasons why you shouldn't start anything with him.*

I'm torn. While his gorgeous grin and cute grooves pull at my heart strings, his continual protectiveness of his brother irks me. No matter what I say, he's always super quick to defend him. *If it wasn't for Lucas, we'd both still be alive.*

Noticing my wiggling fingers, he places his other hand on top of mine to stop me from fidgeting. He's capturing my hand, like he's captured my heart.

"What happened yesterday?" he asks, a serious note to his voice. "I never heard any bangs. Were you only saying that to escape me?"

"No, there were really bangs," I say, taken aback by his assumption. "Only they weren't coming from here, they were filtering in from back home."

"How do you manage to do that?" His brows lift. "Stay in tune with your Zeek body while being here on Earth?"

I shrug. "I don't know, it's not a conscious effort. It's just how it works for me. How do you manage to keep coming back here every single day? That's what I'd like to master."

"It's just how it works for me," he says, throwing my own line back at me.

My gaze flickers between his face and the stadium exit. "Let me know if you see my sister leaving. I want to make sure she gets to her car okay."

He nods, but I can tell he thinks I'm overreacting.

"What was causing the bangs back home? Did you find out? They must have been loud, you looked pretty worried."

"It was Ogre," I reply. "He came to our cavern looking for my sister and when he couldn't find her, he started trashing her nook."

Alex's brows crease. "Seriously?" He appears sceptical. "It would have been around three in the morning?"

"I doubt Ogre knew what time it was," I reply, ignoring his scepticism. "He was extremely high and agitated."

"High and agitated?" He scrunches his nose up. "What kind of Zeeks do you and your sister hang around?"

I shrug. "Ogre's the son of my parents' friend Rae. He's not someone my sister and I hang out with by choice."

"Well with the name Ogre, I suppose he was destined for destruction. Who in their right mind names their kid Ogre?"

"His name isn't really Ogre," I admit. "It's Elgar, I call him Ogre because—to me—he is one, well was one, he's dead now."

Alex's eyes bulge. "What? Dead?" He scratches his head. "How? What happened?"

When I don't answer right away his brows dip in concern. "Did *you* kill him?"

"No," I shake my head. "Of course not. I couldn't even if I wanted to. He's ten times my size.

"Well how did he die?"

"It's a long story," I say. "And to be honest, I don't really know all of the details. What I do know, is, because of him my best friend

Zavier is now clinging onto his life in hospital." Tears prickle the corners of my eyes, causing Alex's expression to soften.

"Oh Rubes."

"Jax is hopeful he's going to pull through, but he looks bad." My eyes meet his, a lone tear now escaping down my cheek. "I mean it, Alex, he looks really, really bad."

"I'm so sorry." His hands tighten around mine. "I don't know what to say."

Unable to stop myself, I admit, "I feel guilty. I've been an absent friend to Zavier the past few days—I haven't meant to be—but there's so much chaos surrounding me. I feel like my life is spiralling out of control."

I know I should stop talking about my Zeek personal life with Alex—*he's a Vallon, he's the enemy*—but I can't help myself, it feels good to finally be able to open up to someone who's not directly involved in the matter.

Another tear spills down my cheek, and he uses the back of his hand to wipe the moisture away. "I'm sure you're a great friend. Everyone here still sings your praises. I don't see why it should be any different there."

He's completely off, but still, I take comfort in his kind words. I'm no longer the popular confident girl I was as Ruby, *I'm a curse.*

According to RJ, the Commander herself labelled me an "abomination". She even killed her own husband because he was willing to stick his neck out for me. I'm a walking death wish to those who dare to stand up for me.

Pulling back from his touch, I straighten. I've let my barriers down. I've allowed things to get too personal.

"I'm sorry, I shouldn't be burdening you with all of this. It's been a rough string of days." I pause and then add, "I'm sure things will get better soon."

"Don't be silly." He brushes back a stray strand of hair from my face, and I shiver. "Talk to me, it's what I'm here for. I'm happy to listen."

"But you're a Vallon," I say.

His relaxed body immediately stiffens. "So?"

"It complicates things."

"It'll only complicate things if you let it."

"It's not only that…" I bite my lower lip. "You're Lucas' twin brother, and Josh's adopted brother. There's so many reasons why I shouldn't even be sitting here with you, never mind burdening you with all of my problems."

Alex lets out a strangled breath as though I've knocked the wind out of him. "What are you trying to say? Do you think because I'm Lucas' twin and a Vallon—you can't trust me?"

"No, of course not, it's just… I don't know what to make of you." I swallow. "I also don't know how I'm supposed to feel about you. There's a part of me that enjoys hanging out with you, but there's another part of me which is scared…" Seeing the raw hurt in his eyes, I rephrase. "No, not scared…wary."

My heart skitters. *Now wasn't the time to bring this up.*

Without responding, Alex lets go of my hand and nods his head to the side, his eyes glancing past me, not at me. "Your sister is leaving."

"Oh…" I crane my neck to look. There she is, stepping out from the double doors with Connor.

My heart sinks. I don't want to leave Alex on this note, I need to say something positive, *but what?* I shouldn't have said anything negative to begin with, not now anyway. If I'm looking to push everyone who cares about me away, I'm doing an excellent job. I've neglected Zavier, made Jax angry, and now I've upset Alex.

Unable to find the right words to smooth things over, I stand. "I'm going to follow them to her car," I say lamely. "I won't be long."

Alex nods, his eyes saying what his voice doesn't, but to my relief, as I make my way over to Jade and Connor, he gets up and follows.

Jade's car is parked a hundred metres down the street, and as we exit the school grounds—following the pavement—Connor races ahead to settle a score with a teammate.

"Hey Tommy," he says, tapping the kid's back with his empty drink bottle. "You owe me five bucks. I told you Adam would get that last shot. You'd better bring the money tomorrow, I wanna buy a sausage roll for lunch."

Tommy spins to face him, his face screwed up mockingly. "Yeah whatever, I'll spit on your sausage roll."

"Tommy," his mother lectures disapprovingly. "Don't say things like that, it's disgusting."

The boys push and shove at each other playfully, laughing and teasing, but eventually Connor steps off the pavement and goes and leans against Jade's black BMW. He swings to face Jade, tapping his pointer to his thumb impatiently.

Recognising the gesture, she pulls out her keys and presses a button, making the car lights flash simultaneously with a beeping sound.

Alex remains a few steps behind me, following silently.

I slow my pace for him to catch up. "I think we should go with them?" I say questioningly, acting as if everything is normal between us. "It's not like we need to stay here."

"You go." He avoids giving me any eye contact. "I've got a few things to do."

I grab his arm jerking him to face me. "Yeah? Like what?"

Clearly surprised, his eyes snap to mine. "What does it matter? Do you even really want me to come?" The shadow of hurt is still evident in his gaze. "If you're too scared to talk to me, then what's the point of being around me?"

He's fighting me on this, but he's still following, which tells me he still wants to be around me. He's just hurt by what I've said.

"I'm sorry, I shouldn't have said those things."

"But you meant them."

He's right, I had meant them. I was scared and confused, and I was trying to push him away, but I realise now that I was wrong. Seeing him like this, withdrawn and barriers up, the fear of losing him has become far greater than the fear of being with him.

A car engine starts close by.

"Come on, there's not enough time for me to explain myself right now." I reach for Alex's hand. "We're going to miss our ride."

Alex does a double take before accepting, and then together we race those extra few metres, managing to slip into the car in the nick of time, before it pulls out from the curb.

As soon as Jade reaches her stencilled driveway Alex dives out of the car.

"What's your hurry?" I ask, diving out after him.

His usual warmth has been doused ever since I offended him. "There's bad memories attached to the song that was playing."

"Oh…" I'd been so busy fretting about how I was going to fix things between us, I hadn't even noticed there was any music playing in the car. Now curious, I ask, "Why? What was the song?"

"It was an old Marilyn Manson song," he says, eyes staring off into the distance. "It's just a stupid song from my past, it's nothing, don't worry about it."

He looks troubled but I don't push for details. I've already upset him enough. Instead I ask, "Are you going to come inside with me?"

"You go ahead," he says. "I'll be in in a minute."

My heart twists, I don't like this wedge I've put between us. I should have kept my mouth shut.

By the time I get to the kitchen, Jade's already got the jug boiling and Connor is helping himself to a *very* large slice of orange cake with lemon icing. The smell of citrus is strong and causes my mouth to water. I used to love orange cake. Especially the ones my mum used to make. *I wonder if this is one of hers.* It looks and smells like one of hers.

"Oy, I said a small piece, not a quarter of the cake," Jade lectures. "I'm about to make dinner."

Connor gives an exaggerated eye roll. "Yeah, yeah."

Clearly annoyed by this, Jade snatches the rest of his slice from his hand. "I'll give you yeah, yeah."

"Hey," he grumbles, the sound of his voice muffled by half eaten cake. "I was eating that."

"You can have the rest after dinner," she tells him. "Now go upstairs and have a shower, you stink."

He shoots her an irritated glance but does as she says.

Unaware of my presence, Jade works her way around the kitchen preparing dinner. As she chops up a carrot into small dollar sized pieces, I'm reminded of the night Zavier cooked me a veggie bake. He was so busy showing off how quick he could chop up a carrot, he'd accidentally nicked the side of his thumb with the tip of the knife.

Thinking of Zavier makes my heart ache. *I hope he's going to be okay.*

"Hey," Alex finally joins me by the side of the bench. "Do you want to stay in here or should we go and sit by the pool?"

Relief fills me. "The pool sounds nicer."

Alex takes a seat at the pools edge, patting the empty space next to him. I leap at the offer.

"I'm sorry," he says. "I didn't mean to wig out on you. I was already feeling like shit about what you said, and then that song coming on in the car was…" He pauses mid-sentence and lets out a long breath. "It was really bad timing."

No longer holding back, I park myself nice and close to him, allowing our outer thighs to touch. "I'm so sorry too. I didn't mean to push you away."

"Look, I get it," he says. "Lucas took your life, and Vallons have done terrible things to Zeeks. You are well within you rights to not trust me. It was silly of me to believe that you could."

"I never said I didn't trust you."

"You didn't have to say it, it was implied."

"I want to trust you, I do." I stammer a second and then add, "I like you Alex… I like you a lot, but given all I've been through, I can't help but be cautious. I'm afraid of letting my guard down, I'm afraid of getting hurt."

His gaze meets mine, eyes intense. "You don't have to be afraid of me. I'm not going hurt you." His hand reaches for my cheek.

"You're all I've thought about for years. You're all I've dreamt about."

My pulse quickens.

"But you hardly know me. All you know are the photos you've seen and the stories you've been told. You don't know the real me."

He chokes out a laugh, his hand slipping from my cheek. "Yeah, well at least they're all good photos and stories. All you appear to know about me is that I'm the twin brother of the monster who killed you, the adopted brother of the guy you once dated, and your greatest arch enemy."

It feels strange hearing him refer to Lucas as a monster. He's usually infuriatingly protective of him.

"You are nothing like your bother," I assure him. "You are kind and compassionate, and you're also *much* better looking."

A smile tugs at the corners of his lips, and his brows shoot up. "You think I'm good looking?"

I blush. "I didn't say that." My eyes trace his face. "But you're okay—I guess. Passable."

Before I know it, Alex's hand is back on my cheek, his smile widening as he gently brushes his fingers against my creamy skin. "You know, you're not so bad yourself," he taunts affectionately.

His smouldering eyes capture mine, appearing far more gold than brown under the harsh orange light of the setting sun.

"You know what, scratch that." His hand slides gently from my cheek to the back of my neck, causing me to shiver. "You're beautiful."

He tilts his head, bringing his lips to meet mine, and I swallow back my qualms. They are soft, luscious, and brush gently at first, but as I reciprocate, the intensity of the kiss increases.

A few negative thoughts try to penetrate my mind, but I fight them off.

*Alex is not a monster like his brother, he is good, I know he is. I like him. I want to be with him.*

Giving up my reservations, I wrap my arms around his neck and pull him eagerly to me, my mouth pressing fervently against his.

Shockwaves rattle my insides, leaving me breathless and shaky.

I'd forgotten how good it felt to be kissed by someone—to be held passionately by someone.

After a long moment starved of air, we both pull back panting, our eyes searching one another's for a sign of regret. *No regrets here.*

"I've waited a long time for you," he says, voice breathy, and without warning, his face disappears, and so do all of my surroundings. *Damn it!*

# 33

# PRETTY IN PINK

## -HARLOW-

"*H*arlow," someone mutters under their breath. There's a hand clasped firmly around my shoulder, giving it a good shake. "Harlow, wake up, we need to talk."

My eyes flick open to find my mother crouching above my bed, her deep Magenta braids falling toward my face.

"Mum?" I sit up in a panic, swatting my way through her thick curtain of braids. "What's going on? What's wrong?"

"Shhh…" She places her fingers on my lips, silencing me, and then glances towards the passageway outside my nook. Her eyes do a thorough scan of the area.

I peer down at my watch; it's three-thirty. I've never known my mother to sneak to my nook in the early morning hours before. It seems out of character. Something must be terribly wrong.

Still appearing nervous, she returns her attention to me. "Harlow, I need you to do something for me." Her tone is soft but urgent. "I need you to go and speak to Floss tomorrow. Convince her to come back home. I don't want your father to find out where she's been staying. I don't want him to cause unnecessary trouble."

I frown. This is not exactly the life-or-death emergency wakeup call I'd first imagined.

Anger burns inside me. I can't believe she's waking me up in the middle of the night to ask me to bring Floss back home—and tonight, of all nights... I'm so mad my blood is boiling.

*Go away,* I shout inside my head. I resent being woken up from a moment of bliss, only to be given an impossible task. *How rude!* I'd rather be with Alex.

My lips tingle with the thought.

"Harlow," she repeats, this time more firmly, and I realise I haven't responded. "I really need you to do this for me."

I grit my teeth. If she was honestly that worried about Floss, she'd go and fetch her herself, not palm the job onto me. Besides, she should know better. Asking me is useless, there's no way Floss will listen to me. She never has before.

"I don't know where Floss is," I lie. "Besides, she'll never listen to me anyway, so what's the point?"

"I know where she is," she says, confirming my suspicions from earlier. "She's staying at Lexan's."

"How did you find out?"

"Lexan told me yesterday."

"Because you two are friends?" An alarming thought comes to mind. Dad says she's been out a lot lately. "Or more than friends?"

She blanches. "Because Floss is my daughter, and he knew I would be worried about her." Dodging any further questions, she swiftly adds, "Please, Harlow, can you at least try?" Her tone is verging on desperate. "I'd like her home by this evening. Things are about to get ugly now that Elgar's been killed, and I'd like our family together as a unit."

I scoff. She wants our family together as a unit. *What a joke.*

"Yeah, whatever," I concede half-heartedly. "I'll try."

In other words, *get lost so I can get back to sleep.*

It's Oscar who arrives to escort me to the art cavern. *Darn. This morning just keeps getting better and better.* Not that I have a problem with Oscar—he seems okay—but the fact that he's here to fetch me, not Jax, tells me Jax is still angry with me.

"Just a sec," I say.

I pick up my crutches and hobble over, being careful not to trip over my own feet. I can barely keep my eyes open. I hadn't been able to get back to sleep again after my mother left, and I'm devastated I didn't get the chance to go back to Earth and rekindle things with Alex.

As I reach Oscar's side, he asks, "Are you okay?"

I have to crane my neck to look up at him. He's not as tall as Jax, but he's not far off the mark. He's the only other Zeek in the colony to make it to the mid-six-foot mark. He has mauve cornrows that finish at his shoulder line, lilac eyes, and a crooked smile.

"Yeah, I'm fine."

He looks me up and down. "Are you sure? Because you don't look so good. Have you slept at all?"

His concern is totally unexpected. He barely spoke two words to me on our walk home yesterday.

"I never look good," I shrug. "What's the difference?"

This seems to amuse him. He flashes me a semi-grin. "You do alright for a Pastel." He gives me another once over and then adds, "Just maybe not today."

As we get to the entry of the art cavern, I'm quick to notice there's no Sphinx dashing out to greet us. It feels odd not having to shield my wounded leg from his wild thrashing tail. My already miserable mood plummets further.

I hadn't considered that by losing Jax as my escort, we'd be losing Sphinx as our security guard. *Come to think of it,* there doesn't appear to be anyone watching over us today.

I'd meant what I said about Jax not spending so much time with me—but at the time I'd said it, I hadn't realised we'd be leaving things on such hostile terms. I hope he will come to fetch me this afternoon—*just this once.* I'd like the chance to smooth thing over with him. I want to apologise for keeping him in the dark.

"I'll see you at five-thirty," Oscar says, and my heart sinks. He's picking me up this afternoon, not Jax.

I force a smile to disguise my disappointment. "Okay, thanks."

Oscar and I are already heading our separate ways, when a thought occurs to me. I lift my crutches and manage a one-eighty on my good leg. "Oscar, wait!" I call.

He pivots back around, his left brow arched.

"I know you're probably super busy, and I hate to ask this of you, but is there any chance we can swing by the medical chamber for a few minutes after I finish up here? I really want to see how Zavier is doing."

He inhales deeply while considering the idea. "Sure," he says. "No problem."

Oscar shows me a much warmer side of himself as we make our way to the medical chamber, telling me how he was in charge of running the day's training session since Jax was busy cleaning up the Elgar mess. I can see why he gets under Zannah's skin; he does like to toot his own horn a lot, but his cockiness doesn't bother me personally. I'm just glad he thinks I'm worth talking to.

I want to ask him if he knows what happened to Trey, but I'm afraid of saying anything incriminating. I don't know what he's been told regarding Ogre's death.

Oscar pauses by the open entry of the medical chamber. "I'll be back in an hour," he says. "Don't you dare leave without me or Jax will have my head."

I smile. "Thank you. I won't leave without you, I promise."

I hobble to the front reception desk. Tansy is working today and greets me with a friendly smile. A small perk I must have earnt by being associated with Jax.

"Hi," I say. "Wh—"

"He's in the same bed as yesterday," she cuts in before I can finish. "He's woken a few times, but because of the meds he's very groggy." Her smile is sympathetic. "I'm sorry about what happened to him. A lot of Zeeks have ended up in here due to Elgar's ruthlessness, but nobody's ever been brave enough to report him to the Commander in case she let him off and he retaliated. Plus, his mother Rae is a force to be reckoned with, and so's your father for that matter." She pauses a moment before adding, "Jax is pretty worried about what's going to happen to Trey, but I think it's safe to say that we are all glad that Elgar is dead. He was a danger to everyone."

I nod in agreement but don't add anything in the way of an opinion. I'm too afraid to share my true thoughts. Tansy might be acting friendly towards me now, but this doesn't mean I trust her.

"What bed is Minty in?" I ask, going back to the original question I had tried to ask before she cut in on top of me.

She does a quick scan of the chart sitting on the desk in front of her. "Bed six," she answers.

"Excellent, thank you."

Minty looks stunned to see me heading towards her bed.

"Hey," I say as I approach. "How's your arm?"

"Sore."

"And your face?"

"Sore."

*Simple one-word responses, excellent!* Still, I persist.

"Is there anything I can get for you?"

"No. Tatum's already brought in everything I need."

I shuffle anxiously on my crutches. I knew this would be awkward, but I couldn't come here to visit Zavier and not her, it wouldn't be right. "Where is Tatum?"

"She's gone home to make some dinner."

"Oh."

*Silence.* Our conversation is done.

"Well I hope you feel better soon. I'm going to go see Zavier."

She nods, and then adds, "If Zavier is awake, can you please tell him that I love him, and that I'm sorry."

*Sorry for what?* I don't ask. Instead, I give a forced smile and say, "Sure thing."

I hobble into the intensive care section of the medical chamber to find a Magenta sitting by Zavier's bedside. At first, I think it might be Ambre—given she'd helped to save him—but as I get closer, I realise with a jolt it's my sister.

"Floss?"

*How is it she is willing to go out of her way to visit Zavier in the medical chamber, and not me?* I don't begrudge Zavier the visitor, but I do *very much* begrudge her.

"What are you doing here?" Resentment drips from my voice.

"What does it look like I'm doing?" she snarls in her usual Floss fashion. "I'm here visiting Zavier, the same as you are."

"That's wonderful," I spit sourly. "You'll make the time to come and see Zavier in the medical chamber, but you never even bothered to come and see me—your twin sister."

I step up alongside her. She's glowering, but that's not all I notice. Big brownish-green bruises mark her face, some yellowing at the edges.

I gasp, "Your face..."

"What do you know, huh?" She forces a plastic smile to go with her cynical tone. "Now you really are the prettier one. Congratulations."

Lexan mentioned that Ogre had given Floss a beating, but I hadn't realised her injuries would be this extensive. She looks like Zavier. Both of their faces are swollen, colourful messes.

"How did this happen?" I ask.

She huffs and turns her face away. "Don't pretend like you care."

Her comment infuriates me. "Unlike you, Floss, I do care."

"Oh really? Because I've been missing for days and I didn't see you roaming the passages searching for me."

"I told Jax you were missing so that he would send his warriors out to search for you, but then Lexan told us you've being staying at his place, so we figured you were safe."

"I bet our parents haven't even asked after me," she says with a bitter edge. "I bet they're not even worried. Our father is too full of himself, and our mother is a selfish coward."

A sad laugh escapes me. "What do you know," I say, "We actually agree on something. That's a first. You're wrong about one thing though—Mum is worried about you. She asked me to speak to you tonight—talk you into coming back home." Admittedly, I hadn't actually planned on doing it. I knew for sure if I were to tell Floss to come home with me, she'd deliberately do the opposite just to spite me. And going by her snarky attitude so far, I have a sneaking suspicion I was right.

She humfs. "Why doesn't she come and get me herself?"

"She said something about not wanting dad to know where you've been staying. I think she's afraid he'd start trouble with Lexan."

"Yeah, I bet she is," she says spitefully.

"What's that supposed to mean?"

Her eyes analyse mine. "You really don't know?"

I swallow. "Mum and Lexan are having an affair, aren't they?"

Floss releases me from her penetrating gaze. "No," she says a little too fast. "They just shouldn't be friends, that's all. Magentas and Pastels aren't meant to be friends."

"If that's true then why are you visiting Zavier?"

"Zavier stood up for me when no Magenta would." She lets out a pained breath. "Perhaps I'm starting to lose faith in our colour system."

"Perhaps that's smart."

Her eyes flick to mine momentarily, and for a split second, I almost detect a glimpse of compassion behind them, but then *snap!* It's gone, and I'm left wondering if I imagined it.

"What happened to your hair?" she asks, changing the subject. Her nose crinkles. "You look like a something the fuegor's dragged in."

I narrow my eyes and groan. *Nice.*

Giving up on speaking to her, I step around to get closer to Zavier. I run my finger along his colourful swollen cheek and my heart sinks. His face is so puffy and marked, it's hard to believe it's him.

When Floss looks away, I sneakily put my hand in my pocket, and pull out Zavier's and my small magical rock. "It's magic," I whisper, as I slip it into his hand. "It'll keep you safe."

"What are you doing?" Floss asks.

"He's completely out of it," I say, ignoring her question.

While a part of me is disappointed that I'm unable to speak to him, another part of me knows it's for the best. Sleep is the best healer.

"He woke up a little while ago," Floss offers. "I couldn't make out much of what he was saying... Except your name," she adds sourly.

Guilt courses through me. "I feel terrible," I admit. "I wasn't there for him when he needed me."

"He'll forgive you." She pouts. "He loves you."

## 34

# ONE BIG HAPPY FAMILY

## -HARLOW-

To my delight, Jax shows up to walk me home. However, he doesn't look nearly as excited to see me as I am to see him. He steps around Floss to join me, and I hear her mutter something unintelligible under her breath.

Oblivious to this, or ignoring it—I'm not sure—Jax says, "I take it you didn't get much sleep?" His eyes examine me, and my cheeks grow hot.

"No, not really."

"I'm not surprised. Neither did I."

I peer up at him to find dark circles surrounding his violet eyes. He looks tired and slightly more drawn, but he still looks good, better than good.

I open my mouth to apologise, but his sharp expression tells me now's not the time.

"I need you to write a statement about what happened with Elgar at your family cavern the other night, and I also need another statement declaring everything that you saw and heard yesterday afternoon in the Bean-Brew Cavern."

"When?" I stammer. "Now?"

"What happened with Elgar at our family cavern?" Floss asks, stepping in closer to join our conversation.

"He stormed in at an ungodly hour looking for you," I say. "And when he couldn't find you, he trashed your nook."

"He did what?" Floss' face flushes with anger.

"He smashed your favourite ornament and snapped the bow Fau gave you."

She stomps her foot like an angry child. "That Avalanche! If he wasn't dead, I would kill him."

"That's enough," Jax says firmly. "While I understand where your anger stems from, you need to keep your emotions in check, especially in public." His eyes scan the chamber to make sure that nobody is eavesdropping. "You two can discuss this topic all you like when you get home."

Floss' face sets in a scowl. "I'm not going home," she blasts.

Her raging outburst catches me off guard. *Has she forgotten who she's speaking to?* I would've expected her to show more restraint in front of the Commander's son. She must be losing her mind.

"Floss, I think you should," I say. "Mum wants you home, and it's not like you can stay with Lexan forever."

Her fists clench into tight balls by her sides. "In case you've forgotten, I don't care what you think."

*Ouch.* Any slight progress we'd made earlier is well and truly gone.

Jax appears dumbfounded. "Is she always like this?"

Not wanting to anger her any further, I shrug, letting my readable expression say what I don't dare to.

"You two can sort this out afterwards," Jax's eyes rest on mine. "but right now, I need you to come with me and write those statements."

"What about Floss?" I ask. "Doesn't she have to give a statement?"

"I spoke to her earlier today. She's already given me one."

"Ahem... I'm right here," she snaps, her eyes darting between us both. "Stop speaking about me as if I'm not!"

Jax takes me to a small office nook at the far left of the chamber. It's much bigger than my sleeping nook and furnished with a decent sized desk and three tall filing drawers. I glance down at the desktop to find there's already a pen and paper waiting for me.

"Write down as much as you can remember, every last detail," he says, all official.

The tension between us is killing me. I want things to go back to how they were. I want us to be sort-of-friends again.

"Jax," I say, my voice quivering with nerves. I need to clear the air before I can concentrate on writing. "I'm so sorry about yesterday. I shouldn't have kept you in the dark. I had considered telling you about Elgar's early hour visit, but I didn't want to cause you any extra worry."

His brows dip. "What I find so frustrating about this," he says, "is I'd specifically asked you if your sister was okay, and yet you still didn't think to share that someone as dangerous as Elgar had come around at an indecent hour looking for her."

"To be honest, until Lexan filled you in yesterday, I didn't know Elgar had beaten Floss, or that she'd even been dating him. I literally had no idea why he'd come to our cavern looking for her. I figured she must have had something valuable he wanted."

The ice melts from Jax's expression and he lets out a long sigh before asking, "Do you have a singlet on?"

*WHAT!*

I gulp. "Yeah, why?"

"Take off your jumper. I want to see how badly he bruised your arms."

I feel self-conscious but do as he says and slip off my threadbare jumper. I gaze down with burning cheeks. Dark blue-green hand-prints mark the skin of my upper arms. He steps over to me, lifting one of my arms up to get a good look at it.

My insides flutter at his touch, and for a second, I forget to breathe. *You're just nervous. You're standing in front of the Commander's son in a worn old singlet. This jittery feeling you're experiencing is natural.*

He tsks. "Silly girl," he says, as he tenderly twists my arm from side to side to examine the extent of my contusions. "How could you keep this from me? These bruises are horrendous. They must be painful."

"I didn't want to worry you," I repeat.

"We can't have these kinds of secrets between us." He releases my left arm and picks up my right. "I've put a lot of faith in you, and I'd like it if you would put some faith in me too."

"I do have faith in you," I assure him. "I just don't like being a burden."

His eyes zone in on mine, bright and intense. "You are not a burden. You might need my help sometimes, but I need yours too."

My heartbeat quickens to a dizzying pace. The intensity of Jax's gaze has me feeling weak. It reminds me of the way Alex gazes at me.

*Stop it!* I scold myself. *You are reading too much into this. Jax is an intense Zeek in general. Besides, I'm sure Alex wouldn't be too happy if he knew you were getting all fluttery about somebody else. You don't have feelings for Jax; he's the Commander's son. He's above you. You just find his God-like presence intimidating, that's all.*

"Talking about needing help," he says, his eyes still locked on mine. "I need you to do a good job writing these statements for me. I want you to dish out as much dirt on Elgar as you possibly can. I have to prove beyond a doubt that he was a ticking time bomb and that Trey did what he needed to do to save the lives of many others. I don't want my mother sentencing Trey to the cell."

"That shouldn't be hard to prove," I say, desperately attempting to settle my fluttering insides. "It's true."

"I know it is, and there are a lot of Zeeks backing Trey, but I'm afraid Rae is going to put up a fight. She hasn't been the easiest Zeek to talk to about this. She doesn't want to believe that her son's death was unavoidable, she believes Trey should be punished for his crime. She also believes that there are others who should be punished too." He pulls out a jar of cream from his pocket, opens it up, and then rubs a small scoop of its contents into my bruises. "This should help with the bruising." Completely oblivious to my out-of-control thoughts and feelings towards him, Jax hands me back my jumper.

I take it from him and quickly slip it back on.

"Elgar's funeral is tomorrow," he says. "So, when I stopped at Lexan's earlier today to get a statement from him and Floss, I picked up the sack of clothes I got for you a while back. I figured you might want to wear something from the sack for the occasion."

I smile. "Thanks."

"The sack is under the desk there," he says, motioning his head to where it's been placed. "Don't let me forget it when we leave."

I make my way over to the desk and pull out the chair to sit, but something inside me still feels unsettled.

"Hey, Jax..." I say and then pause.

He glances over at me, his expression wide and open.

"Could you please speak to Floss for me? Convince her that she should come home?"

"I don't imagine she'll be easily convinced."

"I'm sorry she was so rude to you. I can assure you her spiteful attitude was aimed at me, not you. Like I've told you, Floss and I aren't close. We don't really get along."

An amused smile plays on his lips, causing his dimples to emerge. "I didn't notice."

I grin in return. "Please," I say, clasping my hands together in front of me. "I promise you'll see a different side to her when I'm not around."

"I wouldn't take anything Floss says too personally," he assures me. "Going by what she told me today, she'd been dabbling pretty heavily in Elgar's toxic concoctions for a few months now. Her mental stability is probably a little off."

This explains a lot. Floss and I have never been friends, but she's never been quite as horrible to me as she has been these last few months. I hadn't known she was experimenting with chemicals, I just thought she was becoming more and more bitter towards me due to a build-up of years of resentment. She's always been held back in life because of me, and the older we get, the more apparent it becomes. This also explains how she'd been silly enough to date Ogre. *Gross.* I cringe, still unable to believe she'd stoop that low.

"I didn't know. Thanks for telling me."

He nods by way of response and then leaves.

The walk back to our family cavern is awkward and seems to take forever. Jax walks beside me while Floss mopes behind, defiantly dragging her boots against the floor with every step. Jax had commanded her to return home, informing her there would be heavy consequences if she was to stay on the lower level. Clearly, she's not happy about it. The scuffing sound drives me batty, and I can tell by Jax's clenched jaw it's annoying him too, but neither of us are game enough to complain in case she snaps and takes off in the other direction.

As we get to our cavern entry our father dashes over. However, it's not to greet either of his daughters. *Of course,* he's only interested in Jax.

*Let round three of the humiliating fawning begin,* I announce like a ringmaster, only it's said inside my head.

Floss is more hurt by his snub than I am. "Give me a break," she huffs, and then storms past him.

"Floss." Our mother rushes over to her. "My goodness, my poor baby, look at your face." She tries to embrace her, but Floss gives her a hearty shove.

"Get away from me," she growls. "I don't need your pity. I hate you."

I observe the hurt in my mother's eyes as Floss gives her another shove and then storms off to her nook in a rage. I don't feel even remotely sorry for her, she deserves this kind of rejection from Floss. I understand Floss' anger. If I were Floss, I'd want to push our mother away too.

"I'm sorry, I'm going to have to cut you short," Jax tells my rambling father, causing him to jerk his head back in offence. "I've got a lot to do before Elgar's funeral tomorrow, and not enough time to do it all." He turns his attention to me, which only insults my father further.

"Where's your nook?"

I gulp. "My nook?"

The large hessian sack of clothes is still slung over his shoulder, and I realise with a start, he wants to dump it in my nook.

I feel uncomfortable about him seeing my tiny, near-empty nook, and what makes matters worse is that I didn't even attempt to make my bed this morning. I was too tired and cranky to do anything. I hadn't expected that the Commander's son would be paying my nook a visit—today of all days. *How embarrassing!*

"It's...it's um," I trip on my words. "It's down the passage to the left."

He raises an eyebrow in silent question, before trotting off in the direction I've pointed out.

Hesitantly, I follow him, my cheeks flushing with heat. I pray he will dump the sack by the entry of my nook, and then turn to leave without bothering to peek inside, but I'm not that lucky. Instead he walks straight in, dumping the hessian sack right beside my unmade bed.

Feeling beyond embarrassed, and at a loss for words, I scratch my head. "I...um... Thanks."

His lips curl at the corners in amusement. "I'll see you tomorrow," he says, sounding more like Jax my friend again, rather than Jax the Commander's son. "Try to get some sleep. It's going to be a big day." Before he leaves, his eyes flick from mine to the sack. "You should wear the black fur jacket with the snowflakes. There's a matching set of fur flats at the bottom of the sack. I think it will look good on you."

I nod, my breath catching in my throat. "Okay, sure."

After Jax leaves I remain in my nook, heart thumping and head confused. I don't understand what's come over me this afternoon. The way I've been acting around Jax is completely absurd. I shouldn't feel this nervous around him.

Mum must have gone to see Floss because I can hear them bickering in the background.

In the end Mum says, "Let's not make any rash decisions right now. Let's discuss this matter over dinner as a family."

Dinner is chicklet stew, *certainly not my favourite*. My mother always tends to go heavy on the spices when making it—to the point where it takes my breath away. Even the mere smell of it causes my eyes to tear up.

*Suck it up and eat it or starve*. I bring another heaped spoonful to my mouth and then swallow. I'm not in any position to be picky.

Our father starts on me first, interrogating me about what was in the hessian sack. For a grown man who is highly regarded for his strength and bravery, he seems to be terribly paranoid about the sack's contents. *What does he think is in the sack? Explosives? Ogre's head?*

"It's only clothes," I tell him.

"Why is Jax bringing you a sack full of clothes?" Floss asks with a frown.

Our father pounds the end of his fork down on the table in front of her, making us all jump. "I'm the one asking the questions here, not you."

Floss' eyes narrow. "I'm sorry." Her slitted eyes shift to meet our mother's. "I thought we were playing happy family. My mistake."

Infuriated by her sarcasm, Father drops the topic of the sack to cross-examine her. "I haven't even started with you," he says with a razor-sharp edge. "Enlighten me. What exactly is your involvement in Elgar's death?"

Unfazed by our father's intimidation tactics, Floss sets her cutlery down and glares at him from across the table. "I was nowhere near the Bean-Brew Cavern when he was killed."

He glares in return. "That's not what I asked."

"Trey killed Elgar, you know that, so what's with the ridiculous question? In case you haven't noticed, it was Elgar who hurt me, not the other way around."

"It's your own fault," our father spits, and both our mother and I gasp. "You should have never gotten involved with him. You've embarrassed our family and caused conflict between us and Rae. Rae's been telling everyone we know that she believes you are partly responsible for Elgar's death."

Floss launches up from her seat. "You know what, maybe she's right. Maybe I am partially responsible. If this is true, then I did our colony a favour. I'm glad Elgar's dead, and I guarantee everyone else is too."

Our father launches up after her, fierce, angry energy crackling around him. He gestures violently to the opening of our cavern. "Get out!"

"With pleasure."

Dropping her cutlery with a clang, our mother jumps up from her seat and races over to Floss, who is making a beeline to the opening. "Floss. No. Wait!" She reaches for her. "Don't leave."

Our father thrusts himself between them both and gives our mother a shove, causing her to stumble back a few steps. "Let her go, Krista."

For the first time ever, our mother finds her courage and charges forward to shove him back. "No!"

Floss comes to an abrupt halt, her jaw almost hitting the ground. She's shocked, but not nearly as shocked as our father. He looks like he's been given an ice-slap.

"We are a family," our mother insists, daring to challenge him. "And families stick together, even when times get tough."

She barges past him to get to Floss. "Come on, honey," she says, taking her hand. "Let's see what we can do about your face." Too stunned to argue, Floss allows our mother to lead her to back to her nook.

Our father grunts in rage and storms the other way to his nook, and I'm grateful this is all he does.

After eating the rest of my supper alone and in silence, I take everyone's bowls to the sink, wash them, and then head to my nook. As I pass by Floss' nook I see Mum applying some sort of ointment to her face. I'd like to join them, but I don't. Floss needs Mum's attention right now, and I don't want to spoil their moment. With an empty sigh I continue to my nook and climb straight into bed.

I lie awake, daydreaming about Alex and our magical kiss by the pool. I can still feel his full lips brushing against mine, and his strong, warm hands tenderly caressing my skin. If only he was a Pastel Zeek and not a Vallon, we could be together in both worlds. As it is, I don't know when I'll see him again. I'm hoping it will be tonight.

"Hey," Floss says, poking her head inside my nook with a cautious semi-smile.

I prop my head up to look at her, wondering if maybe I've dozed off and this is a dream. Floss never comes to my nook—*ever*.

"Hey." I feel slightly on edge, but I try to keep my expression casual. I never quite know where I stand with Floss. She's a hard Zeek to figure out.

"Can I come in?"

"Sure."

I shuffle upward into a seated position, while Floss enters and sits at the end of my bed. She hasn't done something like this since we were four—before we started school—before she learnt to hate me because of my colouring.

"Is everything okay?" I ask.

"I know I haven't been the best sister, and I'm not about to start promising anything, but given everything that's happened recently, I'm here to give you some sisterly advice."

Aware of her lack of tact, I brace myself for the worst. "Okay?"

"I think you should call things off with Jax. Zeeks are starting to talk—and you know the drill—if you get caught sleeping with him, you're dead." She shrugs and then adds, "I mean, it's your choice, but I guarantee it won't end well. Jax is the Commander's son. His actions are closely watched."

My back straightens and I blink in shock. "Excuse me?"

"Don't play dumb," she continues, her eyes meeting mine, sharp and serious. "Think about it. I mean really think about it. What happens if you fall pregnant? What will happen to the kid? If it comes out Purple, everyone will know for sure that you two have been breaking the rules and doing the dirty. The Commander might spare her son, but you and the kid will be killed."

I shake my head in disbelief. "I'm not sleeping with Jax."

"Sure, he's just escorting you everywhere and bringing you a sack full of clothes because he feels sorry for you."

I flinch at the idea of being a charity case. "It's not like that. He's looking out for me because he needs my help with something."

"Yeah? And what's that?"

I cringe, knowing I'm unable to share. "I can't say."

Her brows rise. "Really?"

"It's true, and anyway, I have feelings for someone else." The words tumble out of my mouth before I have the chance to stop them.

This revelation seems to aggravate her further. Her eyes slant to mine and she lets out a huff. "Since when?"

"Since…recently."

"Yeah, well if that's the case, then why haven't you asked him out already? He's been pining for you for years and everyone knows it, yet you've done nothing about it." She frowns. "Do you actually really love him? Or are you just in love with the way he's so in love with you?"

"What?"

"Zavier is a great guy," she continues, "and he doesn't deserve to be jerked around. If you are in love with him, tell him, otherwise move aside so that he can find happiness with someone else."

"Floss, you've got it wrong. I'm not in love with Zavier. He's my friend—my best friend. He's like family to me."

"But you said… I thought… Never mind. It's stupid. I'm in here lecturing you about Jax, when all the while I'm…" she shakes her head. "I resent our mother for the predicament she's put us in, and yet I would happily make the same mistake you're both making in an instant. I'm a hypocrite."

I frown. "Hold on a minute," I say, piecing it together. "Are you into Zavier? Is that why you've been staying at his place? Is that why you're so upset?" I don't know how I feel about this. I'm not sure if I'm okay with it. Zavier's *my* friend. *Mine.* If they start getting close, I'll get pushed out. I'll be back to having no one. Besides, they couldn't officially date. To date someone outside your colour status is an offence punishable by death. This is exactly what Floss is in here lecturing me about.

"What does it matter," she answers bitterly. "He's in love with you."

I go to argue the point but stop short. If she thinks Zavier is in love with me, it might discourage her from making a move on him. Instead I ask. "What mistake did our mother make?"

"She made the mistake of telling me I have to go to Elgar's funeral tomorrow," Floss says, cleverly changing the subject. "I don't want to go, but she keeps insisting. She believes it would be the right thing for me to do—*like I care.*" Her words are snarky, but I can see the wheels spinning behind her magenta eyes. "I guess I owe it to her. She did actually stand up for me for once. Who knew she had it in her?"

"I'm not keen on going either," I admit, letting the subject of our mother drop for now. "But I know if I don't go, it's only going to cause further problems with her and Rae."

"Do you really care about mum and Rae's friendship?"

"Enough that I'm going to attend. Besides, it gets us out on the ocean for the day." I give her a nudge. "That's kind of cool, right?"

"Yeah, I suppose." She screws her nose up. "If I don't get seasick like last time."

Last time we went on the boat was when we were six, after our mother's parents had died in a horrific thunder-snow storm south of the caves. Three others had died in that storm too, and as they all died on the same day, their funerals were combined, which meant it was a long day out at sea.

I'd been sad about my grandparents' passing, and I felt sorry for the others, but I have to admit, I'd rather enjoyed having a long day out on the boat. I'd felt alive.

Seeing Floss' grim expression, an uplifting idea pops to mind. "Say, what are you wearing?"

She shrugs. "I don't know, why?"

"Do you want to borrow something from the sack?" I hop off my bed and untie the top. "I'm wearing the black jacket and boots with the snowflakes," I say, "but you can take your pick out of everything else."

"Seriously?"

I nod.

Floss drops to her knees beside me and rummages through the sack, pulling out a few items that take her fancy.

She runs her finger along the silver embroidery of a stylish grey cord jacket with charcoal fur fluffed around the collar. "This stuff looks expensive."

"Well what do you say? Do you want to borrow it or not?"

She eyes me suspiciously. "What's the catch?"

I consider this a moment. *Treat me like a sister, be my friend, show me that you love me.* However, I settle on, "Can you do my hair?"

She glances up at me, something calculating in her eyes. "I tell you what... I'll dread your hair so that you never have to bother doing it again, *if* you let me keep the jacket." She gestures to a matching pair of grey boots. "And those too." She raises her brows. "Deal?"

I nod while she gloats. "Deal."

"I'll go grab what I need." She leaps to her feet, practically bursting into song. "But just so as you know, we're probably going to be up past midnight getting the dreads done."

I shrug. I'm happy to endure another sleepless night if it means I get to hang out with my sister. It would mean the world to me if we could finally be friends.

# 35

# BE GONE EVIL ONE

## -HARLOW-

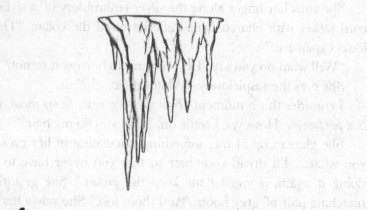

*I* feel myself being pushed and shoved every which way as I shuffle along the over-crowded dock to the boat. I didn't bring my crutches. I figured they'd only be a nuisance. Besides, my calf is good enough to walk on; it's mostly tender to touch.

Floss shuffles along with me, while our parents charge ahead, shouldering their way through the crowd like a pair of ferocious lions.

The wind is strong and causes my new dreadlocks to lift and whip at my face. They are more uncomfortable than I thought they would be. The roots are knotted tight, pulling on my skull. I hadn't known that getting dreadlocks done would be such a painful experience. No wonder Floss was so eager to do them for me, she probably enjoyed inflicting the pain.

I peer upwards and sigh. The weather is a massive disappointment. I'd been hoping for a blue sky and bright rays of sunlight like last time, but all I can see is a dark cluster of angry grey storm clouds. The only upside to this is it reminds me of Alex. "I prefer overcast days," he'd said. "I like feeling brighter than the weather." I try, but I'm unable to share his point of view. The depressing weather merely has me feeling depressed too.

"Oh, Alex," I exhale to myself. I didn't get to see him last night like I'd hoped. *How does he get to go to Earth every single night, yet I don't? It's so unfair.* I miss his golden eyes and cheeky smile. *He's my escape.*

"Watch it!" Floss gives the staunch Magenta in front a shove. "Some of us need to use our toes for climbing, you know."

"Bite me," he says spitefully, keeping his back to her.

Floss grunts in frustration. "Tell me again why I'm doing this?" She flicks a stray braid away from her face. "I hate Magentas, especially Elgar, and I hate boats."

I give her a sidelong glance. "What do you mean you hate Magentas? You are a Magenta."

"Yeah, and it sucks."

I twiddle my fingers. *Okay then.*

"Think of all the warriors you'll get to perv on," I say, aiming for her weak spot.

"I suppose you're right. Not that I can date any of them."

"No, but they're a good distraction."

Zannah and Kieran stand at either side of the suspended footbridge—which connects the boat to the dock—fiercely attempting to keep everyone in order.

"Step back for the lady and her child," Zannah orders to a rowdy pack of Magenta men. "Show some common courtesy."

285

Her voice rings loud and strong, yet it can barely be heard over the continual flapping and snapping of the boats' sails. The larger of the front sails has the official Zeek snowflake symbol on it, painted in a soft blue with a darker blue edging.

As I shuffle over the footbridge, Zannah gives me an unnecessary shove. "Come on, move it," she demands.

I feel aggravated inside, but I keep a poker face.

Up on deck, the crowd loosens a little, but not much. From here we are broken up and ushered to designated areas of the boat, depending on our relationship to the deceased. All of the family members and close friends are taken to the side where Ogre's body lies on an open wooden stretcher, his lifeless frozen skin now a shade of purply-blue. Our parents have been chosen to stand alongside Rae, while Floss and I get ushered to the back of the crowd. *Good.* The further away the better as far as I'm concerned.

As we stand waiting, I gaze about curiously. There are warriors everywhere. Some are spread throughout the crowd to keep us all in check, while others work as crewmen. Jax, Oscar, Electra, and Jax's mother Azazel—the Commander—are the only four Purples standing up in front, on show.

Azazel's features are stark and intimidating. I hadn't known she was coming today. She doesn't attend many Magenta funerals, only a select few have ever made the cut. I imagine Ogre only made the cut due to the controversy of his death, and not because he was deemed worthy. I'm not entirely sure why Electra is here though. She's not a member of the Commanding family, and she's not a warrior. However, I do remember Jax telling me she is under his mother's personal protection, which tells me they are close. She must be here for Azazel, I figure anxiously. I'd overhead her calling me Jax's pet to the prune-faced librarian. *Who's the pet now?*

Everyone talks amongst themselves during the short voyage out. I turn to Floss, hoping to start a conversation but she already looks nauseous.

My eyes are drawn to Ogre's lifeless body. *I wonder what the next planet we reincarnate to will be like. And when my time comes, will I still remember Zadok as I've remembered Earth?* RJ says he remembers the planet he lived on before Earth. I'm curious to know what it was like. I'll have to ask him one day.

Rae gives a long cringy speech about what a wonderful loving boy her son was. *Please!* I think and Floss scoffs. She can't really believe this. They say love is blind, but this feels next level.

*Heaven help the next planet.* They have no idea what they're in for. Some poor unknowing woman will give birth to this horrid monster. I hope for her sake that he grows up to be a very different character, although I can't imagine it.

Zeeks believe our souls need to see life through the eyes of many existences in order to grow and develop, which sounds feasible, but what I've never understood is how we can grow and develop from our last life if we don't remember living it. Most Zeeks aren't like RJ and me; they don't remember their past.

I'd asked my mother about this the day of her parents' funeral and she'd said, "The soul is unlike the mind, it doesn't need memories to develop. Memories are a hindrance. They cause the Zeek to become fixated on what was, rather than what is."

I'm still unsure whether I agree. Besides Zeeks are no better than humans. We may look and live differently, but we are still just as screwed up.

I try to blank out Rae's voice. *This is cringe worthy.*

Hurry up and let this ceremony be done.

After the ceremony's finished, Jax passes behind me. "You might want to check on your sister," he says under his breath, and I wait a minute for him to move on, before scanning my surroundings. It doesn't take long to spot her. She's only a few metres away, hunched over the side rail of the boat. She looks terrible. Her skin has turned a mild shade of green.

"I'm sorry, excuse me a moment," I say to the group surrounding me. Nobody pays me any attention. *Typical.*

I struggle not to fall as I make my way over. The weather has taken a turn for the worse—the wind has picked up, and the water has become extremely choppy.

"Floss, are you okay?" I ask as I get close, but she's too busy heaving over the wooden rail to answer. I place my hand on her back to give it a light rub. "What can I do?"

The boat gives an abrupt jerk, sending a few plates and cups off the tables and onto the deck.

"Get me off this damn boat," she finally groans. "I should never have come. I didn't want to come. Nobody would have noticed if I hadn't shown."

A clap of thunder rumbles, vibrating the deck beneath my feet, and I feel a drop of water splash the tip of my nose.

"If you want a way off the boat, I'd be more than happy to oblige," comes a gravelly voice from behind us as the sky flashes white overhead.

I turn to find Rae glaring at us, her eyes filled with hatred. This is the closest I've been to her since Ogre's death, and I'm not entirely sure what to say. She doesn't look as if she's here for our commiserations.

"Hi Rae, I'm sor—"

"Stop right there," she barks. "Don't you dare say you're sorry when clearly you're not. I know you both had a hand in my son's death, and you will pay for it. I don't care if you are Saul's daughters, I will see to it that you are dealt with accordingly."

I'm not sorry Ogre is dead, she's right about that, but I had been sorry for her loss. I'm not feeling so sorry anymore.

I try to stand straighter, but the relentless rocking and jerking of the boat make it hard to do so. I can barely keep my footing.

"You know that's not true," I say, but my words are drowned out by the rumble of thunder.

"Don't bother trying to deny it. Electra told me all about your scheme."

"Electra?" My heart gives an exaggerated thump. "What scheme?"

My eyes do a quick scan of the deck to find Electra looking right at us, her lips twisted in a wicked smirk. She is seated next to Azazel at Rae's family table.

My eyes flash back to Rae's in panic. "I don't know what Electra has told you, but I can assure you it is a lie."

Floss looks up in confusion but is still too busy heaving and hacking to join in on what's being said. I'm worried about her. She looks like she's about to pass out. I don't want her falling overboard.

"It was you who should have been killed, not Elgar," Rae hisses through gritted teeth. "You were never meant to be allowed to live amongst us. You are an abomination—a curse to us all."

Her insults sound all too familiar. Fear twists like a hot poker inside me. These words aren't hers; they are hand-me-downs. Electra has planted this information in her head. She is using Rae as her puppet.

"That's not..." Floss begins, but her sentence is finished with actual vomit. Some of it doesn't make it over the rail, and lands on her new fluffy boots. She'll want to kick herself once she realises.

As Floss thrusts her torso further forward to continue spewing over the rail, Rae quickly lunges at her, attempting to reef her off her feet.

My chest constricts. I can't believe it. Rae isn't mucking about. She's actually prepared to kill us.

Adrenaline surging, I dive straight onto Floss' legs, forcing them back down before she can topple over the railing. Luckily for me the boat gives another abrupt jerk as I do this, which knocks Rae off balance. Her grip on Floss releases and Floss falls face first onto the deck—straight into her own vomit. She's not going to be happy about this but being soaked in vomit beats being dead.

"YOU!" Rae snatches a fist full of my hair and reefs me to her.

If my skull hadn't already been tender, it sure as hell is now. I yelp in pain. Rae jumps back to her feet and drags me up with her.

"RAE!" I hear our mother scream from afar. "Rae what are you doing?"

Rae lifts me completely off my feet by my dreads and charges towards the side rail. *Crap!* If she manages to get me over that rail, I'm dead. No one here is going to jump overboard to save a Pastel.

Despite the excruciating pain emitting from my skull, I swing and kick, desperately hoping to land a hard one on her.

"It wasn't our fault!" I yell. "You've been misinformed."

My calf hits the side rail and I wince, but to my relief strong hands snake around me from behind, pulling me back towards the deck. Rae still has a grip on my hair, and I feel a harsh yank as I'm pulled in opposite directions. My head hurts so much I want to cry.

*Suck it up. Everyone is watching. You can't appear weak.*

"What do you think you're doing Rae?" Jax's voice is loud and booming. "Let go of her."

Rae's grip on my hair loosens. "You don't understand…"

"Stop! This is not the time or place. You should get back to your family. I'm sure they're worried about you."

"You are as big of a disgrace to our colony as she is," Rae spits. "You're nothing but a pathetic Pastel lover just like your daddy. Your mother ought to be ashamed."

I feel the muscles in Jax's arms bunch and hear the muscles in his cheeks tick. "You should get back to your family," he repeats, his expression carefully blank.

Rae's eyes snap to mine. "This isn't over," she warns.

"Floss!" Our mother finally reaches us, panting breathlessly. She drops to her knees by Floss' side. "Floss, Floss baby are you okay?"

Floss lifts her vomit smeared head and groans. "She should have let Rae throw me in."

Jax places me down gently, his muscles still tight and rigid. The look he gives is sympathetic, and I can see he desperately wants to say something, but there's no need. The look in his eyes says it all. He knows as well as I do if he shows me any added kindness right now, it will cause an uproar. "Krista, I think you should take the girls below deck until we get back to port. It's not safe for them up here."

Our mother nods, the look of hurt and confusion etched in her features.

"I'll get Oscar to meet you down there," he adds.

The feel of someone's hand touching my shoulder startles me upright. My eyes spring open and I immediately swat my arms out in defence. After having Rae try to throw me overboard, I've been completely on edge. Electra clearly wants me dead, and I have no idea how many others she's recruited to help take me down. Jax won't be able to protect me forever. There is going to come a day when someone succeeds in killing me, and sadly, I'm pretty sure that instead of being convicted of murder, they will be given a pat on the back.

"Harlow, shhh." Two strong hands encircle my shoulders. "It's just me, Jax."

My pulse jack-knifes. He can't be in my nook in the middle of the night. Someone might see him and get the wrong idea. Floss said, "Zeeks are already talking." They think we are having some not-so-secret affair.

I can't deny that I'm attracted to Jax—*what girl wouldn't be?* But this doesn't mean I want to sleep with him.

The thought of him being here for more than just my help causes panic to claw its way up my throat. I can't be the desperate gold-digging Pastel everyone believes me to be. I can't be with him in that way, it would be wrong—whorish. Besides, I have Alex. *I want Alex.* I need to get back to sleep so that I can dream my way back to Alex.

Jax's strong, rough hands slide gently all the way down to my elbows before he releases. "How are you? Are you okay?"

I nod, my heart hammering in my chest. "Yeah, I'm okay."

It's not entirely true. My head is killing me, and I feel as if I'm on the verge of having a full-on heart-attack.

"I'm sorry about today." His words sound choked. "I'm sorry I've put you in such a dangerous position. I never thought things would come to this. I thought that with Nix gone, it would be much easier to bring about change, but I was wrong. It was never my intention to put you in danger."

I sit up properly and cross my legs. "Don't blame yourself," I say. "I don't blame you. My defective colouring has put a target on my back from the moment I was born. It was always going to be this way."

His lips tug up into a smile which doesn't quite reach his violet eyes. "You're not defective," he says. "You're unique." He reaches to one of my dreadlocks and twists it between his fingers. "I like your new hair-do, it looks nice."

I swallow hard, my breath catching in my throat. "Floss did it for me. It cost me the grey pair of boots and matching jacket. I hope you don't mind."

He softly places the dread back down. "The clothes are yours; you can do what you want with them."

"These dreadlocks hurt more than I'd expected them to. They feel tight and itchy."

He reaches into his jacket pocket and pulls out a handful of nauclea latifolia roots. "Give it a week, your head will get used to them. Until then, you might want to chew on these." He carefully places them into my hand. "They'll take the edge off."

"Thank you." His fingers brush mine and I quiver. *STOP IT!*

I need him to leave now, before I start confusing my feelings of gratitude for something else. *I don't want him. I want Alex. I miss Alex. Alex knows the truth about my past life. We share a connection.*

Breaking me away from my disjointed thoughts, Jax says, "I'm going to have to do as you and Zannah suggested and keep my distance for a while. I'm copping a lot of heat at the moment, and I don't think it's safe for you to be around me."

Hearing him say this fills me with both relief and dread. It's the right decision for both of us, and I know it, yet all the while I can't help but feel a pang deep inside my heart. I need space from him to get my thoughts and feelings straight, and he needs to prove to everyone that he is the warrior they need him to be.

"The other thing I came here to tell you is that Rae has been officially excused for her behaviour today. My mother insists her actions were those of an ill-informed grieving mother." A soft bitter laugh escapes him. "I tried fighting her on this verdict, but my opinion was squashed. Don't worry," he assures me, as he stands.

"I'll have some of my more trusted warriors looking out for you, RJ, and Floss. I'll make sure they keep you safe."

"You be safe too," I say. *I'll miss you.*

He uses the side of his thumb to stroke my cheek and my insides squirm. This gesture feels dangerously affectionate. "I'll be okay; it's you I'm worried about. Lay low for a while and hopefully everything will blow over soon."

## 36

# LET'S MEET

## -HARLOW AND HARLOW AS RUBY-

"*Y*ou really know how to torture a guy, don't you?"

I'm so excited to hear Alex's voice I could scream.

"I've been trying to get back to you for the past couple of nights, but I couldn't make it happen."

My vision clears, revealing Jade's living room. Connor sits on the lounge with Rueben, both of them tapping away eagerly on a set of videogame controllers.

"Eat dirt," Rueben says as his race car skids past Connor's.

These graphics are incredible. I'm amazed. *It all looks so real.* Peeling my eyes away from the large screen, I look at Alex.

His eyes survey mine with a hint of apprehension. "So, does this mean you didn't leave me mid kiss on purpose?"

I smile "Of course not. Trust me, I wanted to strangle my mother for waking me."

"You seem to have a lot of Zeeks waking you up in the early hours of the morning." His humorous tone is laced with a hint of suspicion.

"If only that was the worst of it," I say. "My life is a complete and utter mess at the moment. I have Zeeks trying to kill me."

His brows shoot up in alarm. "You what?"

"I..."

A loud crash startles us both as Connor throws his controller to the floor in a tantrum. "Screw you!" he shouts, and Rueben sniggers.

"You throw that controller once more and I will confiscate your PlayStation." Jade stands by the kitchen cooktop, her brows scrunched in anger. "I didn't spend big money on that thing just for you to destroy it in a tantrum. Now stop being a sore loser and show some respect."

"Maybe it's best if we get out of here," Alex suggests.

I watch as Connor picks up the controller and plonks back onto the lounge with a sour look on his face.

"I think you're right."

We leave the living room and head outside to the pool.

Alex sits by the water's edge, and I park myself next to him. The memories of last time we were here together flitter through my mind and I blush.

"Tell me what's going on." He wraps an arm around me, pulling me closer. "What do you mean you've got Zeeks trying to kill you?"

I open up, telling him how I'm the only Pastel to be born to a set of Magentas and how my defective colouring has caused bloodshed in our Commanding family. I also delve into the evil plots and betrayals I've learnt about since hanging out with RJ, including how Nix blew up the factory caverns.

"I was supposed to be killed as a baby," I add. "But Arlo fought to keep me alive, and that's why Azazel had him killed."

"This is outrageous," Alex says. "And to think, you were trying to pin my kind as the baddies."

"I'm starting to believe we're all baddies."

"Not all of us," he says.

He ponders with crinkled brows before airing his thoughts. "Why now?" His eyes meet mine, his gaze intense. "I mean, I get how this all started, but what I don't get is why everything is coming to a head now? You've been around for eighteen years. You'd think if they wanted to kill you so badly, they would have done it by now."

"A lot has happened over the past couple of years to make me stand out," I tell him. "Firstly, Jax made sure I was allowed to work with the Magentas which didn't sit well with everyone in our colony—especially his brother, and then when I got attacked by the fuegor he helped get me a job in the library which is a Purple job."

"You got attacked by a fuegor?"

"Yeah," I nod. "But that wasn't the point of the story."

Regardless, he doesn't let it drop. "How badly were you hurt?"

"Not too badly. A Drake saved me before the fuegor could do too much damage."

"Who gave you the brain freeze?" he asks, jumping ahead.

"Electra."

"What's her story? She's a Pastel hater too, I gather?"

"She was Nix's nexus and has since become Azazel's confidante," I tell him. "She didn't want me working in the library, so she gave me the brain freeze to prove a point. She really has it in for me. She tried to have me killed yesterday when we were out on the boat. It was lucky that Jax was nearby. He caught hold of me just as Rae was about to throw me over the rail."

"Geez, Rubes." Alex's hands rise to his temples in distress. "What am I going to do with you?"

"Nothing, you're a Vallon. You couldn't help me even if you wanted to. And besides, you know as well as I do that if you were to step foot on our land alone, you'd be killed."

A sly grin plays at his lips. "I wouldn't be so sure of that if I were you."

"What do you mean?"

"I mean the Slater side of me is tough," he says, giving me a playful nudge.

As the afternoon passes by, I continue to fill Alex in on all the little details, and he is curious as to why Jax is so eager to help me.

"Jax wants to integrate our colour system, and he needs my help," I tell him, but he doesn't seem to buy it.

"If you keep letting him use you like this, you are going to be killed. I know he might be telling you everything you want to hear, but unless he's into you or something, I'm afraid he might be using you as his pawn."

I resent what he's said. *I'm not Jax's pawn, I'm his ally*—or at least I thought I was. I hope Alex isn't right about Jax using me as his pawn. *I can't believe that—I won't.* He's helping me because he cares for me and my fellow Pastels. He wants things to be better for us. I've seen him stand up for us.

"We need to meet."

Alex's outburst comes from nowhere.

I straighten. "What do you mean we need to meet?"

"I mean Slater and Harlow. We need to meet."

"WHAT?" Fear washes over me. "No... I can't... It's not even an option."

"Sure it is. We have to. I know what I can do to help you." The words rush off his tongue. "We should meet at the Spring border tomorrow night."

"It's not possible," I insist. "I have no way of getting out of the caves unnoticed, and besides, even if I could manage it, I'd be killed by fuegors."

"Don't worry about the fuegors. They won't lay a paw on you with me around."

"That doesn't solve my problem of sneaking out. I won't be able to slip out of the caves unnoticed. It's not going to happen—especially now. Everyone's eyes are on me."

An emergency vehicle passes by in the distance, causing the

neighbourhood dogs to howl like a choir. They sound as distressed as I feel.

"Better idea." Alex's pointer finger shoots up. "I'll stay awake. We'll meet in the morning."

"What difference will that make?"

"Do you know a hunter named Saul?"

"Ah...yeah. Saul's my dad."

Alex cocks his head in surprise. "He's your dad?"

Confusion washes over me. "Hold on. How do you know my dad?"

"It's a hunter thing."

That sounds suspect, but I let it slide for now.

"You need to find a way to stow away in his sled," he insists. "And then when they leave it to go hunting, climb out and hide."

"Hide where?"

"It doesn't matter, I'll find you. Trust me. It's what I'm good at."

"I don't know." I'm nervous. Something about this doesn't feel right.

Alex brushes my hair back from my face, his eyes pleading. "Come on," he begs. "I'm not only doing this for you, I'm doing it for me too. You can't die on me. If you die on Zadok, you might not be able to come back here." His hand squeezes my thigh. "We've only just connected, and I don't want to lose you."

He brings up a good point. I'd never thought of that.

"Fine," I concede. "I'll try."

I wake up at five in the morning with knots in my stomach. I can't believe I'm really going to do this. *I shouldn't, but I am.* I'd like to dress nice for Alex, but if I do, it will only attract unwanted attention while I'm trying to escape. Besides, my fruit picking clothes are comfortable. They're what I'm used to wearing when trotting about in the forest.

I'm not sure how I'll react to seeing Alex as a Vallon. Under normal circumstances, seeing a Vallon would terrify me. I forgot to even ask him which colour he was—red, orange, or amber. I hope he isn't a Red; the Reds are the worst of them all.

I try to be as quiet as I can while getting ready. I don't want to wake Floss. If she catches me sneaking out, she might question where I'm off to. She's being a little nicer to me as of late, but I still don't trust her.

After putting on my boots, I carefully scan the passageway outside of our family cavern. It's all clear. I make a dash for the stairs, feeling so anxious I could throw up. I need to hurry and to get to the hunting cavern before someone sees me.

The next few passages on the ground level are clear, but as I get closer to the hunting cavern, I see a small group of Magentas congregating a few metres before the opening.

*Darn.*

They are deep in conversation and don't appear to be moving anytime soon. I flip the hood of my jacket over my hair, and keep my head facing down as I take to the passage.

I sigh a breath of relief as I enter the hunting cave unnoticed and throw back my hoodie. As a child, I used to hate visiting my parents at work. Animal heads line the limestone walls, each on a wooden plaque with my father's name scrawled below it. They are his trophies. *It's sickening.* There are also a bunch of bleached animal bones scattered along the bench which will be used to make buttons, tools and weapons. I know this because my father has a whole stash of bone-made-items at home. He uses some to trade with occasionally, but mostly he likes to collect them and show off.

I open up the seat of the sled. Inside are some ropes and hessian sacks. *I wonder if they'd notice me if I were to hide beneath the sacks.* I'm small; I wouldn't take up much room.

✳

After half an hour of hiding I hear voices enter the cavern. There are a few bangs and slams before the seat lid is opened, and a pile of weapons are thrown in on top of me. I bite my lower lip to stop from crying out. These weapons have rough edges, and they are heavy as hell.

*At least they haven't noticed me.*

The trip out to Spring seems to take forever, and my sides begin to throb from all of the bumping and banging. I hadn't realised how painful this was going to be. I should have brought some sort of cushioning to wrap around me.

"There's a big one right there," my father says with delight, and the sled finally comes to a halt.

*Hallelujah.* I'm not sure how much more hurt and discomfort I can take.

"Krista, you go and distract it and Fau and I will take it down."

He didn't mention Rae's name. She mustn't have come with them. *I wonder if she, Jax, or my parents made that decision.*

The seat lid above me opens and the weapons are grabbed with haste. Their hands graze the sacks I'm lying beneath, but thankfully they don't lift them. I can breathe again.

"Let's go," my father says, and I hear the crunch of their foot-steps receding.

I wait a few minutes before slipping out from under the sacks and taking a peek. I can see my father and Fau, their backs are to me, but I can't see my mother. *Not good.* I can't get caught now, not after the pain it's taken to get here. I scan further until finally I get a glimpse of her. She's creeping up on the deetra from behind. The deetra is beautiful. It looks similar to a deer only it shimmers with golden flecks. My insides churn. *I can't watch this.*

I slip out from the seat compartment and drop to the ground on my toes. It's loud enough that the huskens hear me and turn to investigate, but thankfully my father and Fau are focused solely on the deetra. Sweat drips from my brow. It's time to make a run for it.

I dash to one of the nearby trees, which has a trunk the size of a car, and hide between its large protruding roots. From there I wait, and wait, and wait…

An hour passes and I ask myself for the hundredth time if I've made a terrible mistake by coming here. Alex said he would find me, and I believed him but as I take in my surroundings, I realise how utterly foolish I was. Spring's forest is vast. It'd be like finding a needle in a haystack.

Eventually I hear a few snaps nearby and I tense. *Please be Alex.* I know fuegors don't roam in the daylight but still I'm scared.

Rustling noises join the snaps as something—or someone—moves closer to where I'm standing. My body is trembling like a leaf. I should've brought a weapon.

A shadow appears from above me and I cower.

"Rubes? Is that you?"

My heart pounds erratically inside my chest. "Alex?" I squeak.

I know it must be him, but his voice sounds foreign to me. His accent is similar to that of a German—like all Vallons. It doesn't feel right.

I dare a peek. Swirling molten lava eyes gaze down at me from above, glowing and demonic. I gulp. *What have I done?*

*HE'S A RED.*

# 37

# VERTIC SWITZ

## -HARLOW-

I shrink back with a gasp, nearly tripping over a bumpy section of the protruding tree root. *I've made a horrible mistake.* Alex is my enemy here. A Vallon. A Red. I don't know what I was thinking. *I never should have agreed to this.*

"Rubes, it's okay," he assures me, but I can't even look at him. "It's just me, Alex. You have nothing to be afraid of."

My voice quivers. "But you don't look like you, and you definitely don't sound like you."

A small chuckle leaves his throat. "Yeah, well that makes two of us." He lowers his large black hand to mine, and I flinch. I've never touched a Vallon before—I've never wanted to. Especially a Red. To be this close to a Red is absolutely terrifying. They are the most dangerous of them all.

"Rubes, it's just me," he repeats.

I shake my head, unable to accept his words. "Only it's not you at all. Your name is Slater here, and you're a Vallon. You're my enemy." I shrink back further. "This doesn't feel right. I shouldn't have come."

Without warning, he snatches my hand and pulls me to him in one swift movement. "It's Alex in here," he says, placing my hand on his rock-hard chest. "Not Slater. Don't forget that."

His heartbeats are evenly paced, unlike mine. He isn't scared; he doesn't need to be. Still trembling, I stare at his bare, glowing chest and cringe in fear. The vertic switz markings etched on his skin luminate, like a tribal tattoo that's been needled with the fluid of a red glow stick.

"I'm sorry." I try to hide my fear, but my unsteady voice betrays me. "I wasn't expecting you to be so big, or a Red."

"What does it matter what colour I am?" The accent lacing his words is off-putting. He sounds as terrifying as he looks.

"You know as well as I do that colours mean everything to our colonies. The darker we are, the stronger we are."

"The stronger I am, the better I can protect you." He puts a hand to my cheek, and I flinch. "Come on Rubes, it's me, Alex. Get it in your head. You have no reason to fear me."

He's right, I need to calm down. *He might look like Slater the Vallon, but he's Alex inside. Human Alex. My Alex. I have nothing to be afraid of.*

He doesn't allow my obvious display of fear to hold him back. "You know," he says, his voice light. "You're prettier than I'd imagined you'd be." His eyes sweep over me, stopping short at my threadbare pants. He screws up his nose. "I'm not sold on your outfit choice though."

I let out a weak, breathy laugh. "Yeah...well...you look much scarier than I'd expected."

The sky is crystal clear today, leaving the sun's rays to shine down brightly on his closely shaved skull. "Oh, come on... I don't look that bad, do I?"

"It's your eyes," I say without looking at them. "I don't like the continual swirling irises. It's creepy. They look demonic."

"Phft." His creepy eyes dance mischievously in my direction. "I happen to think they look rather extraordinary. I mean, come on, what other race has irises like this?"

"My point exactly."

He laughs. "Touché."

After taking a few long breaths to calm my nerves, I force myself to take a proper look at him. He's four years older than me here, the same as Jax, but he's a foot taller and bulkier than Jax. All Vallons are bigger and bulkier than Zeeks. *It's Alex inside.* I remind myself. *You don't have to be afraid.*

Creepy irises aside, his features are actually quite appealing. His brows are shaped into perfect arcs, and his cheekbones are high and circular. He looks like Tyson Beckford from the human world eighteen years ago, only bigger, blacker and much, much scarier.

"I guess you look...uh...not too bad for a Vallon," I offer, but my tone lacks conviction.

He rolls his creepy eyes at me. "Gee, thanks. Don't exert yourself."

He might not look or sound like Alex, but his persona is Alex all over. I feel myself relax a little. "Okay fine then, you look terrifyingly handsome."

He gives me a cheeky, devil-may-care smile. "Now that's more like it." His hand grabs mine pulling me closer. "Come on, let's get moving. I've got a few places I'd like to show you before the day's out."

As the next few hours pass and we get to talking, I grow more and more comfortable with this new intimidating version of him. He still looks scary as hell, but I don't feel unsafe. In actual fact, I feel safer than usual. He takes me for a walk through the forest and shows me some of his favourite places to visit. It's all new to me. Most of the areas he takes me to have been marked as Danger Zone on our Zeek maps—and I can see why. Spectacular creatures of all shapes and sizes hide out together in these heavily shaded areas. Some are bird-like, some are lizard-like and others are insect-like—only mega sized. Most of them are luminous, emitting a range of highlighter pinks, greens, blues and purples. But although they are incredible to look at, they don't appear to be friendly. They lick their chops and snap at the air as we pass, some with teeth as big as my hand.

"Bleib zurück," Alex growls, and they all scatter—including the big ones.

I quickly discover that having a Vallon as an ally might not be such a bad thing. If I were to come to these places alone, I would be snapped up for sure.

After leaving the last of his favourite shaded areas, I find a fallen moss-covered-tree-trunk to sit on.

"I'm sorry," I say, "but I need a break. My calf really hurts." I pull my pants leg up to check the bandage. No blood has seeped through. *Good.* I may have overdone it, but I haven't ripped any stitches.

"Can I have a look at it?" he asks.

I feel shy about showing him, but nevertheless I unwrap the bandage. The wound looks good in comparison to a few days ago, but the skin surrounding the stitches is still heavily stained with a yellowy-brown bruise.

Alex crouches down next to me. "Ouchy mumma." He runs his finger alongside the stitches edge. "It sure managed to sink its teeth in, didn't it? You're lucky it didn't rip your whole calf muscle right off."

I cringe at the thought.

"You know," he continues, his tone apprehensive, "I've brought along that *little something* which I believe might help you." His eyes assess mine, gauging for my reaction.

"Oh?" Curiosity fills me. "Well, what is it?"

"Listen…" He glances away, his top teeth grazing his lower lip, "I don't want you to freak out on me, okay."

Just hearing him say this, automatically freaks me out. "Why," I ask nervously. "What is it?"

He pulls out a small glass jar from his pocket and places in my hand. It's the size of my pinkie and contains fluorescent red liquid.

Perplexed, I give the small jar a shake. "I don't know what this is?"

"It's vertic switz ink."

"Vertic switz ink?" I blink in confusion. "I don't understand. How is *this* supposed to help me?"

"It'll make you stronger."

My gaze shifts to his heavily patterned chest, and I tense instinctively. The fluro-red ink looks powerful and suits his lethal physique, but it would look strange on a scrawny Pastel like me. Besides, if anyone saw that I'd been tattooed in vertic switz ink it would cause an outrage. Vertic switz ink is exclusive to the Vallons. It's been laced with the dust of their ancestors and their family members blood.

I attempt to hand the jar back to him. "I can't accept this."

He closes his hand over mine. "Sure you can, I'll do the tattoo for you. I'll draw whatever you want."

"I'm a Zeek," I say, "Not a Vallon. This isn't mine to use."

"It's mine, and I'm giving it to you to use. You must. It's the only way you are going to survive."

A small metallic insect lands on my knee, and I brush it away before it can bite. "How do you even know if it'll work on me? It might kill me before anyone else gets the chance."

"It won't kill you. It'll change your body shape, but it won't kill you. I promise."

"But how do you know?"

"Don't ask me how I know, just trust that I do."

It suddenly clicks. *Oh God!* "You've done this to one of us before, haven't you?"

"No." He shakes his head adamantly. "I haven't done it. I swear to you—but it has been done."

Silence lingers a moment while I try to digest what he's said.

"The paler Pastel slaves weren't surviving on our land," he confesses, his voice strained. "So, our Queen ordered a trial to be done. They injected ten of the palest Pastels with our vertic switz ink to see if it would improve their strength—and it did. The only problem was, they got too strong and tried to rebel against us." He grimaces before adding, "So she put an end to them all."

Bile rises in my throat.

His admission hits home. *Vallons are our enemy. They kill Zeeks like me. Alex might mean a lot to me, but Slater is my enemy. Who knows what he's capable of, or what he's already done?*

As if reading my mind, he says, "I'm not your enemy, Ruby; I'm not going to hurt you." His hand cups my chin. "I'm here because I want to save you. I love you, and I don't want to lose you."

I swallow. *He loves me?* This seems sudden. Not that I'm complaining, I want to be loved.

He leans in to kiss me, and my heart jumps. I'm not sure how I feel about kissing a Vallon.

*It's just Alex,* I lecture myself, for the millionth time today. *It'll be fine; you're safe with him. Pull yourself together.*

As his lips touch mine, I close my eyes and imagine him in his human form. It's the only way I'm going to get through this without freaking out and drawing back on him. I can see his golden-brown irises gazing into mine, shining brighter than usual due to the orange glare of the setting sun. This image sure helps. I push any worries I have aside and allow myself to respond. His lips feel warm, supple and not at all deadly. They are not so different to those of human-Alex's.

He eventually pulls back, and with a breathy voice he says, "Let me do the tattoo for you." His molten swirling eyes plead with me. "It doesn't have to be anything big or exposed." He rests a hand on my thigh, and he gives it a light squeeze. "It could be as simple as a tiny snowflake on your hip."

Contemplating this insanity, I nervously fiddle with the leather bracelet Zavier made for me. The idea of being tattooed with Vallon ink—laced with the dust of Slater's ancestors' and his family's blood—has me feeling apprehensive, but really, *what do I have to lose?* If I go home as I am, I'm as good as dead anyway.

*And think about it,* I urge. *Alex has fearlessly gone out of his way to meet you here. He wants to keep you around. He loves you. He is risking a whole lot to be with you.*

"I'm curious… When you say that the paler Pastels were injected, do you mean that they were literally injected, or were they tattooed?"

"They were literally injected."

"Then why tattoo me?" I ask. "Why not inject me? Wouldn't it be the less obvious approach?"

"The problem is the overall effects are very different. Being injected with the ink isn't as efficient, or as long term effective as being tattooed—which is permanent. When someone is injected with the vertic switz ink, the benefits snap into effect immediately —hard and fast—but instead of the Vallon, or in your case the Zeek, improving and growing stronger as time goes on, the ink dilutes in the bloodstream and the effects will lessen. The Vallon or Zeek will still be improved compared to their original state, but they won't ever be as strong and powerful as what they were when they were first injected. It's only half as effective."

"That might be all I need right now," I say. "Just a quick boost until things settle down."

"I didn't bring a syringe." He strokes my thigh with a slow drag of his fingers. "Plus, I've been told it's a rather painful transition when you are injected. The body doesn't have enough time to adjust to the changes comfortably. It grows and expands at an accelerated rate. The tattoo is the better option for you, trust me. This way you'll remain strong forever."

*Do I trust him? I think so.*

Eventually giving in, I say, "Do you think I could get it done on my inner wrist, so that I can hide it under this?" I tug at the inner part of my bracelet to show him where I mean.

A satisfied smile curls the corners of his lips. "Sure, I could make that work."

"Okay then," I swallow. "Let's do this."

I hastily slide my bracelet off, causing his brows to shoot up in surprise. "Really? Now?"

"Yes, really—and now—before I change my mind."

He pulls out a small leather case from his pocket, and from it, he slides out a long, sharp, needle.

I gulp at the sight of it.

"What are you so nervous about?" he asks in amusement. "This'll be nothing in comparison to that bite on your leg."

"It's not only the pain I'm nervous about, it's everything. I'm crossing dangerous lines right now."

"I'm crossing dangerous lines too. But you're worth it." He takes the jar from my hand and unscrews the lid. "I can't stop Zeeks from coming after you," he says, dipping the needle inside. "But at least if you are stronger, you'll be able to fight them off."

"Does this mean I'll be strong enough to take on a Magenta?" The thought of not being such a weakling excites me.

He nods, and I have to turn my face away to hide my ridiculous grin. "Exactly how strong will this ink make me? Do you think it will make me as strong as a Purple?"

"Honestly," he pauses a moment in deliberation. "I wouldn't be surprised if it makes you stronger. The Pastels who were injected, were able to put up a decent fight against the Vallons who were sent down to kill them. And they were only injected with the amber zertic switz ink, not the red."

*Huh.* My grin widens ear to ear. *Perhaps getting this tattoo done isn't as crazy of an idea, as I'd first thought.*

## 38

# SHE'S MISSING

## -ZAVIER-

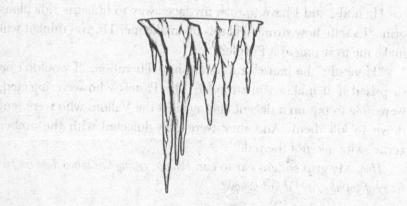

*A* sharp pain slices through my shoulder and then travels down my side, as someone's hand shakes me awake.

"Stop it, Minty," I croak. "I can't come in today, I'm too sore."

"Zavier, it's me, Jax." Jax's voice booms. "I need you to wake up."

"Even worse," I groan. "Go away."

"Zavier, it's important," he stresses. "It's about Harlow."

"Harlow?" I attempt to open my eyes, but they are sealed with gunk. Jax must notice and places a wet cloth in my hand. I wince as I dab at the inner corners near the bridge of my nose. *Frost, it hurts.* I don't know what's happened to me. My whole face feels like it's been taken to with a mallet.

Eventually I'm able to peel my lids open, but not by much. "Why won't my eyes open properly?" I ask in alarm. "And why is everything so blurry?" I blink several times, yet nothing changes, it only makes them sting all the more. "I think there's something wrong with them."

"Your eyes are still swollen," he says impatiently. "It'll be a few more days before you can open them properly."

My ears prick to the sounds of beeps and I panic. "Where am I?" I attempt to sit up, but something stabs at my insides. *Nope, this isn't going to work.* I groan and lay back flat. "Why am I hurting so much?" My gaze flicks to the rails at the side of the bed, followed by machines, and then a long row of beds. *Oh no!* An irrational fear swirls inside me.

"What's going on? Where am I? Am I at the medics?" I try to sit up again but it's another painful fail.

"Calm down." Jax's tone becomes harsh and impatient. "You're causing a fuss."

"Excuse me?" My irrational fear is instantly replaced with resentment. "I'm sorry, Jax," I say cynically. Instead of calling him Jax, I should start calling him Jackass. "I forgot that your problems are more important than mine. How is it that I can help?"

He lets out an exasperated breath. "Have you seen Harlow today? Has she come in to visit?"

My head thumps as I try to think. "I don't know," I say in confusion. "I didn't even know that I was at the medical chamber until now. What am I doing here? How long have I been here?"

Ignoring my questions he urges, "Do you know if she has a special place she likes to go? Or is there a certain place she likes to hide?"

"I don't know... The library maybe?" I frown, as the memory of finding her passed out up the back aisle, comes to mind, and then

I add, "But it's probably not her favourite place anymore. Why? What's going on? Is she in trouble again?"

"Maybe." His eyes scan the chamber before adding, "She's missing."

I feel the shimmer drain from my face.

"Frost." I want to get up and help find her, but I don't think I can. The pain when I move is crippling. "How long has she been missing?"

"I'm not sure *exactly*. Floss said the last time she saw her was before she went to bed."

"Well what are you going to do?"

"The only thing I can do. Keep searching until I find her. I just hope she's still alive."

# 39

# SNOWFLAKE TATTOO

## -HARLOW-

*J* stare at the letter J inside the small fluorescent snowflake and smile. The red ink appears to be glowing brighter than ever due to the shade of the tall trees.

"It's perfect," I say.

When I'd first asked Alex to add the letter J into the snowflake pattern, he was weird about it—this is—until he realised it was Jade's initial. I think he thought I was getting the J to represent Jax.

He stands up straight, and stretches his arms out above him, causing his shoulders to crack. "That wasn't so bad, was it?" A yawn leaves his mouth, and I notice his teeth look very white in comparison to his dark chocolate skin.

I shake my head. "No, it just feels a little warm."

His eyes glow bright, like our tattoos, but the skin around them has sunken since this morning. He looks tired.

After popping the ink jar and needle back into the leather case, he steps out of the shadows to stretch his long legs. He's not wearing much, only a pair of khaki harem shorts, and leather strappy sandals—which match the sash which hoists his weapon.

"Now remember, the full effects of the ink's power aren't instant," he reminds me. "It'll kick in gradually over the next few weeks. So, until then, please promise me you'll be careful."

I don't know whether I will last a few weeks, but I nod and promise anyway.

"I already feel a little different," I admit, jumping to my feet with a new-found confidence. "I don't feel as weak or scared."

"That's good, I'm glad," he says, however a flash of worry crosses his face, contradicting his enthusiasm. "But I still wouldn't try anything on anyone yet if I were you. Give it time. It might be a placebo effect."

"Maybe," I say, shrugging.

The setting sun blazes down, reflecting magnificently off his shiny dark skin, and I feel as if I am seeing him through a new light. I stare despite myself, a fresh sense of appreciation washing over me.

His Vallon physique no longer looks as terrifying as I'd first thought. It looks beautiful—striking. Even his molten eyes don't bother me anymore, I find them fascinating.

"Thank you," I say. "I appreciate you doing this for me."

He gives a crooked smile. "Now that I have you, I'll do anything to keep you. You seriously have no idea how much you mean to me. You're all I've thought about for years."

He'd said something similar to me when we were sitting by the pool. "You're all I've thought about for years," he'd told me. "You're all I've dreamt about."

"Why me?" I ask curiously. "There are plenty of fish in the sea, and I'm sure Slater," I refer to his Vallon form in third person, "has his fair share of women chasing him." I slip my bracelet back onto my wrist, as he chuckles over this comment. "I don't understand why you find me so special?"

"You know." He crosses the space between us in two long strides. "The first time I ever saw you, I thought you were an angel. You looked glorious dancing by the fire pit, with your sparkly silver dress reflecting the flickering flames." His molten irises burn even brighter as he pushes a loose pink dreadlock, back from my face. "Seriously, you were so beautiful and spirited. It took my breath away watching you."

"Are you saying it was love at first sight?" My cheeks flush with heat. "Is that even a real thing?"

"Probably not." Now it's his turn to blush, although it's hard to see given how dark his skin is. "It was probably more like lust at first sight, but that lust soon grew to love when I learnt more about you. Everyone spoke about you for years after you were gone, so I over-heard a lot. They all sang your praises."

"Oh yeah? What exactly was said? And by whom? You do realise that people generally tend to romanticise the dead, right? You probably fell in love with me over a bunch of half-truths."

"Do you remember Lucas' caravan?" he asks, and I nod, not liking where he is going with this. "Josh used to come across almost every single evening until he met Sarah, and you were all he ever wanted to talk about."

"I was?"

He nods. "And trust me, he had a lot of really nice things to say."

Regardless of everything Alex has told me about Josh, I still struggle to imagine him getting all sentimental over me. I didn't think he had it in him. I guess it goes to show I never really knew him all that well.

"You were all Lucas ever talked about too," Alex adds, and I find myself wishing he hadn't. "Not only to Josh, but to himself." I squirm at the thought of Lucas talking about me, whether it be nice or not. "He and Josh got a bunch of your photos printed off, and then put them up on the shelf, above the suede lounge." Unaware of my disgust, he grins. "My favourite picture of you was the one where you were posing with a silly face by the three sisters. I liked how the wind had picked up your hair, and made it..."

Suddenly noticing my troubled expression, Alex's grin fades and he cuts his sentence short. "You know what, forget it." He shifts back a step. "By the look on your face, I'm guessing what I've said, has come out a lot creepier than I'd anticipated."

A pang of regret fills my chest. I shouldn't have been so blatant with my disgust. He probably thinks it's directed at him, but it's not. It's directed at Lucas.

"I'm sorry." I place my hand on his. "I didn't mean to upset you. Please continue."

"What does it matter how or why I fell for you?" He avoids looking my way. "You're never going to feel the same way about me. You are always going to be wary of me—and my intentions —because of my schizophrenic brother. And you know what, I get it. What he did to you was..."

"Stop," I say, putting my hand up to cut him short. "You're right." His head jerks to face me, hurt evident in his eyes. "What does it matter how you fell for me? The fact is, you did, and you are here now—helping me, despite the consequences." No longer afraid, I reach for his waist and pull him to me. "You are nothing like your brother. I've already told you that. You are the good twin —kind, compassionate and cute—even as a Vallon." The corner of my mouth quirks up. "I'm so sorry if I've made you feel any other way."

His expression grows vulnerable—which is a rare sight indeed, given he's a Vallon. "Do you really mean that? Or are you just trying to make me feel better?"

"Of course I do. I can't thank you enough for everything you've done for me. You're basically my hero." I glance away for a moment, embarrassed by my own admission. "You've risked your own life to save mine, and I'm not entirely sure I'm worth it. I mean, look at me... I'm a lousy little Pastel for crying out loud."

A hint of a smile plays at his lips. "I think you underestimate yourself. Even as a Pastel, there's still something about you."

He bends down to kiss me, and without hesitation, I respond. His lips brush delicately at first, but as my hands wrap around his neck—pulling him to me—his kisses become deeper and more fervent. His large Vallon hands slide from my waist to my lower back, strong and powerful, yet they caress me with care—as if I am a delicate porcelain doll he doesn't want to break. Eventually his lips leave my mouth to trail the curve of my neck, and I gasp with a shiver. It's been over a lifetime since I've been touched this way. It feels good; I feel wanted. I lap up the sensation.

He draws back, picking me up by my waist to lift me to him. I cling to his warm arms, and a sense of urgency swirls through me.

For reasons I can't fathom, I want to be with him. Like *really* be with him. I'm no longer afraid of his new exterior, or the consequences or repercussions that could come from our two different races uniting. *I want him, I need him. I need him to want me.*

I slide off his sash and put up my arms for him to pull off my jumper. He hesitates, giving me an *are you sure* look, before doing so. Our kisses intensify with heat and passion, and my singlet follows.

His eyes of molten liquid pools gaze deep into mine, making my heart beat faster, only this time it's with desire, not fear. "Is this really happening?" he asks, his breaths coming out in rasps.

I let out a self-conscious, breathy, chuckle. "Why not? We might as well make the most of our time together before I'm killed tomorrow."

He rolls his eyes. "Your humour sucks, you know that? You should work on it."

"Oh, just shut and kiss me, won't you, you're ruining the moment."

His brows shoot up. "I'm ruining the moment?"

I push my pointer to his lips. "Shhh…" I say, and then lean back in for another kiss.

❋

*Wow!* My hearts races with lingering passion and ecstasy. Never in my wildest dreams would I have imagined that my first sexual experience in this world would be with a Vallon—furthermore, a Red. If anyone had told me this a week ago, I would have laughed in their face. The idea of a Pastel and Red falling for one another is completely outrageous. I know this—everybody knows this. We are entirely different races—worse yet—we are each other's archenemies. *We don't belong together.*

Although I must say, for a connection which is supposed to be *so* wrong, everything I'd just experienced had felt *so* right.

We curl up together by the foot of a large protruding tree root, big spoon, little spoon—or should I say, large spoon, tiny spoon. Our bare bodies press tightly together, and I can feel the warmth of his glowing vertic switz heating up my back like a hot water bottle.

We chat for a while, mainly about how completely insane our relationship would seem to our opposing races, before going on to consider the ramifications we'd face if we were caught in this *very* compromising position. The suggestion of being caught like this has my nerves on edge, but Alex laughs it off, saying that the incredible moment we'd shared was well worth any punishment he'd be made to face.

He also makes a joke, saying, "How awesome is this? I almost feel like I have two girlfriends, Ruby the human and Harlow the Zeek."

I smile at his comment, but I can't say I feel the same way. Regardless of what form he presents in—to me—he is only ever going to be Alex, *not Slater.*

After a while of chatting back and forth, I flip over, and notice Alex's eyelids are beginning to droop. I give him one last kiss and say, "You should go to sleep. I'll keep a lookout in case anyone comes looking for us."

"Are you sure?" he asks, and I nod.

"I'm sure."

"If you start to get nervous about anything, wake me, okay? I don't mind."

"Okay."

I'm already nervous, but I refuse to admit it. I hadn't been too keen on spending a night in the forest, especially in the danger zone, but Alex had assured me we would be fine. That he would easily be able to protect me from any lurking predators. I'd appreciated his confidence, but after my last terrifying run-in with a fuegor, I can't help but be wary. The continual sound of snaps and crackles in my ears are a constant and solid reminder that we are not alone out here. Scarier still, every so often a growl joins the ruckus, and I hold my breath in fear. *Fuegors.*

Pushing the thought of predators aside, I wonder if anyone from Summer or Winter will come out here looking for us. I don't know how popular the Slater side of Alex is, or how much he would be missed by his fellow Vallons, but I'm pretty sure the only Zeeks who would even care that I was missing would be Zavier and possibly Jax.

*I wonder how Zavier is doing. Is he awake? Does he know Floss likes him?* I'm still not sure how I feel about this revelation, but I guess it's not my place to say anything, especially now. I only hope if anything happens between them, they're careful not to flaunt it, and more importantly, I hope that Zavier won't let it stand in the way of our friendship. He's the only true friend I have. I can't afford to lose him.

I manage to stay awake and on lookout until daybreak. A few creatures rustled around in the bushes near us, but thankfully none had come into view. Alex had told me they'd be too afraid of his illuminating vertic switz to come right up to us. He'd said that he was the greatest predator in the forest, and all of the animals knew it. Under these nerve-wracking circumstances, I'd been glad he was right.

By six A.M. the glorious pink light of dawn filters in through the tree branches above, and even though I'm very much enjoying being able to catch a sunrise on Zadok, I can't hold my eyes open any longer. Without remembering to wake Alex first, I relax my guard and succumb to sleep.

# 40

# THIS CHANGES EVERYTHING
## -HARLOW AS RUBY AND HARLOW-

"inally!" Alex snaps. "I've been calling and calling you!"
A cat hisses nearby and he yells, "Get lost!"

*What's going on?* I wonder. *Why is he so agitated?*

I blink twice over to clear my vision. Jade sits on her lounge with a glass of wine in her hands, and alongside her is my box of treasured things—and Lucas. *Oh, no!*

Billy my bear, lies askew on Lucas' lap, along with one of my old soccer presentation photos. I hate that Jade has let him pick through my things again. I don't want his filthy mitts tarnishing what little is left of me. *They are my things God damn it! MINE. He has no right to touch them.*

Alex paces behind them looking as if he's about to explode. "Can you believe this?"

"No," I answer. But what I find even more unbelievable than this disturbing scene in front of me is his volatile reaction to it. He's usually the one telling me not to worry, that Lucas is okay now, that he's on meds and that he hasn't had a…

It hits me like a slap to the face. "There's a drink in Lucas' hand." *Jade, what have you done?*

"Yeah." Alex nods in agitation. "And it's his fifth."

This can't be happening. My insides twist. "Well, what do we do?"

"We need to get him to leave, before he has another one and completely loses it. Even as it is, I'm already seeing the early signs of his aggression surfacing. We don't have much time."

"Is Byron here?"

"No."

"Well, where is he? Is he far?"

"I don't know." He throws up his hands in frustration. "And we don't have time to chase him down. We have to do something —*NOW!*"

"Okay." My body trembles with stress. "We need to make him leave," I repeat. I push my fingers to my temples, hoping to come up with a solution, but I'm too shaken to think straight. "How in the world are we going to do this? It's not like we can just pick him up and carry him out."

"Oh don't-I-know-it," he says with annoyance. "I've spent the last half an hour trying to pick this idiot up, but I'm not like you, I can't make contact."

"What? Me?"

"Yeah." He stops pacing to look at me. "Do you remember the first day you saw me?" he asks, and I nod. "You made your sister's car window shoot up—remember?"

"Ahhh…Ye…ah. So?"

"You need to use that poltergeist trick on him. Move him, or push him, or…I don't know… Scare him. It doesn't matter what you do. We need to get him out of here, before he does something we all regret."

"I don't know if I can," I say in a panic. "I can't control it. It only happens…"

"You know, you remind me a lot of her," Lucas' slurred comment instantly steals my attention away, stopping me short. "In fact, I could easily mistake you for her if I didn't know she was dead."

Jade cringes. "We might have looked similar," she agrees, uneasily. "But our personalities were like chalk and cheese."

Lucas lifts the box from between them and dumps it on the coffee table with a thud. "Enough with this junk," he slurs. "It's fuckin' depressing." He picks up Billy bear and tosses him carelessly onto the half-eaten cheese platter.

"Is everything okay?" Jade asks. Her brows are dipped, and her posture has become rigid. I can tell by her body language she's troubled by his sudden change in behaviour but is trying desperately to play it cool.

He flashes a deranged smile, exposing his yellowing teeth. "Never better."

"Ruby, you've got to do something," Alex warns. "He's on the verge of completely losing control—look at him."

Alex is right. I recognise the madness in Lucas' eyes. *Far out Jade; you have no idea of the danger you've put yourself in. I wish you hadn't let him back into your life.*

More afraid than ever, I try desperately to grab his arm, but it's hopeless; my hands slip straight through. The scent of stale cigarettes mixed with sweat wafts from his shirt, making me want to gag. I screw up my nose. *Just breath in through your mouth.*

I make another attempt, and another. "This isn't working. I'm getting nowhere." My eyes snap to Alex in desperation. "You've got to help me."

We attempt to grab an arm each. *No luck.* Meanwhile, Lucas shuffles closer to Jade.

"You even have the same eyelashes as her," he says, his gaze much too intense for my liking. "They are long and thick, like the lashes of a camel."

For every few inches he gains, Jade shifts in the opposite direction—until finally she stands. "You know I think I'm going to have to call it a night," she says, faking a yawn. "I'm buggered from all of that paperwork I had to do this morning."

"You can't call it quits on me now," he says. "The night's still young. Let's just have one more drink."

She shakes her head. "I don't think that's such a good idea. Connor has basketball practice early tomorrow morning, and I promised him I'd watch."

Lucas cocks his head, fixing her with his psychotic gaze. "You're lying."

Jade flinches. "Excuse me?"

He rises from the lounge, completely oblivious to Alex's and my efforts to stop him. "You're lying to me. You're trying to get rid of me."

"No, it's not that, it's..."

His tongue clicks as he waves his pointer in front of her face. "Excuses, excuses. Admit it. You think you're above me because you live in this fancy-fuckin'-house with your fancy-fuckin'-car."

"What, no... I..."

Without warning, he hurls his wine glass at the wall causing it to shatter and the three of us to jolt in surprise. "You're a liar."

"You know what, that's enough," she finally snaps. "You need to leave."

"Mum?" Connor's voice calls from upstairs. "Is everything okay down there?"

"Yeah Honey, just stay—"

"Rueben," Lucas calls over the top of her. "We need to leave now. It seems we are no longer welcome."

"—up there please. Everything is fine."

"Okay, one sec," Rueben calls back. "I've almost finished the level."

Lucas nostrils flare in anger. "RUEBEN, I said we are leaving. Get your arse down here now before I kick it to kingdom come."

I can see panic written on Jade's face. "Oh, actually, I spoke to Josh earlier, and he said Rueben could stay the night." It's obvious she's making this up, and Lucas sees straight through it.

"You're lying again."

Her hands tremble at her sides. "Please go. Byron should be home soon, and I don't want any trouble."

"Lies, lies, lies…"

He charges towards her and she instantly back-peddles—but stops suddenly—with a yelp.

Shards of smashed glass glisten from the floorboards, and as she jerks her foot up, I detect blood spilling from her heel. Lucas takes advantage of her mishap. His filthy hands go straight for her neck.

*No!*

Alex and I leap at him frantically, unintentionally smacking into each other, as we do everything we possibly can, in an attempt to get him to let go of my sister.

"STOP," I shout. "Let go of her."

"Why did you have to do this?" Lucas says with a growl. "Why did you have to make me angry?"

Oh no—not again. *Dear God, please don't let him kill my twin.*

Jade splutters against his grasp. "Connor help," she manages, but it's barely distinguishable. "Ring…" she gasps, "triple…" she gasps, "zero." Her delicate fingers tug at Lucas' meaty sausages to no avail.

Tears prickle at the corners of my eyes. My worst fear is coming to life. *He really is going to kill her.*

"You bastard." I charge at him with all of my might, not realising that Alex has launched at him—full force—from the opposite angle. Our heads collide with a bang and we both topple to the floor. *Ouch.* I cradle my head and groan.

"Shit, Rubes." Alex shuffles over to me on his knees. "Are you okay?"

I nod against my hand. "I'm fine."

I'm not really fine. I'm far from it. But I refuse to give up on my sister.

"All we are doing is hurting each other," Alex hisses through gritted teeth. "We need to do something else."

I leap to my feet—a few leftover stars distorting my vision. "Like *what* exactly?" I don't mean to snap at him, this isn't his fault, but I'm frantic. I need to save my sister before it's too late.

"Why don't you try throwing something at him?"

Rueben comes moping down the stairs but abruptly pauses mid-landing to gawk in shock. "Uncle Lucas, what are you doing? Let Mrs King go."

Ignoring his nephew, Lucas' grip around Jade's neck tightens, causing her skin colour to shift to a mild shade of blue.

I scramble to pick up the TV remote to throw it at his head, but again it's a fail. I'm so frustrated, I want to scream.

"Connor," Rueben calls with a screech. "Connor, come. Your mum's in trouble." He takes to the next run of stairs, his face a mix of emotions as he races down them. "Uncle Lucas, please, let her go."

Lucas lets out a loud, guttural, howl. At first, I'm confused about what's happened. Rueben hasn't got to him yet.

I whirl around to find him crumpled forward, cradling his package, and understanding fills me. We twins must think alike. Jade's managed to kick him right where it hurts, just as I had all of those years ago. *I hope it buys her more time than it did, me.*

Connor comes flying down the top run of stairs. "What the heck?"

"Stop," Jade yells. She is free from Lucas' mitts, but her voice still comes out strangled. "Go back upstairs. Quick. Hide."

Rueben hurries over to scoop her up, and I'm glad it's him, not Connor. He's taller, and much bulkier. He looks strong enough to carry her the distance. "Hold on to my neck," he says.

Connor waits at the middle landing, urging Rueben to hurry, before helping him with Jade the rest of the way up.

Lucas doesn't stay immobilised for long. He rights himself and goes charging up after them.

"Come on," I yell to Alex—taking up the chase. "We have to go with them."

I remain hot on Lucas' heels the whole way up the stairs.

"Quick, he's coming," Rueben says, and I see his lower arm slip though Connor's bedroom door before slamming it behind him.

A click of a lock sounds, along with a few bangs, and I imagine they are putting blockades across the entryway.

Lucas makes a beeline straight to Connor's door and bangs on it hard with the back of his fist. "It didn't have to be this way Jade." His familiar words are like a stab to my guts. "It didn't have to come to this."

He waits a moment to listen, before banging again. "Jade! Open up. I won't hurt you this time, I promise. I only want to talk."

*Don't do it Jade,* I think. *His words mean nothing. He's a killer.*

I gaze at Alex. He looks as distressed as I feel. "I'm going in," I say, and he nods.

"I'll stay out here and keep an eye on him."

I slip through Connor's door to see that they've wedged his desk in front of it.

Jade sits on Connor's double bed, tears streaking her face, and Connor sits beside her, his arms wrapped around her shoulders.

"Don't worry mum, it's going to be okay."

Rueben has his phone out and on speaker, and I hear a woman on the other end say, "We are sending someone out now. Stay where you are and try to keep calm. We'll be with you as soon as possible."

*Easy for her to say.*

Lucas' bangs grow more ferocious, as does his tone. **"JADE! OPEN THE GOD DAMN DOOR BEFORE I SMASH IT TO PIECES!"**

Rueben shoves his phone back into his pocket with an unsteady hand. "I'm so sorry, Mrs King. I've never seen my uncle act this way before. He's usually the quiet type." He scratches his head, ruffling his curls. "He mainly hangs out in his caravan watching TV or listening to that Mysterious Universe podcast. My mum calls him a hermit crab."

"It's not your fault, Rueben."

"Ruby," Alex shouts from the other side, "Ruby, watch out. He's about to smash down the door."

Next thing I know there's a deafening crunch, and the tip of something metal emerges through the doors surface.

Jade screams and the boys turn white. The metal recedes as fast as it's entered, and a hand emerges, going straight for the handle.

Quick to react, Rueben picks up one of Connor's basketball boots, and hurls it at Lucas' hand.

There's a groan, and his hand recedes, but the piece of metal instantly returns—punching through another hole, and then another, and then another.

"He's going to break in," Jade says, leaping up from the bed. "You boys have to hide. Quick. I don't want him to hurt either of you."

"What about you mum?" Connor asks.

"Don't worry about me." She puts on a brave face. "I'll be fine."

Rueben rushes to Connor's shelf, to pick up one of his larger basketball trophies to hand to Jade. "Use this if you have to Mrs King."

A string of loud crunches continue as Lucas persists on turning Connor's door into the image of a large cheese grater.

"Thank you, Rueben," Jade says, "Now hurry and hide."

Connor is already squashing himself into the hanging part of his wardrobe, so Rueben goes for the next best place, and crawls underneath his bed.

After another few big hits, the door bursts off its hinges taking out Connor's flimsy little desk as it flies into the room with a crash. It passes through me, but thankfully misses Jade by a matter of centimetres. *Phew, and not phew.* My sister might have been spared this round, but Lucas has made it in.

"There you are." A predatory sneer pulls at the side of his mouth, and Jade gulps. The piece of metal he'd used gleams in his hands, and I can see what it is now—a large broken lamp stand.

"I'm sorry," Alex says, stepping out from behind him. "I couldn't stop him."

Lucas edges towards Jade and despite all of my other failed

attempts, I charge at him once again, only to crash into Alex. It's no use. No matter how hard I try, I can't seem to make contact.

"It was you, wasn't it?" Jade's voice wobbles. "You killed Ruby."

"I was in love with your sister," he confesses, and my blood runs cold. "But she didn't love me back." He keeps edging forward, forcing Jade to reverse closer and closer to Connor's double hung bedroom window. "I didn't want to kill her, but she made me so angry."

Tears spill from Jade's eyes. "How could you do that to her? To all of us? We trusted you. We thought you were one of our friends."

"I was never anyone's friend. I was a tag along. Nobody wanted me around; they only put up with me because I was Josh's 'poor adopted brother'."

"That's not true."

"Stop lying to me. All everyone ever does is lie to me." He lunges at her with the lamp post, but she manages to knock it aside with Connor's trophy. Thrown by her defence, he stumbles slightly, and the post drops from his hand.

Righting himself, he lets out a sickening, psychotic laugh. "Very good, you got me. Not to worry, I don't need the lamp post anymore. I've got you right where I want you." He dives straight at her, and I'm afraid he's going to push her through Connor's window.

*What can I do? What can I do?* I think franticly. *Hurry.*

Instead of trying to stop Lucas, I hurl myself at Jade, attempting to push her aside. *It works.* She stumbles to the side and falls. A split second later, a loud smashing sound fills my ears as Lucas crashes headfirst into the glass. Blood trickles from his forehead and nose, and as he turns to face us, I notice there's a long gaping laceration on his right forearm.

His eyes zoom in on Jade's, ablaze with fury. "What the fuck was that?"

Jade looks rattled.

"Mum?" Connor bursts out from the wardrobe wielding a metal school ruler. "Mum, are you okay?" He moves towards her, but she motions for him to stop.

"I'm fine. Get out of here. Now. Run!"

Lucas lunges towards Jade, and Connor charges over to him in a rage. "How dare you hurt my mother and my aunty. I never even got to know her because of you."

"Connor, no!" Jade cries.

This isn't going to end well. Connor isn't strong enough to take on Lucas.

Alex jumps between them, both arms raised, but it does nothing to part them.

I rush to Jade who is insanely rushing towards them.

"Wait!" I yell, even though, I know she can't hear me. "I want to help." As I get closer to her, I feel a strange pulling sensation, and for an instant everything goes black.

"Ahhh," I hear Connor yell, and my vision returns just in time, to see him fall to the floor with a thump.

*No not him, he's too young to die. Please let him be okay.*

*Hold on, where the hell has Jade gone?* My eyes give a quick sweep of the room, I'm surprised she's not rushing to his aid.

With Connor now down, Lucas turns his attention to me. Confusion fills me. He's looking right at me—as if he can literally see me.

"Ruby?" Alex calls, seeming bewildered. "Ruby, what's happening?"

I hardly know myself.

Lucas snatches at my arm, and to my astonishment he makes contact. *What the hell?*

Acting fast, I use my free hand to whack his, twist free and then I kick him in the kneecap as hard as I possibly can. He groans, his feet becoming unsteady once more, and then without missing a beat, I dive straight at him, forcing his body backwards.

"No!" Alex yells as Lucas' body topples through Connor's window with a crash.

I hope Lucas has fallen all of the way, and is not hanging onto the eaves, but before I can check, everything turns black.

I feel a forceful snap—like I'm being pulled from something—

and then all of a sudden, my vision clears again to find Jade standing in front of me. *Weird.*

"Ruby, that was you?" The fractured tone of Alex's voice makes my heart ache.

I veer to find him staring right at me, his eyes withered with hurt. "How could you do this to me?" His whole frame is flickering in-and-out. "Do what?" I ask, and then the light inside my brain switches on. If Lucas dies, Alex's spirit might leave with him. He might never be able to come back. Dread sweeps over me and a lump grows in my throat, thick and suffocating. *This can't be right. I can't lose him.*

Jade's head whips around to face me—catching me completely off guard. "Ruby? Is that you?"

I do a double take. "Jade? You can see me?"

A flicker catches the corner of my eye and I glance back at Alex in time to see him disappear altogether.

*No! Oh God no. What have I done?*

My eyes snap open to find Vallon Alex writhing beside me.

"Alex?" I bolt upright, automatically rushing to give his bulging black-and-red bicep a squeeze. "Alex, what's happening? Are you okay?" When he doesn't respond right away, my grip tightens, and I give his whole arm a firm shake. "Alex, please…wake up…talk to me. You're scaring me."

His head jerks up with a start, and I jolt. He appears disorientated at first, but after a few exaggerated blinks his expression clears, and then darkens.

"You killed him." Are the first words to leave his lips, and I shudder. "How could you do this to me? Especially, when I've gone out of my way to help keep you safe. Now I'll never be able to go back there again. I'll never see my brother again."

"I'm so sorry. I hadn't known that by killing Lucas, I'd cut your link to Earth. I was only trying to save my sister and nephew. I acted on pure instinct. Lucas was going to kill them." Tears well in my eyes, as I process the devastating consequences of my actions.

"I understand you were trying to save your family," he says with a bitter edge, "But there was no need for you to push him out of the window. You could have just knocked him out and then restrained him until the police got there. You didn't even try to talk him down. You deliberately rushed in and used your sister's body as a weapon to kill him."

I hadn't deliberately used Jade's body; it was unintentional. I didn't understand what was happening at first. I'd wondered where she'd disappeared too.

"I panicked," I say. "I wasn't thinking straight. I saw an opportunity to stop your brother from killing anyone else, and I took it. I didn't realise what the ramifications would be."

Alex scrambles to his feet, his gaze homing in on mine accusingly. "I saw it in Jade's eyes—your eyes—you wanted to kill him. You purposely shoved him out of the window."

"It's not true." I let out an anguished breath. "And even if it was, could you really blame me? Your brother was a murderer; he killed us both, and if I hadn't stopped him, he would have killed Jade and Connor too." The image of Connor hitting the floor with a thump, enters my mind, and I pray he's okay. "I'm sorry that I've hurt you by hurting Lucas—I'm devastated—but your brother brought it on himself. He wasn't a good person. He was a killer—you saw it yourself—he was about to strike again."

"He wasn't born a bad person," Alex says in his defence. "Our parents made him this way. You have no idea of the torture we went through as kids—especially him."

"Again, I'm sorry," I say, feeling angered by his response. "But a torturous childhood doesn't give him the right to hurt or kill others." I slip on my singlet. "You might have forgiven your brother for what he did to us, but I haven't, and I would never have forgiven myself if I didn't do everything in my power to stop him from hurting my family."

"I've never forgiven Lucas for what he did to you. It eats at me.

But I know he doesn't mean to do the things he does. He has a mental illness."

Okay, now I'm feeling *really* angry. *What a cop out!*

"Yeah, well why don't you tell this sorry excuse to eighteen-year-old Ruby," I spit. "I'm sure she was more than willing to pay the ultimate price for his shitty childhood." After slipping on my pants, I pull my legs to me, and cross my arms over them, squeezing them tight. While I truly am completely and utterly devastated over what I've done to hurt Alex, I'm also infuriated with him for once again jumping to his brother's defence.

Alex was there. He saw how the evening was playing out; Lucas is a monster. I don't understand how he can stand there defending him or how he can say he loves me and is willing to risk everything for me, yet still be protective of my killer. It makes no sense. I feel like he is putting his love for his brother before his love for me. It has me questioning if he really does care about me and my feelings as much as he says, or if he's just in love with the idea of loving me.

I grit my teeth in resentment. "You know," I add, my body starting to shake. "If it wasn't for your brother, I would still be alive in a world I love with family members who actually love me. I wouldn't be a pathetic little Pastel who is once again on the verge of being killed." My fingers strain as my grip on my legs tightens. "Your brother took my life for cruel and selfish reasons. I only took his so I could save three others."

He yanks up his harem shorts with haste. "I'm not saying that what Lucas did to you was okay by any means. I'm disgusted by the awful things he did. I'm just saying... You know what, forget it. Forget everything."

He picks up a rock and pegs it at a nearby tree, causing a bird to flap away in fright. In this moment he looks terrifying, and I cower.

"I guess this is it then." His harsh tone makes me shudder. "If I can't go back to Earth then this isn't going to work. Ruby and Alex are finished."

"What?" Hearing him say this causes my heart to crumble. Surely he doesn't mean it. This can't be the end. I might be extremely mad with him, but I don't want to lose him. *I can't.* "Don't say that," I plead. "There's got to be a way you can go back to Earth without having to use your brother as a connection—like a loophole or something?" My words come out rushed and frantic. "We'll work it out."

"This isn't some stupid video game, Ruby. There are no cheats or loopholes. This is real. You killed Lucas—he's dead—which means I'm no longer attached. I risked everything to come here for you because I loved you, and I wanted to help save you, and now the Alex side of me has been obliterated—by you of all people."

"That's not fair, and you know it. I didn't know this would happen. You could have warned me."

"Would it have even made a difference?"

"I..." I hesitate a split second too long before adding, "Yes, of course it would have."

"Goodbye, Ruby," he says, and then storms off into the thick of the forest, without even giving me a final glance.

# RUBY RED

## COMING SOON...

July 15th 2021

# ABOUT THE AUTHOR

Born in Queensland, Australia, 1984, Nikki Minty rose into this world with a wild imagination. As a young girl, she would lay in bed with her family of a night, co-telling stories about the big bad wolf and his turbulent adventures.

# NAKED
## INSIDE OUT

*From Penthouse Centerfold
to 13 Years of Stage 4 Breast Cancer:
The Drop-Dead Story of*

Victoria Lynn Johnson

*Photo by Bob Guccione*